Thread
of
Fear

LAURA GRIFFIN

POCKET STAR BOOKS

New York   London   Toronto   Sydney

Pocket Star Books
A Division of Simon & Schuster, Inc.
1230 Avenue of the Americas
New York, NY 10020

This book is a work of fiction. Names, characters, places, and incidents either are products of the author's imagination or are used fictitiously. Any resemblance to actual events or locales or persons, living or dead, is entirely coincidental.

First Pocket Star Books paperback edition October 2008

POCKET STAR BOOKS and colophon are registered trademarks of Simon & Schuster, Inc.

For information about special discounts for bulk purchases, please contact Simon & Schuster Special Sales at 1-800-456-6798 or business@simonandschuster.com.

Cover design by Lisa Litwak; cover photograph © Ed Freeman / Getty Images

Manufactured in the United States of America

10 9 8 7 6 5 4 3 2 1

ISBN-13: 978-1-4165-7063-9
ISBN-10:   1-4165-7063-2

"I've got another witness," Jack said. **"Nine-year-old boy. He saw the killer dump the body."**

Fiona closed her eyes and counted to ten mentally.

"I need you to interview this kid for me, get a picture of the guy."

She wouldn't look at him. She couldn't. He had this way of bulldozing right over her.

Jack's hand closed over hers. It was big and strong, and she could feel the heat from him move up her arm into every part of her body. But she knew he was using these touches to wear down her resistance. He was a determined investigator—she'd seen that firsthand. He'd do whatever he needed to, including lie and probably fake emotions, in order to solve his case.

And she still didn't know why this case meant so much to him.

"You drove all the way to Austin to ask me this?"

"I thought I'd have better luck in person." She stole a glance at him and saw a boyish smile playing at the corner of his mouth. "You have a hard time telling me no."

Praise for *One Last Breath* by Laura Griffin

"Enticing . . . a fun read and a promising career kickoff."
—*Publishers Weekly*

"Laura Griffin hits all the right notes . . . compelling characters, unexpected twists, and a gripping story from the first gasp to the last sigh."
—Roxanne St. Claire, author of *First You Run*

Thread of Fear is also available as an eBook.

Also by Laura Griffin

ONE WRONG STEP
ONE LAST BREATH

And look for

WHISPER OF WARNING

Coming Spring 2009
from Pocket Books

For Lois

ACKNOWLEDGMENTS

Thank you to the many people who helped with the research for this book, including Chris Herndon, Phyllis Middleton, and Tracy Pullan. I am particularly grateful to Lois Gibson and the dedicated professionals in the—hopefully, expanding—field of forensic art. Also, thank you to Kevan Lyon and Abby Zidle for their ongoing support and for believing in this story.

And finally, a special thanks to Leonard Folgarait for teaching me to love art, in all its forms.

PROLOGUE

******at 11:25 PM ♥shelB
joined the room

♥shelB: ne1 wanna talk?
Justin5: waddup girl
♥shelB: nothing good
Justin5: been waiting 4u
♥shelB: who's in here?
Justin5: just us   •
♥shelB: where's Kylie from
NYC
Justin5: dunno why dont u
have a picture?
♥shelB: im getting 1 soon
Justin5: good u sound sexc
ru?
♥shelB: lol
Justin5: seriously
♥shelB: thx
Justin5: your parents let u
stay up this late?
♥shelB: its just my mom and
she doesn't care
Justin5: wheres your dad

Justin5: ru there?
♥shelB: he died last year
Justin5: j/k?
♥shelB: no 4 real
Justin5: how?
♥shelB: car crash
Justin5: that sux
♥shelB: my mom said he fell asleep but he was drunk she always lies 2 me
Justin5: that's so weird
♥shelB: y?
Justin5: my dad died in a car crash 2 last year
♥shelB: no way
Justin5: we have so much in common i really want 2 meet u
♥shelB: i want 2 meet u2
Justin5: where do u live
♥shelB: mom here GGN!!
Justin5: later then

******at 11:32 PM ♥shelB left the room

CHAPTER

I

Fiona Glass was trained to notice faces, but even if she hadn't been, she would have noticed this one.

The man watching her from across the crowded concourse was a study in contrasts, from his receding hairline to his youthful, ruddy cheeks. His hair was strawberry blond—the same color as Fiona's—and a smattering of freckles covered the bridge of his once-broken nose.

But it was his eyes that really captured her attention. They were brown and serious and fixed squarely on her.

Fiona halted outside the arrival gate, creating a pileup of deplaning passengers.

"Sorry," she muttered, tugging her black roll-on bag out of the flow of traffic.

"Miss Glass?"

She glanced into the eyes that had been boring a hole in her just moments before.

"Garrett Sullivan, FBI," he said.

A special agent. His charcoal suit and forgettable tie should have been her tip-off. Fiona draped her coat over her arm and hitched the strap of her attaché case onto her shoulder so she could shake the hand he'd offered.

"I didn't know someone was coming to meet me," she said, pulling her hand back. "I was planning to take a cab."

The side of his mouth ticked up. "Didn't want you to get lost."

"Aren't we going to the police station?"

"Change of plan." He commandeered her suitcase and led her into the river of people, creating a path for her in his wake. He wasn't tall—probably five-nine—but he was bulky in the way of an athlete who had let things slide.

"Any checked bags?" he asked over his shoulder.

"No."

He obviously wasn't going to fill her in yet, so Fiona simply followed him through the concourse. Glancing around at all the harried business travelers, she smoothed her French braid and adjusted her lapels. She didn't like suits, but she wouldn't dream of wearing anything else to a meeting with police and FBI agents, most of whom would be men. Those occasions called for drab, wrinkle-resistant clothes, which she kept in the carry-on bag that lived in her car. Today's gray suit was double-breasted and had the added advantage of concealing her figure. She looked tailored. Conservative. Professional.

She looked like Sullivan.

"We're going to the house," the agent finally explained. "The media wanted fresh sound bites for five o'clock, so there's a press conference scheduled at police headquarters in twenty minutes. Things are quiet at the residence now, and we thought it'd be a good time to get you out there."

"Okay." Fiona blew out a breath and mentally adjusted

her expectations for the evening. She'd hoped to be thoroughly briefed on the case before she met with the child. She didn't want to go in unprepared. All she knew about this kid was that he was "highly traumatized," which could mean anything.

They passed the escalator leading down to ground transportation, and Fiona stopped. "Don't we—?"

"We're out here."

He led her to a roped-off area near a bank of metal detectors and X-ray machines. A line of passengers snaked back and forth, their boarding passes and IDs held out for inspection. A security guard gave Sullivan a crisp nod, then unclipped the nylon strap from the stand and waved them through. Less than a minute later, Fiona stood on the curb beside a white Ford Taurus that had been illegally parked in the passenger-drop-off lane. Sullivan waved at the orange-vested guard patrolling the sidewalk as he opened Fiona's door.

She slid into the car, discombobulated by the change of plan but grateful to be whisked away from the airport so efficiently. Fiona hated airports. They were inevitably bipolar—filled with people either frantically stressed out or morbidly bored.

She fastened her seat belt and stowed her attaché and coat at her feet. The interior of the Taurus felt warm, meaning Sullivan couldn't have been waiting long inside the terminal. For some reason that came as a relief. Sullivan slammed her suitcase into the trunk and then opened the driver's-side door to admit a gust of chilly air. Georgia wasn't known for its bitter winters, but the entire South was in the midst of a cold snap. Even Austin was expecting snow tonight.

Fiona watched the agent settle in behind the wheel. She placed him at thirty-eight, maybe forty years old.

"Tell me about the case," she said.

He turned up the heater and pulled out into traffic.

"Shelby Sherwood. Age ten. Last seen by her brother Monday afternoon."

"And she was taken from her home?"

"Yep. Man came to the front door. Rang the bell, we think."

So far he was only repeating what Fiona already knew from CNN this morning. She typically avoided news broadcasts, but she'd been surfing for weather updates, and the story had caught her attention. At the time, she hadn't imagined that a few hours later she'd be abandoning her Survey of Western Art class to rush to the airport.

"Tell me about the witness," she said.

Sullivan twisted his body around to retrieve something from the backseat, all the while steering the car onto Interstate 85.

"Colter Sherwood. Age six. Was home from school watching *Power Rangers* in the living room when Shelby answered the door." He flipped through the file in his lap, taking his eyes off the road and making Fiona's heart palpitate. "First-grader at Green Meadows Elementary. Same school as his sister."

Sullivan unclipped something from the manila folder and passed it to Fiona. It was a color copy of Shelby's school photo, the one that had been all over the television this morning. Shelby's straight brown hair hung past her shoulders, and she wore a purple and pink striped T-shirt. The photograph made Fiona uneasy. Shelby's expression wasn't the carefree smile of a typical ten-year-old girl. Neither was it the sullen look you might expect from a middle-schooler. It was a tense smile, very self-conscious. Fiona studied the girl's tightly closed lips.

"She has braces?"

Sullivan glanced at her, startled. "How'd you know that?"

"You can tell from the picture. She's trying to hide them. What's with the makeup?"

His gaze shifted back to the road. "I noticed that, too. Not exactly age appropriate, huh?"

"For a fifth-grader? I wouldn't think so. Especially if her fifth grade is part of an elementary school like you said. You guys need to get a photograph of Shelby in braces circulating, pronto."

"We're working on it. Apparently Shelby hasn't smiled for the camera since the braces went on."

"How old is this picture?"

"September, I think."

Four months probably wouldn't make much difference in the girl's appearance, assuming she hadn't cut or dyed her hair recently. Still, they needed a photo with the braces.

A horn blared as Sullivan skated across two lanes of traffic. Fiona glanced over her shoulder.

"Are we late for something?"

"I'm trying to get you to the house while the media's distracted," he said. "No one knows you're here, and we'd like to keep it that way."

"That's going to be tricky when we release a sketch of the subject tonight."

"That's *if* we release a sketch. We're not sure the brother saw anything."

Fiona looked up from the photograph, surprised. "Then why am I here?"

"His beanbag chair was parked in front of the television, not fifteen feet from the front door, but he says he didn't see the guy."

"And why don't you believe him?"

"Because when the mother came home from work, the kid was distraught. Shelby was missing, and all he kept saying was, 'I didn't see him.' That's pretty much all he's said for the past two days. No one can get anything else out of him—not his mom, not the cops, not the shrink we brought in. He's freaked out, so we're pretty sure he saw *something*. That's why we called you."

Fiona stared down at the school portrait and shook her head.

"What? You don't think you're up to it?"

She lifted her gaze, and Sullivan was smiling at her.

"Aw, come on," he said. "You're supposed to be magic with traumatized kids. It's all in your file. You're the rising star in forensic art."

Fiona pressed her lips together and looked away. "This is my last case. I'm retiring."

The car filled with silence as he digested this. She hoped he wouldn't press her on it. She didn't want to explain. All she wanted right now was to do her job and get back on a plane.

She glanced over. Sullivan was eyeing her with amused disbelief.

"*You* want to retire. You're what, thirty?"

"Twenty-nine."

He tipped his head back and laughed, and Fiona's spine

stiffened. She didn't expect him to understand. But she didn't owe him an explanation.

"Who's home with Colter?" she asked, changing the subject.

His smile disappeared. "The mother and grandmother."

"And the dad?"

"Deceased. Drunk-driving accident about a year ago."

"Okay."

"Mom hasn't left the house since Monday night," he continued. "Doesn't want to be gone in case there's a call. She's convinced Shelby has her cell phone with her, although we haven't confirmed that."

"And is Mom a suspect?"

He cast her a sidelong glance. "Mom's always a suspect."

"You know what I mean. Any weird behavior? Boyfriends who don't check out?"

"So far, no. Everything we've got indicates a stranger abduction."

So Sullivan had leads he wasn't sharing. Fiona wasn't surprised. Her job was to provide information, both visual and otherwise, to investigators, but the information tended to flow one way. Most detectives she'd worked with operated on a need-to-know basis, and the artist didn't need to know anything not directly related to the drawing.

A muffled snippet of Vivaldi emanated from the pile near Fiona's feet. She dragged her case out from beneath her coat and rummaged around until she found her phone. The caller ID showed a Texas area code, the same one that had popped up on the screen three times today. It would be that detective again. He'd left three brief messages, and she'd been putting off calling him back. She needed to get this over with.

"Fiona Glass," she said briskly.

"Hello, ma'am. I'm Jack Bowman with the Graingerville Police Department." He paused, as if he wanted her to say something, maybe offer an excuse for not returning his calls. She didn't.

"You're a tough lady to get ahold of."

"What can I do for you, Mr. Bowman?" Fiona's stomach clenched, dreading what he'd say next. They had a murder. An abduction. A serial rapist on the loose . . .

"Well, we've got a homicide down here, and we'd like to get your help." His voice sounded relaxed, with a hint of Texas drawl. But Fiona sensed something more from him, a steely determination that told her he was going to be a difficult person to refuse.

"I'm sorry I can't help you, Mr. Bowman, but I'm on another case at the moment." She felt Sullivan's gaze on her as she said the words. "You'll have to call someone else."

Silence. This was so much harder than she'd expected. She held her breath and prayed he wouldn't tell her about the victim.

"Well, that's just it, ma'am. There isn't anyone else."

She cleared her throat. "You might try calling Nathan Devereaux with the Austin Police Department. I'm sure he can recommend—"

"He recommended you."

Fiona's grip tightened on the phone. She'd *told* Nathan she was retiring. What was he trying to do here?

Suddenly the car slowed as Sullivan exited the interstate.

They drove through a few stoplights, and Fiona looked out the window. They appeared to be entering a bedroom community like so many others that had cropped up on the outskirts of American cities. The landscape was a series of strip centers, mega-markets, and cow pastures. Every telephone pole and stop sign was adorned with yellow ribbons and MISSING flyers bearing Shelby Sherwood's picture.

"Ma'am?" Jack Bowman's voice jerked her attention away from the girl's face. "You still there?"

"I'm sorry, Mr. Bowman. I can't help you."

She snapped the phone shut and shoved it back into her bag. As she zipped the attaché closed, her hands trembled. She flattened her palms on top of her thighs and took a deep breath. She needed to focus on the task ahead. This was her last case. She needed to get it right.

We've got a homicide down here. How many times had she heard those words? Too many to count. She didn't want to dwell on it. She didn't want to think about the words Jack Bowman *hadn't* said, because she'd heard those before, too, from the detectives who called her from all over the state, and lately, the nation. *We've got a young woman* . . . they usually said. And the woman had been raped, or murdered, or beaten to within an inch of her life. Maybe her child saw it happen. *The witness is highly traumatized, and we heard you can help* . . .

Sullivan approached an intersection and entered the left-turn lane.

"Is this it?" she asked.

"Yeah."

Fiona leaned forward and peered out the window at the residential street. All the homes looked alike—small, red-brick one-stories with garages dominating the fronts. The entrance to the neighborhood was marked by a young magnolia tree and a sign that said ROLLING HILLS.

Fiona glanced over her shoulder at the strip center they'd just passed. She spotted a convenience store.

"Can you do a U-turn?" she asked.

"Sure. Why?"

"I'm not dressed for this," she said. "I need to stop and change."

The homes of missing children are charged with a peculiar energy. Parents wait for their sons and daughters thinking unthinkable thoughts, and their desperation is like a current in the room. Their energy is powerful, galvanizing scores of perfect strangers to tromp through woods and pass out flyers and tie ribbons. But it doesn't last forever, and as the days and weeks and months tick by, the energy fades.

Fiona knew the odds. She knew that in all likelihood she could visit Shelby's house a year from now and the energy would be gone completely, snuffed out by a single phone call.

She surveyed the Sherwood home as she walked up the driveway. The concrete path leading to the front entrance had been cordoned off by crime scene tape, the doorbell and doorjamb dusted for fingerprints by hopeful investigators. The yard had no landscaping to speak of, save a leafless gray sapling whose slender trunk had been wrapped with a big yellow bow.

A handful of B-team reporters kept an eye on things while their colleagues covered the press conference downtown. Most waited for something to happen in the comfort of their vans, but a few milled around on the sidewalk talking and smoking. Sullivan ignored their inquisitive glances as he sauntered up the drive with Fiona at his side. There was nothing going on here, his gait seemed to say, nothing new to report.

"Another member of our CARD team's on the way over," Sullivan said, his voice low. "She's in charge of releasing the drawing, so I'm sure she'll have some questions for you after the interview."

"You're with CARD?"

"Yep. They put four of us on this one."

"Good for them," Fiona said, impressed. The FBI's Child Abduction Rapid Deployment team was an elite group, and she was surprised Sullivan hadn't mentioned he was part of it before now.

They mounted the back steps. A forgotten Christmas wreath made of plastic holly decorated the Sherwoods' door. Sullivan rapped lightly on the windowpane beneath it as Fiona stood behind him on the stoop, stealing glimpses of the backyard through weathered slats of fence. She saw a sliver of patio, some yellowed grass, a blue-and-white swing set.

Her icy fingers tightened on the handles of her brown leather case. She'd left her coat in the Taurus, along with her luggage, which now contained a neatly folded pantsuit. She'd changed into jeans, white Keds, and the navy Mickey Mouse sweatshirt she'd bought in Anaheim years ago. Her prim French braid was long gone, and her hair now hung loose around her shoulders.

The door squeaked open, and a thin brunette woman stood on the threshold. Matching streaks of blond framed her angular face, and she held a cigarette behind her. She looked like a barely adult version of Shelby. Fiona was startled by her young age and the fact that she'd answered the door herself. Most people in these situations had protective relatives standing guard.

"Afternoon, Mrs. Sherwood. This is the forensic artist I told you about, Fiona Glass." Sullivan stepped aside to make room for Fiona beside him.

The woman nodded a greeting, her gaze wary but not unfriendly. "Y'all come on in," she said, opening the door wider.

Fiona entered the small breakfast room. It smelled of Pine-Sol, as if someone had just finished mopping. The blinds were sealed shut, and the only light shone down from a fixture above the kitchen sink. So often, it seemed, these houses were dimly lit, as if the people within had an aversion to bright lights. Fiona had observed this phenomenon enough times to think there must be some psychological explanation for it, but she wasn't a psychologist and had no idea what it might be.

A vacuum hummed to life in another part of the house. Shelby's mother leaned back against the Formica counter. She wore low-rise jeans and a long-sleeved black T-shirt. Beige woolen socks covered her feet.

"Y'all want anything?" she asked, nodding at the endless row of bundt cakes and casseroles sitting on the counter. "It's just me and my mom and Colter. No way we can eat all this."

"I'm fine, thanks," Sullivan said. "How is he today?"

The woman took a long, pensive drag on her cigarette, then reached over to tap ash into the sink. "Pretty much the same. He asked for Froot Loops this morning, but that's been about it. He's playing in Shelby's room now. I told him you were coming."

"If it's all right with you," Fiona said gently, "I'd like to talk to him one-on-one. It seems to work better that way."

The young woman pitched her cigarette butt into the sink and gazed at Fiona for a long moment. She started to say something, then stopped herself and looked at the floor. She crossed her arms and cleared her throat before looking up at Fiona with glistening blue eyes. Again, Fiona was struck by her resemblance to Shelby.

"We can certainly leave the door open if you'd be more comfortable, Mrs. Sherwood. But I'd like to minimize distractions."

"Just call me Annie," the woman said, swiping at her cheeks. "And whatever you need to do is fine." She pushed off from the counter and padded out of the kitchen.

As they walked through the house, Sullivan paused briefly to show Fiona the living area just off the front door. It contained a royal blue sectional sofa, an oak wood coffee table, and a matching entertainment center. A large television inside the cabinet was tuned to CNN, but the sound was muted.

"Colter was seated there," Sullivan said, pointing to a denim beanbag chair beside the table.

"And the lighting conditions?" Fiona asked.

"The blinds were open," Annie said from the doorway. "And the overhead light was on." She flipped the wall switch to demonstrate, and the room brightened considerably.

Fiona looked from the beanbag chair to the front door.

Sullivan was right. The boy almost certainly saw something.

Annie led them to the bedroom wing of the house, which was even darker than the rest and smelled like stale cigarette smoke. "My mom's been cleaning nonstop," she said as they neared the vacuum noise that drifted from one of the back rooms. "She drove up from Albany Monday night."

Annie paused beside the first doorway. "Colter, hon. The artist lady's here to see you."

Fiona glanced into the bedroom and saw a boy with sandy blond hair sitting cross-legged on the carpet. He wore green Incredible Hulk pajamas, and Fiona wondered whether he was ready for bed or simply hadn't dressed today. He didn't look up from his project, a multilayered Lego structure that appeared to be some kind of staging area for his many plastic dinosaurs.

Annie gazed at her son for a few moments before shifting her attention to Fiona. "Well. I guess we'll leave you to it."

Fiona nodded and entered the room. The lilac-painted walls matched the floral-print spread and pillow sham on Shelby's twin bed. A white wicker desk sat beneath a window, and Fiona noticed gray smudges on the windowsill where someone had dusted for latent prints. Beside the bed was a second windowsill, also smudged. Gold thumbtacks were pinned to the woodwork, each spaced about one inch apart. From every tack dangled a woven bracelet made of brightly colored embroidery thread. The intricately patterned bracelets were in various stages of completion, and Fiona stared at them a moment, thinking they were just the sort of thing she'd enjoyed making as a kid.

She chose a spot on the carpet far enough away from Colter to give him a sense of space. He still hadn't looked up from his dinosaurs or in any way acknowledged that he had a visitor.

"Hi, Colter," she said casually, mirroring his cross-legged posture on the floor. "My name's Fiona. I'd like to hang out with you for a while if it's okay."

Colter said nothing, but he stole a glimpse of her from beneath his cowlick.

She unzipped her leather case and pulled out a wooden board. It was four boards, actually, fitted together with brass hinges. Folded, the board measured twelve inches by twelve, the perfect size to fit inside a carry-on bag. Fiona unfolded the flaps and slid several brass fasteners into place, creating a two-foot-square work surface. Her grandfather had created the drawing board in his woodshop last summer, and Fiona considered it a clever feat of engineering. The brass fasteners that held the pieces rigid also served as clips for photographs or other visual aids. There was a shallow groove for pencils, and a notch at the top where a light could be attached if needed.

Colter didn't look up, but his hands had stilled.

Fiona pulled out a cardboard tube and unrolled a thick sheet of vellum-finish watercolor paper. She clipped it to the board and then dug a graphite pencil from her bag, along with a small container of Play-Doh. She spotted her *FBI Facial Identification Catalogue* and placed it within easy reach on the carpet. She preferred to work without it, but sometimes it came in handy when young children or non-native English speakers struggled to describe something they'd seen. A six-year-old boy might not know the term "receding chin," but he could point to a picture.

Fiona then rummaged through her collection of Beanie Babies and selected a soft green dragon with purple spikes on his back. It was the closest thing she had to a dinosaur, and she plopped it on top of her drawing board. She made a quick sketch of the dragon and glanced at Colter. His attention was riveted to her paper.

"What's your favorite dinosaur?" she asked him.

He tipped his head to the side, giving the question ample consideration.

"Mine's triceratops," she told him, quickly drawing one. It ended up looking more like a rhinoceros than a dinosaur, but she had Colter's attention.

"I like velociraptor," he mumbled.

Fiona's heart skipped a beat, but she nodded gamely. "I'm not sure I know that one. Is he the guy in your hand there?"

"That's pachycephalosaurus."

Whoa. So much for limited verbal skills. Fiona took a closer look at the dinosaur toys and noticed they'd been divided into camps. Her prehistoric animal trivia was rusty, but she was pretty sure he had them grouped into meat eaters and plant eaters.

Colter scooped up several of the dinos and scooted closer to Fiona. "Here," he said, dumping them on the carpet beside her. "These are the best ones."

One by one, Fiona drew each plastic toy, quizzing Colter about them as she went. He was a font of information.

"I draw people sometimes, too," she said as she shaded a

T-Rex. "I'd like to draw the person you saw at the door after school Monday. You think you could help me do that?"

Colter sat across from her on the carpet now. He bowed his head.

Fiona removed the dinosaur picture and replaced it with a clean sheet. She brought her knees up and rested the drawing board on them so he wouldn't be distracted by it. "Will you help me, Colter?"

"I didn't see him," he muttered.

Fiona tried to keep her voice relaxed. She didn't want Colter to sense the pressure, although clearly he already did. "It's okay," she said. "Just tell me anything you can."

He sat inert.

"Colter? Do you remember someone coming to the door Monday?"

A slight nod.

"What color hair do you remember?" Asking about characteristics in the abstract was less threatening, and hair color was the trait most witnesses talked about first.

"Brown," he whispered.

Brown hair.

"Okay." She leaned forward to hear his quiet voice. "What else did you see?"

"He was big."

"All right. That's good, Colter." But she didn't start drawing yet. Lots of people would seem "big" to a child seated on the floor, particularly a scared child. "Can you remember what he looked like?"

The silence stretched out as Colter stared at his lap. A tear splashed onto his pajama pants, and he rubbed it in with a pudgy thumb. Fiona's chest tightened.

"He said not to tell."

"It's okay to tell me, Colter. What else do you remember?"

"He made Shelby cry." The boy's voice caught, and he hunched his shoulders.

"It's okay." Her heart was breaking. "Take your time."

"He sticked his knife in my face!" A sob erupted from the depths of his little body. "He said don't tell about him or he'll come cut out my tongue."

CHAPTER

2

Jack hadn't expected her to be so young.

He watched Fiona Glass from across the darkened room, gathering details and filing them away in his brain: five-eight, average build—though it was difficult to tell because of the suit. Hair, light brown. Skin, pale. Full, pink lips illuminated by the glare of the slide projector.

He listened to her talk, not really caring about the words, as she stood beside the lectern and clicked through slides. Her voice was clear and confident, no discernable accent. He knew she was from California, but her businesslike demeanor didn't gel with his idea of an art teacher from the land of fruits, flakes, and nuts.

She turned to face the class, and her gaze skimmed over the bodies slumped in chairs throughout the lecture hall. She used a laser pointer to highlight something on the screen, something that excited her, judging by her tone. But the windowless room was warm and dim, and Jack knew from his own college days how that combination could put a person to sleep, especially one who'd been up half the night drinking beer.

Unfazed by her students' drowsiness, she continued to hammer away at her point about humanism. She made another visual sweep of the room, and this time her gaze landed on him. Her speech faltered a moment, and he could tell she was wondering why a guy his age had appeared in her lecture hall to eavesdrop on a discussion of Florentine painters.

A bell sounded in the outer hallway, and the room jolted to life. Students stood, yawned, stretched, and shouldered backpacks so they could be on their way to the next gig.

Jack leaned against the wall and waited until the last sloppy coed had trudged out, leaving him alone with Fiona Glass.

She had her hair pulled back in a fancy braid. With efficient movements, she packed her slide carousel into a cardboard box and loaded it into a briefcase. Then she threw her coat over her arm and crossed the carpeted lecture room to his place by the door.

"May I help you?"

"That depends," he said, looking her up and down. From a distance, she resembled a tax attorney, but up close like this he could see there was more to the story. That dull brown hair was actually more of a reddish gold, and the body he'd dismissed as average was straining against her suit in all the right places.

"Depends on?" She watched him impatiently, and he could see she didn't appreciate the way he was checking her out.

"Are you Fiona Glass?"

"Yes."

"Jack Bowman." He held out a hand. "We spoke on the phone."

She glanced down at his hand but didn't take it. Amused

by her attitude, he propped a shoulder against the wall and crossed his arms.

"I thought I made myself clear," she said tersely. "I'm not taking any more cases right now."

"That's not what you said," he pointed out. "You said you were on another case right *then,* and I have to assume that's finished because I saw your drawing on Fox News yesterday."

She huffed out a breath. "Mr. Bowman—"

"Jack."

She rolled her eyes. "*Jack*—"

"Why don't we go have a cup of coffee? I'll tell you about my case."

"As I said on the phone, Jack, I can't help you. You'll have to find someone else."

He studied her face. She felt annoyed with him—that much was clear. But he was picking up something else here, too. Like she was afraid of him for some reason.

Okay, fair enough. Six-foot stranger corners her at her workplace and demands a meeting. Hell, she sketched perverts and murderers for a living. Maybe she was skittish with men. He decided to try a different tactic.

Jack reached into the back pocket of his Levi's and pulled out a leather billfold. He opened it and slipped out a dog-eared business card. He gave it to her. Since moving back to his hometown, Jack had found few occasions to use the cards because most people he dealt with knew him on sight. But this woman needed reassurance.

"I'm the police chief in a town called Graingerville, about two hours south of here. That's my contact info. I understand you're busy, but I've known Nathan Devereaux for a lot of years, and he thinks you can help me. I trust his opinion. I don't want anyone else."

A wisp of hair fell over her face as she studied the card. She was obviously torn, so he decided to back off temporarily.

"Think about it and call me."

She looked up at him, and her hazel eyes showed concern. He could tell there was some kind of battle going on in her head.

"This . . . homicide you mentioned. You've got a witness?"

He had her.

But he didn't want to scare her off by telling her the full truth. "By the looks of things, yes. A woman who survived a previous attack."

She paused a minute. Took a deep breath. "Okay, I'll hear you out. But I'm not promising anything."

He couldn't repress a smile. His investigation was completely stalled, and she had no idea how much he needed a break.

"Thank you." He nodded politely.

She checked her watch. "I've got forty-five minutes before my next class. Let's sit down somewhere, and you can tell me about your case."

The Java Stop across from campus was packed with students seeking caffeine, free Wi-Fi, and procrastination. Fiona made a habit of stopping there between her two art history classes, which convened three days a week. She figured it was the perfect place to hold a meeting with a man she didn't know from Adam.

"How long you been teaching at the community college?" Jack asked as they settled into chairs.

He had to turn sideways because his legs didn't fit beneath the diminutive table. He'd shed his brown leather jacket with the shearling collar and now wore merely a gray flannel button-down tucked into jeans. His brown hair was short—almost a military cut—and his scarred work boots looked out of place beside the café's chic Scandinavian furniture.

"This is my fourth semester." Fiona blew on her skinny latte and looked around, noticing the many female gazes lingering on Jack. "I teach survey courses Monday, Wednesday, and Friday and spend the rest of the week in my studio." At least, that was her goal. She couldn't remember the last time she'd had an uninterrupted day to paint.

Jack wrapped his long fingers around a cup of plain black coffee. He had a farmer's hands—strong, tan, and callused. She wouldn't have picked him for a cop. He didn't wear a wedding band, and she wondered if he'd ever been married.

His gray-blue eyes watched her watching him over the brim. His look was direct, penetrating. He didn't miss much, Fiona realized as she gulped her latte. The foam scalded a path down her throat.

"Doesn't leave much time for police work, I don't guess."

"I'm trying to focus on my painting now," she said. "I sold a few pieces recently, and I've got a gallery showing coming up soon."

He didn't say anything to this, just lifted his steaming cup and took a sip. Fiona had paid for both drinks because she didn't want to owe him anything. She'd predicted the gesture would irk him, and it had. There was something old-fashioned about him.

Jack watched her for a long moment, and she tried not to shift in her seat.

"If you don't mind my asking, why would a woman with your reputation be looking to change careers?"

She did mind his asking, but she didn't want to seem rattled. She wasn't accustomed to having coffee with attractive men, and her social skills needed honing.

"I spent six years training to be a painter. Police sketches were just a way to pay the bills."

He frowned. "And you've got that covered now, that's what you're saying? You no longer need the cash?"

Fiona bristled. He made it sound so shallow, like it was all about money. But then, what else would he think, given what little she'd told him? No one understood her desire to be a painter, least of all the cops she knew. And although he might understand about the emotional toll her job was taking on her, she didn't want to discuss that with him. He'd see her as weak.

She squared her shoulders. "I thought we were here to talk about your case."

Jack leaned back in his chair and folded his arms over his chest. It was a muscular chest, and it went well with his broad shoulders. As an artist, she couldn't help noticing these things. She'd also noticed he had a prominent jaw and a slight cleft in the center of his chin. Wonderful bone structure. Good lips, too.

"Victim was discovered Tuesday."

Fiona abandoned her wayward thoughts. "Do you have an ID?"

"All we know so far is that she's a Hispanic female, probably sixteen or seventeen years old, according to our ME. She was sexually assaulted, strangled, and left in a pasture on the edge of town. No missing persons report that we can turn up. Course sometimes those don't get filed right away."

"Except that she's a minor," Fiona stated. "Most parents don't take long to report their kids missing."

He cocked his head to the side. "True. But she could be a runaway or maybe someone up from Mexico. We aren't certain about her age."

"Okay. And you said something about a surviving victim?"

He looked down into his coffee and nodded. "Another teenager. Mexican heritage. She was taken captive and sexually assaulted over a period of days. She'd been beaten and choked repeatedly before she managed to escape."

His eyes remained downcast, which Fiona found unusual for a seasoned police chief. She put him at late thirties, maybe younger. Police work packed on the years. She'd met twenty-three-year-olds at the LAPD who had seen more violence than many rural sheriffs. Maybe murders were a rarity in Jack Bowman's little community. If only the rest of the world could be so lucky.

"So you think you're looking at a serial killer?" she asked. "Someone who targets teenage girls?"

He lifted his gaze. "Possibly. Right now it's just a hunch. One I'd damn sure like to disprove."

"Did you submit it through ViCAP?"

"No hits."

"None at all?" she asked, surprised. The FBI-run database was massive.

"Well, one actually." He furrowed his brow. "But it was twelve years back."

"And?"

"And the man convicted of that crime was sentenced to forty years. He died in Huntsville last spring."

"So what's the feds' theory?"

His jaw tightened. "No idea."

"But don't they typically get involved with serial killers?"

Jack scoffed. "So far I've got one dead body, and it's sitting unclaimed in the morgue. Not a lot of folks clamoring for a big investigation."

And yet the chief of police had driven all the way to Austin to hire a forensic artist for his case. Fiona had to admire Jack's determination to seek justice for this victim, unidentified or not.

"Surely San Antonio PD must be willing to lend a hand here," she said. "They're the closest metropolitan area, right?"

Jack studied her face, and again she felt the power of those gray-blue eyes. "You're not from around here, are you?"

She gulped. "I grew up in California."

"I live two hours away from the Rio Grande, Ms. Glass."

"Fiona."

He nodded. "Fiona, then. Law enforcement agencies in this state, particularly in my area, are up to their necks in drug running, gang wars, and illegal immigration. Not to mention your regular stream of meth addicts and pedophiles. So far, all I've got is one un-IDed victim. How much help do you think I'm gonna get tracking down some guy who may or may not have been involved in a previous assault?"

"Not much."

Jack nodded. "That's why I need you. I think the crimes are connected. I think we're dealing with someone skilled and practiced, although I can't prove it."

"But my sketch won't give you proof of anything. It's just a tool."

"I realize that, but maybe it'll put us on the right track."

Fiona sighed, and Jack leaned forward. "Look, I'd really like to get a picture of this guy circulating before he gets a hankering to kill another girl. The only witness I have has been through hell. You've got a reputation with kids and rape victims. I know there're other artists around, but I want you."

Fiona took another sip of her latte and found it bitter. She pushed it away.

Another day that had started bright and sunny had turned bleak before her eyes. Another murder. Another witness. Another chance to torture some woman by mining her memory banks for the most horrifying moments of her life.

"Will you help me?"

She looked up at Jack Bowman, at the determined set of his mouth. She'd known it over the phone—he was a difficult man to refuse. The force of his personality was pulling her in.

But it wasn't just his personality. Fiona's gaze dropped to the hand wrapped around his coffee cup, and she wondered again if he had a woman in his life. Not that it mattered, anyway. Fiona didn't get involved with cops. She'd learned that lesson the hard way and didn't need a refresher course. She looked away.

She couldn't believe she was even considering this. She

barely knew this man, and she'd made a commitment to changing her life. She was really going to make a break this time. No more death and violence and evil faces haunting her everywhere she went. If she didn't stop now, there'd be no end to it.

"Fiona?"

"Let me think about it," she told him. "I'll call you with my answer."

Jack Bowman's words were still echoing through her mind when she unlocked the door to her loft apartment in downtown Austin. She dropped her briefcase and coat on the wooden bench beside the door and kicked off her sensible flats. Then she locked her deadbolt and fastened the chain.

Home.

She was out of her suit jacket in two seconds. She untucked her silk camisole from her slacks, crossed the living area, and dumped her mail onto the stone-topped bank of cabinets that separated the kitchen from the rest of the loft. Just walking through her apartment improved her mood. It was her island of tranquillity. Her first weekend here, she had painted the walls celadon green and bought wheat-colored sisal rugs to add warmth to the Saltillo tile floors. The soft colors relaxed her.

She pulled open the refrigerator and breathed a sigh of relief when she spotted the bottle of Sauvignon Blanc with a few sips remaining. It had been a long, tedious day, wrapped up with a two-hour faculty meeting and a three-hour stint in the library scrounging up slides for Monday's lecture. She was ready to unwind and shift into painting mode.

Fiona emptied the remaining wine into a glass and

perched on a bar stool so she could thumb through her mail: the usual flyers and bills, plus a letter from her grandfather, who lived in nearby Wimberley. His letters were easy to spot because of the spare handwriting—always in black ink—and the faint pencil lines he drew with a ruler before addressing his envelopes. A former structural engineer, her grandfather had an extreme Type A personality, but Fiona adored him, which was more than she could say for the rest of her family. Despite their fifty-year age gap, she and Granddad knew each other well. Fiona knew, for example, that the envelope from him would contain a clipping from the *San Antonio Express-News* detailing some misfortune that had befallen a single woman living alone somewhere. That would be it. No letter, not even a sticky note. Just an article he hoped would make her settle down and marry some nice young man.

Fiona sighed and tossed the letter aside. The only other item of interest was a plain white business envelope hand-addressed to "Glass." It bore a return address she didn't recognize in Binford, Texas. She took a paring knife from her chopping block and sliced open the top.

A small slip of paper fell out, a sheet from one of those pocket-size spiral pads. Fiona picked it up and read the wobbly block lettering scrawled across it: GET READY BITCH. ILL COME 4 U.

She dropped the note on the counter. Then she snatched up the envelope again and reread the return address. "Binford." The postmark said "Binford" also. She didn't know of any prisons in Binford, but that didn't mean a prisoner hadn't written this. She'd received hate mail before back in Los Angeles—different from this letter, though. Those disturbing missives had been mailed from the home of a convicted murderer's brother, and they had ceased after Fiona moved to Texas. She hadn't received anything threatening in nearly two years.

God, could this be happening again? Was she going to spend the next six months looking over her shoulder and dreading every trip to the mailbox? She didn't have the stomach for it.

She grabbed the portable phone off the counter and dialed a number she knew by heart.

"Devereaux."

"Nathan, it's Fiona."

"Well, speak of the devil." His voice sounded cheerful, meaning he wasn't on duty.

"I have a question for you. Do you know of any jails or prisons in Binford, Texas?"

"Binford, huh?" His tone became serious. "That's in east Texas. No lock-up there, unless you're thinking of the town jail, which I would guess has about one cell and a cot. Why?"

She paused, reluctant to tell him but knowing it was pointless to lie to a man who'd been a homicide detective for the past ten years. "I got a letter today."

"Threatening?"

She chewed her lip. "Maybe 'harassing' would be a better word."

"What did it say?"

"I'll show it to you." She cleared her throat. She hated asking for favors. But he'd asked her for plenty since she'd started freelancing for the Austin Police Department. "If I bring you a list of the APD cases I worked on, can you check to see if an address in Binford pops up?"

"No problem. I'm on tomorrow, so go ahead and drop it off along with the letter. We'll check for prints."

She let out a relieved breath. "Thanks."

"And don't touch it. Put it in a bag—"

"I know the drill."

"So," Nathan said, and she knew what was coming. "I hear you told ol' Jack Bowman to take a hike."

"I didn't tell him to take a *hike*. I just declined to get involved in his case. I left him a voice mail at his office with the name and number of someone I know up in Dallas."

"Jack wants you. He thinks you're the best in the business, that you'll use kid gloves with his rape vic."

"Gee, I wonder where he got that idea?"

He laughed. "Yeah, well, I brag on you every chance I get, sweetheart. You've helped clear more cases than half the cops we got working here."

"I'm really ready for a change, Nathan. I need—"

"I know what you need, and it's not more time alone. Call Bowman back. Give him a hand with this one."

Her irritation was mounting. It always annoyed her when men second-guessed her decisions, as if she didn't know her own mind. More than one relationship she'd been in had run into trouble over this very issue.

"I appreciate the compliment, but please don't send me any more cases." *Or detectives.*

The phone beeped, and Fiona welcomed the interruption. "Can I talk to you tomorrow at the station? I've got another call."

"Sure, see you then."

She switched to the next call and didn't even have time to say hello.

"What are you doing?" her sister demanded.

"Right now?"

"Yeah, right now. Right this second."

Fiona stared at her untouched glass of wine. It was probably warm by now. And after that, she was fresh out of distractions for the evening. "Not much," she said glumly.

"Perfect! You're coming with me to the Continental Club."

Fiona groaned. A crowded, noisy nightclub filled with wannabe rock stars was the dead last place she wanted to be tonight. And Courtney probably just wanted her there so she'd have someone to talk to before she picked up whatever guy was on her radar screen this week.

Either that or her car wasn't working again and she needed a ride.

"Fi? You there?"

"Tonight's no good, Courtney. I've got papers to grade. And I was planning to paint—"

"Fio*na*! What are ya, eighty? I swear to God, you're always doing chores or some bullshit *craft* project or—"

"Hey!"

"Come *on*. I'll even buy you a drink."

Fiona bit her lip. Felt tempted. Thought about the forty-two essays awaiting her on the European Renaissance. If she read one more paper citing Dan Brown as an authoritative source on Italian frescoes, she was going to scream.

Plus it was Friday night, and she felt lonely. Coffee that afternoon had been the closest thing she'd had to a date in months, and she was beginning to feel like a shut-in.

"Okay, I'll go."

A squeal pierced her eardrum. "I *knew* you'd come! Wear

something fun, okay? Not one of your Laura Bush getups."

Fiona gritted her teeth.

"Oh, and hey, my car's out of commission, so you can drive."

Jack rode the elevator up to Fiona Glass's swanky loft apartment and wondered what the hell he was doing. He didn't have time for this shit. He had a desk piled with paperwork, an officer out on maternity leave, and an unsolved homicide waiting for him back in Graingerville. And he'd wasted a full day driving up here to sweet-talk a cranky art teacher.

The elevator doors dinged open, and Jack glanced around. This floor had six units, and hers was on the left at the end. Nathan had given him her address over a steaming platter of barbecue brisket at the County Line. That was moments before she'd called Nathan's mobile phone to tell him about some letter she'd received and ask him not to send her any more cases.

Yet here he was.

All his life Jack had had a hard time taking no for an answer. His mother had taught him if he wanted something badly, he should show up in person, ask politely, and then ask again. And again. And again, if necessary. It was the Bowman family credo, the one that explained why his sisters had sold more Girl Scout cookies than anyone else in town, and why their drill team fund-raisers always generated enough money for trips to South Padre over spring break. The Bowmans could sell milk to a dairy cow, and Jack refused to accept failure after one attempt. He stopped in front of Unit 4A and mustered a charming smile.

The door swung open before his knuckles touched the wood.

Fiona jumped back. "What are you doing here?"

Holy hell, she'd ditched the suit. In a very big way. Jack stared, slack-jawed, at the two creamy scoops of flesh disappearing into folds of purple fabric. He managed to drag his gaze away from her cleavage only to get hung up on her shiny red lips. The cherry on top of a sundae.

"Jack?"

Then she stepped into the hallway, and he noticed the boots.

Plenty of women in Graingerville wore boots. The western kind. These were black leather lace-ups that went clear to her knees, with skinny heels about four inches tall. A black miniskirt hugged her hips.

"Hel-*lo*? Earth to Jack?"

He snapped his attention to her face. "That's . . . quite an outfit, Professor."

Scowling, she shrugged into a long black coat that covered everything up to her chin. Then she turned her back on him so she could lock the door.

All that hair hung in waves around her shoulders. It was reddish blond, or blondish red. There was a word for it, but damned if he could think of it when most of his blood had left his head.

She spun around to face him. "I thought you went back to Graingerville."

Jack cleared his throat. "I was on my way out of town, and I realized I forgot to mention something."

She made a point of looking at her watch. "I'm late to pick up my sister—"

"Where are you parked?"

"The garage."

He flashed her a smile. "How about I walk you to your car? Then I'll leave you alone, promise."

She huffed out a breath. She seemed to do that a lot when he was around.

"Fine." She slid her keys in her pocket and started down the hall. "What did you forget to mention?"

"I forgot to tell you about the poppies."

"The poppies." She stopped in front of the elevator, jabbed the Call button, and turned another scowl on him. "What poppies?"

The elevator doors slid open, and he stepped in beside her. She pressed the button for the lobby.

"We've got the best poppies in the entire state. Right outside Graingerville. Artists and photographers come from all over. We even have a festival."

She was looking at him like he was nuts. And she was right. As sales pitches went, this was a little out there.

Her eyebrows arched. "And you thought I should know this *why*?"

"Nathan told me you're a nature painter." Wow, she had a pretty mouth. He wondered if she planned to use it on anyone tonight. "The best fields are off the back roads. I figured I'd give you a private tour. You can bring along your painting stuff, maybe do something for your show."

The doors dinged open, and she strode across the lobby to the side entrance. Her heels made little clicks on the marble floor, and the sound reminded Jack just how long it had been since he'd gone to the trouble to ask out a woman.

He pushed the door open for her, and they entered the

breezeway to the garage. A cold gust of air lifted her hair off her shoulders. Jack darted his gaze around as he walked her down a row of parked cars. This garage needed better lighting and a security camera.

She halted in front of a white Honda Civic. A hybrid, no less. "Let me get this straight. If I agree to help you with this case, you'll give me a tour of the *poppies*?"

He rubbed his jaw. "Now, I hadn't thought about a trade. But it's a good idea. Course, we'd still pay your drawing fee. Whatever you normally charge."

"Don't poppies grow in the spring?"

"Yeah. So?"

She shook her head, but he saw the smirk on her face. She pulled her key chain out of her pocket, and he noticed the whistle attached to it.

He frowned. "You know, a tube of Mace can be a lot more effective. You can pick one up at any hardware store."

She tipped her head to the side. "I'm aware of that, but I'm in and out of airports all the time, so I settle for this."

Jack's personal security device of choice was a SIG P229, which trumped the hell out of a panic whistle. But he doubted Fiona cared for guns, being a California girl.

She opened her door and stood there watching him for a minute. "You don't give up, do you?"

"Nope."

He rested his hand on the door. Their fingers brushed, and a little quiver of something passed between them. He caught her look of alarm.

She slid behind the wheel and shoved her keys in the ignition.

Jack leaned his forearm on the Civic's roof and looked

down at her. She was moments away from caving, he could tell by those pursed red lips.

"Okay, I'll do it."

He smiled, and she started the engine.

"How about ten A.M. tomorrow?" he suggested. "You can meet me at the Graingerville police station. It's a two-hour drive from here, an hour forty if you speed."

She tugged the door handle, and he stepped out of the way. She pulled the door shut and lowered the window a few inches. "Eleven. I'll probably get in late tonight, and I've got an errand to run in the morning."

"You driving home alone?" It was none of his damn beeswax, but he had to ask. He'd spent nine years on a major metropolitan police force. Women leaving bars alone at night were easy pickings.

"*That*," she said, "is none of your business."

He stepped away from the car as she put it in gear. "Right. Well . . . be careful."

She smiled up at him. "I'm always careful."

CHAPTER

3

The sky outside Fiona's window was still black when she gave up the charade of sleep and tossed back the covers.

It was futile. Nothing would be gained from another two hours in bed besides a stiff neck. She wrapped herself in her green satin robe, slipped on her flip-flops, and shuffled into the kitchen to start a pot of coffee. As the machine hissed and gurgled, she stared down at her feet.

Why can't you go barefoot like normal people? You're so freaking anal.

Aaron's words came back to her, and she felt relieved that they no longer mattered. So what if she couldn't stand bare feet, or loud music, or empty milk cartons left in the fridge? Those were *her* preferences, and it was no longer anyone's concern if she was anal, or picky, or flat-out impossible to live with.

She was alone now and better off.

The coffee finished brewing, and she poured a mug while mentally rearranging her day. She'd swing by the police station, as planned, but instead of delivering the letter to Nathan personally, she'd leave it for him at the front desk, along with her list of cases. That would give her a jump on this morning's road trip and also save her from a conversation she didn't really want to have. At least not yet. Once she'd finished this last job—once it was *totally* complete—she'd march into Nathan's office and tell him she'd officially retired. Period. No more referrals.

Less than an hour later, Fiona exited police headquarters and returned to her car. It was still dark. Once inside the Civic, she flipped the heater to high and rubbed her hands together, wishing she'd remembered gloves. As the car warmed up, she skimmed the directions she'd printed off MapQuest. Estimated trip time, two hours and thirteen minutes. By eight o'clock, she would be entering the bustling metropolis of Graingerville, Texas, population 10,320.

With any luck she'd beat Jack Bowman into work.

She didn't know why, but the idea of one-upping him—even in such a minor way—pleased her. She supposed it had to do with his talking her out of what she'd thought was a firm decision. She'd really, truly intended to refuse him. She had, in fact. But when he'd told her this case involved teenage girls, she'd lost her backbone. All it took was one more nudge, and he'd had her.

She suspected he'd planned it that way.

Despite his tough-guy persona, Jack seemed unusually sensitive for a cop. Fiona had picked up on it when he'd talked about those girls in his town, as if he felt personally responsible for what had happened to them. She'd met a lot of dedicated cops over the years, and most of them displayed a certain detachment that enabled them to do their jobs day after day. Jack didn't seem detached. On the contrary, he seemed personally invested in this case. Fiona recognized the signs because she had that tendency, too, which was one of the reasons she longed for a break from law enforcement.

She took the on-ramp for Interstate 35 southbound and cast a glance at Town Lake as she crossed the bridge. Even at this early hour, people were out jogging on the spotlit path by the water.

She'd intended to exercise today. But making it to the gym—just like making time to paint—kept falling off the agenda as her life got busier and busier. If it wasn't a faculty meeting or a student-teacher conference, it was a late-night phone call from some detective who needed her help yesterday. A few high-profile cases, a few big arrests, and Fiona's forensic art career had taken off, leaving her barely enough time to keep up with her day job, much less devote a few hours to the painting she loved so much. And her fitness regimen? Her feet hadn't touched a treadmill in months. She needed to get back to the gym. Although, judging by Jack's tongue-tied reaction last night, she still had a few assets worth noticing.

A pair of headlights flashed in the rearview mirror. She squinted against the glare as the driver closed in, beaming her with his brights.

"Jerk," she muttered, adjusting the mirror. It looked like a pickup, the testosterone-mobile of choice in the Lone Star State.

He continued to blind her, so she relented and swerved into the right lane.

Fiona's shoulders tensed as the truck passed her, horn blaring, and swerved in front of her. He flipped her off and then gunned his engine, sending back a puff of exhaust.

Her breath whooshed out as the taillights faded. It was a

tailgater, for God's sake. She needed to get a grip. She took a deep breath and rolled her shoulders to ease some of the tension.

The inky purple sky was turning yellow in the east as Fiona exited the interstate a short time later. She passed several dumpy gas stations before finding one that looked sufficiently new and well lit. She needed something caffeinated to keep her alert for the remainder of the drive.

A cow bell clattered against the door as she entered the store.

"Mornin'. Help you find anything?"

She glanced at the clerk behind the counter and shook her head. She'd been in Texas two years, and the unwarranted friendliness of strangers still caught her off guard.

After grabbing a Diet Coke, Fiona paused in the snack aisle beside a box of Nutri-Grain Bars. She passed over the healthy stuff for a king-size Snickers and headed for the register. After all, breakfast was the most important meal of the day. As she dug through her purse, she felt someone behind her. She glanced over her shoulder and froze.

She'd sketched this man.

Her brain scrambled for a context. Was it an Austin case? Los Angeles? Her gaze swept over his features, searching for a clue. He had a hooked nose and a high forehead. Thinning brown hair . . . She *knew* she'd sketched him.

Or had she?

She watched him pull out his wallet, trying desperately to remember—

"That be all, ma'am?"

At the clerk's voice, the man's head jerked up. He caught Fiona staring at him and arched his brows. "What?"

She'd never seen him before. She'd never sketched him. He wasn't some wanted fugitive, just some regular guy buying gas.

"Ma'am?"

Fiona whirled around. The clerk was watching her expectantly.

"I'm sorry." She slapped a five on the counter and rushed from the store.

Jack's nationally renowned forensic artist arrived early and in a foul mood.

"You sure you don't want some coffee?" Jack asked, as they exited the station house.

She glared at him. "I repeat: *no*. If I change my mind, you'll be the first to hear about it."

"Suit yourself." He shrugged into his official cold-weather attire—a khaki windbreaker that matched his uniform. It wasn't heavy, but it kept him from freezing his ass off.

They descended the steps and started across the parking lot. Fiona's breath turned to steam in the brisk morning air, and he wondered why she hadn't worn something warmer than a turtleneck. Not that he minded the way it fit her, but she had to be freezing.

Jack led her to his pickup. She'd wanted to take her car, but after much wrangling he'd convinced her it'd be easier if they just rode together. He wanted to give her a feel for the town, and anyway, it was a short trip.

Now he wondered if he could stand her that long.

He popped the locks with his remote. After driving a two-toned Buick for nearly ten years, Jack was now the proud owner of a stone gray Ford F-250 with leather interior. It was a nice truck. And he'd decided to use it this morning because he wanted to keep a low profile, not because he wanted to impress Fiona, who seemed determined to bust his balls today.

Jack opened the passenger's-side door, and she sighed as she looked inside the cab. He offered her a hand getting in, but she batted it away.

Well, shit.

He rounded the front of the truck and hitched himself behind the wheel. "Someone get up on the wrong side of the bed this morning?"

She shot him a pissy look. "Stressful trip."

Jack turned his key, and the V8 hummed to life. "What, like car trouble?"

"No. On my way out of Austin some wacko practically tried to run me off the road."

"Nathan told me you got a mail threat. You think . . . ?"

"Different wacko. This was just some idiot out joyriding in his truck."

Not a fan of trucks, then. Jack cranked *his* truck's heater and adjusted the vents toward Fiona. As he exited the parking lot, he waved at Lorraine Snelly, who was crossing Main Street. She gave him a nod, no doubt curious about his passenger. Jack resigned himself to the unavoidable reality that his new "friend" would be the hot topic of conversation at Lorraine's lunch counter later today.

"Tell me about the witness," Fiona said, her voice crisp. He'd noticed she had different tones for different settings, just like she had different wardrobes. Besides the pine green turtleneck, she wore jeans and practical brown ankle boots today. He missed the spiky black ones from last night.

Jack reeled his thoughts in. "Her name's Maria Luz Arrellando. Lives just outside town."

"You have jurisdiction there?"

"No. But she was abducted from Graingerville, so it's ours."

"Okay. Give me a sense of the crime. I want to make sure I steer clear of her triggers."

"Triggers?"

She opened the leather case she'd brought along and scrounged around for something. "You said she'd been sexually assaulted. Most rape victims suffer from posttraumatic stress disorder. Some experience feelings of panic set off by unexpected reminders of the attack." She pulled a cell phone out of her bag and fiddled with the setting. "I met a teenage victim once who'd been drugged with a hypodermic needle. I was interviewing her in the hospital the following day, and a nurse walked in with some meds in a syringe. The girl went ballistic."

Jack glanced at her, realizing she still had some major misconceptions about this case.

Misconceptions he'd helped foster.

"You planning to medicate my witness?"

She rolled her eyes. "No. I'm just saying, help me prepare. Give me a feel for where she's coming from. What can you tell me about her attack?"

Okay, time to come clean.

"Well, for starters, she was abducted late at night, from a road not too far from here. Guy pulled up in a gray sedan and offered her a ride, which she accepted because she was cold."

Fiona shook her head, probably having heard this sort of thing before. In all his years of policing, Jack had never been able to understand how people could be so reckless with their safety.

"Instead of taking her home," Jack continued, "he pulls off into some brush and ties her up with this tough green twine. Blindfolds her. Then he takes her to an unknown location and keeps her there for about two days. She's in and out during the assaults. He's force-feeding her something—she thinks it's cough syrup. Finally she comes to, and he's gone. She gnaws through the twine, grabs some clothes, and manages to escape. Some deer hunters pick her up about forty miles from here."

Fiona sighed.

"What?"

"I didn't know she'd been sedated. That could affect her description."

"She insists she got a good look at the guy right off. Then later when she was in and out. Fact, she says she faked being out of it at some points so he'd go easier on her."

Jack took the highway leading south out of town and picked up speed. Acres of farmland stretched out on either side of them. The fields looked soggy and desolate.

The recent freeze had wreaked havoc on several of the region's crops, most notably the citrus. Not an hour south of here, groves of navel oranges and ruby reds had been decimated by the ice. At first, area growers had attempted to battle the frost. Farmers had pumped water into the fields to raise the ground temperature and circulated warm air with giant fans, but after the frigid temperatures dragged on, the effort became hopeless. After salvaging what little they could, they'd ruefully said good-bye to all the rest.

Jack had grown up on a farm and knew firsthand it

was a tough business. But knowing that didn't make things easier when disaster struck. The repercussions of last week's three-day dip into the teens would be felt throughout this area for years.

The Tejas Fruit sign loomed up ahead, and Jack slowed slightly. On a typical January day, the place would be bustling with delivery trucks and people, but hundreds of workers had been let go recently, and the pack shed looked strangely quiet.

"We're almost there," he said. "Anything else you need to know?"

"Yes. Has she been interviewed before by a sketch artist?"

Jack had expected the question. He popped open the console between the front seats and pulled out a manila envelope. "She talked to one of our officers at the time. He came up with this."

Fiona opened the envelope and pulled out a computer-generated drawing. It showed a Caucasian male somewhere between twenty-five and fifty. He had bland, unremarkable features and reminded Jack of the father from those Dick and Jane books kids used to read in school. Except instead of smiling, the guy stared blankly out into space.

Fiona frowned at the picture. "This is completely generic. It could be anybody."

"I know. The kid who came up with that—guy by the name of Lowell—he'd never interviewed a sexual assault victim before. I'm guessing he was a little out of his league."

Fiona looked at him, appalled. "How could you let this happen? She needed to talk to someone experienced. Preferably a female. If you don't have someone on staff, you should have brought someone in—"

"Believe me, I know. But I wasn't in charge then—"

"And don't even get me started on this computer program! To get a useful sketch you need a good interview with a trained artist. You can't just tell some rookie to sit down at the computer and slap together a face like it's Mr. Potato Head. A woman was *raped*!"

Clearly this was a hot-button issue for Fiona. Jack watched her, waiting for the rest of his words to sink in.

Suddenly her brow furrowed. "Did you say you weren't in charge when this was done?"

He cleared his throat. "I was working property crimes in Houston at the time."

"How long ago was the abduction?"

"Eleven years."

She went still. The only sound inside the truck was the low-humming heater.

Jack cut a glance at Fiona. She stared at him, mouth agape, her eyes wide with disbelief.

He looked back at the road. The Arrellando property lay up ahead, just beyond a set of railroad tracks. Jack pulled off to the side of the highway and parked beside a barbed-wire fence.

"Eleven years," she repeated.

He turned to face her. Saw the color rising in her cheeks. He'd thought she'd be pissed, but he realized now he'd underestimated the extent.

Nothing to do now but have it out with her.

"That's right." He nodded. "Eleven years."

She laughed, but there was no humor in it. In fact, he was pretty sure those were tears glistening in her eyes.

"I can't believe you did this," she muttered. "Does Nathan know about this?"

"What do you mean?"

"Does *Nathan,* our mutual *friend,* know you dragged me here under false pretenses? That you lied to me and lured me down here on some wild-goose chase?"

"It's not a wild-goose chase."

She turned in her seat to face him straight on. "*Not* a wild-goose chase. You're deluded, you know that? You've pinned your homicide investigation to a fantasy. I *cannot* provide you with a usable drawing based on an eleven-year-old memory!"

"Why not?"

"Why not? Do you have any idea—"

"I've been doing some research. Someone drew that famous sketch of the Unabomber based on a sighting that was seven years old. It was a good sketch, too. They went back and superimposed it on Ted Kaczynski's photograph and—"

"*Seven* years is different from *eleven* years!" Her cheeks were flaming now, and she had some freckles on her nose he hadn't noticed before. "Even if I got a good sketch—which is a huge if—I'd have to do an age progression—"

"I hear you're good at that," he cut in. "You did one on that kid up in Idaho. Helped his mom track him down after the stepdad took him." Jack hoped flattery was the way to go here. Everything else he'd said seemed to be fueling her anger.

"Don't you dare pull that crap on me."

Or maybe not. "What crap?"

"That false flattery crap!"

"It's not false if—"

"I don't want to hear it." She folded her arms over her

chest and turned to face the windshield. "You purposely misled me. You smooth-talked me into coming here."

"You're right, I did." He watched her profile. "I didn't think you'd take my case if you knew how much time had elapsed since the other crime."

"You were right. This is crazy. What you want is impossible."

"I don't believe that, and neither do you. I think you want to try, but you're scared of failure. Scared you'll ruin your track record."

She turned toward him, her eyes sparking again. "I can't believe you said that. You don't know anything about me!"

"I know you're good," he said firmly. "You're the best at what you do. Like it or not, you've got a reputation. Especially with rape victims."

Jack looked through the windshield and saw the gray tin roof of the Arrellando house less than a football field away.

"Lucy went through hell," he said. "For years afterward—"

"Who's Lucy?"

"Maria Luz." Jack glanced at Fiona. She was listening. "She goes by Lucy. One of the worst parts of her ordeal was that so many people didn't believe her. They thought she made up some tall tale, created the whole thing for attention."

Fiona's eyebrows shot up. "A tall tale? You said she was beaten and choked—"

"She was." Jack paused, trying to figure out how to phrase it. He couldn't believe he was trying to defend the town that had done this to one of its own.

Of course, not everyone felt like he did—that all the

people who considered themselves part of this community actually belonged here.

"Lucy was pretty rebellious growing up," Jack explained. "Her parents, they're strict Catholics. They were always real religious, especially her dad. Just before the abduction, Lucy had a fight with him. Stormed out of the house. She wasn't seen for two days, and I guess plenty of people figured she ran off. When those hunters found her, some folks didn't believe she'd been held against her will. They thought she'd taken up with a rough guy, maybe even gotten what she deserved."

Fiona shook her head and looked away.

"You could say Lucy got a raw deal. From the cops. From the people around here." Jack clenched and unclenched his jaw. "Even from her dad. I don't think he's ever believed her. It was her mom who made her fill out the police report, and that was days after the fact. Too late for a rape kit."

Fiona leaned her head back against the seat and sighed. "And you want *me* to fix all that. Now. Eleven years later. That's impossible."

"Fiona, look at me."

She looked at him, and he knew that he still had a shot. His words had affected her—he could see it in her eyes.

"I strongly believe—no, make that *know*—Lucy's case is related to this other homicide," he said. "I've got too many similarities to ignore. And you know what that tells me? That tells me some guy with ties to this community is a rapist and a killer. And he thinks he can hurt girls around here because they're soft targets. Maybe they're illegal or their families don't trust cops or they slip through the cracks some other way. But I think he's experienced. I think he'll do it again. I need to catch up with him before he does."

Fiona looked down.

"Just come talk to her. Hell, we're practically at her house. Give her an hour. If nothing comes of it, you can go back home and forget this whole case. No hard feelings."

She bit her lip.

"Please?" As the word left his mouth, he realized just how rarely he said it.

She nodded slightly.

"Thank you." He blew out a breath and thrust the truck into gear. "You'll be done with all this before you know it."

Lucy Arrellando lived a stone's throw away from a railroad crossing in a white clapboard house with a corrugated roof. A dusty black Cavalier sat in the driveway. The small yard was surrounded by a chain-link fence, and Fiona immediately noticed the BEWARE OF DOG sign attached to it.

Jack unlatched the gate and held it open for her. He seemed unconcerned by the prospect of a dog, unlike Fiona. She'd had a deep-rooted fear of dogs—even little yappy ones—ever since a Scottish terrier had bitten off a chunk of her neck when she was a child. She stayed close to Jack's heels, resisting the urge to hold on to his jacket, as they made their way up the gravel path to the door.

The home was a typical postwar tract house, similar to the neighboring ones paralleling the railroad tracks. The row of houses stretched for miles, it looked like, their tin roofs packed together in an orderly line. The closely built structures seemed out of place in the midst of so much open space.

Fiona glanced anxiously around the yard. No dog. No barking. Just a giant pecan tree that shaded the property.

From its lowest limb dangled a tire swing, and at the base of the tree sat a rusted red wagon. Fence or not, she hated to think of a child playing so close to the tracks.

"We're pretty early," Jack said, climbing the steps. "The men are at the refinery, though, so it shouldn't matter."

Fiona was just digesting the implications of his words when the screen door squeaked open. She looked up to see a stunningly beautiful young woman standing on the threshold with a baby on her hip.

The woman cast a quick glance in Fiona's direction before settling her brown eyes on Jack.

"You're early," she said sourly.

"Is that okay?"

"I guess it'll have to be, won't it?"

They exchanged a look loaded with meaning, and Fiona instantly felt uncomfortable. There was some subtext she wasn't getting here, but she couldn't very well ask about it.

The baby squirmed and filled the silence with a wet gurgle.

The woman's gaze returned to Fiona. She gave her a brief up-and-down appraisal before stepping backward into the house and nodding for them to come inside.

When they were all three standing awkwardly in the hallway, Jack cleared his throat. "Lucy, this is the artist I told you about, Fiona Glass."

Lucy shifted the baby to a front carry, effectively precluding the possibility of a handshake. Fiona was good at reading body language, and Lucy's was loud and clear.

She turned her back on her guests and walked to the rear of the house. Jack followed, seeming to know exactly where he was going.

Fiona hitched her attaché case higher up on her shoulder and trailed behind them.

Why did it matter that the "men" were gone? Who lived here besides Lucy, and what sort of threat did they pose to this meeting? Once again Fiona felt her chest tightening with frustration. Jack had kept just a few too many things secret about this job, and she didn't appreciate it one bit.

They ended up in a bright, spacious room at the back of the house. It looked like an add-on that was being used as some sort of workshop. A tabletop sewing machine occupied the far corner. Shimmery white fabric cascaded from the machine and pooled onto the carpeted floor. Behind the sewing table, bolts of white, ivory, and pale pastel material were arranged neatly on a unit of plastic shelving. A varnished plywood table filled the room's center, and lined up to one side of the smooth work surface were plastic trays, each containing an assortment of beads, sequins, and pearls.

"Sebastian's napping," Lucy said, settling the infant into a playpen near the sewing station.

No one bothered to introduce the baby, who wore a lavender fleece sleeper and matching cap. As soon as Lucy put her down, she snatched up a teething ring and brought it to her mouth. She was probably about nine months old, Fiona speculated, watching her sit up among her toys. She was a beautiful baby, wide-eyed and alert.

"Jack!"

Fiona whirled around just as a dark-haired little boy charged into the room. He hurled himself at Jack's knees and wrapped his arms around them.

"Hey, sport." Jack mussed his hair. "Thought you were sleeping."

The boy grabbed Jack's hand and tugged. "You wanna see my Nintendo DS? I got it for Christmas!" The child, who looked to be about four or five, gazed up at Jack with unabashed adoration.

"Sounds good," Jack said, making eye contact with Lucy. "Where's Dolores?"

"Working. They all are." Lucy turned to Fiona, addressing her for the first time. "I assume you want to do this in private?"

"That's usually best."

"Then Jack can watch Sebastian." She nodded at the playpen. "Vanessa won't bother us."

Jack conveniently left the room with Sebastian before Fiona could pull him aside to explain a few things.

Such as, how come this felt like a hostile interview?

Fiona turned to face Lucy. They were about the same age, but Lucy dressed much younger. She wore tight jeans with frayed cuffs and a gray T-shirt that conformed to her generous breasts. She also wore half a dozen silver studs in her left ear, a silver chain belt, and ballet flats, also silver. Her straight hair hung to her waist, and Fiona wondered how she kept it out of her way while she was sewing.

If, in fact, this was her workroom.

"Are you a designer?" Fiona asked, glancing around.

Lucy tipped her head to the side and looked at her a moment before answering. "Seamstress."

"But you do your own designs?" Fiona eyed the drawings lined up neatly on the table beside a box of well-used Prisma pencils.

"Yes." Lucy followed Fiona's gaze. "Most of my girls want something custom. So that's usually what I do."

Fiona stepped toward the table and set down her attaché case. "May I?"

Lucy nodded.

Fiona took a closer look at the gowns that had been sketched with a skilled hand.

"Wedding dresses?"

"Quinceañera."

Fiona nodded. She'd heard that a girl's fifteenth birthday was an important milestone in the Mexican culture, much like a coming-out ball.

"These are beautiful," she said, studying the elaborate beadwork and draping involved. "Expensive, too, I'd imagine."

Lucy shrugged. "I make a living." She walked across the room and retrieved a Sunkist out of the minifridge beside the back door. "Want one?"

Fiona nodded, more to be sociable than because she was thirsty. She tried to avoid sugary soft drinks—if she was going to consume empty calories, she preferred them in the form of chocolate.

Lucy handed her a cold orange can and then walked over to the padded office chair behind her Singer 6000. Fiona picked up her case and decided to take a seat on the low beige sofa just across the room. This arrangement put Lucy at a higher vantage point, which Fiona hoped would make her feel more in control. She also hoped Lucy's proximity to her work would provide a good distraction. Rape victims tended to avoid direct eye contact during the interview and sometimes wanted something to occupy jittery hands. Although Fiona didn't ask them to detail the attack itself—just the perpetrator—many volunteered the information anyway, which could make for a highly emotional conversation.

Of course, this attack occurred eleven years ago, so Fiona was in uncharted waters here.

She popped open the Sunkist and took a sip. The too-sweet flavor reminded her of middle school and agonizing hours spent alone at the end of a lunch table. She placed the drink on the floor at her feet.

Lucy flipped the light switch on her sewing machine and scooted her chair close to the table. "Sebastian and Vanessa are my sister's kids. I usually watch them while she's working."

"You all live here together?"

Lucy nodded. "My sister, my brother-in-law, my older brother. Plus my parents. Everyone's on shift today."

The baby gurgled from the playpen, and Lucy looked over and murmured to her in Spanish.

Then she glanced at Fiona, and her expression hardened. "When Jack called me yesterday, I told him he was crazy."

"I told him that fifteen minutes ago."

Fiona had decided to be brutally honest. Lucy seemed like the straightforward type. And Fiona didn't want her getting her hopes up about what they could accomplish today.

The corner of Lucy's mouth quirked up. "So he didn't tell you, huh? That this was a cold case?"

"Not until this morning."

Lucy shook her head. "Typical Jack."

Fiona felt a prick of annoyance at the implied intimacy. Clearly, Jack and Lucy had a history of some sort, and Jack had purposely avoided mentioning it. Fiona busied herself getting out her drawing board and pencils, the whole time mentally cursing him. She didn't think she'd ever been so misinformed about a job before.

When the board was ready, she took a deep breath and tried to clear her mind. This was her last case, and likely one of her most challenging. She needed to focus.

"That last picture was all wrong," Lucy said. "I told the cops that over and over, but they didn't listen." She tipped her chin up and stared at Fiona with a challenge in her eyes. "But, shit, what do I know, right? I'm just the witness."

"I'm not a cop," Fiona stated. "I'm an artist, same as you."

Lucy shrugged and loaded a spool of white onto the machine. She dampened the end of the thread with her tongue and carefully maneuvered it through the eye of the needle. Lucy's hands were sure and steady, which was uncommon for this sort of interview. The sewing machine whined into action as her foot pressed the pedal.

"Jack really wants to get this guy," Lucy said, not looking up from her work.

"What about you?"

The machine stopped. Lucy's eyes lifted, and Fiona recognized the look in them, something almost feral.

"Sadistic fuck tortured me for two straight days. I want him to burn in hell."

Fiona nodded. Selected a pencil. "Do you remember him well enough to describe him?"

Lucy pressed her lips together, gazed down at her work. The needle became a blur as she fed the white fabric beneath it. "Yeah."

"Because it's okay if you don't. If you can't remember something, just say so. We'll do the best we can."

"I remember." She shook her head. "Little details, too. Like it just happened."

The mind was strange. It stored away some things from long, long ago, and jettisoned others from as recently as yesterday. Fiona could recall the exact outfit she'd been wearing when she watched the World Trade Center collapse. She remembered the precise color of the sky that morning, the coffee mug she'd held in her hand as she stood before the television. Yet if someone asked her what she'd worn to the movies two weeks ago, she'd have no idea.

Emotional trauma, especially fear, cemented memories. It was one of the body's survival mechanisms, she'd learned.

"Tell me about his face," Fiona said. "Whatever you can remember."

The machine stopped. Lucy's hands stilled on the fabric, and she stared off, past the windowpane to the wintry day outside.

"I remember all of it," she said quietly. "It's tattooed on my brain."

"So? What'd you get?"

Jack's deputy sighed on the other end of the line. "This isn't as easy as you think, J.B. Some of this shit, you need to have a warrant."

Jack propped a hip on the wooden railing surrounding the Arrellando porch. He glanced at his watch. An hour and forty minutes, and they were still back there drawing.

"So problem-solve," Jack insisted. "Come on, Carlos. That's the beauty of small-town policing. We can cut through some of the red tape."

Carlos muttered a curse in Spanish. "Why don't you go

talk to her? You're the pretty face around here. I'm the guy with the beer gut and six kids."

Jack smiled. "Don't forget the wife."

Another curse.

"Okay, so Norma won't cooperate," Jack said. "She's not the only one over at Parks and Wildlife. What about Melvin?"

Carlos didn't say anything, and Jack realized his mistake. Melvin was something of a racist. He didn't talk about it openly, but it became apparent whenever the old man dealt with the two Hispanic officers in Jack's department.

"Forget it, I'll talk to him," Jack amended, glancing at his watch again. He had so much to do today, and he hadn't made a dent. Now he'd probably spend an hour shooting the shit with Melvin in the Texas Parks and Wildlife Bureau's local office, trying to talk him out of a list of every bubba in the tricounty area who'd applied for a deer license eleven years ago. Maybe he'd delegate this job to Lowell.

As leads went, this was pretty thin. But Jack had reviewed Lucy's original police report a dozen times in the last few days, along with the statements provided by the hunters who found her after the abduction. She'd been picked up in a remote area northwest of here accessed by a few ranch roads and surrounded by thousands of acres of flat brushland. Deer country. And no one working the case at the time had checked out who owned the land or had access to those deer leases. According to Lucy's statement, she'd been held in some sort of small trailer, the kind you hitch to a vehicle, the kind many people kept at their deer camp. Lucy had said the trailer hadn't been hitched to a vehicle at the time of her escape. The trailer could have been anyone's, but an officer should have at least attempted to find out if it might have belonged to someone who had reason to be on the acreage near the pickup site.

And if Jack could cross-reference *that* list with a list of drivers who had gray Chevrolet Caprices registered to their names eleven years ago . . .

Of course, the car Lucy described could have been stolen. Or maybe the perp owned the car, but had no connection to the property where he'd taken Lucy and he was just squatting there for a few days. Still, it was worth a try. This guy was local. Jack felt it in his bones.

The vehicle, the nearby property owners, the hunters—all these aspects of the case should have been checked out over a decade ago, but they weren't. Of course, the lead in the case back then was more interested in where his next doughnut was coming from than where the killer might be hiding. Jack couldn't change the past, but he could avoid a repeat performance. This time around, there would be no sloppy police work, no half-assed investigating. This time around, the Graingerville Police Department—all six of them—would do the job right.

"J.B.? You listening, man?"

"Sorry. What?"

The screen door screeched opened, and Fiona stepped out of the house.

"I said I got a lead on that twine from our victim. The fluorescent green that Lucy described? They used to carry it at hardware stores all over the Southwest, plus Wal-Mart."

Lucy followed Fiona onto the porch with Vanessa on her hip again. Neither woman looked at Jack. As he watched,

Fiona reached over and squeezed Lucy's hand, and then Lucy—to Jack's astonishment—pulled Fiona into a hug. They whispered back and forth for a moment and then stepped apart.

"So we got a break there," Carlos was saying.

Shit. "Sorry, can you repeat that?"

"I said, *you can't get it anymore!*" Carlos evidently thought Jack was having trouble hearing. "Now they only manufacture it for a few customers. Stopped mass distribution about six years ago."

Lucy gave Jack a curt nod and went back into the house. Fiona descended the steps and waited in the yard, her back to him.

"So that narrows it down to specialty stores. Farming supplies, mostly. You can find green all over, but for this exact color, you gotta really look."

"It's a good lead," Jack said, watching Fiona's shoulders tremble in the biting wind. Why the hell hadn't she brought a jacket?

"I'm on my way in now," he told Carlos. "Don't go anywhere because we need to discuss the ME's report."

"You got it."

Jack disconnected and shoved his phone into his pocket. Fiona started across the path, and he had to stride to keep up with her.

"Fiona?"

She didn't turn around. "Can we go now, please? I'm cold."

She pushed through the gate and stood beside the pickup, gripping her art case and shivering. Jack popped the locks and opened her door for her. Not making eye contact with him, she stowed her bag on the floor and climbed into the truck. She stared straight ahead at the windshield.

"Where's your coat?"

"In my car." She looked at him. "I spilled something on it earlier."

Her nose was red, as were her cheeks and her eyes. She was crying.

Jack reached over her lap and snagged a crumpled flannel shirt from the back of the cab. He shook it out and handed it to her.

"Put this on," he said, and closed her door.

He went around and climbed behind the wheel, reviewing the exchange he'd just seen between Lucy and Fiona. Jack didn't know Fiona very well. He didn't know her at all, really, except what he'd read on the Internet and what he'd learned from Nathan. But Lucy, he knew. And she was—hands down—the least *huggy* woman he'd ever been around. She did not squeeze, kiss, cuddle, or do any of that warm-fuzzy shit in public, and especially not with women. Lucy was a loner and a hard ass and, according to many people, a bitch.

Yet obviously Fiona had bonded with her.

Jack steered onto the highway and cast an apprehensive glance in Fiona's direction. She'd put on his shirt and flipped up the cuffs, but still the thing damn near swallowed her. She sniffled. He didn't see any tears, but she dabbed her nose with the back of her hand.

Jack popped open the console and retrieved a stack of Dairy Queen napkins. He stuffed them into the cup holder and passed one to her.

"Thanks." She took the napkin and did one of those dainty nose blows. "Sorry. I'm usually better at this."

"At what?"

"I don't know. Compartmentalizing."

"It's a rough case," he offered. Understatement of the century. Lucy's ordeal was as vicious as he'd ever come across, and it was amazing she'd lived through it. Looking at it now, Jack doubted that had been part of the perp's plan.

Fiona folded her hands in her lap and took a deep breath. "So . . . You guys have a motel around here?"

"Sure. What for?"

She looked at him. Her eyes looked emerald green now because she'd been crying. "I need a quiet place to work. I've still got to refine the preliminary drawing and do the age progression."

Holy shit. "You got a drawing?" Jack had pretty much talked himself out of that hope.

"I got something." She looked at her hands. "The question is whether it's usable. I don't really know yet. I'll have to spend more time on it and make a judgment call."

Jack focused on the road, trying to seem open-minded. In reality, it wasn't Fiona's decision. If he paid her fee, he'd do what he wanted with the picture.

"How long does the age progression take? Maybe you could work at the station house."

Fiona stared out the window. "I prefer to work without distractions. And this could take a while. Especially if I do another subject."

Another subject . . . ?

She looked at him. "You were planning to ask me, weren't you?"

He debated whether to answer that truthfully. He'd misled her about pretty much everything from the get-go, and this was no exception.

"I hadn't counted on it," he said. "If you don't want to—"

"Don't make excuses. You can't work a homicide without an ID."

She was right. The victim's identity was a critical missing piece in this puzzle. But Fiona looked drained. He hadn't expected this case to have such an impact on her, and guilt needled at him.

"You want to go to the motel first?" he asked. "Maybe take a nap or something?"

She shook her head, looked away. "I don't need a *nap,*" she said. "Just take me to the morgue."

CHAPTER

4

Shelby Sherwood's abductor had rented a Chrysler mini-van in Minneapolis yesterday afternoon.

An hour later he'd checked into an Econo Lodge in Bangor, Maine, and at 7:15 this morning he'd been seen buying super-unleaded gasoline at a Shell station in Tucson. The clerk who took his twenty said he looked exactly like that drawing on the news, except maybe heavier and with a ponytail.

Garrett Sullivan downed his last gulp of truck-stop coffee and flipped open the file on the Taurus's front seat. Since Fiona's sketch had been released three days ago, leads had been pouring in by the hundreds. The guy's in Nashville. No, Roanoke. Someone just sold him a set of snow tires in Peoria . . .

A dedicated team of cops and volunteers had spent hours sifting through all the tips. The promising ones resulted in police visits, and a small handful of those interviews had netted information worth pursuing. It was tedious work, and stressful because one overlooked lead could be the only one that mattered. Everyone who worked child abductions was haunted by the Polly Klaas case. Just hours after the twelve-year-old was snatched from her slumber party, police detained a man on a trespassing complaint at some property not thirty miles from Polly's house. Unaware that the man was wanted on a parole violation, the police helped him pull his car out of a ditch and sent him on his way.

Weeks later that trespasser—Richard Allen Davis— confessed to killing Polly and led investigators to her body.

Child abductions were a nightmare, but Sullivan remained hopeful, in large part because of Fiona Glass. He had faith in her drawing, and now that he'd finally met her, he understood how she'd earned her reputation.

Psychic, some said. Others called her telepathic. When these high-profile cases came up, those labels got a lot of media play. Sullivan dealt in facts, not magic. Fiona wasn't psychic, but she *was* gifted. He had no doubt that when they finally tracked down this UNSUB, he'd be a dead ringer for the picture she'd drawn. The woman was highly intuitive. He'd seen her in action, spied on her methods while standing silently outside the bedroom where she'd worked with Colter Sherwood. She had amazing instincts with people, somehow knowing precisely how to coax out vast quantities of information they didn't even realize they possessed.

Sullivan flipped through his file until he found the brief write-up on the woman he was about to meet. He reviewed a few key facts before getting out of the car, leaving the file behind on the front seat. He liked to do interviews empty-handed. People tended to clam up when they thought he was taking notes, although most times that's exactly what he was doing. Sullivan locked the Taurus, crossed the sidewalk, and entered Second Go Round.

The resale shop's owner led Sullivan to the back as she reiterated what she'd said in the preinterview.

"It's Ron," she declared. "I'm sure of it. It's like I told that agent on the phone, I got a knack for faces. There's not a doubt in my mind."

She shoved aside a rolling clothes rack and stepped through a narrow doorway. Sullivan followed her into the dimly lit back office.

"'Scuse the mess," she said.

The room smelled like mildew and vanilla air freshener, and "mess" was something of an understatement. Giant piles of clothes lined the cinderblock walls—shirts, pants, dresses. A large black bin on wheels was filled to the brim with shoes. Another similar bin held child-size jackets and coats. Along the very back wall, a set of clear plastic boxes overflowed with socks, belts, and other items Sullivan couldn't make out. It was difficult to see clearly. The sole light in the room came from an antique-looking floor lamp with a fringed yellow shade.

"He used to sort the merchandise," the shopkeeper said. "People drop off whatever. It's all mixed up." She nodded toward several clothes racks crammed with hangers, but no clothes. "I been short-handed since he left. 'Specially with the New Year's rush—people cleaning out closets and whatnot."

The back door had been propped open with a rusty shopping cart, and Sullivan wondered whether this was for light or ventilation. He stepped over a pile of men's sweaters. "You said he filled out an employment application? Do you have it on hand?"

"Sure." She walked over to a black metal desk hardly

visible beneath a heap of papers. "I got it filed here somewhere."

Sullivan mentally composed a description of the witness. Her platinum blond hair was twisted atop her head
in some kind of bun, and several frizzled strands fell in her
face as she shuffled through the desk. She'd given her age
over the phone as forty-nine, but Sullivan put her closer
to sixty.

"Here it is!" She tugged a paper loose from the drawer
and held it out for him.

"Thank you." He took the form and stepped closer to
the back exit where the light was better.

Ron Jones. The handwriting slanted sharply left. *339
Elm St*. A phone number had been listed, then crossed out
repeatedly.

A prickle of anticipation traveled down Sullivan's spine.
Practically every piece of information on the form looked
invented.

"You check out these references?" Sullivan asked.

"Heck, I was just happy to get an applicant." She fisted a
hand on her hip. "This isn't exactly dream work, and I cain't
afford to pay more than minimum wage."

Sullivan's pulse quickened as he scrutinized the form.
"Ron" had listed a ten-digit social. "You ever see his driver's
license? A Social Security card?"

The shopkeeper shook her head. "He said he'd lost his
card, but he was getting a new one. He was American,
though—I could tell that just by looking. So I told him not
to worry about it." She bit her lip guiltily. "I always paid him
in cash. I'm not real caught up on some of my tax stuff, to
tell you the truth."

Sullivan didn't comment, so of course she hurried to fill the silence.

"He just seemed like a regular guy, you know? Until he quit coming last week. No forwarding address, nothing."

"How did he get to work?"

"The bus." She gazed up at the ceiling and tapped her chin, as if trying to remember. "I can't recall what line."

Sullivan glanced around the room. "You have a computer on the premises?"

"Sure, out front."

Investigators were working the theory that Shelby had met someone in an Internet chat room during the weeks prior to her abduction. "He ever use it that you know?"

"Every now and then he would, if we weren't busy. But most days he stayed back here. Real quiet type."

Sullivan glanced out the door, which led to a service drive. His heart was pounding like it did sometimes when a lead panned out.

"You give him a key?" he asked.

"No. But he closed up a couple times, so I'd lend him my hide-a-key, and he always put it back. Like I say, I never had any problems with him."

Sullivan poked his head outside.

"That's where we get all our drop-offs," she explained. "I come back and quote them a price. They either take it or leave it."

He surveyed the surrounding area. Across the driveway was a narrow strip of grass, then the edge of another parking lot. The shopping center about forty yards away included a Mailboxes, Etc., a sandwich shop, and a ballet studio. A trio of girls was standing outside. They huddled against the cold in bulky jackets, their legs bare except for pale pink tights. A white SUV pulled up to the curb to collect them.

Sullivan took out his cell phone. His supervisor answered on the first ring.

"It's Sullivan. I'm over here in Birmingham."

"And?"

"And I think we've got something."

Fiona entered the autopsy suite and sent a silent thanks to whatever thoughtful staffer had just left here.

While she had been signing in and receiving a visitor's badge, someone had transferred Jane Doe from the cooler to a gurney in the autopsy room, which was a relatively bearable sixty degrees. A metal folding chair had been set up for Fiona alongside the sheet-covered body. Having put in many grueling hours under much less hospitable conditions, she appreciated such considerations and attributed them to Jack. From the moment he'd ushered her into the Grainger County Administrative Building, it had been apparent he was a popular man around here. It shouldn't have surprised her, really. He had that confident, easygoing way about him that made the men want to talk sports and the women want to flutter their lashes.

Fiona crossed the room, which seemed blessedly quiet for a county morgue. She glanced around, quickly taking in the stainless steel tables and sinks, the lights and hoses, the metal cart neatly loaded with sterilized tools, and felt vaguely comforted. From county to county and state to state, these rooms all had a sameness about them.

She took a small plastic container from her bag and unscrewed the lid. After dabbing some Vicks under her nose, she sat down and felt the cold, hard chair through her jeans. She shivered briefly, and was grateful to Jack once again for the loan of his flannel shirt.

She snapped on a pair of light blue surgical gloves. Then she pulled the cloth back from the face and tucked it in around the girl's shoulders, all the while going through the mental routine she used to ease herself into the task. Hispanic female. Estimated age, sixteen or seventeen. Height, five-foot-two. Weight, one hundred and six pounds. Name, unknown. These details and others had been provided in the preliminary autopsy report, which the medical examiner had shared with her. The report also had been accompanied by several well-intentioned but practically useless Polaroids.

Many autopsy photos were taken with the victim lying down, giving little thought to scale, lighting, or the effects of gravity. To get a useful picture, the photographer would have to wait for rigor mortis to pass, then prop the body up, letting the tissues hang naturally, and strategically place a ruler or some other object to show scale. But many morgues didn't go through all that, meaning Fiona was usually better off drawing directly from the body itself if it was available rather than a photograph.

Fiona spent a quiet moment now simply looking at the girl.

She'd been pretty, Fiona saw right off. The brown, slightly shriveled appearance of her lips and eyelids didn't mask her attractiveness to someone accustomed to seeing death. Her right temple and upper lip showed several moderate lacerations, and a series of dark, oblong contusions encircled her neck, evidence of the manual strangulation detailed in the

ME's report. Another telltale sign—the tiny red dots visible at the corners of her eyes. The bruising around her cheeks and jaw told Fiona that her last hours had been painful. If Lucy's experience was any guide, they'd been horrific.

For the first time in weeks, Fiona felt glad for the cold. Homicide investigators liked cold weather, particularly in Texas, where they more frequently dealt with heat, humidity, and abundant insects. In this case, the recent frigid temperatures, combined with the body's quick discovery, had cooperated to minimize decomposition. The ME estimated she'd been found between eight and twelve hours after death. He'd also noted that the finger marks encircling her neck were consistent with an attacker who had large hands.

Fiona squinted at the girl's face, trying to see beyond all the signs of violence and visualize the way she'd been in life. The critical identifier would be the arrangement and proportion of her features—not necessarily the details of the features themselves. Correct proportion was more important than a perfectly reproduced nose or eye. This was the reason some criminals could be apprehended on the basis of a blurry surveillance tape. It was the overall impression of the face that mattered most when it came to recognition.

Once a tentative ID was made, police could use more conclusive means to get a definite match. Fiona was the middleman here, and her drawing would be the bridge that linked this lonely corpse to a living, breathing family somewhere. At least she hoped so.

She spent a few moments selecting her drawing materials and then stood up to begin the sketch. She rested her board on her hip so she could peer around it at the girl.

She started by lightly sketching the heart-shaped face, then blocking out the features. Working from top to bottom, she sketched in the brow line, the eyes, and then the delicate nose. Gradually she built up more and more detail until the picture started to resemble the subject. When the eyes and nose were refined sufficiently, she moved on to the mouth.

With a latex-covered finger, Fiona peeled back the girl's lips and examined the teeth. Her upper lateral incisor was missing, but the ME had concluded this injury occurred around the time of death. It wasn't a physical characteristic that could be used to help identify her, so Fiona ignored it. She spent a few moments repositioning the chin, trying to correct for the slack-jaw effect that could make a dead body appear quite different from a living person. Once she had an idea of what she wanted, she sketched in what she hoped was a naturalistic mouth and then leaned back to study her work.

Not bad.

Finally, she added the most challenging feature of all—the ears. The vast majority of her suspect sketches were men, so drawing ears realistically was a skill she'd been forced to learn early in her career. In this case, the ears might be important because the victim had two piercings in each lobe, which could be helpful for identification.

Fiona's legs felt stiff, so she sat down and did some shading. For a few minutes she added highlights and shadows with an array of umber-toned pencils.

"Cold enough for ya?"

Fiona glanced up into the kindly brown eyes of the Grainger County ME. Dr. Russell Jamison was white-haired and grandfatherly and had a big, bulbous nose. Fiona had met him when she'd arrived, but he'd seemed to be on his way out, and she hadn't expected to see him again.

"I'm okay." She suppressed a shudder. "Nice and quiet today, huh?"

He glanced around his empty work room. "So far, so good." He winked. "I'm not making any plans, though. Something tells me we're in for a big night out on the roads. What do you want to bet we get a tree hugger by nine o'clock?"

Fiona raised her eyebrows but didn't comment. In her experience, medical examiners had a strange sense of humor. To some, it might seem like Jamison was looking forward to a break from the boredom, but Fiona gave him the benefit of the doubt. Jack had described him as "highly dedicated," and Fiona took the doctor's meticulous autopsy notes as corroborating evidence.

"So," she said. "You didn't find any tattoos?" Fiona always made separate drawings for nonfacial tattoos, then left it to investigators to decide whether to share those details.

"Not a one," the doctor said, shoving his hands into the pockets of his khaki pants. In a padded green windbreaker and CCA cap, he looked ready for a fishing trip.

"And her hairstyle? I couldn't tell much from the picture."

Unfortunately for many victims, especially women, the process of washing the body during autopsy eliminated the possibility of re-creating a hairstyle. Again, the Polaroids had provided no help here, but Fiona didn't want to criticize.

Jamison frowned. "It was a mess. Blood, debris, tangles. I'd go with straight, parted down the middle."

Fiona mumbled something noncommittal. She'd been paying attention all day, and the current trend for area teenagers seemed to be a side part, so without better information, she decided to go with that.

Jamison stepped closer to her chair, and Fiona's neck tensed. She disliked people looking over her shoulder as she worked. But she didn't want to complain.

"Sure is a pity, someone so young," Jamison muttered behind her. "And the animal activity . . . Don't think she'd been out there long, but something sure got to her. I'd say a stray dog or a coyote."

Fiona let her gaze slide to the jagged tear at the girl's clavicle, just above the Y-incision. In the report it was described as a postmortem animal artifact, and Fiona had been trying to erase it mentally for the sake of the drawing.

Suddenly her eyes burned, and she had to blink rapidly.

"It really is a pity," the doctor repeated. "I got a granddaughter about her age."

Fiona didn't say anything, sensing he wanted to talk.

"I know this may sound strange . . ." he continued.

She cleared her throat. "What's that?"

"I wanted to ask you if you could, you know, in your drawing there, you think you could make her smile?"

Jamison was clearly uneasy with the sentimental request. But what he didn't know was that Fiona heard it all the time, from medical examiners, and beat cops, and giant, tough-as-nails detectives.

Some cases were like that.

She took a deep breath and looked at the girl, who bore a not-so-surprising resemblance to Lucy.

"I'll do my best," she said.

• • •

Jack hesitated outside Fiona's motel room, thrown off by the conspicuous lack of light coming through the curtains. Could she be asleep? It was 8:45, and she'd told him to come by at nine to have a look at the drawings.

He knocked softly, torn between not wanting to bother her and needing to get his hands on those sketches. He leaned close to the door and listened. The only sounds he detected were from the trucks speeding down Highway 44 and the muffled laugh track on the television two rooms over.

The door jerked back.

"I was just thinking about you," a wide-awake Fiona said.

"Oh, yeah? Why's that?"

She motioned him into her room. The only light came from a clip-on lamp attached to a wooden easel. He hadn't seen the easel earlier. She must have had it stashed in her car.

"I'm just finishing up here, and I need some info," she said.

Jack caught a strong chemical smell as he closed the door. He followed Fiona across the room, noticing that she still wore his shirt.

"Her personal effects are at the lab," she said, "so I had to go by the report. It says she was wearing 'four-centimeter dangle earrings, feather design.' Are we talking actual feathers or something made of metal, like maybe silver?"

Jack closed his eyes briefly and envisioned the crime scene. An earring had been hanging from the victim's left ear when the techs zipped her into the bag. The second earring was found later, tangled in her hair. Jack had watched the ME remove it at the start of the autopsy.

"Metal," Jack said. "I think it was silver, but it could have been something else."

"Any other earrings? Maybe some studs? She has two holes in each ear."

"That was it for jewelry."

Both feather earrings showed traces of dried blood and were currently being analyzed at the state crime lab. Also at the lab were samples of forensic evidence collected from the victim's body, as well as the plaster cast of a tire tread Carlos had created at the crime scene. Jack expected to get a full report on everything in a few days—give or take a year. The state lab was notoriously backlogged, but Jack didn't have an alternative. The Graingerville Police Department couldn't afford its own laboratory. It could barely afford a Coke machine.

Fiona pivoted toward her drawing. Her hair was knotted at the top of her head, and she'd stuck a pencil in it to hold it in place.

"I know it seems minor," she said, "but it's important to get the personal effects right. Sometimes a piece of clothing or jewelry can be the key detail that prompts recognition."

Jack studied Fiona's drawing of a smiling, dark-haired teenager. The picture was in full color.

"How'd you do that?" he asked, awestruck. It looked nothing like the brutalized corpse he'd seen . . . and yet it did.

"Do what?"

He gestured to the eyes, the smile. "Get her to look alive."

"It took some time." Fiona regarded her picture with a critical gaze. She picked up a bottle of Liquid Paper from the easel tray, shook it, and carefully added a tiny white dot to each iris, making the eyes look even more realistic.

"That's the hardest part with postmortem drawings," she said. "The look of life; it's very elusive. But without it, even someone who knew her well might not see the resemblance. Real people are animated. Without that spark, even if you're working from a good-quality photograph or a body with relatively minor trauma, it can be tough to get an ID."

Jack watched her, admiring the confident way she talked about her work. She radiated strength. And yet she seemed fragile somehow, too—maybe because his shirt was miles too big for her. And then there was the childish bracelet she wore on her wrist. It was woven out of red and orange thread and reminded Jack of something his young nieces would make.

"Where will you distribute this?" Fiona asked.

He shifted his gaze back to the drawing. "The fruit-processing plant, for starters. The refinery. Workers around here have a fairly tight network. If she's been here any length of time, someone's likely to know her."

"Jamison said he rehydrated the fingertips to get you a good set of prints. I assume no luck with the thumbs?"

"Nothing with the DPS," he said. "And no criminal record."

Fiona nodded. "She might be too young for a driver's license. She looks fifteen to me."

Jack looked at the drawing again. "I'll also get this out to law enforcement agencies, plus some shelters and churches with outreach programs."

"Any evidence of drug use?"

"No," he said. "And no signs of malnutrition, either. Wherever she came from, she had people taking care of her."

Fiona sighed quietly beside him. It was such a hopeless sound, and again Jack felt guilty for getting her involved in this. She was a pretty woman, and he suddenly wanted her back in Austin painting pretty pictures instead of spending her time down here up to her elbows in death and gore. She wasn't suited for this job.

"Are you finished with the perp yet?"

She flinched—just slightly—but Jack caught it. "Almost," she said.

She crossed the room to a cheap wooden bureau and switched on the light there. Beside the lamp were a can of spray fixative and a charcoal drawing of a man's head and shoulders.

"This is the original," she explained, "based on Lucy's description."

Jack studied the picture. The man had dark, shaggy hair and a wide nose. His complexion looked rough, pockmarked even. Shadows surrounded his deep-set eyes.

"He's not familiar to you, is he?"

He looked at Fiona, who was watching him intently.

"No," Jack said. He evidently hadn't hidden his disappointment well. And now he felt foolish for harboring such an unrealistic expectation. What had he been thinking? That he'd get some famous artist down here, and snap, she'd draw a picture of the guy who sacked groceries at the Pick & Pack?

Real investigations didn't work that way. At least, none

of his ever had. Homicide cases were about long hours, thorough police work, and logical thinking. And even then, much of it amounted to luck.

Maybe he'd expected Fiona to be his good-luck charm. He'd let himself believe that if he could just get her involved, all the pieces would fall into place. He realized, with a growing sense of shame, that he'd been watching too much TV news. He'd actually bought into the hype about her.

"Lucy believes her attacker was probably in his twenties."

Fiona lifted the picture and pulled another drawing out from beneath it. This picture showed the same face, but heavier and with a thicker neck. The hairline had receded, and the wrinkles bracketing his mouth had deepened.

"This is a ten-year age progression." She overlaid a sheet of clear acetate, suddenly giving the man facial hair and glasses. "Here's a variation."

Jack nodded his approval.

Then she pulled out yet another drawing, only this one showed a much thinner man than the previous two. His bones were pronounced, and his cheeks looked gaunt.

"This is another possibility," she said. "It all depends on his health. Maybe he's an addict of some sort and he doesn't eat much. Or maybe he's put on a hundred pounds. I have no way of knowing." She glanced up at him. "Here's another detail that might interest you: Lucy said she remembers smelling cigarettes during her ordeal, both on his breath and in the room. This guy is a smoker, or at least he was eleven years ago. I don't know if that helps or anything, but I thought you'd want to know."

Jack nodded, surprised he'd never thought to ask about a

detail like that. It wasn't in the police report. Yet another clue everyone had missed so many years ago. It was almost as if no one had investigated a goddamn thing.

She returned her attention to the sketch. "The best age progressions start with a photograph. I usually use school portraits for kids and mug shots for perpetrators. I also like to use photos of siblings and parents, too, if they're available. That makes it easier to predict how the person is likely to age. In this case, the original image is a drawing, unfortunately."

Jack blew out a sigh. He hadn't really considered all that.

"Because of all the ambiguity," she said, "I can't recommend you release any of these suspect sketches to the public. There are just too many unknown factors, too much time has passed. And you don't even know for sure we're dealing with the same man who attacked Lucy, right?"

He met her gaze, set his jaw. She was right, but he had a hard time admitting it. He wished he could plunk down some sort of proof the cases were connected, but at this point everything was circumstantial. Maybe when the labs came back—

"Jack? I'm afraid I have to advise you not to use any of these."

"Well, they're my drawings now, right? I reckon it's my call."

She jerked back, stung. The rapport they'd been building since this afternoon vanished. "Well, no. I don't think it is." She shifted in front of the sketches, physically blocking his view.

Now it was Jack's turn to get his hackles up. "I hired *you*," he reminded her. "That means your work product is my property."

She crossed her arms. "If you want to get technical about it, you haven't paid me yet, so I *reckon* these drawings belong to me."

This was a dead end. He should have known better than to piss her off, but he'd been feeling testy all day, and this latest disappointment only added to the mood.

"Fine," he said, turning away from her. "You win. If you say don't use 'em, we won't use 'em."

She didn't reply, and he knew she was waiting to hear the catch.

"You mean that?" she asked finally. "You're going to trust my opinion on this?"

"Hey, you're the expert. If you think they're no good, they're no good." *Shit.* He'd really been hoping for a break here.

"I didn't say they're no good. I just—"

"Can't have it both ways, honey. They're either usable or they're not."

"That's not true at all. You can still use them within the department. If you find another witness, for instance, I could compare the two descriptions to determine whether they're consistent enough."

Another witness. Right. "I'm not holding my breath," he said sarcastically.

"Okay. Another possibility would be if you start homing in on a suspect, you can compare the picture to whoever you're looking at. I'm just not comfortable using these pictures publicly." She gestured to the drawings. "They're all over the map! He's fat, he's thin, he's balding, he's not. Not to mention the description that generated these was based on a highly problematic witness."

"Problematic. What, you don't believe her either?"

Her body stiffened. "Of course I believe her. I mean from a legal perspective. Eleven years have passed since Lucy saw her attacker. What if you go public with this and the guy you end up arresting looks nothing like any of these drawings? A defense attorney would have a field day! He'd say you arrested the wrong guy, or there was obviously someone else involved. You could torpedo your own case."

Jack rubbed the bridge of his nose. He was tired. And hungry. And sick of this investigation, although it had barely gotten off the ground.

"Shit," he muttered, sinking onto the bed.

Fiona's arms dropped to her sides. "I'm sorry I couldn't do better. But I told you from the beginning, there are a lot of circumstances working against us here."

"I know, I know." He combed his hands through his hair. Then he glanced around the spartan little room. This fleabag motel wasn't winning any awards, but it was the best Grainger County had to offer, since Fiona hadn't wanted to blow a sizable chunk of change at Cold Creek Farms, the fancy B-and-B in the neighboring town.

Jack watched her standing there looking limp and deflated in his oversize shirt. Being alone with her in this motel room was starting to get to him, too. He suddenly had a vision of her wearing just his shirt and nothing else.

"Are you hungry?" he asked abruptly.

Her eyebrows arched with surprise. "I'm . . . no, actually. I already ate."

Jack spied the M&M's wrapper on the bedside table next to a bottle of Evian. Evidently, she was a real health nut.

"You mean you ate something real, or you gobbled down gas station crap?"

She looked wary now, and he realized he wasn't making much of an impression here. His dating skills were a little out of practice.

He stood up and stepped closer, and her tension picked up. "May I take you out to dinner, Fiona? To a real restaurant, with all the food groups?"

She had a smudge of charcoal on her cheekbone. He reached out to rub it with the pad of his thumb, and there it was again—that little zing of electricity.

She stepped back. "Thank you. But I don't date cops."

He laughed and hooked his thumbs through his belt loops. "Is that a fact?"

"Yes."

He shrugged. "Okay, don't call it a date, then. How about a meal? You do eat, don't you?"

He could see her wheels turning, trying to come up with an excuse. "I thought you had your hands full with the investigation—"

"We all need fuel. And I've been running on empty for about"—he looked at his watch—"fourteen hours now. There's actually a fairly decent restaurant right next door."

She bit her lip, looked around.

"Come on." He smiled. "Just a quick bite. I'll have you in bed by ten."

She tipped her head to the side, clearly not liking the innuendo. Then he saw the faintest trace of a smile and felt a warm shot of lust. She was definitely getting to him—those pink lips and that smooth, pale skin. But since when did he have to work this hard to get a woman to say yes?

He stepped closer. "That was a joke," he lied.

She looked up at him, still wary. "A *quick* bite. I have to get up early tomorrow to drive home."

"I promise," he said. "I would never keep a girl out past curfew."

CHAPTER

5

Fiona's mouth started watering the second she stepped into Becker's. The place was dark and warm and smelled like frying onions.

Jack didn't wait at the hostess stand, but steered her directly to a booth at the back of the dining room. Fiona slid into the polished wooden seat, relieved to be off her feet after so many hours standing in front of an easel.

She heard a crack, and a shout came up from the back room.

"It's a pool hall, too?" she asked.

"Food, drinks, pool. They've got a beer garden outside, although it's closed now. Live music on Saturdays in the summer."

"Sounds nice," Fiona said. She hated beer, but the food and the music sounded pleasant. It was fairly crowded tonight, and she took that as a good recommendation.

A waitress stopped by and asked for their drink orders. Jack had arrived at Fiona's motel room wearing jeans and a faded black sweatshirt, so she guessed he was off the clock for the evening.

"White wine, please," Fiona said.

The waitress lifted a brow. "I'll see what we got."

Jack flashed the woman an apologetic smile and ordered a Budweiser.

When she disappeared, Fiona gave him a quizzical look. "White wine? I thought that was pretty basic."

"Round here basic means beer."

She shuddered. "I hate beer."

He shook his head and opened his menu. "Well, please don't tell me you're a vegetarian, or we're flat out of luck."

Fiona skimmed the list of food. Lots of sausage and potatoes, chicken fried steak, hamburgers. The popular vegetable seemed to be sauerkraut. When the waitress reappeared, Fiona ordered the Fried Chic-N-Salad, hold the Chic-N.

"That's it?" Jack asked, after she left. "You come all the way down here, and you won't even let us feed you some cholesterol?"

"I like salad."

He clinked his beer bottle against her wineglass. "Guess you can take the girl out of California, but you can't take the California out of the girl."

She smiled, thinking about how her grandfather also liked to tease her about being from the Left Coast. She wondered what Jack would say if she told him she'd actually spent the first seven years of her life in Wimberley, Texas, a town a third the size of this one, which locals touted as "a little bit of heaven."

She took a sip and looked at him over the rim of her glass. He was staring at her with those intense gray-blue eyes.

"What?"

"Nothing." He frowned down at his beer. "I was just

feeling bad about earlier. You know, misleading you. I'm sorry."

She leaned back against the booth and folded her arms over her chest.

"What?"

"You're not sorry," she said. "You wanted me to help you with your case, and I helped you with your case. You just feel guilty now because you're getting to know me, and I'm not some anonymous person you can manipulate anymore."

His eyebrows tipped up. "Damn. All that in two days. You a psychiatrist, too?"

"No."

He watched her for a moment. "Okay, you're right, I'm not sorry. I'm glad I got you down here, but not for the reason you think."

He gave her a warm, lingering look, and Fiona felt a rush of heat. How long had it been since a man looked at her that way?

She sipped her wine, gathered her courage.

"So. What's between you and Lucy?"

The warmth disappeared. He flicked a glance over her shoulder, then met her gaze. "Nothing."

The lie hung there in the air, and Fiona felt something sink inside her. She looked away from him. This was one reason she didn't date cops. They lied far too easily.

An elderly man walked up to their table. His belly hung over the top of his jeans, and he wore a western-style shirt and a John Deere cap.

"Evening." He nodded at Jack and cast a curious glance Fiona's way. "Y'all probably want to eat in peace, but I told the wife I'd stop over and complain about those teenagers been vandalizing cars over at the theater."

"This the Dough Boys again?" Jack asked.

"They're a buncha hoodlums. I spent nearly all morning cleaning biscuit dough off my truck. You need to get on this, Jack, or I'm gonna have to take my Winchester along next time."

"Take it easy, now," Jack said. "I'll have a talk with them."

"I'm serious. Folks got a right to go to the show without getting their cars pelted."

When the man left, Jack cast a glance at Fiona, and she thought he looked embarrassed.

"Is it my imagination, or did he just threaten those kids with a rifle?" she asked.

"Ah, he's just blowing hot air. He doesn't really care that much, but his wife's hell on wheels. She was watching his performance from a few booths up."

Fiona glanced over her shoulder and saw a woman seated across from the John Deere guy. Hell on Wheels had big hair and a blue rinse. She eyed Fiona suspiciously, perhaps wondering where Jack had picked up an outsider.

"I don't know how you do it," Fiona said. "I'd go crazy in a small town."

"It's not that bad."

But Fiona thought he had to get tired of it, or at least annoyed. Here he was trying to run a murder investigation, and the citizenry was more concerned about teen pranksters.

"So, you were saying?" she asked. "About you and Lucy?"

"There's nothing to say."

A low buzz sounded, and he reached for his hip. "Damn," he muttered, checking his phone. "I've got to get this."

Saved by the cell.

She pretended to enjoy her wine as he took a call from someone named Carlos. As soon as he disconnected, she knew dinner was over. Yet another reason she didn't date cops.

"I have to go see about something," he said, signaling the waitress. "We can get this to go."

Fiona nodded and collected her blazer and purse off the seat beside her. She'd returned Jack's shirt when they'd left the motel. She didn't owe him anything now except an invoice, and she planned to e-mail it to him.

"It's okay," she said, sliding from the booth.

And it was, too. The last thing she needed was another dead-end relationship with a man who didn't know what honesty was. She was finished being lied to.

Jack stood up and spoke briefly with the server before returning his attention to Fiona. "We'll do a rain check."

She slipped her arms into her blazer and pulled the lapels together protectively. "I don't think that's a good idea."

His eyes narrowed. Clearly, he wasn't used to getting the brush-off.

"I've got too much going on right now, and so do you."

For a moment, he just stared at her. "Let me walk you back."

"Not necessary, it's just next door." And she didn't want him to pick up on her disappointment.

"You sure?"

"I'm sure." She plastered a smile on her face and thrust

her hand out. "Thanks for the drink, Jack. It was nice working with you."

The disappointment was still lodged in her stomach the next morning as she rode up the elevator to her apartment. She'd been willing it away all morning, trying to focus on all the things she needed to do besides brood over her non-existent love life, but the feeling remained. She'd genuinely liked Jack. He was an attractive man, in more than just the physical sense, and it had felt good to be around someone who understood about her work.

The elevator doors dinged open, and she trudged down the hallway, telling herself she needed to quit being so optimistic. Given that she'd been raised by a woman who went through men like other women went through shoes, it was pretty mind-boggling for Fiona to realize that deep down somewhere, she was a romantic, that deep down she actually believed she might meet a man someday who would fit with her for the long haul. She needed to wise up.

Fiona neared the end of her hallway, flipping through her keys and silently cursing her neighbor's tastes in music. Who listened to Usher at 10:00 A.M. on a Sunday?

As she approached her door, she realized the noise was coming from 4A. Fiona jammed her key in the lock and felt her stress level climbing even before she stepped over the threshold.

A pizza box sat on her coffee table, surrounded by empty beer bottles. A half-eaten bag of Oreos lay abandoned on the sofa beside a balled-up throw. On the end table sat one of her favorite sculptures, a hollowed-out egg that harkened back to art school and Fiona's Barbara Hepworth stage.

The glossy ceramic creation had been transformed into an ashtray.

Fiona dropped her attaché and purse beside the door and stalked over to the stereo to switch off the power. Then she snatched up the sculpture, took it into the kitchen, and dumped the stinky contents into the trash can.

"Hey, I was listening to that."

Fiona glanced up to see Courtney slouched against the doorway to her bathroom. She wore a black satin blouse—one of her nightclubbing outfits—that she hadn't bothered to button over a red bra and panties.

"A little loud for Sunday morning, don't you think?"

Courtney rolled her eyes. She turned to face the bathroom mirror and pulled a brush through her long auburn mane. When she reached for the straightening iron, Fiona's eyes widened.

"You brought your stuff?" she asked, alarmed. Courtney occasionally crashed on the sofa when she was too drunk to make it home from downtown, but if she'd packed, then this was a premeditated visit.

Her sister released a lock of hair from the iron and admired the way it fanned out, straight and shiny, across her shoulder.

"I'm thinking of going for some color again. What about raspberry?"

A classic evasion tactic. "Courtney? Are you moving *in*?"

She lifted a shoulder casually, never taking her eyes off the mirror.

"Please don't tell me you got evicted."

Her sister turned and planted a hand on her hip, as if this were totally implausible. "You're such a drama queen. God."

Fiona tried not to bite a hole in her tongue. She walked over to the bathroom and took note of the three matching cosmetics bags sitting on the lid of her toilet. Courtney was here for an extended stay.

Fiona took a deep, cleansing breath, and didn't feel cleansed at all. "What happened?"

Her sister leaned toward the mirror and darkened her golden lashes with mascara. "Fucking Texas Gas Service. They cut off my *heat*. Do you believe that? In the dead of *winter*."

Fiona absolutely believed it. They probably hadn't received payment in months.

"Anyway, it's just for a few days. Just until this freeze lets up." Courtney pulled open a drawer and helped herself to a pair of earrings. "Hey, can I borrow these? I'm having brunch with David."

"Who's David?"

She removed her gold dangles and replaced them with Fiona's pearl studs. "You met him the other night. Trial attorney from Dallas?"

"He was an attorney?" Fiona conjured up an image of the leather jacket–wearing heartthrob from the Continental Club. The only lawyerly thing about him had been his gold Rolex, which Fiona had assumed was fake.

"His conference ends this morning. We're having brunch at the Randolph Hotel."

"The Randolph." Not Courtney's usual stomping grounds.

She breezed past Fiona into the bedroom corner of the loft. "You have anything conservative I can borrow? A sweater set or something?"

Fiona watched as her sister rifled through her closet. She shrugged out of the black satin blouse and selected a gray cashmere cardigan.

Fiona eyed her rumpled sheets, cringing inwardly. "Did you bring him back here last night?"

"*No.* He had to meet a client for drinks after dinner." Courtney buttoned up the sweater, leaving open two more buttons than Fiona would have. Any man with a pulse would notice the sliver of red lace visible between Courtney's breasts. She snagged her black miniskirt off the floor and shimmied it over her hips. Then she strode past Fiona into the living area.

"You seen my shoes?" She snatched up the throw and tossed it over a chair. After retrieving a pair of black heels from beneath the coffee table, she turned to face Fiona.

"I know you're pissed," she said. "But it's just for a few days. I promise."

Fiona resigned herself to at least a week of chaos and distractions. She had three canvases to complete before her art show. And the tranquil mind-set she needed for painting would be impossible to achieve with Courtney kicking around.

"Three days," she said firmly. "That's *it*, Court."

Courtney gave her a dazzling smile and pulled her into a hug. "Thanks. You won't even know I'm here, I swear."

Fiona looked over her sister's shoulder and counted the beer bottles on the coffee table.

"Who was here with you last night?"

Courtney pulled back and whirled around, avoiding eye contact. "Have you seen my purse?" She traipsed across the room, showing off the legs that attracted men like David at bars. "It was *just* here. I saw it—"

"Courtney?"

She stepped into the kitchen and looked at Fiona across the counter. "Aaron was here for a little while."

"Courtney!"

She rolled her eyes. "What was I supposed to do? Kick him to the curb?"

"Yes! That's exactly what you should have done!"

"Well, I tried to, okay? But he's persistent. He says he misses you and he wants to apologize."

"I can't believe you let him in here."

"I didn't. He still has a key."

Fiona's cell phone started ringing, and she pulled it out of her purse, which was on the floor. She didn't recognize the number—not a good sign.

She flipped it open. "Fiona Glass."

"Fiona, it's Garrett."

She paused, trying to place the name.

"Garrett Sullivan? FBI?"

"Of course! Sorry, I just—" She watched Courtney rummage through the junk drawer in the kitchen. "What?"

"I need a nail file," Courtney whispered.

"Top of my dresser."

"Excuse me?" Sullivan asked.

"Not you. Sorry." She took a deep breath and tried to collect her thoughts. Special Agent Sullivan. This would be bad news. "Did you find her?" Her chest tightened as she asked the question.

"No. But we have a suspect now, thanks to you."

Fiona let out a breath. "You're kidding."

"I'm serious. And he's a dead ringer for your drawing, too. Have you seen the news this morning?"

Fiona flipped on her only television, a thirteen-inch Sony that sat on her kitchen counter, and switched it to CNN. It was a weather report, but she watched the scrolling headlines on the bottom of the screen, knowing it would come on sooner or later.

"Our man's name is Keith Janovic, aka Ron Jones. His employer recognized him from your drawing and called it in."

Sure enough, the headline started crawling across the bottom of the screen: "Authorities are seeking Birmingham resident Keith Janovic for questioning in the Shelby Sherwood abduction case. While not officially calling him a suspect, an FBI spokesman said he is a 'person of interest'..."

"He's not a suspect?"

"It just became official," Sullivan said. "The media hasn't caught up yet. But we've matched prints at his workplace to a partial found on the Sherwoods' doorbell. He's the man. Now we just have to locate him."

Courtney sashayed toward the door and grabbed her black trench coat off a hook in the foyer. She blew a kiss at Fiona as she made her escape.

Fiona shifted her attention back to the television. "And what's his story?"

"Twenty-five. Loner. Busted a few years ago for some rubber checks, but no history of violence."

"That's interesting."

"Lives in a rat hole. Collects child pornography. Hasn't been seen in ten days."

Fiona sighed and sank onto a bar stool. She hated these cases. "How's Colter?"

"A little better, from what I hear. He's talking to our shrink some, at least. Mom says he's having nightmares, though."

Fiona fidgeted with the woven bracelet at her wrist. Colter had given it to her Monday, and Annie had insisted she keep it, saying her daughter would want her to have it. Shelby loved making them for friends, apparently.

"Anyway, I called to say thank you," Sullivan said. "This is a major breakthrough, and it wouldn't have been possible without your work."

Her stomach fluttered, and she knew what was coming. She waited a few beats.

"Is there something else you need me to do?" she prompted.

"Do?"

"Yeah, I mean . . . you just called to thank me?" If so, it would be a first. Investigators rarely bothered to thank her. Or if they did, it usually happened right before they hit her up for help on another case. She didn't take it personally, really. She knew how overworked they were.

The silence stretched out.

"Fiona?"

"Yes?"

"You really have no idea how talented you are, do you?"

She didn't know what to say. Guilt tugged at her.

"I hope you'll reconsider your career plans," Sullivan said. "We really need you out here in the field."

Fiona watched the TV screen, where coverage had shifted to a podium crammed with microphones. The Atlanta police chief stood behind them, looking haggard but hopeful as he answered reporters' questions.

She was reminded of one of the reasons she did this work. She liked putting that flicker of hope back in people's eyes.

The flip side was seeing it fade away in the weeks and months from now when it became evident Shelby Sherwood wasn't coming home. Even Keith Janovic's capture, if they ever did capture him, couldn't make up for that.

Fiona turned off the television. "Thanks, but I meant what I said about moving on."

"Let me know if you change your mind," Sullivan said, and she heard the disappointment in his voice. "It was a privilege working with you."

"Thanks." She squirmed in her seat, not liking the favor she was about to ask. Sullivan was on a high-profile case, which meant exceedingly long hours. He probably had way too many balls in the air to be worried about making extra phone calls. "Would you mind getting in touch again? If you find out anything about Shelby?"

It had become personal at some point. Fiona had tried not to let it, but that never worked out.

"We'll find her," he said somberly.

"I know."

Jack stared at the ME's report on his desk, trying to glean any kernel of information he'd overlooked. Until the labs came back, this was the best he had to go on in terms of physical evidence. The cast of the tire tread, the green twine, and the biological evidence collected during autopsy all had been sent out for analysis. Now it was time for some low-tech, back-to-basics detective work.

Fortunately, that was just the sort of work Jack excelled at. Fitting the puzzle together. Finding missing pieces where no one else had thought to look.

Unfortunately, he had very few pieces to work with at the moment.

Still no ID on the victim, although he fully expected Fiona's postmortem drawing to solve that problem. She'd managed to translate a mutilated corpse into a smiling portrait. Someone would recognize her, and when they did, Jack would have an insight into the killer's mind. How did he select his victims? Where did he operate?

In Lucy's case, she'd just been wandering down the road on a bitter December night. She'd been cold, distracted. Too emotional after another fight with her parents to think about her personal safety.

What about Jane Doe? Had she simply been out walking alone near Graingerville? The clean, bare soles of her feet, plus the conspicuous lack of evidence in the field where she'd been dumped, told Jack the murder most likely had occurred elsewhere. Reinforcing this theory was the ME's conclusion that the victim's injuries had been sustained over the course of several hours, meaning the killer probably had held her captive somewhere else. But where? And why would the murderer dump the body on the outskirts of a town where someone might spot him coming or going? It was a ballsy move, and it bothered Jack.

He wondered where the killer had found her. Probably not a bar. As Fiona had pointed out, the girl looked young, maybe even younger than the ME's report concluded. She wouldn't have gotten served anywhere around here.

She could be a runaway, or a prostitute, or both.

But the physical findings didn't bear that out. She'd been healthy, with the obvious exception of her final hours. She'd been well nourished, free of sexually transmitted diseases. She'd had straight white teeth and a cavity that had been filled at some point.

She was young. Hispanic. And beautiful, if Fiona's picture was accurate. Those were three traits Jane Doe shared with Lucy, three traits Jack couldn't get out of his mind. The similarities gnawed at him, made him uneasy for the simple reason that this was south Texas, a place where cultures collided, where tempers and resentments flared hot, especially during hard times. If beautiful Hispanic girls were being targeted around here, Jack knew this wasn't a simple sex crime. They were dealing with something more complicated. And whatever it was, he felt sure the ramifications were going to rock his world.

As if they hadn't already.

Jack rubbed his fingers over his eyes and tried to focus. Pipe dreams of a lunch break at Lorraine's had faded hours ago. Now the best he could wish for was something from the vending machine to reenergize him for the mountain of neglected paperwork he faced this afternoon. For the past week, he'd virtually ignored everything unrelated to the Jane Doe homicide.

"Edna Goldby's out here. She wants to file a complaint with the chief of police?"

Jack glanced up to see his youngest officer, a woman fresh from the police academy in San Angelo, standing in the doorway. She wore a neatly pressed uniform with all the right gadgets and weaponry clipped into place. Regulation female hairstyle. Shiny black shoes. She'd obviously been paying attention when they taught Cop 101, but she'd missed the class on Gatekeeping.

"Handle it, Sharon," he said testily. "It's probably her neighbor again. The guy's Weimaraner keeps getting at her chickens."

"I already told her you were in."

"Tell her I'm on the phone," Jack said. "Hey, did Lowell ever track down that list from TPWB? He was supposed to get it to me yesterday."

"You mean that thing with the hunting licenses? It's in your in-box."

Jack shuffled through his tray and found the list beneath a few neglected case files. The damn printout was at least an inch thick. He sighed.

"So . . . about Mrs. Goldby?"

Jack glanced up. "Take her statement. Then pay a visit to the neighbor at the end of your tour." Maybe a little grunt work would teach Sharon how to prioritize.

Jack's phone rang, and he reached for it gratefully. He dismissed Sharon with a nod.

"Bowman."

"J.B., it's Mary Ellen down at the school."

Jack smiled. The principal of Graingerville Elementary School was one of the few people Jack liked calling him J.B. The fact that she'd given him her virginity in the back of her father's Chevy Suburban twenty years ago probably had something to do with it.

"What can I do for you, honey?"

Mary Ellen was married, but they still flirted on the rare occasion they crossed paths.

"I've got a fourth-grader sitting outside my office. His teacher brought him in right before bus pickup."

Shit, what next? Was he going to be called out to settle fights on the playground? After years scraping bodies off the streets in Houston, the realities of small-town policing were pretty amazing.

"His name's Brady Cox," she continued, "and I'm afraid he's in some trouble."

Jack frowned. This wasn't Mary Ellen's typical friendly tone. "What's going on?"

"Well, I'm hoping you can tell me. I'm looking at his drawing here on my desk. Done with colored pencils? It's really quite good. Remarkable, in fact, given his age—"

"Mary Ellen—"

"It's a naked woman, J.B. She's wearing green handcuffs and lying in a field. You want to come have a look at this?"

CHAPTER
6

Thank God she was home.

Jack rapped on Fiona's door for the second time, doubting she'd be able to hear him over the music blaring inside her apartment. He didn't know what he'd expected her tastes to be, but hip-hop hadn't made the list.

He glanced at his watch and cursed. Then he tried the door and was surprised to find it unlocked.

"Hello?"

He stepped into the foyer, scanning the messy apartment for any sign of Fiona or the offending stereo. It was a one-room loft, with high ceilings, Mexican tile floors, and a big wrought-iron bed situated on the far side, beside a window.

"Fiona?"

She came out of the bathroom wearing nothing but a few scraps of black lace. She let out a shriek, and Jack realized two things: this woman wasn't Fiona, and he'd made one hell of a mistake letting himself in here.

"Who are *you*?"

Jack jerked his attention to her face. "Excuse me. I'm looking for Fiona Glass."

Shit, was he in the wrong apartment? He darted his gaze around, looking for clues.

"She's not home." The woman plunked a hand on her hip. "You want to tell me who you are?"

"Jack Bowman."

She turned and flipped off the stereo, startling him with a full view of her shapely butt.

Jack turned around and pretended to check out Fiona's kitchen. "You know where I can find her?"

He heard shuffling behind him and hoped she was putting on some clothes. The afterimage filled his brain: leggy redhead. Pale skin. Full breasts.

If this woman wasn't related to Fiona, he'd eat his badge.

"You can turn around now."

Jack did. She'd pulled on a short black robe.

"She's at work. She should be home soon, if you feel like waiting."

Did he feel like waiting? No, but he'd driven an hour and forty minutes just for a conversation, so he might as well. Otherwise, he'd wasted an entire evening in the midst of a homicide investigation.

"I'll wait." He shoved his hands in the pockets of his leather jacket. "If you don't mind."

She shrugged. "Suit yourself."

He turned his back on her again and wandered into the kitchen. A bowl of fruit sat on the counter alongside an open bottle of red wine.

"You're a friend of Fiona's?"

"I'm her sister."

Jack looked over his shoulder again. Fiona's sister wasn't in much hurry to get dressed.

"You both live here?" He'd only noticed one bed.

"Just visiting."

He felt her watching him as he continued his tour of the kitchen. Taped to the refrigerator was a *Far Side* cartoon and a postcard from Florence, Italy. It showed a famous painting of a naked woman with wavy red hair standing on a seashell. The woman reminded Jack of Fiona, and he had to fight the urge to flip the card over and see who'd sent it to her.

"You want a drink?"

He glanced over his shoulder. "No. Thank you."

Jack made his way to the corner of the apartment, where a large canvas rested on a paint-splattered easel. The loft seemed to be divided into quadrants by functions: cooking, sleeping, lounging, and painting. The floor in this corner was covered by a heavy drop cloth.

Fiona's sister sauntered up beside him and looked at the picture. "So what do you think?"

He studied the painting. It was blue. And green. And plenty of colors in between. There were concentric circles that reminded him of ripples on water, but the picture was too abstract for him to know for sure what she'd been aiming for.

"I like it," he said truthfully. Something about the colors, all those greens and blues merging together, felt peaceful. "Is it finished?"

"I don't know. You'll have to ask her." She turned to look at him, tilting her head to the side. "You're a cute one. Where'd Fiona meet you?"

"Mutual friend."

"So you're a cop, huh?" She stepped closer, and he smelled her perfume over the paint thinner.

He held his ground. "What makes you think I'm a cop?"

Her lip quirked up at the corner. "You're all cops." She

turned back to face the painting. "So, I suppose this means Fiona's off the wagon. I should have guessed."

"Off the wagon?"

"You know, working again. She said she planned to quit, but she's said that before. She always goes back."

Jack stared at her, intrigued. She smiled up at him and lifted a brow. "She's addicted to saving the world. Or hadn't you noticed?"

Jack looked back at the easel. Behind it, a much larger canvas leaned against the wall. This one was heavier on the green and showed reflected grass, like you might see at the edge of a river or lake. He decided he'd been right about the water thing.

"So, *Jack.*" Her voice turned sultry as she eased between him and the painting. She shifted her shoulders, and the robe parted, giving him a view of skin and lace. "Are you a detective?"

"Yes." He kept his voice cool, his attention glued to her face. She had hazel eyes—like Fiona's—but hers were outlined in black. She looked like a sexed-up version of her sister.

"And has Fiona seen your gun yet?"

Jack frowned down at her. "You're something else, you know that?"

"So I've been told." She trailed a long, copper-colored fingernail down the front of his flannel shirt. It came to rest on his belt buckle.

"What's your name?"

"Courtney." She shook her hair back, and her robe parted some more.

"Listen, Courtney—"

Jack heard a noise and whirled around. Fiona stood in

the doorway, holding a briefcase and looking perplexed.
Shit.

"Hi, there." He forced a smile and wondered why he felt guilty. He hadn't done anything wrong.

"Hey, Fi." Courtney turned toward her sister, and Jack noticed she'd finally managed to tie her belt.

Fiona gave Jack an apprehensive look. "What brings you here?"

"I came to take you to dinner." He walked over to her. "I owe you a rain check, remember?"

She set down her briefcase beside the door. Then she shrugged out of her coat and hung it on the hook in the foyer. She wore another one of those tax attorney outfits, a navy blue blazer and slacks. Her hair was pulled back in a braid again.

"I'm not really free tonight. I was planning to get some work done."

Unbelievable. He'd just driven two hours. He stepped closer and lowered his voice. "You'd have more fun with me."

She gazed up at him. Her cheeks were tinged pink from the cold. Her gaze veered to Courtney. "Have you eaten yet? You want to come with us?"

Jack gritted his teeth. He turned around to face Sister Sexpot, praying she wouldn't say yes. He wanted Fiona alone. For a number of reasons.

"I've got plans already. But thanks for the invitation, Jack." She smiled, and he knew she'd read his mind. "You guys stay out as late as you want. I won't wait up."

Fiona chose a restaurant just blocks away so she wouldn't have to argue with Jack about who should drive. The place had the added benefit of being a sushi bar, which she felt sure he would hate. He had come to Austin because he needed something, and she wanted him as uncomfortable as possible while he asked for whatever it was.

The hostess suggested a cozy, candlelit table beside a waterfall, but Fiona asked for two seats at their bar. The granite counter faced an enormous tank filled with color-coordinated fish. Jack pulled out a bar stool for Fiona and nodded impassively at the knife-wielding chef behind the counter. Then he sat on the stool beside her and gazed blankly down at his menu.

"They have great *hamachi* here," she said cheerfully.

"Hmm."

"Or the *unagi* is always good. Do you like eel?"

"I've always been partial to *kajiki*."

Fiona tried to mask her surprise. "You eat sushi?"

He shrugged. "Not lately."

The waitress stopped by, and Fiona ordered a glass of Sauvignon Blanc. Jack ordered a Budweiser, and didn't even comment when it was delivered a few moments later in a slender blue glass.

He rested an elbow on the bar and turned to face her. He was wearing flannel again, and jeans, and work boots. Everything about him clashed with the restaurant's trendy decor, but instead of looking out of place and uncomfortable, he simply looked more masculine, more in charge than ever. Fiona felt a spurt of irritation and dropped her gaze to her menu. She'd always had a weakness for in-charge men, and this one was throwing all her sluggish hormones into high gear.

"How come you didn't invoice me for the postmortem drawing?" he asked.

She took her time answering. The reasons were complicated, and she didn't feel like explaining. "I do pro bono work sometimes. It's no big deal."

She glanced up as she sipped her wine and saw him watching her intently. His eyes matched the water in the aquarium, and she felt annoyed with herself again for suggesting this place.

"I want you to invoice me."

"Why?"

"Because I need us all squared up so I can ask you to do me a favor."

The waitress came by for their orders, and Fiona took advantage of the interruption to shore up her defenses. Another favor. Another job. She was going to have to find a way to say no to him, and every one of her attempts so far had failed.

"You want to hire me again," she said when the waitress left.

"That's right."

"I don't want you to. I don't want Nathan to hire me or the FBI or anyone. I need to move on, Jack. I—I've got a show coming up, and I'm nowhere near ready for it. It's a major opportunity, and I can't afford to blow it."

"I've got another witness," he said, as if she hadn't even spoken. "Nine-year-old boy. Name's Brady Cox. He saw the killer dump the body."

Fiona closed her eyes and counted to ten mentally.

"I need you to interview this kid for me, get a picture of the guy."

She wouldn't look at him. She couldn't. He had this way of bulldozing right over her resistance. She didn't know how he did it, exactly, but she was pretty sure it had to do with eye contact.

She stared at the fish—all vibrant shades of scarlet and vermilion and gold—schooling and swirling through the water. They reminded her of flames. They reminded her of the red and orange bracelet she wore on her wrist and all the reasons she couldn't let herself get sucked in again, because if she did, she'd never find her way out. She'd start watching CNN. She'd lose the ability to sleep and find herself lying in bed at night with the faces of child torturers looming above her.

Jack's hand closed over hers on the bar. It was big and strong, and she stared at it, feeling the heat from him move up her arm into every part of her body. She didn't look at him, didn't want to acknowledge this first. If she did, she'd be acknowledging more touches to come. And she couldn't, not when she knew he was using those touches to wear down her resistance. He was a determined investigator—she'd seen that firsthand. She *admired* that about him. But that meant he'd do whatever he needed to, including lie and probably fake emotions, in order to solve his case.

And she still didn't know why this case meant so much to him because he'd refused to tell her.

"You drove all the way to Austin to ask me this?"

"I thought I'd have better luck in person." She stole a glance at him and saw a boyish smile playing at the corner of his mouth. "You have a hard time telling me no."

She pulled her hand away and took another sip of wine. She felt him watching her, probably planning his next move.

Why was she actually considering this? What had happened to her backbone?

She placed her glass delicately on the bar and looked him right in the eye. If he lied to her again, she was out of here. For good. Screw Jack Bowman and his case, screw her friendship with Nathan. If this man lied to her one more time, she was going to get up and simply walk out.

"What's between you and Lucy?" she asked.

He looked surprised. Then wary. Then he looked away.

He thumbed the base of his beer glass, turning it in circles on the bar. "We had a thing once. A long time ago."

He glanced up at her, and she knew he was telling the truth.

"When? Before her attack?"

He nodded.

"How old are you?"

"Thirty-five."

"And she's—"

"Twenty-nine."

Fiona did the math. The age gap was a little weird. It wasn't illegal, but it was cutting it close.

"She was barely eighteen at the time," Jack provided. "And no, I'm not proud of it." He looked down, shook his head. "Shit, I can't explain it. It just happened. It started one summer, and then it just kept going. We'd been talking about her moving to Houston to be with me."

He looked up at her. "Everything changed after her attack. She closed me out. Started drinking heavily. I didn't know how to help her, really, and then after a while I stopped trying."

He stared at his beer. "I'm not proud of that, either."

Fiona watched him, and for the first time felt as if he was being completely straight with her. And then she disliked herself for making him do it.

God, she was messed up. Honesty was the big issue for her, it was *the* sticking point, and now that this man was finally being honest with her, she felt bad for asking it of him.

The sensible thing to do would be to tell him no. To save herself a slew of headaches and make him find someone else to help him.

But she didn't want to do the sensible thing. She wanted to help Jack.

Jack who'd finally been honest with her.

"I'll talk to your witness," she said suddenly.

His head jerked around. "You will?"

"I'll come tomorrow. You want to meet at the station? Or the boy's house?"

He grimaced. "This kid's home life's a mess. We're best off at the station."

"Let's do it early. If we get something useful, you can release it to the media in time for the afternoon and evening broadcasts."

"Thank you." He nodded. "I mean it, I really owe you one."

She looked at the fish again, composing a painting in her mind. It was a waterscape with not just blues, but fiery oranges and reds swirled in. It was beautiful.

And she'd probably never take the time to paint it because Jack Bowman had pulled her back in.

• • •

Jack somehow managed to talk her into a drink after the sushi restaurant. Not wanting to give her time to change her mind, he picked the closest bar he could find, a tiny pub just across the street. The place was overheated and smelled like stale beer, but he glimpsed a dartboard in the back.

Jack took her hand and led her to an empty table near it. "Wine again?" He pulled the chair out for her and helped her off with her coat.

"How about a whiskey sour?"

A whiskey sour. He kept his opinions to himself. At least she was kicking back a little. "I'll be right back."

He took a few minutes to get their drinks at the bar, along with a set of darts, and returned to the table. She'd taken off the blazer to reveal a silky white shirt that was a lot more interesting.

"Here you go." He set down their drinks, but didn't join her at the table. "You ever throw darts?"

She looked at the box of darts. "No."

"I bet you'd be good at it."

He thought she was going to resist the challenge, but she scooted her chair back and stood up. She took a swig of her drink and plunked it on the table. "You're on."

He dropped his jacket over a chair and moved beside her in front of the board. "This isn't a power game," he explained. "It's about technique."

"In other words, I have a chance of beating you?"

"Ah, probably not. But it'll be fun to see you try." He took a dart and threw it gently, hitting the outer bull by some amazing stroke of luck.

She smiled up at him, and he got a warm feeling in the

pit of his stomach. Maybe it was the alcohol, but she'd lost her snippy attitude. "Okay, my turn."

He handed her a dart. She took it and squinted at the board, then leaned forward.

"Wait. You're leaning." He guided her shoulders back and eased her pelvis forward slightly. "You need a stable stance."

She took a deep breath and threw the dart, hitting a three just beneath the inner ring.

"Not bad," he said. "Most first-timers barely hit the board."

"I want to go again."

He smiled and handed her another dart. She stepped forward, eagerly.

"Hey, now. No cheating."

She dropped her gaze to the floor, noticed the line, and stepped back behind it. Then she bit her lip and sent a dart sailing three feet above the bull's-eye.

"Oops."

"It's okay." He retrieved the darts.

"You do some," she said. "Let's see what you've got."

He managed three respectable throws, even hitting a triple twenty, which she didn't seem to realize was a big deal. He pulled the darts out and nodded for her to take a turn.

"So how'd you end up in Graingerville?" she asked. "You seem like you'd be more at home on an urban police force."

"My dad got sick a few years back. Cancer. I was coming home a lot, helping out my mom."

He watched her almost nail the bull's-eye, then send one into the wall. Her aim was erratic. He eyed her blouse again, and noticed she'd unbuttoned another button, showing some skin. Her flirting was erratic, too.

"You were saying?" she asked, snapping his attention back to the conversation. "About coming home a lot?"

"So then the chief's job opened up, and I decided to stay."

Her face grew concerned. "How'd it turn out with your dad?"

Jack looked at the board and swigged his beer. "He died 'bout eighteen months ago."

"I'm sorry."

"Warm-up's over," he said, changing the subject. "Let's keep score now. You go first."

She threw a few times while Jack explained the scoring for Cricket—which was a little complicated for her liking—and she suggested they play first person to one hundred points. Fiona wasn't great, but she wasn't terrible either. Mainly, he just found himself enjoying her company. She was fun when she wasn't working. She kept smiling at him, and he wondered why he'd let himself go so long without a date.

"So why's your sister staying with you?" he asked. He was curious about Courtney, particularly her comments earlier. It sounded like Fiona had had previous boyfriends who were cops. It also sounded like she wanted a break from cops as much as she wanted one from police work. He intended to change her mind.

"She drops in sometimes," Fiona said, not looking at him. She focused her concentration on the board and threw one smack into the bull's-eye.

"Oh my God, *look*!" She turned and gave him an excited hug, which would have been great except for the dart in her hand.

"Careful, now." He took it from her. "Hey, that's a beauty. Guess I'm getting whipped."

"Beginner's luck," she said, beaming.

Her smile was contagious, and he grinned down at her. "You're gloating."

"No, I'm not." She picked up her glass, but it was empty. "I'm just enjoying the fact that you were so smug when we started. And now I'm kicking your butt."

He liked her this way—relaxed and confident and loose around him. He nodded at her drink. "Want another one?"

She shook the glass, rattling the ice cubes. "I'd better not." She put it on the table. "I've got to get up early."

And with that, the mood changed as she seemed to remember why they were here together. She had a boy to interview tomorrow. A homicide to work.

She glanced at her watch. "We should go."

She looked a million miles away as they left the bar and walked back toward her apartment. They passed a gap between buildings, and an icy gust of wind whipped through. Jack wrapped an arm around her shoulder and pulled her into him, and after an instant of resistance, she settled against his side.

"I saw your pictures," he said. "Back there at your place."

She didn't say anything, but he felt her shoulders tighten.

"They're good," he added lamely.

She looked up with a wry smile. "You sound surprised."

"Not really. Nathan said you painted nature scenes. I'd expected some portraits, too, I guess."

"I don't like portraits."

"You're kidding."

"No."

"But you're really good at them. And I've only seen a few examples."

She looked away. "I try to avoid people."

"Antisocial?"

"Just when it comes to art. Too many sidewalk sketches on Venice Beach, I think. Tourists and wiggly kids."

He pictured her seated at an easel beside a sunny beach in California. It was a nice image. Much better than the image of her seated beside a gurney in the morgue.

"It was a good place to start," she continued. "Taught me to work quickly."

"But you burned out?"

"Yes. Now I'd much rather paint something peaceful."

They strolled down the street, ducking their heads against the biting wind. He pulled her closer.

"I wish this cold would end," she said.

He could feel her shivering, even under the coat and blazer. "You miss California?"

Her cheek rested on his jacket, and he could smell her hair—something sweet, like peaches. He couldn't believe she'd let him get this close, even just for warmth.

"Not really. Seventy-two and sunny all the time gets boring."

He tried to follow the conversation, but he was distracted. He kept thinking about peeling off all those layers and warming her up the right way. He pictured her flushed and sweaty from sex, and his body reacted.

"Central Texas gets big, dramatic thunderstorms," she said. "I love those."

Christ, were they really talking about the weather? This

was pathetic. What he wanted to talk about was where he'd be spending the night.

Although he shouldn't even be here. He needed to be at work early, and even though he wasn't technically on call tonight, being chief meant he was in charge twenty-four/seven. He should get back in case something happened.

But he wanted to stay with Fiona. All night. And not get a wink of sleep.

"Is this you?" Her footsteps slowed as they neared his truck, which he'd parked at a meter in front of her building. She stopped and turned to face him, stepping back so his arm fell away from her shoulders. A lock of hair blew across her face, and she peeled it away.

"So I'll see you tomorrow then? Nine A.M. at the station? I'll try to get there a few minutes early, before Brady."

He tried to read what she wanted. Her words were telling him to take a hike, but her eyes were telling him something different. They were dark and liquid and wide with anticipation.

He eased closer, resting his hand on the cold metal of the truck and trapping her against his body. Her breath caught.

"You in a hurry for me to leave?" He stroked his hand up the lapel of her coat and then rested it against the bare skin of her neck, right where her pulse thumped. She had a faint scar there.

"Jack—"

"Invite me up." He leaned in and kissed her temple. She smelled sweet. He wanted to find out how she tasted. He wanted some of that lush, pretty mouth.

But she turned and looked away. He followed her gaze

to the top floor of her building. She seemed to be focused on the corner apartment where the lights were blazing. "Courtney's there."

"Maybe she left."

"No, I just saw a shadow by the window. She doesn't usually go out until late."

Jack sighed. He'd only just met Courtney, but so far he wasn't a fan.

Fiona slid her hands beneath his jacket, resting them at his waist. He felt the light pressure of her thumbs through his shirt, and his blood stirred some more.

She hadn't said no. She just hadn't said yes *tonight*. It was a subtle distinction, but he knew it was progress.

"Tomorrow then," he said, hoping she knew he wasn't just talking about work. He took her hand and tugged her toward her building.

Her brows arched, and her feet stayed planted.

"What?" he asked. "You expect me to leave without walking you to the door?"

She eyed him skeptically.

"Where I come from, a man doesn't dump his date on a street corner."

Reluctantly, she let him lead her to the entrance to her building. "This wasn't a date. I don't date cops."

He pulled the door open for her and smiled. "You keep right on saying that if it makes you feel better."

"Here she is."

The night manager held up a key.

Sullivan took the key ring from him with a latex-gloved hand. The other keys jangled together as the agent unlocked

Room 103. Careful not to mar any prints on the knob, Sullivan kept the key in the lock and used it to push open the door.

"And you're sure it was vacated yesterday?" he asked the manager.

"Yesiree. He cleared out Tuesday morning. Only person been in here since was the maid."

"Thank you for your help tonight," Sullivan said, donning a pair of paper booties. He gave the man a nod. "I'll take it from here."

The manager pushed his bifocals farther up on his nose. Although it was twenty-eight degrees out, he wore a lightweight tracksuit and loafers without socks. He seemed to be oscillating between curiosity about what Sullivan was about to do, and a pressing need to get back to the space heater in the front office. "I'll get out of your way then. You lemme know if you change your mind about that coffee."

He shuffled off, and Sullivan turned to face the room that was the last known location of Keith Janovic. He'd been sighted by a fellow lodger nearly thirty-six hours ago as he was leaving this motel, and Sullivan was just now making the scene.

Thirty-six hours for the tip to get passed up the channel. Thirty-six hours for the trail to grow cold. Thirty-six hours for a maid to make her way into this small, dark hole and unwittingly eliminate clues.

Sullivan turned on the light and entered the room, closing the door behind him to keep out the cold and the curious gazes of other lodgers. Lucky for him this place wasn't at full capacity. It was one of the many no-tell motels along Interstate 20, and the man now calling himself George

Green reportedly had been the only other person to rent this particular room in a week.

He'd been alone, by all accounts.

The couple who called in the tip and the two motel staffers who had seen him all reported the same thing: a mid-twenties man, tall and heavyset, who appeared to be traveling solo and drove a burgundy Mercury Cougar. The car itself was a huge lead, one being followed up on at this very moment by several Atlanta-based agents.

Sullivan, meanwhile, had been sent to secure the scene. He'd rocketed down I-20 westbound and made it even before the techs who had been called out to gather evidence.

His gaze scanned the room, taking in the signs of a recent cleaning: the ammonia smell, overlaid with cinnamon air freshener, the freshly folded washcloths stacked on the bathroom counter, the cable brochure propped neatly on the TV set, where it might entice someone to order a skin flick. Sullivan planned to check the motel records to find out what, if any, programs had been requested by 103 this week.

He stepped toward the bed, opened the nightstand drawer, and saw a giveaway pen and a Gideon Bible. He made his way to the vanity and flipped on the fluorescent light above the sink. The porcelain bowl gleamed at him, but still bore rust stains from years of use. He pulled out the trash can and looked inside, but saw only a plastic bag lining the empty can. He stepped into the cramped bathroom. More cinnamon assaulted his nostrils. More freshly folded towels, these large enough for the average five-year-old but not for an adult. A bar of cheap, plastic-wrapped soap sat forlornly on the side of the tub.

A knock sounded at the door, and Sullivan crossed the

suite, wondering just how many DNA profiles could be lifted from the carpet alone. Despite the room's apparent cleanliness, it was just the sort of setting that drove the forensics guys up a wall. Evidence was everywhere—fibers, fingerprints, hairs, and semen. It wouldn't be a lack of evidence in a place like this, but an overwhelming abundance of it that would make their task difficult.

Sullivan jerked open the door, expecting to see a pair of crime scene technicians wearing paper shoes.

Instead, it was a woman. Mid-thirties. She wore a brown leather coat and had spiky blond hair.

"Are you George?" she asked breathlessly. "Sorry I'm late, but I got here soon as I could."

CHAPTER

7

Fiona showed up looking like a teenager. Jack watched her enter the station house, taking in the ripped jeans, the faded black T-shirt, the dingy sneakers. He'd told her last night Brady Cox was a discipline case who had problems with authority, and Jack suspected she'd chosen her outfit with Brady in mind. She looked like the exact opposite of an authority figure, the antithesis of someone who collaborated with the nation's top law enforcement officials on a regular basis. Only her leather art case hinted at who she really was.

"I have an appointment with Chief Bowman," she told Sharon. As the resident rookie, Sharon got to sit closest to the reception counter and deal with the whiners and wack jobs who dropped in from time to time.

Jack crossed the bullpen—which in this humble jurisdiction consisted of a few mismatched desks and file cabinets.

He caught Fiona's eye, and she smiled, taking some of the punch out of her bad-ass look. He lifted the hinged divider that separated reception from the main office. At his old precinct in Houston, cops were separated from visitors by metal detectors, armed guards, and bulletproof glass, but in Graingerville life was more low-key.

"Come on back," he said, nodding toward his office, aware that every gaze in the room was fixed on Fiona. All of his subordinates had heard about the hotshot FBI artist he'd hired yet again, in the hopes she could help crack their case. Every last one of them was skeptical.

She passed the break room just as Carlos came out, and the deputy chief sloshed coffee on himself as he stepped back to admire Fiona's butt.

Jack shot him a look. "No interruptions. And the only visitor I want to see is Brady Cox. You're in charge of distracting his mom while we do the interview."

Jack pulled the door shut as he entered his office, no doubt fueling the fires of speculation already burning around town. Placing bets about Jack's sex life—or lack of one—had been a popular pastime ever since he'd taken the chief's job and moved back to Graingerville. Even his own mother and sisters weren't above the gossip. It was one of the reasons he tried to get the hell out of Dodge whenever he wanted a woman's company.

Fiona stood beside his window, staring through the glass. Jack took one look outside and predicted precipitation by late afternoon. Having grown up on a farm, he'd been paying attention to clouds all his life, and it amazed him how oblivious city people could be to something as basic as weather.

"Forget your coat again?"

She turned around. "Where do you normally conduct interviews?"

His lip curled at her tone of voice. All business. Like he hadn't asked her to go to bed with him just last night.

"*Normally,* we use the break room." Not that they normally had many interviews to conduct. Most of the stuff they dealt with was such small potatoes, it didn't merit a formal interview. But on rare occasions when one was called for, the break room worked best, provided Jack could keep his officers from streaming in and out to use the Coke machine.

Fiona cast a critical look around the room. Her gaze paused on the framed photograph sitting on his desk, then moved to the bulletin board beside the door.

"I'd prefer here," she said. "The lighting's good, and it's nice and comfortable. We need to get rid of those, though." She nodded at a series of mug shots pinned to the corkboard. It was a collection of area dirtbags, plus the FBI's Ten Most Wanted. Jack knew the nation's most notorious baddies weren't likely to set foot in Graingerville, but he kept them clearly visible as a matter of pride. He'd paid his dues at one of the largest law enforcement agencies in the country, and he took his job seriously, even if most days it consisted of nuisance complaints and petty theft.

"You think the mugs will spook the witness?"

"Not necessarily," she said. "But it's better not to suggest an image. I want to know what Brady remembers on his own."

Jack nodded. "Okay, what else? I'll bring another chair in. And have the phone routed to voice mail so it's quiet."

She stowed her purse on the floor beside his file cabinet. Then she lifted her art case onto his desk and started unloading supplies. Her hair fell in a wavy curtain around her face, and he wondered why she wore it pulled back all the time. It looked much better like this.

"We don't need another chair." She glanced up. "Unless

his mother insists on being present. Can you persuade her to sit outside?"

Jack propped a shoulder against the wall and crossed his arms. "Shouldn't be a problem. But *I'd* like to sit in, if it's all the same to you."

"It's not."

"Not what?"

"Not all the same to me. This child saw something disturbing. He's probably scared, even if he's acting tough. The last thing he needs is some puffed-up cop giving him the third degree."

"Puffed-up?"

She sighed. "No offense, Jack, but you come on a little strong. I've been around cops a long time. I understand the swagger and the arrogance, and I know it serves a purpose."

"Do you now?"

"But you have to understand how it can be interpreted by a victim. It's intimidating. It stifles open conversation."

Jack clenched his jaw, not sure which insult to deal with first. "This kid's not a victim," he reminded her. "He's just a witness."

"Fine, he's a witness. But a traumatized one. I don't want you hanging around making him uncomfortable."

"Who says I make people uncomfortable?"

She glanced up at the ceiling, clearly exasperated. "Jack, come on."

"I'm friendly. Ask anyone in town."

Her eyes sparked with indignation. And damned if he wasn't getting aroused.

"Jack, you're six-one, built like a brick . . . wall. And then there's that look you get."

"What look?"

"Please." Her eyes pleaded with him now. "I'm an experienced interviewer. And I'm asking you to leave us alone. It's the best thing for the witness."

Back to the witness again. The victim. Jack cared about that; he really did. It was one reason he'd been so determined to get Fiona down here to talk to Lucy. But Lucy actually *was* a victim. And this investigation was too important for Jack to keep tiptoeing around everybody. All this touchy-feely crap was starting to piss him off.

"I need to hear this kid's story," he said. "He's my best lead."

"I understand. And I'll tell you everything. You can even videotape us, if you get permission. But I don't want you in here."

Someone tapped on the door, then pushed it open. Carlos poked his head in sheepishly, and Jack glared at him.

"Sorry, J.B., but Brady's mom's here."

Jack turned to Fiona, who still had that plea in her eyes. Goddamn it, he couldn't say no to her. She had better be right about this.

And if she wasn't, he'd just have to hang on to the kid when she was done so he could milk him for more information.

"Give us two more minutes," he told Carlos. "Then send Brady in. I'll talk to his mother."

Carlos cleared his throat. "That's the problem. I just talked to her. She said Brady's run off."

Fiona's stomach growled, and she glanced at the clock. Four hours, and still no Brady. And each time she thought about going out for a break, she convinced herself to wait another twenty minutes. Every cop on Jack's force was looking for the boy. They *had* to find him soon. In a town this small, how hard could it be to find a kid tooling around on a purple dirt bike?

She looked down at the papers fanned out across Jack's desk, grateful she'd had them stashed in her car. At least the morning hadn't been a total waste. She hadn't helped apprehend any murderers, but hey, she'd managed to grade three dozen essays, meaning she might actually squeeze in some painting tonight, assuming she could get back to Austin in time.

She jotted some comments in the margin for one of her students, and her gaze wandered over to the photo by Jack's phone. Two girls with their arms hooked around each other smiled out at the camera. By Fiona's guess, they were seven and nine. They had Bowman features, from the gray-blue eyes to the square jaw, and Fiona wondered for the umpteenth time whether Jack had ever been married.

The thought made her uneasy, so she shifted her attention to the stack of mug shots on Jack's file cabinet. He'd removed them from the bulletin board at her request, but not before she'd had a chance to look. Fiona made a habit of paying attention to faces, and without really trying, she'd memorized Jack's collection in a matter of minutes. Most of them were from the FBI's Ten Most Wanted List.

Fiona had her own top ten list of sorts—an array of rapists and murderers whose faces appeared to her in the wee hours of the morning, no matter how hard she tried to shut them out. They were from cold cases, mostly, from some of the toughest investigations she'd ever worked, the ones that hadn't ended in resolution. Lucy's abductor had recently been added to the list. And whenever Fiona started to feel sorry for herself because her job had filled her head with such horrible images, she'd think about the victims. She'd wonder how *they* were sleeping—if they were lucky enough to be alive. Many weren't so lucky. In those cases, Fiona wondered how their parents fared at night, and she knew she had it easy.

She returned her attention to her papers and tried to concentrate.

"Good news," Jack said, sticking his head in.

"You found Brady?"

"Yep." He smiled. "Sharon spotted him inside the video arcade at Dot's Truck Stop. She's bringing him in."

"You make it sound like he's being arrested. I don't want this to be a hostile interview."

Jack scoffed. "With this kid, everything's hostile. But Sharon's working on him. She took him through the drive-through at the Dairy Queen and promised not to write him up for truancy if he behaves himself."

"Does he have a history of ditching school?"

"His principal tells me he's one unexcused absence away from repeating fourth grade." He checked his watch. "Hey, you hungry or anything? You want a Coke?"

"No," she said, although she was famished.

"Well, sit tight. They'll be here soon."

Fifteen minutes later, Fiona was seated across the desk from a sullen nine-year-old, the best link anyone had between an unidentified girl and the man who'd choked the life out of her.

Brady had made quick work of his Hunger Buster with cheese, and now was finishing off a greasy pile of fries. His lunch smelled heavenly, and Fiona was practically drooling from sitting so close to it.

"I saw your drawing," she said. "You're really talented."

He eyed her with suspicion as he dipped a fry in ketchup. At her urging, he'd taken Jack's comfy swivel chair, which put him in the power seat. Fiona was in the stiff, plastic chair on the other side of the desk.

"You have a good eye for detail."

Brady didn't say anything. He chomped the last french fry and washed it down with a slurp of soda. Then he pushed back from the desk. After a quick spin in the chair, he leaned back and propped his feet on Jack's blotter. His sneakers were richly embellished with graffiti, and Fiona noticed with a sinking heart that it looked like gang writing.

"You ever had art lessons?" she asked.

He squinted at her through his shaggy brown bangs. "You mean like painting?"

"Or drawing."

"No."

"Well, you're very good at it."

He shrugged.

"I'd like to talk to you about the picture you drew. You told your teacher you were up in your tree fort when you saw the girl?"

No comment.

"What were you doing up there in the middle of the night?"

Silence.

Fiona plopped her elbow on the desk and rested her chin on her fist. "When I was nine, we lived in an apartment. I used to sleep out on the fire escape when I didn't feel like being home."

Brady took his feet down and opened Jack's drawer. He helped himself to some paper clips and started fiddling with them.

"That was in L.A., though. So it wasn't nearly as cold as it is here right now. I hope you had a sleeping bag or something."

He shrugged. "I had my Spurs sweatshirt. Plus my coat."

"Does your mom get upset when you go out like that?"

Brady fashioned one of the clips into a triangle, carefully adjusting the metal ends to maximize the tension. "Sometimes." He placed it on the desk—just so—and it shot into the air with a *ping*. "Did yours?"

"She didn't always notice. But when she did, I'd get in trouble."

Brady went to work on another paper clip. "You don't seem like a cop."

"I'm not. I'm just here to talk to you about the man you saw from your tree house, see if we can get a picture of him."

Ping—another clip went flying. Brady picked up yet another one, avoiding eye contact. "I didn't really get a good look. It wasn't hardly light out."

"But you got a good enough look to remember the girl?"

His cheeks reddened, and for the first time, he actually looked his age. He chewed his lower lip, then hazarded a glance up at Fiona. "She was naked. I didn't make that up. He took her out there that way."

"I know, Brady. You wouldn't make up something like that."

He glanced down at his paper clip. He kept fidgeting with it, but this one wouldn't cooperate. "She was dead, too. I couldn't do nothin'."

"I know."

He glared up at her. "It was too late for 911. She was *dead*. Just like on TV, with her eyes all popped open."

"I know."

He tossed the paper clip aside and snatched the straw from his paper cup. He twisted it around his thumb.

"Let's talk about the man, Brady."

He mumbled something.

"What?"

"I can't draw him. This is stupid. I already tried drawing him, and I can't."

Fiona leaned forward, trying to keep her voice even. "You don't have to draw him, Brady. Is that what you thought?"

Confusion filled his eyes.

"Is that why you ran away?"

He looked down and unwound the straw from his thumb. "I'm not supposed to draw him?"

"You don't need to draw anything," she said. "That's my job. All I need for you to do is talk to me."

He looked up warily, and she could tell they'd bridged the gap. "I guess I could do that," he said.

"All right, then." She felt her chest loosening with relief as she reached for her sketch board. She smiled at Brady, and got the faintest trace of a smile in return. "Just tell me what you saw."

• • •

They had a break. Jack knew it the moment Fiona stepped out of his office. The good-bye she exchanged with Brady was casual, but the expression on her face told Jack something big had happened. It was all he could do to keep his cool as Sharon guided Brady and his mom into the break room to fill out paperwork.

He followed Fiona back into his office and closed the door.

"We got him," she said, grinning.

"Are you sure?"

"Have a look at this." She gestured to a drawing on his desk.

Jack took one glance and felt his heart skip. "Holy shit."

"I know." She smiled triumphantly. "Isn't it uncanny?"

"Are you sure about this? I mean, it's not just because you talked to Lucy?"

"I swear it's good. I always go into a second interview aware of that possibility, but this isn't a hybrid image. Brady's description was completely independent. And it's the same guy."

It was, indeed, the same guy. He looked just like Lucy's attacker, except older.

Jack whistled. "It's your age progression to a T. The heavy version."

"I mean, I couldn't believe it. He was just *brimming* with details. Look at the nose. The eyes. I got a freaking *tattoo*!" She snatched a drawing pad off the desk and flipped it open.

"No kidding?"

"Our guy has a swastika on his left forearm." She handed him the pad. "Brady originally said it was a spider, but I showed him some pages from my tattoo catalogue, and he picked out the swastika."

Jack stared down at the drawing, stunned. The swastika was unusual, with arrow points at the ends of the arms. He couldn't believe Brady had come up with this. It was too good to be true.

And maybe it was. "How'd the kid see all this?"

Fiona shook her head. "He was paying attention. I mean, *really* paying attention. God, what would you do if you saw someone dumping a body? And Brady was stuck there, up in his tree fort, trying not to make a sound as the whole thing unfolded. He thinks it took about fifteen minutes, from start to finish. And it was right after dawn."

Jack stared down at the stylized hate symbol. He guessed Fiona had drawn it on a separate sheet because it wasn't part of the face. "This tattoo is helpful. I can run it through some databases. Is Brady sure it was on his forearm? It was in the thirties that night. I would have thought the guy'd be wearing a coat."

She nodded. "I asked the same thing, but he insists. Said the man was wearing one of those down vests and a sweatshirt. He was carrying the body, and by the time he made it from the road all the way to the drop site near the fence, he was breathing heavily. Brady says he laid her on the ground, pushed up his sleeves, and went to work arranging her."

Jack recalled the crime scene, the way the victim had been positioned provocatively, her legs splayed. It was one of the reasons he'd known, immediately, they were dealing with someone theatrical. Some attention-seeking fuckhead who wouldn't stop. Not until he was forced to.

Jack looked up at Fiona. She was clearly on an adrenaline rush. "How much time do you need?" he asked. "You know, to finish this up?"

They both glanced at the clock. It was nearly three. They could still make the five o'clock broadcast, provided they held a news conference at 4:30. But Jack had to get on the horn quick, if he wanted to round everyone up.

"I need fifteen minutes to refine it," she said. "Twenty, tops."

"You got it. Now just tell me one more thing." He squeezed her shoulder, praying she'd kept her end of their bargain. "Please, *please* tell me you got it on videotape."

She smiled. "You really think I'd forget something like that?"

Jack swerved into a reserved parking space at City Hall and glanced at the clock on the bank building downtown. It was 4:20. They were cutting it close if they intended to make the five o'clock news. But Jack hadn't wanted to put this off until tomorrow—he was determined to get this picture out today.

He got out his official vehicle—a tan and green Explorer with GRAINGERVILLE POLICE DEPARTMENT painted across the door—and surveyed the lot for familiar cars. Carlos was here already. And Lowell and Sharon had just pulled up in a patrol car. He spotted the dinged hatchback belonging to the guy who ran the local radio station, and Doc Jamison's ancient station wagon, which sometimes doubled as a hearse.

But where the hell were the news vans? He'd called every media outlet in central and south Texas. Barring something with sexier footage, like a factory fire or maybe a five-car pileup, he'd expected a full turnout. He'd called ahead to have a podium set up in the large meeting room typically used by the city council. But this looked like a far cry from standing room only.

Lowell and Sharon strolled up with their chests thrust out, both in freshly pressed uniforms. Lowell hitched up his patent leather gun belt, and Jack remembered what Fiona had said about puffed-up cops. She was right. They both looked like they had a pole up their ass. Come to think of it, he knew a lot of cops who looked that way.

Shit, did *he*? He glanced down at his starched uniform, his shiny badge. He'd even shaved for the occasion. But did he swagger around like that? No way.

At least he didn't think he did.

"Pretty thin," Lowell observed.

Jack scowled at the parking lot. "I thought this was a slow news day. There something going on I don't know about?"

"Radio's been quiet," Sharon said.

A white Honda turned into the lot, and Jack watched as Fiona slid out of the car dressed once again in her attorney clothes. But it wasn't a tax attorney this time. More like a crack trial lawyer. She strode up the sidewalk in tall black heels and a charcoal suit. Her skirt was short enough to reveal a pair of very nice legs that, until now, Jack had seen only in his imagination.

She nodded hello. "No television yet," she said, casting a worried look in Jack's direction. "You called them, didn't you?"

"Yep."

Jack told his officers to go inside to check the podium setup. He needed a minute alone with Fiona.

"You're disappointed," she stated.

"Something's up. There should be way more people than this." He scanned the area again and spotted a white van in the distance, slowly making its way down Main Street. As it got closer, he discerned the logo for the CBS affiliate out of San Antonio. It parked, and Jack watched a blonde climb out of the van. She wore a snazzy red pantsuit and stood out like a beacon on this slate gray day. Jack didn't recognize her.

"There's one, at least," Fiona said.

"They sent their second string. We're not the lead story."

The woman fluffed her hair in the van's side mirror as her cameraman dragged his gear from the back.

"I assume you all don't have a public information officer," Fiona said.

"You're looking at him."

"Well, you know how this goes, right? It's up to you to decide what information to release. I won't discuss the case; I just stand beside the easel. I don't talk unless someone has a question specifically related to the sketch or the drawing process."

"Good." Jack needed control over this thing. The media could help, but they could also harm the case if he wasn't careful. "I've told everyone else to keep it zipped, too."

"I'm sorry it's not a better turnout."

Jack looked down at her and noticed the worry line between her brows. "Not your fault," he said. "You've done everything you can."

"That's why I came."

Was that the only reason? He was hoping he could talk her into staying the night, even though her official work here would be finished as soon as the press conference ended.

In his peripheral vision, he saw the TV crew approaching, and he knew he was about to get blasted with questions. But he couldn't take his eyes off Fiona. She'd put on makeup—not a lot, just enough to accent her eyes and her lips. She looked beautiful. And she smelled good again. She reached up to stroke his earlobe, and his heart kicked.

"Shaving cream," she whispered, and smiled.

"Chief Bowman, is it true you've had a break in your murder case? Have you positively identified the victim?"

"I'll be happy to discuss that inside, if you'll head into the briefing room."

Jack turned back to Fiona, but she was already gone.

CHAPTER
8

Fiona had been to enough press conferences to know today's was a bust. Only a handful of reporters had shown up, and most of them were from regional newspapers that published weekly. But worse, they barely had any television. Only CBS carried the story, and it was relegated to a twenty-second sound bite at the bottom of the broadcast.

She eyed the barroom TV from her cozy booth. Tired of ignoring her hunger pangs, she'd stopped for a meal at Becker's before getting on the road back to Austin.

"Here you are," the waitress said, placing a glass of iced tea in front of her. "That cheeseburger'll be right out."

Fiona thanked her and caught a glimpse of the man seated at the bar. He wore a green camo baseball cap pulled low over his face, and he'd been watching her for the past ten minutes. Maybe she should tell the waitress she wanted her food to go. Avoiding the man's stare, she busied herself adding lemon and sweetener to her tea.

"You must be famous."

She glanced up. The camo guy peered down at her from beneath the bill of his cap. He wasn't tall, but he had wide shoulders and big, meaty hands, one of which was wrapped around a Bud longneck.

"Excuse me?"

"Yeah, I saw you." He jerked his head toward the TV above the bar. "Six o'clock news. That thing with the Mexican girl."

He slid into the booth across from her, and Fiona felt a flutter of unease. "So, what, you from the FBI or something? They send you down to solve the case?"

"I'm a forensic artist. Chief Bowman hired me to do the suspect sketch."

"An artist, huh?" He took a swig of his beer and plunked it down on the table, as if he intended to stay a while. "You don't look like an artist."

She was curious to know just what he thought an artist should look like, but she didn't want to prolong the conversation.

"Here we go." The waitress reappeared with Fiona's food. The cheeseburger was the size of a dinner plate and was accompanied by a mountain of seasoned home fries. Fiona was dying to dig in, but first she wanted to get rid of the barfly.

The waitress shot him a stern look. "You're not bothering this nice lady, are you, Hoyt?"

Hoyt smiled and gave the woman's rear end a pat. "Nah, I'm just being friendly. You know me. Hate to see a pretty girl settin' all alone."

"Aren't you sweet?" the waitress said, rolling her eyes at Fiona.

"Hey, she tell you she's a police artist? She drew that picture on the news."

"That was *you*?" Her eyes lit up, as if she were meeting

a celebrity. "I heard we had someone down from Austin, working on Jack's case."

Fiona forced a smile.

"I bet Jack's steamed, isn't he? Upstaged by Randy again like that." She lifted a brow in Hoyt's direction.

"Yeah, ol' Jack's probably spitting nails right now."

"Who's Randy?" Fiona couldn't resist asking.

"Randy Rudd," Hoyt said. "Our county sheriff. He and Jack sometimes get crosswise on account of their territories overlap."

The waitress nodded at Fiona. "That big drug bust on the news tonight? That was Randy. He's always running for reelection, so he loves to get in front of the camera whenever something big happens."

Fiona tried to recall the top news story this evening. She'd caught only the tail end of it: something about a raid on a methamphetamine lab. Some sheriff had seized equipment and made a few arrests.

But surely the timing was a coincidence. How could the Grainger county sheriff have known Jack had a break in his case? And that he'd be releasing a sketch to the media this afternoon? Fiona herself hadn't even known for sure until after the interview.

"Well, don't let us keep you." The waitress shot Hoyt a pointed look, then turned a smile on Fiona. "You enjoy your dinner, now."

Fiona mustered a pleasant expression for Hoyt. "It's been nice chatting with you."

He leaned forward on his elbows. "You look like a lady who knows her way around a stick. What say we shoot some pool later?"

"Thanks, but I don't think so."

He let his gaze drop to her breasts, and she regretted taking off her jacket when she'd sat down.

"Look, I don't mean to be rude," she said, "but do you mind if I eat my dinner?"

"Nah, go right ahead." He nodded at her plate, but made no move to leave.

"I mean, alone?"

His expression hardened. He watched her coolly as he took a swill of his beer. Then he slammed the empty bottle on the table, making the silverware jump. Fiona jumped, too, which seemed to please him.

"You know, I never got your name." He held out his hand.

She glanced at it, debating the wisdom of further ticking off this guy. She gave his hand a brief shake. "It's Fiona."

"Fee-yo-na." He tested the word on his tongue. "It's real nice to meet you, Fee-yo-na. You come find me if you change your mind about pool."

He slid out of the booth and nearly bumped into a stout older woman holding a plate of pie.

"Quit bothering the customers, Hoyt." She set the pie beside Fiona's tea and scooted into the space Hoyt had just vacated. Good God, where was the waitress? Fiona needed a bill.

"Ginny Kuzak," the woman said. "I'm the cook. Allyson tells me you're that police artist down from Austin."

"That's right." She glanced longingly at her food and wished she'd gone to a drive-through.

"Well, welcome to Graingerville. It's a nice place to live, most times. We don't usually get all this murder and mayhem. I'm just sick over what happened to that poor girl."

Fiona studied the woman's plump face, surrounded by gray curls. She wore a white, grease-splattered apron and looked like she'd been on her feet all day.

"The apple pie's on me," she said. "I want to thank you for coming all the way down here to help Jack like this. I've known that boy thirty-five years now, and I haven't ever seen him so wrapped up in something. Course it's personal to him, but he probably already told you about all that."

The waitress stopped by, and instead of requesting a to-go box, Fiona found herself asking for a glass of wine. Ginny seemed to want to sit for the foreseeable future, and Fiona didn't think she could wait another minute to get some food in her system. She bit into a fry, and sighed at the crunchy, salty goodness of it.

Ginny smiled. "That's my grandmother's recipe. You won't get anything that compares over at Lorraine's."

Fiona didn't know who Lorraine was, but she kept eating. "You were saying?" she said after another bite. "About this case being tough for Jack?"

This was a shameless fishing expedition, but who else was she supposed to ask about him? He was so tight-lipped about everything, and she was curious. If she asked Nathan, he'd just tell Jack she'd been inquiring, and she didn't want to let either of them know she cared. Her interest was completely unprofessional, and it would compromise her reputation with the guys over at APD.

"Well, I assume you heard about the Arrellando girl? Jack may not have told you, but they were sweethearts way back when, and everyone knows it's been eating at him for years how no one ever solved her case." Ginny leaned forward conspiratorially. "Now some folks think there never was much case to *solve,* but I don't believe all that. What girl goes out and lets somebody knock her around that way?"

The waitress delivered a glass of wine. She seemed amazingly attentive, and Fiona figured she was eavesdropping.

"Sure, I know it *happens.*" Ginny waved a hand, as if batting away a gnat. "But that Arrellando one's a tough cookie. She wouldn't put up with that. She was attacked, you ask me, and I don't care what all they say about her."

Fiona picked up her burger. Ginny seemed to be on a roll, and Fiona had no desire to interrupt.

"Anyway, if what happened to those gals is connected, Jack'll get to the bottom of it. That boy's a good cop. Always has been. That stuff back in Houston was blown way outta proportion."

Fiona tried not to look too curious. All she knew about Jack's years in Houston was that he'd worked homicide at some point, and that Nathan had helped train him.

"It sounds like you know Jack and his family pretty well."

Ginny nodded. "They're fine people. Salt of the earth. Course they're a stubborn bunch, too, every last one of them. And you never met a more persistent man than John."

Fiona swallowed a succulent bite. The meat was perfect, the cheese warm and gooey. The bun was homemade and toasted with just a hint of butter. It was the best burger she'd ever put in her mouth, but she didn't want to interrupt Ginny by telling her so. She dabbed her lips with a napkin. "And John is . . . ?"

"Jack's daddy. Cotton farmer. He was a hardworking, hardheaded SOB, and Jack takes right after him. Takes after him in other ways, too. Got more than his fair share of good looks." Ginny smiled, suddenly looking younger and less worn out. "But I bet you already noticed that, right?"

Jack spotted her at the back of the bar. She had an empty wineglass in front of her and looked to be deep in conversation with one of his mother's best friends.

He sighed.

"They've been at it half an hour now," Allyson said, wiping down a booth near the hostess stand. "But we just sat a big table, so you'd better tell Ginny to hustle it back to the kitchen before Ralph pitches a fit."

Allyson cut another look at him and seemed to notice his jeans. "You off tonight? My brother's having some people over to watch UT basketball, if you're interested."

"Thanks, but I've got plans." Jack stripped off his jacket, trying not to make a puddle on the oak plank floor. It had started sleeting outside, and the roads were a mess. He predicted an injury accident by midnight.

He made his way to the back, nodding at friends and acquaintances wedged into booths. Kenny Chesney played on the jukebox, and a shout went up from the poolroom in back as someone sank a shot. He stopped at Fiona's table.

"You bad-mouthing me again, Ginny?"

Ginny looked up, and her face went from surprised to guilty in about half a second.

Jack slid into the booth right beside Fiona, and she beamed at him.

"What?"

"Oh, nothing." Her eyes sparkled with amusement. "Ginny's just filling me in on a little background info. I didn't know you had a *rabbit*."

Jack glared at Ginny. "I don't." He picked up Fiona's fork and stole a bite of her pie.

Ginny tipped her head to the side and folded her arms over her chest.

"Great pie, Gin." He took another bite. "Hey, Allyson wanted me to tell you you're needed in the kitchen."

She stood up and pretended to be in a huff. "Don't you lie to this girl, Jack Bowman. She's a smart one." She bestowed a smile on Fiona. "Nice meeting you, hon. You come on by here again next time you're in town."

When she finally left, Jack gave Fiona a long, steady look. She had her elbow resting on the table and her cheeks were flushed, probably from the wine. Her suit jacket was crumpled up beside her, and she wore a cream-colored blouse that was a tad see-through.

"Good thing you decided to stay. The roads are bad tonight." He draped an arm over the back of the booth and picked up a strand of hair that had come loose from her braid.

"I just stopped for dinner. I'm going back after this."

Jack forked up another bite of pie. "What all did Ginny have to say?"

"Oh, not much. Just how you used to be a real big shot in high school."

"Hmm."

"And how you led your football team to the state championship. Very impressive."

Fiona obviously didn't know much about football. Jack's team had been good, but Grainger High was only a 3A school, not exactly a powerhouse. That winning season was still well remembered around town, though. And his role as quarterback during the glory days had made him pretty popular. It was probably the reason the town council had overlooked his age when he'd applied for the chief-of-police job.

Jack stroked a finger down Fiona's neck and wondered what else she'd heard about him. Knowing Ginny, it hadn't all been good. "Don't believe everything Ginny says. She has a tendency to stretch the truth."

Fiona lifted an eyebrow.

"Get you a beer, Jack?"

He glanced up at Allyson. "I'll have a Budweiser. And a piece of this pie. À la mode, please."

Fiona scrunched up her nose. "Beer with *pie*?"

He looked down at her, resisting the urge to lean down and kiss that nose. "Sure, why not?"

She shook her head and reclaimed her fork. He watched her take a dainty bite, then run her tongue over the corner of her lip. Just sitting here watching her eat was getting to him. If he had any sense, he'd move to the other side of the booth and give her some space, but it had been a long, grueling day, and her hair smelled just a little too nice. So instead, he inched closer, brushing his thigh against her knee. She gazed up at him and sank her teeth into that plump bottom lip. He didn't know for sure what she was thinking, but he could make a guess.

"Here you go."

Jack dragged his gaze away from Fiona's mouth and thanked Allyson for his order. The service sure as hell was prompt tonight.

When she was gone, Jack looked at Fiona. Her attention was fixed on her dessert, as if she didn't want to look him in the eye. He dropped his hand under the table and touched her knee. Her skin felt warm and soft, and she wasn't wearing the panty hose he could have sworn she'd had on earlier. Either she'd taken them off someplace, or her legs were naturally smooth.

"You've been drinking," he murmured, and slid his hand around to the inside of her thigh. "How much wine have you had?"

She shot him a glare and pushed his hand away. "*One* glass. I've got to get on the road."

"I'm thinking you should stay here. We can get you a room." He laced his fingers through hers and rested their hands on his lap. She gazed up at him, and the color in her cheeks deepened.

"Hey there, J.B."

Carlos stopped at the table. If Jack could have killed a man with his thoughts, he'd have done it right then and there.

"What's up, Carlos?"

His deputy squeezed right on into the booth, and Jack clenched his teeth. There was no such thing as privacy in this town.

"Ma'am." Carlos gave Fiona a nod. "Sorry to interrupt, J.B., but I talked to my cousin over in the sheriff's office."

"And?"

"And the raid went down at four o'clock. TV guys got a tip-off to be on standby, just like you thought, so that's how come they got footage of Randy making the collars."

Fiona tugged her hand away, and Jack realized he'd been gripping it.

"Sharon's still at the station," Carlos continued. "She went ahead and faxed out the sketch to all the news people who missed the press conference."

"Which is pretty much everyone," Jack said.

"Lowell volunteered to work a double shift, covering phones. But so far, not much response. Just a few crazies who called to say it's their relative back from the dead or some bull."

"That happens a lot," Fiona put in. "And it only gets worse once the sketch really gets into circulation. Still, you never know when the call you need will come in."

"When it does, we'll be ready," Carlos assured her. He eyed the pie, and Jack pulled it closer and took a hefty bite to make his point. Carlos was coming off an extended dinner break, and Jack hadn't eaten all day.

Fiona picked up her jacket and purse. "Will you excuse me, please?"

Jack frowned. "Where you going?"

"I need to use the restroom," she said, and he knew she just wanted an excuse to get up. But he scooted out of the booth anyway and watched her walk past the poolroom to the very far back.

"You coming in tonight, Chief?"

Jack sat back down. "Maybe. Late."

Carlos stared at him, knowing exactly what he was up to.

Shit, so what? Jack had been working round the clock since this case had come in. He'd barely eaten. He'd barely slept. His only breaks had been driving his ass all the way to Austin to hire a forensic artist, and as far as relaxation went, that sure as hell didn't qualify. Jack was so tightly wound right now, he was about to snap, and his frustrated libido wasn't helping. He needed some relief, and he'd already decided the form he wanted it to take.

Carlos was still staring at him, probably hoping to guilt him into coming in.

"You've got me on call," Jack said. "If something comes up, I'm there before you can blink."

"I know it, J.B."

"Then what's with the look?"

"I've never seen you like this."

"Like what?"

"Like a man who's thinking with his *palo*."

Fiona splashed water on her cheeks and stared at her reflection. What was she doing here? She should be home right now, preparing for her art show in the soothing comfort of her loft apartment. Instead, she was in Podunk, Texas, in the cramped bathroom of some redneck bar fighting off an alarming attack of lust.

Jack Bowman wanted to sleep with her. He wanted to check her into some seedy motel and set her world on fire.

And he could do it, too. Whenever he touched her, whenever he so much as *looked* at her with those intense blue eyes, she started smoldering inside.

It was just sex. It would be raw and physical and probably just what she needed to wake her up from the frigid state she'd been in ever since she'd walked in on Aaron and that groupie from the Continental Club. The instant she'd seen them together, a frost had settled over her sex drive.

But Jack had melted it. It had happened the moment she noticed him watching her from across her lecture hall.

He'd stood there in the shadows, leaned up against the wall, looking dangerous and determined and much too cocky. Just the type of man she made a habit of falling for.

But she wouldn't fall for Jack. It would just be sex.

She heard the toilet flush and straightened away from the mirror. She adjusted the lapels of her tailored jacket and smoothed her skirt. She dabbed away the mascara smudges under her eyes and tidied her hair.

The woman at the sink beside her wore tight black Wranglers and a low-cut sweater. She opened a tube of lipstick and smiled at Fiona in the glass. The twang of country guitar music came through the thin paneled walls.

"They're crowded tonight," Fiona said, wondering why she felt compelled to make small talk with a complete stranger.

The woman blotted her lips on a tissue and smiled. "Five-dollar pitchers every Thursday. Ralph always gets a crowd." She winked at Fiona, and squeezed past her and out of the restroom.

When she was gone, Fiona looked at herself again. She didn't belong here. She didn't fit in with these people who were open and friendly and lived on farms and drank beer.

But then again, maybe she was being a snob. Or being too uptight. Courtney was always telling her she needed to lighten up and let herself have fun.

I'm thinking you should stay here. We can get you a room.

A room. At a cheap motel. Funny how he hadn't asked her back to his house, to the little two-one he lived in not far from the Bowman homestead and his widowed mother. He hadn't asked her to meet his sisters, both schoolteachers, or his nieces and nephews, or in any way to enter his life.

What he'd asked for, she realized, wasn't so different from what Hoyt had asked for. *You look like a lady who knows her way around a stick. What say we shoot some pool later?*

Jack wanted sex. And she did, too. But if she slept with him, where would it get her? Nathan would hear about it for sure. And in no time she'd go from being a respected APD consultant to a locker-room joke. It had happened before. Law enforcement was a boys' club. As a woman, Fiona had to work ten times harder than the men just to be taken seriously as an artist, to build a reputation as a professional. And that hard-earned reputation could vanish in a heartbeat if she took her clothes off for the wrong guy.

She should drive back to Austin.

Fiona yanked open the door to the hallway and walked past the poolroom. The corridor was dim, and she nearly missed the dark figure lurking in the alcove beside the pay phone.

"I was beginning to think you fell in."

Her heart lurched as he emerged from the shadows. The neon sign on the wall cast his face in a bluish light. His strong features looked even more dramatic than usual—the cheekbones, the lips, the prominent chin. She had to get out of here.

She glanced at her watch. "I really need to—"

"Oh, no you don't." He took her hand and pulled her into another alcove, this one stacked with boxes and metal kegs.

"You're trying to flee the scene again," he said, easing her back against the wall with his body. His gaze dropped to her mouth.

"Jack. Please."

He smiled slightly. "So polite." He cuffed her wrists and

pinned them to the wall beside her shoulders. She gazed up at him and felt his breath warm against her forehead. He smelled like rain and beer and woodsy aftershave, and she missed being this close to a man, missed it so much she ached. And he must have read what she was thinking, because he kissed her.

She should have known he'd dive right in. That he'd take control of everything and that he wouldn't ease back until he'd completely dragged her under. She heard the din of the crowd, the thrum of the jukebox. The wall at her back seemed to vibrate, and Jack pressed her against it, pinning her with the weight of his body, making her dizzy with the force and the heat and the taste of him. His hand slid down over her thigh and tugged at the hem of her skirt. And that's when she realized her own hands were free, no longer trapped against the wall, but draped limply on his shoulders.

He moved his mouth to her neck and said something against her throat.

"Hmm?"

"Peaches," he muttered. "You smell like peaches."

She lifted one knee, frustrated by the confines of her skirt, and those strong fingers moved to help her, jerking the fabric up even farther and hitching her leg up to rest at his hip. His jeans rasped against her skin as she moved against him.

"You're burning up," he said. "I swear to God, you're so hot."

She felt hot. And feverish and nearly hurting with the need to get him closer. He sucked on the sensitive skin just below her ear, and she felt the pull deep in her body. She wanted him right now, right this very second.

God, what was wrong with her? They were in a *bar*.

"We're in a bar," she whispered.

His mouth moved back over hers, and for a moment, she forgot everything but his wonderful, avid tongue.

Crack! The sound of pool and people snapped her back.

"Jack." She turned her head away, and watched, horrified, as bar patrons filed back and forth in the hallway. Could they *see* them in here? They were deep in the shadows, but still.

Jack's hand glided up to her breast and his pelvis rocked against her.

"Jack!" she hissed. "Jack, we need to stop."

He stopped, his palm cradling her breast, his thumb poised just above her nipple. He seemed to recover his sanity, and he eased away from her, letting her knee drop down.

"We have to get out of here." She pulled her skirt down and stabbed her foot around, searching for her shoe. It must have fallen off when she'd wrapped her leg around him.

God, what was she thinking?

He laced his fingers together behind her neck and looked down at her. "Go next door." His voice sounded hoarse. "Get the same room as last time. I'll be right over as soon as I clear the bill."

She stared at him in the dimness, at the hungry, impatient look in his eyes. No one had ever looked at her like that, like if he didn't have her in the next minute, he'd simply combust. That was how she felt, too.

"Hurry." She stood on tiptoes and kissed him. "If I think about this for long, I'll lose my nerve."

CHAPTER

9

The air outside Becker's felt cold, doubly so because her skin was already damp with sweat. The bar had been warm. She'd been overheated all through dinner, and Jack hadn't helped matters when he'd slid up beside her and started copping a feel beneath the table.

She glanced across the parking lot to the run-down motel next door. If their sign was any indicator, they had a vacancy. If their parking was any indicator, they had way more than one. And Fiona was about to walk into the front office and request Room 22, where she'd stayed last time and where tonight she intended to have scorching hot sex with a man she barely knew.

Well, she sort of knew him. He'd become less of a stranger after her talk with Ginny. But she still didn't really *know* him, and given the geography and everything else between them, she didn't realistically expect that to change. Maybe that was why this felt so exciting. Her lips were still swollen from his mouth, and her skin tingled.

Her foot sank into a pothole, and she yelped as freezing water filled her shoe. She braced her hand against a truck so she could take off her pump and shake it out.

"Fee-yo-na."

She whirled around. Hoyt stood beside the Dumpster at the edge of the lot. He wore the familiar camo hat and a jacket, and it looked as though he'd stepped out for a smoke.

Or had he followed her out?

"Hi, Hoyt," she said, feigning comfort she didn't feel.

He tossed his cigarette away and walked toward her, and she noticed he wasn't very steady on his feet. Fiona resumed her path down the row of trucks, wishing she could remember for sure where she'd parked.

"You promised me a game of pool." He caught up to her, and she darted her gaze around for any sign of Jack.

"We'll have to do it next time," she said, walking faster. She spotted the bumper of her little white car just up ahead.

"Hey!" He gripped her elbow, hard, and panic zinged through her. He jerked her close to him. "I'm *talking* to you."

God, he was drunk. And angry. And they were alone in a sea of pickups.

"Okay, you win." She forced a smile, although her heart was pounding furiously. "Let's go back inside. You can break."

He clenched her arm tighter, and she smelled beer and tobacco.

"Hoyt, you're hurting me."

A slow, mean smile spread across his face, and she knew he had no intention of letting her go. Every self-defense class she'd ever taken came flooding back to her, but all the moves and tactics churned together in a big soup. Suddenly, she remembered her high heels. On a burst of adrenaline, she stomped his foot.

"*Shit!*"

He dropped her arm, and she lunged away. But a yank on her ponytail toppled her backward onto the asphalt. Pain shot up from her tailbone, and tears sprang into her eyes. She heard a *thud,* and then something heavy slammed against the truck. Above her was a blur of denim and leather as Hoyt wrestled with someone against the pickup.

Jack.

Fiona scrambled to her feet just as Hoyt planted a fist in his face.

"Oh my God!" she shrieked, rushing forward. "Stop!"

An elbow jabbed into her chin and she reeled back against a car. Jack launched himself at Hoyt, and the next instant they were both on the ground in a tangle of limbs and grunts.

Fiona gripped the side of the truck and tried to shake off the dizziness.

"You're under arrest, asshole!" Jack's voice was muffled as he struggled under Hoyt. He was fighting off punches with one hand and reaching for something with the other. His handcuffs? A weapon?

"Stop it!" Fiona screamed. She spotted her purse on the ground and snatched it up. "Stop it right now!"

Jack managed to roll on top, but Hoyt cuffed him across the nose and regained control. She saw a flash of metal and a line of blood streaming from Jack's nostril. Did someone have a *knife?*

Fiona thrust her hand into her purse and yanked out her gun. "I said *stop it!*"

She aimed it right at Hoyt's chest, but his attention was fixed on Jack.

Jack glanced up at her, and in his moment of shock, Hoyt landed another blow.

"Hoyt!" she squeaked.

Finally he looked up at her, and this time Jack seized the opportunity. Another flash of metal, and Hoyt's left wrist was handcuffed.

"What the fuck?" he stammered, looking from the handcuffs, to the gun, then back to the handcuffs again.

Jack got to his feet, dragging Hoyt with him. He wrenched Hoyt's arm back behind him and shoved him against the nearest truck. *"You* are fucking under arrest." Jack clinked the empty bracelet on Hoyt's other wrist, and then glared at Fiona. "Put that thing away!"

Fiona's hands were frozen around the revolver. She lowered it and let out a deep breath. Suddenly her legs felt weak, and she slumped against the side of the truck.

Jack shook his head and whipped a cell phone out of his back pocket. He punched a button and brought it to his ear.

"Carlos? Yeah, it's me. I'm bringing in Hoyt Dixon on a drunk and disorderly, plus a raft of other shit."

Hoyt squirmed against the truck and turned his head. His right eye was cut and bleeding, and he spat a curse at Fiona. Jack clapped his ear and snarled something, then he got back on the phone. "Send Sharon over here to escort Fiona Glass to her motel room. Make sure she brings a first-aid kit."

"Jack, I don't need—"

"Not a word." He gave her a pointed look as he hauled Hoyt out from between the cars. "Come wait inside for your ride."

She blew out a breath and zipped her gun back into her purse. She tasted blood in her mouth, and her chin stung, but the last thing she wanted was Sharon rushing over to babysit her. "Jack, this is ridiculous. I don't need—"

"Just do it," he said. "I'll come find you as soon as I'm through."

She thought about arguing, but he seemed to be at the end of his patience. And even if she didn't need a first-aid kit, *he* certainly did. Blood trickled from his nose and his eyelid was already starting to swell as he recited Hoyt's Miranda rights. So instead of arguing, she simply complied.

A faint siren came from the direction of the police station. The noise got closer, and people stepped out of the bar to check out the spectacle. It was going to be a long night.

Jack glanced at the crowd, then back at her, and she could tell he knew what she was thinking. "I mean it, Fiona. Don't even think about taking off."

Jack did another visual sweep of the area, and knocked on Fiona's door. Her car was still at Becker's, so it was possible she'd actually followed his instructions and let Sharon give her a ride.

She opened the door looking disheveled. She still wore the last remnants of her suit, but her hair was down and the heels had been replaced with yellow flip-flops.

"You didn't ask who it was."

She rolled her eyes. "There's a peephole."

He brushed past her and into the room. She'd turned on the bedside lamps and cranked the heater up full blast. Her coat and blazer were draped over a chair, and a rolling suitcase was parked beside the bathroom.

Maybe she'd intended to stay the night after all.

"That was quick," she said as she bolted the door.

"I let Carlos handle the paperwork." He pulled her close to the bedside table and lifted her chin with his finger. "What happened to your lip?"

"I caught an elbow. It's fine, really. I've been putting ice on it."

He took her hands and turned them up. She had some minor scrapes on her palms, but she'd cleaned them. He knew her tailbone must hurt like hell. He'd come out of the bar just in time to see Hoyt yank her backward by her hair, and twelve years of police training had flown out the window as Jack had shot across the parking lot in a blind rage. Beating the living shit out of Hoyt had been his only thought.

His mistake. He should have handled the situation like a professional.

He swallowed the bitterness in his throat. "Sharon said you don't want to see a doctor."

"I don't."

"Are you sure you're okay?"

She sighed. "I'm fine. It's just a few scratches."

Just a few scratches. Yeah. And it could have been a lot worse.

Jack shoved his hands in his jacket pockets and wandered to the other side of the tiny room. Anger was pumping through his system with a force that scared him.

"That's quite a gun you're packing, Professor." He spotted her purse on the dresser and nodded at it. "Mind if I . . . ?"

She waved at it. "Help yourself." Then she walked over to the vanity and lifted the lid off an ice bucket. She started transferring cubes to a clear plastic bag.

Jack unzipped her purse. It was small and stylish, made of supple black leather. He never would have guessed she carried a fucking cannon around inside it.

"Where'd you get this?" he asked, pulling out the revolver. It was a Ruger .357 with a six-inch barrel.

"My grandfather."

He checked the cylinder. Loaded. "Who's your grandfather? Jesse James?"

She didn't say anything, and Jack looked up. She was watching uncomfortably as he handled her gun.

He slid it back into the purse, and replaced it carefully on the dresser. "How long you been packing that thing?"

"Three years."

He crossed his arms. "You want to tell me why?"

"Not particularly."

"You have a permit for it?"

"Yes."

"You know how to use it?"

"Yes."

"Who trained you?"

"My grandfather."

Jack was trying. He really was. But his frustration had about reached the boiling point. He was pissed at Hoyt, and Fiona, and most of all at himself. He'd told her to leave the bar alone. Yes, this was Graingerville, but there were assholes everywhere, as Hoyt had so aptly demonstrated.

Fiona took a few steps toward him and raised a tentative hand to his eyebrow. She touched the skin just above his cut, and he flinched.

"I'll make you a deal," she said softly. "I'll tell you about the Ruger if you let me take care of that eye." Without waiting for an answer, she slipped her hand into his and led him to the bed. He sank down onto the edge and watched, silently, as she shuffled through a small box on the counter. Sharon, evidently, had followed orders and left Fiona with a first-aid kit.

She returned to the bedside and put some tubes on the table, along with the ice pack she'd made. Then she pulled the lamp closer for better light.

"Is that a toothbrush?" he asked, frowning.

"Yes."

She picked up a tube of what he'd thought was ointment, but was actually Colgate. She squeezed some onto her fingertip and dabbed it around his left eye, right where the bruise was forming. After rubbing it in, she cupped his face in her hands and tilted it up. She had soft hands. He watched her eyes in the lamplight as she gently stroked the toothbrush over his skin.

"This how they treat shiners in California?"

She smiled, but her attention didn't leave his bruise. "The peppermint stimulates circulation and helps break down the blood clot under the skin. Same with the toothbrush." She did a few more strokes, and he held his breath when she got to the really sensitive part just above his eyelid. "With any luck, this won't show too badly tomorrow. A little concealer, and you might even be okay in public. In case you have a news conference."

Jack looked up at her uneasily. "Where'd you learn that?"

She shrugged. "Just something I picked up along the way."

He watched her face. For whatever reason, she'd erected her wall of privacy with the big KEEP OUT sign.

This woman confused the hell out of him. She was aloof one minute, then compassionate the next. She abhorred violence, but she carried around a gun that could put a hole the size of a baseball in someone. She spent her time making big, beautiful oil paintings and portraits of hardened killers. She dressed herself up in staid business suits, but underneath she had the body of a Playmate.

And the more time he spent around her, the more she drove him crazy. What had she been thinking tonight? Jesus, did she think he needed her help taking down Hoyt Dixon? If something had gone wrong after she'd whipped out that gun, a parking lot scuffle could have turned deadly.

"Fiona." He caught her wrist in his hand, and she looked at him finally. "What's with the gun?"

She didn't say anything.

"We had a deal."

She glanced down, cleared her throat, then met his gaze again. "A couple years ago in L.A., I worked on the case of some gang members who were involved in a drive-by. I testified at their trial, too. One of them—after he went to prison—he started harassing me through some of his contacts on the outside."

"Define 'harassing.' "

"Threatening letters. Obscene phone calls. Someone broke into my apartment and vandalized everything. It freaked me out."

"So what happened?"

She pulled her hand loose from his and put the toothbrush on the nightstand. "The guy was behind bars, and no one could ever trace anything back to him. I talked to my supervisor about it, but I think people thought I was just paranoid. Maybe I was."

Jack could tell she didn't believe that. If she felt certain about the source of the threat, she was probably right. Jack was all for good, hard evidence, but he believed in gut instincts, too.

"Anyway, I stopped taking cases for a while. Went to visit my grandfather for a few months, get some R and R. When I went back to Los Angeles, things subsided for a little bit. But then it all started up again, and I didn't feel safe anywhere. Pretty soon after that, I decided to move."

She pressed the ice pack to his eye, and he winced. "Keep that on there for a few minutes," she told him, replacing her hand with his own.

She walked back to the sink, and he watched her, thinking about what she'd been through. She'd dealt with some major lowlifes in her career and had every reason to be cautious.

She came back with some ointment.

"And what about Courtney?" he asked. "Was she already here, or did she come along for the ride?"

"We moved together." Her face looked carefully neutral. "She'd had enough of California and wanted a fresh start."

A fresh start. How come he felt like he was getting the abbreviated, sanitized version of that story?

"This'll help your nose," she said, dabbing ointment below his nostril. He'd cleaned up some already at the station house, but he'd been in a rush.

"So what's going to happen to Hoyt?" she asked.

"He'll spend the night in jail. Probably take a good day

or two before he can round up someone willing to bail him out again."

"He's a repeat offender?"

"He's a repeat fuckup. He drinks too much and makes a habit of picking fights."

She pursed her lips, and he wondered if she thought he didn't take tonight's events seriously.

"Don't worry, he's in a whole new world of hurt this time. He assaulted two people tonight, both law enforcement officers."

Fiona raised an eyebrow at the description, but didn't say anything.

"He'll be charged. The prosecutor'll probably want to make an example of him, and if he doesn't, I'll do my best to persuade him."

Fiona gazed down at him tiredly.

"Come here." Jack tossed the ice pack aside. He put his hands on her hips and pulled her between his knees.

"I'm not finished patching you up."

"Yeah, you are." He tugged the silk loose from her skirt and slid his hands underneath. Her skin was smooth and warm, and he felt her shiver. He pushed the shirt up and watched her eyes. "Let me see you," he whispered.

She stared at him a moment, then lifted the shirt over her head. It made a soft whoosh as it landed on the bed beside him, and then she was standing there, finally, without all those layers covering her up.

"You're so pretty." He reached up to cup her breast, thumbing her nipple through the creamy lace. He eased forward on the bed and reached for the other one. Her bra had a tiny pink rosebud just between her breasts, and he pressed a kiss into the sweet skin right above it. He ran his hands down over her hips again and then reached around her waist to find her zipper.

"On the side," she whispered, guiding his hand.

He pulled the zipper down, then slid the skirt over her rounded hips. She had another rose just below her navel, and when he kissed the skin above it, she sucked in a breath. He trailed his mouth down, tasting her skin, and his phone buzzed.

She froze.

Jack looked up at her as it buzzed again. He swore vividly and fell back on the bed. He jerked the phone out of his pocket and saw Lowell's number on the screen.

"What?"

"There's a woman just come in here. Nola Fuentes."

Jack sat up. "Yeah?"

"Well, it took a while to understand her at first. She's crying and carrying on. Finally Carlos came in from that fender bender in front of the Texaco? I got him to talk to her."

Fiona reached for her shirt and pulled it over her head. Next the skirt came up, and Jack sent her a look of apology. Her face was a mask of composure.

"Spit it out, Lowell."

"It's our Jane Doe, Chief. This woman says the picture on the ten o'clock news is her daughter."

CHAPTER

10

Natalie Fuentes. Natalie.

All day long, the name had been echoing through Fiona's mind.

Natalie. It was such a young-sounding name, so full of promise. Natalies were beautiful, smiling girls with lots of friends, girls whose phones never stopped ringing and whose lockers were always surrounded by people. Girls named Natalie had bubbly personalities, and long silken hair, and dates to the homecoming football game every fall.

She knew it was an illusion. How could a name determine a person's life? But Fiona had feelings attached to names, and in her mind—up until today, at least—*Natalie* had been one of the happy ones.

According to Jack, Fiona's illusion hadn't been far from the truth, either. During her early-morning drive back to Austin, Jack had called. He'd apologized again for leaving abruptly and then had given her an update on the victim.

Natalie Fuentes had been an honor student and captain of the Meyersberg High School cheerleading team. Fifteen months ago, she'd been nominated for the homecoming court. Five months ago, she'd enrolled as a freshman at San Pedro College in Hamlin, Texas.

Two weeks ago she'd been raped, brutalized, and strangled, then abandoned on a frozen patch of grass off Highway 44.

Neither Fiona nor Dr. Jamison had pegged her age correctly. Natalie was a short, slightly built eighteen. She'd been on her way back to school after Christmas break, but she'd never made it. Her mother hadn't heard from her in twelve days, but she said that wasn't unusual. Her daughter studied hard and had a busy social life.

Natalie's body would be released to her family by the end of today.

Usually, when a victim's identity finally came through, Fiona felt a sense of closure. Some family somewhere would lay their loved one to rest, and Fiona would feel a small measure of satisfaction for helping make that possible, for being one of the people who gave the victim back a name and a bit of dignity.

But Fiona felt no closure today. On the contrary, she'd spent the better part of this chilly Friday blazing with red-hot anger. So she'd come home from work, thrown on her rattiest jeans, and decided to do the only thing she knew that would help.

Now she lined up all her supplies, loaded her gun, and went to work.

Pop. The recoil shocked her hand. *Pop. Pop.* Her arm tingled with it. *Pop.* With every pull of the trigger, she felt a tiny release of tension.

The door opened, and Courtney waltzed in. She looked at Fiona and stopped cold. "What happened?"

"What?" Fiona looked down at the wood and aimed. *Pop.*

Courtney tossed her purse and coat on the sofa. "You're upset. You always stretch canvases when you're upset."

Fiona frowned down at the frame in her hands. She didn't realize anyone had noticed. She'd thought it was her secret stress buster.

"Crappy day?" Courtney prompted.

"You could say that." Fiona put down the staple gun and turned the wooden frame ninety degrees. "You want to help?"

"Sure."

"Right here," Fiona directed. "Pull as tight as you can."

Courtney sauntered over and positioned her hands on the frame. She'd helped with this chore before, so she knew how important it was to get the linen as taut as possible. The fabric had to be stretched tightly across the wood, but not so tightly it would tear at the staple points. Fiona turned the frame frequently, so the fabric would pull more evenly over every side.

Courtney held the linen beneath her thumbs. "This is a big one."

"Tighter."

Courtney pulled it tighter.

"Your hands are all chapped," Fiona said.

"Comes with the job."

Her sister had been through a wide variety of jobs in the beauty industry. In her current position as a hairstylist at an exclusive salon, she worked with chemicals all the time and washed her hands frequently.

"Is this for the show?"

"It's the focal point. It's supposed to be the largest canvas in the Blanco River series."

"Wow," Courtney said. "No wonder it's so big."

Fiona had the four-by-six-foot composition all planned out. She'd *had* it planned for weeks, but hadn't had time to get started until tonight—which was crazy, considering this was to be the centerpiece of her entire exhibit.

"How's the detective?" Courtney asked.

Fiona blew out a sigh. "He's not a detective. He's a police chief."

"So where is he tonight?"

"Working on a case."

"This the Jane Doe thing down in Hickville?"

"Natalie Fuentes." Fiona positioned the staple gun. *Pop.*

"Huh?"

"Her name's Natalie Fuentes. They IDed her late last night. College freshman. She was a cheerleader." *Pop.* "One of the little ones, you know, who go on top of the pyramid."

They rotated the frame again, and Courtney pulled another section of fabric. She was good at this, always had been. A properly stretched canvas was the first step to a good painting. One of Fiona's first instructors at Art Center in L.A. had drummed it into her head: no gaping fabric, no puckers, no tears, and for God's sake, make your staples straight!

"It's called a flyer."

Fiona looked up. "What?"

"The girl on top of the pyramid. She's the flyer. She's the lightest one, so she gets tossed around the most. Sometimes twenty feet in the air."

Fiona lifted her eyebrows. "How do you know that?"

Courtney had steered far away from the cheerleaders during high school.

"Some of my clients bring their daughters in for highlights." Courtney shrugged. "I can tell you anything you want to know about the glam high school scene."

Fiona shook her head at the irony. She and Courtney hadn't run with the cool crowd back in high school. Fiona had been the quiet misfit, and Courtney was the promiscuous one whom the guys sought out and the girls hated.

Pop. Pop. Pop.

"Okay, that about does it." Fiona stepped back to look. "Not bad, either. Thanks for helping."

"Sure."

Courtney stripped off her sweater as she crossed the apartment. "You mind if I borrow something to wear tonight? I'm having dinner with David."

Fiona eyed the lotus tattooed on her sister's shoulder. "I thought he lived in Dallas."

"He does. But he's had a lot of business in town lately." Courtney smiled over her shoulder. "I think he likes me."

Fiona leaned the canvas against the wall and followed Courtney into the bathroom. Her sister swept back the shower curtain and turned on the water to heat.

"And do you like him?"

Courtney wouldn't look at her, which was always telling.

"Is he a nice guy?"

"Yeah." Courtney took off her earrings. "He treats me well. He talks to me. Tells me about his cases. His job's really interesting."

Fiona remembered this guy was a lawyer. Knowing her sister, she'd be talking about going to law school next week.

Not that Courtney wasn't smart enough to do whatever she wanted—she was. She just didn't have much follow-through.

"Stop worrying," Courtney said.

"I'm not worrying."

"Yes, you are. I can see it. Chill out, okay? It's not like I'm getting married or something."

"Where'd you get your tattoo done?" Fiona asked, changing the subject.

"What, the lotus?"

"You have more than one?"

"Yeah, I've got a yin-yang, too." She tugged down her skirt and showed her the black-and-white disk just below her left hip bone. "I got that, like, a year ago. Both times I went to a place downtown."

"Hmm . . ." Fiona rubbed her fingers over it. "Did it hurt?"

"Not too bad." Courtney grinned. "Why? You want one?"

"I'm just curious." Fiona leaned back against the sink. "Say I wanted to get a swastika? Could I just show up somewhere and get one, or is that taboo?"

Courtney flipped the toilet lid closed and sat down to take off her shoes. They had narrow black ankle straps and stiletto heels that looked fabulous but probably felt miserable.

"A taboo tattoo," Courtney mused. "I think that's an oxymoron."

"So I could just get anything I want?"

She shrugged. "I don't know, really. You'd have to check. I've never seen anyone ask for neo-Nazi shit. It might be something they don't talk about, but they'll do it in a back room or something."

"And where would I go?"

Courtney grinned. "You really want to do this? I'll go with you."

"You will?"

"Sure, it'll be fun. We could look at tats, piercings. This is for an investigation, right? You're not really going to get one?"

Fiona wrinkled her nose.

"Don't be so judgmental," Courtney said. "I happen to think you'd look extremely hot with a navel ring. Jack would probably take one look at it and have an orgasm."

"We're not sleeping together." Yet.

"Whatever. I'll take you to one of the ink places on Sixth Street." Courtney glanced at her watch before taking it off and tossing it on the vanity. "We need to go soon, though. I'm meeting David at nine."

Fiona heaved a sigh and buried her face in her hands. "God, what is *wrong* with me? I'm supposed to paint tonight. Instead, I'm going to go traipsing around tattoo parlors." She looked up at Courtney. "If I don't get these pictures finished soon, I'm going to blow my whole career before it even gets off the ground."

Courtney lifted an eyebrow. "Which career is that?"

"My art career! The one I spent six years training for. The one I've been dreaming about since I was a kid. I'm throwing it all down the drain, Court!"

Courtney tipped her head to the side. She had that look of understanding, the one nobody else in the universe had ever had except for her. "You already have a career. You're good at it, too."

"But I'm trying to get *out* of that."

"Are you really? Seems to me if you really wanted out, you'd be out by now."

The Egyptian Cat perched at the end of Sixth Street, just beyond a series of crowded bars and thumping dance clubs. Fiona followed Courtney inside, relieved to get away from the throngs of college students and the bitter night air.

The room was warm. Intricately patterned fabrics were draped over the light fixtures, giving the space a muted glow. Sitar music surrounded her, and she felt like she'd entered an Indian restaurant instead of a tattoo parlor.

"Not what I expected," she said, slipping off her coat. At the back of the room hung a saffron yellow curtain, and from behind it came a low buzzing noise.

"I know. Isn't it great?" Courtney led her to a wall of drawings. Almost all the designs looked Eastern. Fiona caught a few Celtic symbols. Some hieroglyphics. Where were all the naked women and biker symbols? This place seemed a little high end for their purposes.

"I love the incense here," Courtney said, as they perused the drawings. "It gives you something to think about besides the needle."

Fiona sent her a skeptical look. She doubted anything would take her mind off the needle except a shot of morphine.

"This would look good on you." Courtney pointed to a Chinese character. "It means double happiness. Maybe it would cheer you up."

Fiona turned to her sister. "I'm cheerful."

"Right."

"What's that supposed to mean?"

"You're too serious lately. You need to destress. Have some fun."

"I have fun," Fiona said, defensive now.

"You haven't had fun since you and Aaron broke up."

"That's not true."

"All you do is work all the time. And you're avoiding men."

"No, I'm not."

Courtney gave her a "yeah, right" look. "So what happened to Jack the other night? Why didn't you bring him home with you?"

"*You* were there."

"I was on my way out. You should have asked him up. He's very nice-looking. And I think he'd be good for you. He seems trustworthy."

Fiona bit her tongue. She didn't need relationship tips from Courtney. Her sister's longest-term boyfriend had lasted three months.

"Don't get upset." Courtney's expression softened. "I'm just saying, you should start dating again. Loosen up some. Not everyone's out to hurt you."

A man with short-cropped dark hair ducked out from behind the curtain, saving Fiona from a response. He had olive skin, a muscular build, and two full sleeves of black tribal-looking tattoos.

"Hey, there." He stepped closer and zeroed in on Fiona. "You need some help?"

She was speechless. Men typically gravitated toward

Courtney first. It must be the outfit. She was wearing a low-cut crimson sweater with bell sleeves and tight, hip-hugger jeans.

"We have some questions for you," Courtney answered for her. "But we don't want to keep you from a client or anything. You busy?"

"We're slow tonight." He smiled, and focused again on Fiona. "What can I do for you?"

She cleared her throat, trying not to stare at his lip rings. "I'm wondering about your designs here. What all do you do?"

That sounded vague, but she felt flustered. He was looking at her with those sensual black eyes.

"Anything. What did you have in mind?"

"What about swastikas?" she blurted, and his eyebrows shot up.

"She means, hypothetically," Courtney put in. "Would you *do* a swastika? If someone asked you?"

He looked from Fiona to Courtney and back to Fiona again. "*I* wouldn't. But that's me, personally. You could get someone else to do it. Not here, though."

"Where could I go?" Fiona asked.

His gaze drifted over her. "You don't seem like the swastika type. Have you thought this through?"

"It's not for me. I'm just doing some research."

He seemed to relax at this, and smiled again. "Good. You strike me as more of an artist."

Fiona glanced at Courtney. How could he know that?

He crossed his arms and seemed to be looking at her strawberry blond hair. "I could see you with something Celtic. Maybe a cross. Or a tree of life."

"I don't want a tattoo."

"Why not?" he asked.

"Yeah, why not?" Courtney echoed.

Fiona floundered for a reason.

"She thinks they look trashy," Courtney said in a stage whisper.

"I do not!"

Her sister rolled her eyes.

"It's just that it's too permanent," Fiona explained. "I get bored with my shower curtain after six months. Plus, I'm a wimp about pain."

The man smiled. "It's not as bad as you think."

"Yeah, I barely felt my last one," Courtney said. "But we could always get you drunk and come back. There's a shot bar next door."

Fiona gave her sister a pointed look. "I came here to ask questions."

"See what I mean? Much too serious." She sighed. "I'm going to look around."

Courtney wandered off, and Fiona turned back toward the man.

"Go ahead." A smile spread across his face. "Ask me anything you want."

Jack hated the stereotype, but desperate times called for desperate measures. And besides, Sunrise Donuts had great coffee. Jack was on his second cup of the morning—and his third chocolate-iced doughnut—when his cell phone buzzed.

"Did you know that one of the largest tattoo parlors in the nation is less than an hour away from you?"

Jack pulled the phone from his ear and checked the number. Yep, it was Fiona. "You want to repeat that?"

"I said, one of the country's largest tattoo parlors—well, actually, they call it a *studio*—it's off I-35, not fifty miles away from you. I spent my whole morning there, and it was *fascinating*."

"Is that right."

"Some of the piercings would make you lose your lunch, so I spent most of the time looking at tattoos. They do everything—exotic animals, tribal designs. You can even copy something from a famous celebrity. Did you know the Rock has a Brahma bull on his right biceps?"

Jack steered through downtown, noting it was unusually quiet for a Saturday morning. He chalked it up to weather. "Are we talking about the wrestler?"

"That's the guy. The bull symbolizes virility. It's an extremely popular tattoo design in central Texas, I'm told."

"Very interesting, Professor. Course that probably has nothing to do with football."

"With what?"

Jack sighed. "Never mind. Hey, if you're thinking about body art, I should warn you that place has been slapped with fines by the health department for using dirty equipment."

But Jack knew she wasn't interested in a tattoo. In fact, he knew exactly why she'd hauled her pretty butt all the way down here. She was running down the swastika lead.

He pulled into the parking lot at the station and slid his truck into the chief's space. "I thought you were planning to paint all weekend."

"I was. I will. I just started thinking about something, and I wanted to follow up."

Jack cut the engine and stared through the windshield. He dreaded going inside. His desk was stacked a foot high with paperwork, and he didn't give a shit about any of it. All he wanted to do was solve the Natalie Fuentes homicide. It had been a focus before, but now that he had the victim IDed, it was becoming more like an obsession. Natalie had been a vivacious, energetic young girl, much like Lucy had been before her attack.

"So you spent your Saturday morning at Texas Ink."

"Yes."

"And let me guess," he said, "you took some drawings with you and flashed them around."

"Nobody recognized him. But I have a lead for you."

Jack gritted his teeth. It wasn't just the logjam of work that was bothering him. It wasn't just that Fiona had told him she needed to spend the whole weekend painting, and then obviously had changed her mind. It was that her involvement in this case was starting to make him uncomfortable.

Hell, it made him more than uncomfortable. He hated it. He wanted her to stick to oil painting and leave the investigating to the investigators.

"Jack? Don't you want to hear about my lead?"

"Let's hear it."

"There's a guy over at Texas Ink. They call him Viper. I don't know his real name, but I've got an address. The official policy over there is that they won't do neo-Nazi stuff, but if you track down Viper, he'll set you up. He works privately out of his house, apparently."

"Sounds legit."

"It's probably not," she said. "But he gets a lot of traffic. Listen, here's the good part: the woman I talked to said she recognized the swastika."

"The one with the arrows?"

"That exact design. She said she's been to Viper's studio, and he's got it posted up on the wall."

"Fiona, did it ever occur to you that our guy *might* not have gotten tattooed locally? There are thousands of other places he could have had it done, starting with the state pen."

Silence. Shit, he'd hurt her feelings.

"Look, I know you're just trying to help—"

"It's a *lead*. That's all I'm saying. Now do you want it or not? If not, I'll head over there myself—"

"Give me the address." Goddamn it.

"Do you want company?"

"No." Which was a complete lie. He wanted her company in the worst way, but he didn't want her anywhere near Viper or his pit.

"Fine, then. He's at 2200 Dry Creek Road. That's in Borough County, north of you."

"I know."

"She said the house is hard to see from the road, but you can't miss it. The mailbox is painted with a Confederate flag. Are you sure you don't want help with this?"

"Completely." Jack got out of his truck and slammed the door. If he needed help, he'd enlist Lowell or Carlos. Or even Sharon the greenhorn.

"Thanks for the offer, though," he added diplomatically.

"Well . . . I guess I'll get back to work, then. Bye."

She disconnected before he could try to talk her into having dinner with him sometime in the next century.

Jack mounted the steps, eyeing the portly Latino man standing beside the entrance. He wore jeans and a light-weight windbreaker, and he was probably freezing his ass off if he'd been standing out here any length of time.

"Chief Bowman?"

"Yes?"

He stuck out his hand. "I'm Father Alvaro from Blessed Sacrament Church down in Hamlin."

Jack shook his hand, noting the black and white collar peeking out from beneath his jacket.

"Everyone calls me Father Al," he said, smiling.

"What can I do for you, Father?" Jack couldn't believe this guy had driven all the way up here. Hamlin was more than eighty miles south, and Jack had zero to do with Nata-lie Fuentes's funeral arrangements.

"I need to talk to you about one of my parishioners."

"Miss Fuentes?"

"No." He frowned. "I've heard of Natalie, of course, but I'm sorry to say she never joined our church."

"Come on inside," Jack said, opening the door.

Father Al cleared his throat. "Actually, I was hoping you would come with me."

"Come where?"

"To Hamlin. I'd like to introduce you to some people who live in one of the *colonias* down there."

"Okay." Jack didn't like where this conversation was heading. The *colonias* were slums north of the border, where many immigrants lived. "Who are they?"

"I'm afraid I'm not at liberty to say."

Jack arched his brows.

Father Al looked apologetic. "They're not comfortable with police officers, and they want to make sure they can trust you before they ask you to help them."

"Help them what?"

"You see, they saw you on the news last night, and they're hoping you can help them find their little girl."

CHAPTER

11

Jack jerked open the door to the Grainger County Sheriff's Office and stepped inside. The place was empty except for the potbellied deputy talking on the phone and the pit bull guarding Randy's office.

"Afternoon, Myrna." Jack approached her desk, which sat strategically in front of her boss's door. "The sheriff in?"

She chewed frantically, swallowed. Jack had caught her biting into a Hostess Cupcake.

"He's left for the day." She cast a disapproving look at Jack's shiner. "I can take a message for him, if you like."

"Funny thing. His wife thought I'd find him here."

"You just missed him." She glanced at the envelope Jack was carrying and held out her hand. "Got something to drop off? I'll see that he gets it."

Jack pulled his phone from his pocket. He dialed a few numbers, and a buzz emanated from behind the sheriff's door.

"Well, what do you know? Sounds like he's in."

Jack strode past Myrna and yanked open the door. The sheriff was leaning back in his chair, boots propped on the desk.

He scowled. "Goddamn it, Jack. You can't just burst in here."

In two strides, Jack was looming over the sheriff's desk. He flung the envelope at his chest.

"What the hell is this?" Randy sat up, his face reddening.

"Veronica Morales."

"*What?*"

"Veronica Morales," Jack repeated. "Nineteen-year-old from Hamlin."

Randy squinted at him and tossed the envelope on his desk. "Is that supposed to mean something to me?"

"Shit, I guess not." Jack plunked his hands on his hips. "Let me refresh your memory. She went missing New Year's Eve six years ago. Last seen at Three Forks Barbecue in Grainger County. Her parents reported her disappearance to you, and you told them to take a hike. You remember now, *Sheriff*?"

Randy glanced past him, and for the first time Jack noticed someone else in the room. Bob Spivey was lounging comfortably on Randy's sofa, cowboy hat beside him, brim up. The gray felt Stetson—which he swapped for a white straw one every summer—was the mayor's trademark.

Jack nodded. "Bob."

Spivey quirked an eyebrow. It probably wasn't good politics to have a throwdown with Randy in front of his father-in-law, but Jack didn't particularly give a fuck at the moment.

He turned his attention back to Randy. "You should check out that file there. It's chock-full of good information. This girl's parents talked to two people from the restaurant who saw Veronica get into a gray sedan around six P.M. on New Year's Eve. That was the last anyone ever saw her."

Randy had recovered some of his composure, but his cheeks were still splotchy. He waved a hand at the envelope. "They should have filed a missing persons report."

"No shit? That's what I said, too. Thing is, they tried to. Repeatedly. Until one of your lazy deputies got annoyed and threatened to call INS."

Randy leaned back in his chair. "That didn't happen."

"Didn't it? You might want to check out that file. Turns out, mom and dad thought to write down the deputy's name. They also went back to Three Forks every day for months after Veronica disappeared and took down the license numbers of every gray sedan they could find. They visited hospitals, homeless shelters. Unfortunately, they didn't visit any more police stations because they were scared their whole family would get deported."

"More where they came from," Spivey said. "Whole damn border's like a sieve. Our social services are collapsing under the weight of these people."

Randy opened the envelope and sifted through Mrs. Morales's handwritten notes. "Shit, this is all in Spanish!" The sheriff came to a photograph of Veronica and paused briefly. "Hell, I remember it now. Gray sedan. She got in the car with him."

"Exactly my point," Jack said.

"Jack, this doesn't amount to shit. This *woman* got into a man's car of her own free will. She's an adult. She can go wherever she gets a mind to."

"Did you ever stop to think this disappearance might be related to my homicide case?"

Randy propped his feet up again, like he was ready to hear a good yarn. "How's that?"

"My victim is a teenage girl. Hispanic. Her body turns up one cold winter morning in Grainger County. Veronica Morales is a teenage girl. Hispanic. She goes missing one winter evening in Grainger County. Last seen getting into a gray sedan. Lucy Arrellando is a teenage girl. Hispanic. Abducted one cold winter night in a gray sedan. You seeing a pattern here?"

Randy shared a knowing look with his father-in-law, and Jack had to battle the urge to sock him in the jaw.

"You sure this isn't personal?" Randy asked.

Jack took a deep breath. "I guess in the sense that I *personally* try to do my job, then, yeah, it's personal. Looks like you don't know anything about that. Fact, looks like Veronica's parents have done your job for you. They took a glance at the evening news, connected the dots between three separate incidents. Kinda like police work. Maybe you should give them a badge, fire some of the dead weight around here."

"Better watch it, Jack." This from the sofa.

Jack turned his attention to the mayor. "You got something to add, Bob? You want to tell me how to run a homicide investigation?"

Spivey stood up and positioned his hat on his balding head. "You're skating on thin ice here. Running your mouth off about cold cases and sloppy police work. Calling press conferences. Getting half the town all riled up. Getting in bar fights—"

"Hoyt *assaulted* a woman in a parking lot!"

Spivey's eyes sparked. "And what did you do about it, huh? Did you respond like the chief of police? No, you tried to bash his skull in! I'm hearing noise about police-brutality lawsuits!"

"That's horseshit," Jack said. "Hoyt Dixon can't even spell 'police brutality,' much less file a lawsuit. And the guy's been brawling in bars since he could see over the counter."

Spivey walked to the door and turned around. "You get a grip on yourself, Jack. You're not in Houston anymore. We like things nice and quiet around here, and we don't need you running around stirring things up, causing a panic." He jabbed a finger at Jack. "And Hoyt Dixon might not know how to spell 'police brutality,' but you can bet your ass his lawyer does."

Fiona exited APD headquarters and hunched her shoulders against the wind. She blew out a sigh, and her breath turned to frost.

What was up with this *weather*? Texas was supposed to be mild in the winter, yet she'd been freezing for the past two weeks. She was getting tired of pants and boots and itchy wool scarves. And if that weren't bad enough, she was developing a severe allergy to her sister. Fiona squinted her eyes against the wind and wished for a warm front.

And a hot cup of coffee.

And a week of uninterrupted sleep.

She tried not to stumble as she made her way down the concrete steps. Her eyes felt gritty and swollen from fatigue. She'd stayed up until 1:00 in the morning painting. Finally she'd crashed—fully dressed—on top of her bed, only to be awakened three hours later by Nathan, who apologized for calling so early, but who could sure use her help on a robbery-homicide.

Fiona had gone. She didn't know why, really, after all the noise she'd made convincing him she was giving up police work. Maybe she'd never make her choice stick because she didn't have the guts to say no to anyone.

See Exhibit A, her sister, who had been living in her apartment for a week and had contributed nothing in the way of groceries or housework, but who *had* spent a remarkable amount of time downloading music onto her iPod.

Or maybe Courtney was right. Maybe she hadn't managed to quit because, in her heart of hearts, she didn't really want to.

Fiona approached the parking meter and rummaged through her art case with numb fingers. Forget coffee, she'd just go straight home and tumble into bed. The only thing more heavenly than sleep, at this point, would be a warm body to tumble into bed with.

"Morning."

The familiar voice had her whirling around. She looked Jack up and down, and for a moment it seemed as though he'd popped right out of her daydream. "What are you doing here?"

"I've got a meeting with Nathan." He sat back against her trunk and crossed his ankles.

She stepped toward him and reached up to touch his eyebrow. "Looks like my home remedy didn't work. How's it feel?"

"Fine."

She dropped her hand and clutched the handle of her

art case so she wouldn't be tempted to touch him again. Nathan hadn't mentioned a meeting with Jack. Maybe the detective wasn't clued in to the fact Fiona had taken more than a professional interest in his friend.

"Why are *you* here?" Jack asked.

"Nathan called me in on a robbery-homicide."

Jack frowned and looked at his watch.

"Convenience store," she explained.

One of the cops upstairs had made a crack about the twenty-three-year-old clerk working the graveyard shift, and Nathan had politely asked him to shut the fuck up.

"I should warn you, he's in a terrible mood." She noticed the thick manila folder tucked under Jack's arm. "You're here to talk to him about your case?"

"Yep."

"Any new developments?"

"Not really."

She glanced away, hoping to hide her expression. She didn't know how she knew he was lying, but she did.

Jack sighed and stared over her shoulder at the police station. He looked as exhausted as she felt. This case was clearly getting to him.

"You know, he's pretty swamped up there right now," she said. "You want to get some breakfast or something? Wait until things die down?"

He seemed to consider it for a moment. Then he checked his watch again. "I wish I could." He stepped away from her car. "But I really need to get on this."

He *did* have a new lead, he just didn't trust her enough to share it. Some detectives were like that—very guarded with details around outsiders.

She hadn't realized Jack still thought of her that way.

"Well." She managed a smile. "See you later then." But when? When would she ever see him later? That was the whole problem. That, and a severe lack of sleep. Her nerves were ragged, and she was being hypersensitive. She fished her keys from her art case and punched the button to unlock the car.

Jack opened her door for her, and she tossed her attaché inside. He looked like he wanted to say something, but she needed to leave before she got emotional, so she started the car.

"Bye, Jack. Good luck with your investigation."

Sleep wouldn't come, so Fiona gave up and decided to paint. She pulled on her favorite old jeans, slipped into a tank top, and selected a CD. Maybe the Cowboy Junkies would mellow her out. She picked up the canvas she and Courtney had stretched, which she'd painted with a coat of gesso yesterday afternoon. The canvas was ready now, all stiff and white and pristine. It was time for the big one. No more procrastinating. She could feel that hum in her veins that told her today would be the day she created something good.

The canvas was too large for her easel, so she leaned it up against the wall and sat down cross-legged in front of it with her paints.

A blank canvas. It was both daunting and exciting. This was to be the focal point of the Blanco River series, so she combed through her supplies, looking for sap green, olive, and raw umber.

But her gaze was drawn to the hot colors. She picked up cadmium red and scarlet. The colors felt emotional to her—both angry and beautiful, volatile and passionate. She spotted ultramarine blue and indigo and thought of Jack's eyes as he'd sat beside her on that bar stool the other night. He was an impressive man. She could admit that now, in the privacy of her solitude. Jack Bowman impressed her. She respected his persistence, his dedication to his job. She respected his moral code, or whatever it was that made it impossible for him to think of a victim in his town as somebody else's problem.

And he was attractive. She remembered his hands on her last night, the heat of his mouth. She remembered the way her body had warmed to him, like it was stirring awake again after a long nap alone. Suddenly she knew what she wanted to paint, and it had nothing to do with the Blanco River, and it was going to be amazing.

She squeezed some ultramarine onto her palette and added linseed oil, then a touch of turpentine to thin it out. She would use the "fat over lean" method, layering the glazes, making sure each layer was oilier than the one before. The effect would be a vibrant, shimmering field of color. She selected a wide, sable-hair brush and stroked it over her cheek. It felt silky and sensual, and she couldn't wait to saturate it with blue.

CHAPTER

12

A knock sounded at the door, jarring Fiona out of her zone. She glanced at the clock. She'd been painting for hours, but it seemed like only minutes had passed. The canvas was an expanse of watery blues and grays, save the empty white swirls where she planned to add carp. When the blue dried sufficiently, she could start—

Tap! Tap! Tap!

The door. Right. Someone was here.

She stood up and stretched. Her legs were stiff, and she swayed slightly as all the blood rushed to her feet. She picked her way across her messy apartment and checked the peephole.

Jack.

Her heart did a leap.

And then she wiped the smile off her face and told herself to calm down. She shouldn't get excited. He was probably here on business. Probably something about the case.

She glanced at her clothes and knew it was futile to try and primp. She unlocked the door and pulled it open.

"Hi."

He looked her over, and his lip curved up at the corner. "I caught you at work."

She stepped back to let him in. "Yes, you did."

He entered her home, and she felt a touch of nervousness. He was going to see her painting. And her messy apartment. And her unmade bed.

He glanced around, noticing everything, but then his gaze settled on her and he smiled. "You've got paint on your nose."

Her hand flew to her nose, and she ended up with cerulean blue on her fingertips. "Sorry." She crossed the apartment to her easel, where she'd hung a rag. She dunked the corner into some turpentine and headed for the bathroom. "Just a second."

After a few moments, she was slightly more presentable.

Jack was standing in her kitchen now, reading the *Far Side* comics on her refrigerator. He turned around. "I was wondering if that offer still stands."

"You mean breakfast?" She glanced at the clock. It was just past noon.

"Or lunch. Whatever. Or we could go for a walk. You probably need a break from these fumes."

She sniffed the air, and realized he was right. She'd neglected to open a window because of the cold, and her nose had gone numb to the smell. "That sounds good. Just let me change."

"Why?"

She smiled. "Because I look like a hobo."

"You look fine." He snagged her coat off the hook in the foyer. "Here, come on."

She hesitated a beat, then decided the hell with it. There weren't any miracles she could work with her hair and her face in five minutes anyway, so she might as well go as she was. She slipped into some sneakers and let him help her on with her coat.

They left the apartment and rode the elevator down to street level. As soon as they got outside, Fiona took a deep breath of fresh air. She felt relaxed and rejuvenated. Sometimes a good session of painting was better than a full night's sleep.

She turned to Jack. "You hungry?"

"Not really. You?"

She shrugged. "Not really."

Fiona scanned the area. It was too early for a drink. They could sit in a coffee shop. Or they could head down toward the water. It was another drab day, but the temperature seemed to have inched above freezing.

"Come on," she said, striking out toward the bike path that led to Town Lake. "I know a good route."

They walked the first ten minutes or so without talking, and she got the feeling he had something on his mind. Maybe he wanted to tell her about his new lead or bounce some ideas off her. She waited until he was ready to talk.

"You get called out of bed a lot?" he asked, finally.

He was referring to the robbery-homicide. She scooped her hair out of her face and looked at him. "Sometimes."

"And I guess you travel a lot, too, huh? When the FBI calls?"

"Sometimes." It had become much more frequent lately, but she sensed he didn't want to hear that.

"It's a rough job. Maybe you should stick to painting."

She scoffed.

"What?"

"It's pretty interesting to hear you say that after all the

lengths you went to convincing me to work on your case."

They neared the lake now, and Jack gazed out over the water. It was just as gray as the sky above it. "I've been re-thinking that. I'm starting to feel sorry I got you involved."

They walked for a while, and she absorbed what he'd said. He was sorry he'd gotten her involved. Her work had led to two major breaks in the case, yet he regretted hiring her. Did he regret getting to know her, too? Did he regret their budding relationship, or whatever this was?

What was this?

They didn't live in the same town. They didn't have similar backgrounds. They had almost nothing in common except their work and a professional acquaintance—one who could single-handedly ruin Fiona's reputation with APD if he ever got wind she was sleeping with a detective on a case.

Jack stopped beside a spindly sycamore. He shoved his fists in his pockets and looked at the ground. Then he looked at her.

"I won't be asking for any more of your help on this," he said. "I apologize for twisting your arm in the first place, 'specially after what happened with Hoyt."

"That wasn't your fault."

"I know. But I'm sorry anyway. He's facing charges right now. Don't know if they'll stick, but I'll do whatever I can to see that they do."

She didn't get this. Was this about guilt? Or maybe fear? Was he starting to feel some unwelcome attachment to her?

Was this about Lucy?

A jealous lump rose in her throat. She cleared it away. "Are you still seeing Lucy?"

His eyebrows arched. "Huh?"

"Are you still involved with her?"

"What does she have to do with anything?"

"I don't know. You tell me."

"What did Ginny tell you, anyway?"

She huffed out a breath. "Nothing."

"I told you, she stretches the truth." He looked at the lake. "Anyway, there's nothing there. Not anymore."

Fiona's hands balled into fists inside her pockets. He was *lying* again. It was so obvious. Why couldn't he give her a straight answer about this woman?

Maybe because he was still in love with her.

"I need to get back," she said, and started retracing their steps.

He quickly caught up to her. "Hold up a minute. Why are you upset?"

"I'm not upset."

"Bullshit."

She shot him a hostile look.

"Look, I don't know where you're getting all this about Lucy, but I didn't come here to talk about her. I came here to tell you you're done with my case. And to ask you to give police work a rest."

"Oh, I see." Her stride lengthened as her anger grew. "You think you can give me career advice now?"

"No."

"That's what it sounds like."

"I'm asking you as a friend. To give yourself a break from cases. I don't think it's good for you. You look tired."

She halted and whirled around. "Let's get something straight, Jack. You're not my friend. My career is none of your business, and just because you hired me on some case doesn't mean I want your advice."

He stood there, looking down at her, and she could see his jaw clenching and unclenching. He wanted to say something, but he probably knew she was about two seconds away from telling him to go screw himself.

She took a deep breath, and tried to summon some tact. "Why don't you take yourself, and all your advice, and go back to Graingerville?"

Jack stared at the bulletin board in his office, and knew he was missing something. He could feel it. He gazed at all the evidence spread out across the wall and knew he'd failed to register some key bit of information that would bring the fuzzy picture into focus.

These crimes were connected, he felt certain. And after hearing all about the case, Nathan had agreed. The detective had ten years' experience working homicide, and Jack trusted his opinion. Unfortunately, though, all that experience hadn't generated any new insights. The best Jack had gotten out of his trip to Austin had been a reminder to keep hammering away at motive. What had prompted the killer to choose these particular girls? Who and where was he likely to strike next?

Jack gazed at the bulletin board, cataloguing the similarities among the crimes. The victimology was alike, the MO. Even the damn weather was the same from case to case. But it was the proximity of the crime scenes that bothered him. He stared at his map again, zeroing in on the section where Mesquite Creek cut through the southwest corner of Grainger County. Lucy had been picked up by her abductor not half a mile from the creek. The body of Natalie Fuentes had been found off Highway 44, less than a mile from the same location. And Veronica Morales was last seen at Three Forks Barbecue, a restaurant about five miles north of where the creek intersected Highway 44.

The killer was local. *Had* to be. Why else would someone fixate on such a concentrated area? Whoever Jack was dealing with had some connection, some tie to Grainger County.

But if so, why didn't anyone recognize him?

It couldn't be Fiona's drawing that was the problem. Both Lucy and Brady agreed it was practically a photographic likeness of the man they'd seen.

But the only other explanation Jack could think of—and just thinking of it depressed him—was that the killer *wasn't* targeting Grainger County. Maybe he was going around all over the place, picking up girls and torturing them, and for whatever reason, the crimes weren't getting reported.

"Got that tire tread for you, Chief."

Jack tore his attention away from the map and saw Lowell standing in his office doorway. Jack caught the disapproval in the officer's face as he took in his boss's appearance.

Okay, so he looked like shit. He had a black eye still. He hadn't been home to sleep or change clothes since yesterday morning, and his jeans and rumpled flannel weren't exactly regulation attire.

"What'd you find, Lowell?"

He handed Jack a Polaroid of a tire. "Took that crime scene photo over to the guy I was telling you about at NTB. He's a whiz with tire treads. It's really something."

Jack stared down at the photograph of the brand-new BFGoodrich tire. The shot looked to have been taken right inside the tire shop, and someone had jotted down all the specs beneath the picture. The state crime lab probably used a more scientific method to identify tread marks, but Jack wasn't willing to wait three decades for someone to get around to his case.

"He thinks this is it?"

"Swears it," Lowell said. "It's an all-terrain tire. Standard on at least a dozen SUVs and pickups starting about two years ago. Then of course, you got people who put the new tires on older models, so it doesn't really tell us anything for sure about the vehicle."

Jack nodded. "Yeah, but this is for what? A seventeen- or eighteen-inch wheel? Too big for your standard car."

"That's what my buddy said, too. We're looking for a light truck, a Jeep, or an SUV. Not a sedan or a coupe, unless it's some kinda tricked-out ride." Lowell paused for a minute, as if he expected Jack to say something.

"Good work."

"So if that's all for tonight, you mind if I . . . ?"

Jack glanced at the clock. Damn, it was after nine already. The entire weekend had gone by in a blur.

"Yeah, you get on home. Hey, and thanks for running down that lead with the tattoo artist."

Lowell scoffed. "That guy Viper's a freak show, but he doesn't look like the drawing. Said he couldn't remember anyone who does, and I think he was telling the truth."

Lowell had a fairly good bullshit meter, which was why Jack had sent him out there when he got sidetracked with the Morales family.

"I hate body art," Lowell continued. "You couldn't pay me enough to let some nut job near me with a needle."

"I hear you," Jack said. He didn't mind tattoos on other people, but he'd never once been tempted to get one. "Anyway, thanks for the help."

After Lowell left, he ducked into the break room and fed some quarters into the Coke machine. He had mountains of paperwork to catch up on, but he'd most likely spend the night poring over the Natalie Fuentes file.

The victim had been driving a Hyundai Elantra at the time of her disappearance, and Jack had put a BOLO out on the car as soon as he'd gotten the details about it from her mother. He'd also compared the standard Elantra tires to the imprint found at the scene where her body was dumped, but the two didn't match. It sounded like the killer was in a truck or SUV with large tires, which, in rural Texas, didn't narrow things down much. Maybe he'd stopped using the gray sedan—not surprising, given that Lucy's attack had occurred eleven years ago. Most people didn't keep cars that long.

Jack wished they had more on the current vehicle. He wondered if Brady could be of any more help here. The boy had told Fiona he'd heard a "loud" engine, but that he didn't really get a look.

Of course, he'd also told Fiona he didn't get a good look at the perp. That was right before he gave her an extremely detailed description of him. Fiona had a way with witnesses, but Jack would be damned if he asked for her help again.

The front door burst open. Jack poked his head out of the break room and saw Sharon standing in the foyer shaking rain off her sleeves.

"You still on?"

"Yeah." She wiped her muddy boots on the mat by the door. "I was on my way back from that domestic and I saw some activity out toward White Tail Road."

Jack had heard it come over the radio. One of the sheriff's deputies was out there checking on a disabled vehicle. "Any injuries?"

"Car looks fine, except for a flat tire. I think you'll want to come take a look, though."

"That's a good mile out of town. We don't have jurisdiction."

"You're going to want jurisdiction," Sharon said. "The disabled vehicle's registered to Marissa Pico."

Jack's stomach tightened. "The senator's daughter?"

"That's the one." Sharon finger-combed her wet hair. "Her purse and cell phone are still sitting in the front seat, but there's no sign of Marissa, and there's blood inside the car."

CHAPTER

13

Fiona's nerves started jumping the second she pointed
her car south toward Graingerville.

Jack hadn't called her. Her assistance on the Natalie
Fuentes case had been *requested. Immediately.* But instead
of Jack Bowman showing up at her door to ply her with his
unique brand of persuasion, Special Agent Ray Santos of
the FBI had made the invitation by phone.

And Fiona had accepted.

She'd stepped out of her afternoon art class, taken a
three-minute phone call from Santos, and jumped right in
her Honda.

And now she barreled down the interstate thinking of
Jack. He'd put his heart into this case, and whether he realized it or not, it had just been ripped away from him.

She suspected he knew. And she suspected he was
pissed. Royally. The Grainger County Sheriff's Office, in
conjunction with the FBI, was now leading the investigation. According to Santos, federal and local investigators
were looking into the murder of Natalie Fuentes, as well as
two suspicious disappearances in Grainger County, on the
theory that the incidents were connected. What had started
out as a determined effort on the part of one small-town

police chief had just turned into one of the biggest joint law enforcement efforts in the state, because whether by plan or happenstance, the man Jack was hunting had finally made headlines.

Grainger County's latest missing woman was twenty-five-year-old Marissa Pico, the youngest daughter of Ben Pico, prominent south Texas rancher and longtime member of the Texas Senate.

Fiona took the Highway 44 exit, passing the now-familiar truck stop where she'd bought coffee a few days before. She wondered if she'd be pulling in again tonight for a shot of caffeine before making the drive home, or whether she'd end up staying the night.

With Jack.

Given their last conversation, she highly doubted it. Which was better, anyway, because she needed to get things back on a professional footing with him. She'd gotten too emotional yesterday—probably due to a lack of sleep—and she regretted it now. She wouldn't let it happen again. She was here to work, not worry about her personal life.

She smoothed her lapels and checked her face in the mirror. Her hair was back, her makeup minimal. It was just the look she preferred when she dealt with law enforcement types, but it was all wrong for a meeting with Brady Cox. And the suitcase she normally kept in her trunk was parked inside her apartment, awaiting laundry day. She'd have to improvise.

The highway cut a path through the fields, through the never-ending rows of shriveled plants. Fiona gazed out, wondering what sort of plants they were and if there was any chance at all they'd survived the freeze. She knew nothing about agriculture, and as the endless acres raced by, she felt the full force of her ignorance.

She was an outsider here.

Unlike Jack—who seemed just as at home in a sushi bar as he did behind the wheel of his super-macho pickup truck—Fiona wasn't adaptable. She needed the city. She needed congestion. She needed masses of people where she could lose herself and simply exist, anonymously, without the constant scrutiny of others. Courtney called it a defense mechanism, and maybe it was, but sometimes Fiona didn't want roots or relationships. Sometimes all she wanted was her own company and the tantalizing option of remaining nameless.

WELCOME TO GRAINGERVILLE. PLEASE DRIVE FRIENDLY.

She passed the road sign, remembering her talk with Ginny just a few days ago. She'd said Jack was a hardheaded man, just like his father, and that his family were the salt of the earth.

It was a quaint description, but Fiona had no trouble believing it. She wondered how such a man would stand up to the onslaught of federal investigators, politicians, and reporters who would be chomping at his heels by the end of today.

Fiona drove through downtown, past the police station, and the library, and the familiar Texaco station where she'd stopped for gas during her first visit. She turned into the parking lot of the Grainger County Administrative Building and spotted a row of news vans already lined up in the spaces nearest the entrance. Their antennae towered over the parking lot, transmitting images of Graingerville to satellites hovering high above the earth.

Fiona took a deep breath, smoothed her hair, and braced herself for the circus.

Randy Rudd was in his element. Surrounded by microphones and cameras, he seemed bigger, taller, swollen to nearly twice his usual size by all the attention.

Of course, it could be the lifts. Jack watched from the side of the meeting hall, arms crossed, as the Grainger County sheriff took the stage. He wore his extra-special ostrich-skin boots plus his usual ten-gallon hat. The overall effect was that the five-eight lawman appeared six feet tall. He straightened the microphone unnecessarily, made eye contact with key television reporters, and aimed a somber look at his audience. Everyone sat anxiously awaiting news from the Man in Charge.

This was such bullshit. Both Randy and the mayor had done a complete 180. The Natalie Fuentes case had gone from being a pesky annoyance for Jack to deal with to priority number one in the flash of a camera bulb.

Jack scanned the room, trying not to grind his teeth to nubs as Randy spouted sound bites. Jack told himself it didn't matter. So the mayor had sidelined him, so what? So the bastard had threatened to have his badge if he so much as sneezed in front of a camera? Evidently, the black eye wasn't good for PR. Ditto for Jack's surly attitude. He didn't give a shit, really, as long as he still had access to the case. Randy and the mayor could have the publicity; Jack simply wanted an arrest. And if Randy needed to be the guy slapping the cuffs on him, so be it. If Randy needed to pose with a bunch of FBI hotshots, virtually guaranteeing his reelection next November on a tough-on-crime platform, that was fine with Jack, too. But what Jack *wouldn't* tolerate—not for one minute—was some pencil-dick sheriff stepping in and messing with the actual police work. Randy was a politician to the core. He was skilled in front of a camera, but what he knew about homicide investigation couldn't fill a thimble.

Sharon sidled up next to Jack and gave a barely audible whistle. "Who's *that*?" she asked.

He followed her gaze to the line of agents and sheriff's deputies standing off to the side, behind Randy.

"Who?"

"The suit," she said.

Randy's admin, who stood on Jack's other side, leaned forward. "He's FBI," Myrna said. "Special Agent Santos."

The two women exchanged a look Jack had seen before, usually when his sisters discussed Colin Firth or Brad Pitt.

"I wonder what he's packing," Sharon muttered, and Myrna snickered.

Jack shot Sharon his stern chief-of-police look, and she promptly shut up. Then he turned his attention to the fed. Ray Santos, of the San Antonio VCMO unit, stood silently behind the sheriff, watching the room with an eagle eye. This was the guy whose brilliant idea it was to get Fiona back down here to reinterview Brady Cox. Jack had checked out his background. Santos had a PhD in psychology, but instead of analyzing case files from some basement at Quantico, he had spent the past five years on the Violent Crimes and Major Offenders squad in San Antonio, which told Jack two things: Santos had some real, down-and-dirty police work under his belt, but there was a strong chance he spoke psychobabble.

Fucking feds. Jack welcomed their resources on this case, but he didn't want to waste time sitting around a conference table talking about how their perp was probably a bed wetter at age ten. They needed to catch the son of a bitch, not profile him to death.

Randy droned on, taking full advantage of his captive audience. Jack's gaze traveled over the gaggle of reporters, who had come from near and far to get a piece of the story. The print guys wore jeans and button-down shirts with cheap ties. The TV ones—mostly women—had dramatic hair and expensive white teeth. Jack almost didn't notice the woman in beige seated way at the back. Unisex clothes, no smile, but Jack's pulse picked up the second he saw her.

Fiona sat rigidly in her chair, hands folded, listening as Randy assured his viewing audience that "come hell or high water, the Grainger County Sheriff's Department will bring Marissa home."

Fiona winced at the statement. She would be thinking what Jack was: that Randy was way out of bounds making a pledge like that. Marissa had been abducted. Violently. Quite possibly by the same person who took Natalie Fuentes. So if Marissa was alive at all right now, she was likely being tortured by a sociopath. And if she wasn't alive—if he'd already raped her and strangled her and ditched her body—her remains might never be found. Like Veronica Morales, she could be gone for years. Or forever.

And yet Randy stood there swelled up like a toad and promised Marissa's parents—and millions of television viewers—he could bring her home.

Fiona glanced over and caught Jack watching her. A heated look passed between them, and he wondered what she was thinking. Was she pissed off at Randy, like he was? Or was she still angry about his "advice" yesterday? Or maybe she was annoyed because she'd been roped in again.

He didn't think she was upset over that. He was getting to know her now, and he'd learned she was dedicated. Committed. She had a personal stake in every one of her cases. And just like him, she probably wouldn't get a good night's rest until the clues came together and their man was arrested.

Fiona looked down and fidgeted with her sleeves as the audience erupted into a chorus of questions. Randy fielded them, one by one, somehow managing not to make an ass of himself as he discussed investigative procedures and forensic evidence he knew almost nothing about. Jack watched Fiona, with her ugly suit and no-nonsense hairstyle. At some point he'd begun to view all her clothes as disguises, and this one in particular really irritated him. She was hiding from him, and everyone else, thinking if she presented a cool enough front, nothing would get to her. Not the case. Not the victim.

Not him.

The press conference finally ended, and Fiona stood up and gathered her purse. Her body language said she intended to leave, and he decided then and there he wasn't going to let her.

"Miss Glass?"

Fiona stepped away from the mob of reporters and spotted a dark-haired man in a business suit striding toward her. She'd noticed him at the press conference, as had every woman in the room, she guessed.

"Agent Santos." She held out her hand.

"So it's true." He gave her hand a firm shake, which she appreciated. "There's a rumor about you, you know."

"What's that?"

"That you're psychic."

She pulled her hand away, suddenly uncomfortable. This man was handsome, but the intensity of his gaze made her self-conscious.

She cleared her throat. "So. You want me to talk to Brady?"

He continued to stare at her, and she had the strangest sensation he was trying to read her thoughts.

"I talked to Garrett Sullivan early this morning," he said. "He's very impressed with your work. Says you're one of the best interviewers he's ever seen. That you have a way with young children."

Fiona clutched her purse. She'd never been easy with compliments. "How's his case going?"

"Well. They've got an interesting new lead."

"Any word on Shelby?"

"I haven't heard."

A man bearing a tripod on his shoulder exited the meeting room, nearly knocking Fiona in the head. Santos took her by the elbow and steered her away from the crowd. His gaze never left her face.

"I'd like you to sit down with Brady again," he said. "See if you can learn more about the vehicle in the Fuentes case. See if he can provide more information about the suspect's clothing, too. Maybe he was wearing something distinctive that could give us a lead—maybe a hat or jacket with a logo on it."

Fiona glanced past the agent. Jack was watching her from the other end of the corridor, and he had that same heated look he'd had during the press conference.

She turned her attention back to Santos. "I'll do the best I can."

She managed to escape the building without being recognized by any reporters. She pulled out her phone and called Sullivan, who answered on the first ring.

"Sorry to bother you," she said.

"It's no bother, but I can't talk long."

"What's up with Shelby? I just met your friend Santos, and he said you've got something."

"Yes and no," Sullivan said, and her hopes dwindled. "We've found a Meridian, Mississippi, woman who got a call from Janovic."

"Okay."

"He wanted to set up a meeting about buying a used car. He'd seen her ad in the paper, apparently."

"And?"

"And she showed up at his motel as scheduled, but Janovic had taken off. Most likely, he noticed his face all over the news and got spooked."

"Was he with anyone?" Fiona held her breath.

"We don't think so. The good part is, this woman provided us with a cell number. He's using a stolen phone, and we've managed to track a few calls made on it during the past few days. Looks like he's heading west. We don't know where, precisely, but he's on the run, so we're expecting him to make a mistake soon."

From the corner of her eye, Fiona saw Jack leaning

against the building, arms folded over his chest. He was watching her, waiting for her to finish the call and probably eavesdropping, too.

"Obviously, all this is confidential," Sullivan said. "I shouldn't be telling you."

"Understood."

"Listen, I have to go now."

"Thanks for the update," she said hurriedly, but he'd already hung up. She tucked her phone inside her bag.

"I thought you had class today." Jack stood in front of her now with his hands on his hips. He was in street clothes today, no holster or badge in sight. The skin above his eyebrow had gone an interesting shade of green.

"Your eye looks terrible. Is that why they pulled you off the case?"

"I'm not off," he said. "I've just been instructed to steer clear of the media."

Fiona studied his face—the firm set of his jaw, the hard look in his eyes. He was still fighting it. He didn't realize the sheriff and his cadre of federal investigators had effectively taken it away from him. Jack had no resources, questionable jurisdiction, and very little manpower. Given the politics and publicity involved, the FBI would probably fast-track all the lab results, which was good, but they didn't have to hand results over to Jack. Same went for witness interviews and any helpful information that could be gathered from the FBI's vast computer databases.

Jack was outmatched, but he didn't seem to know it yet.

"You're here for Brady," he said, when the silence had dragged on too long. "You plan to talk to him like that?"

She looked down at her suit and flat beige shoes. "I've got some jeans in my car, but I may need to borrow a shirt or something."

"All right. You should be prepared, though. He doesn't want to be interviewed."

"How do you know?"

"The good sheriff already tried talking to him this morning. Brady basically told him to fuck off."

"He *did*?"

Jack sneered. "Called him a 'bonehead asswipe,' I believe it was. Same difference."

"Well, then. He's more observant than he lets on."

But Brady wouldn't talk to Fiona, either. She spent half an hour with him in Jack's office, and all she could get out of him was some snide commentary about his gym teacher's sexual orientation. Finally, she decided to back off. After jotting down her cell phone number in case he suddenly remembered something, she let him leave the police station with his mother. From Jack's window, she watched the boy stuff the slip of paper into his back pocket, where it would probably stay until it disintegrated in the washing machine.

"No luck?"

She sighed and turned to face Jack. "None. What does your evening look like?"

"Same as always. Work."

He was a workaholic, just like she was. It should have been a strike against him, but it wasn't. She tended to trust men with a strong work ethic. Her father had been that way.

She turned back to the window and checked the sky. It

was nearing dusk. Soon the lighting conditions would be similar to those Brady had had up in his tree fort when the killer had dumped the body.

"I want to check something at the crime scene," she said. "Let's go for a ride."

He stared at her for a moment, probably debating whether to try to talk her out of whatever she had in mind. Finally, he pulled out his keys. "Fine, but I'm driving."

Five minutes later, they were cruising down the road in Jack's pickup. He was quiet. He seemed to be in a testy mood, and Fiona guessed he was frustrated with both the sheriff and the investigation.

Not to mention her presence here.

But that was too bad. Investigations were a team effort, and he was just going to have to get over himself.

She turned up the heater and got a blast of warm air. "Smells like rotten eggs," she said, making a face.

"Hydrogen sulfide. Comes from the oil and gas wells. See the pump jacks?"

"It's awful. How can people stand it?"

"Depends on your perspective," he said. "Some folks call it the smell of money."

After a few miles of silence, he pulled onto the shoulder and parked beside some bushes. Fiona glanced around as she climbed out of the truck. The air was chilly and damp. A handful of homes were clustered along a two-lane road where it intersected the highway.

"Over there is the drop site." Jack pointed out the spot beneath the elm tree where Natalie's body had been found. Fiona stared at the sad patch of grass for a moment and then turned away.

"Where does Brady live?" she asked, gazing out toward the houses.

"Just over there." He pointed to one of the small brick homes. "His dad took off a couple years back. His mom has a steady stream of boyfriends in and out."

Fiona felt a pang in her chest. It always took her off guard like that.

"I don't think he spends a whole lot of time there." Jack stopped beside a row of trees and underbrush lining the fence that divided the two properties. He gestured to a giant pecan tree. "There's the fort."

She looked up at the tree. High amid the branches was a small wooden platform surrounded on three sides by scraps of weathered plywood. The ladder leading up to it consisted of about a dozen crude boards nailed to the tree trunk. Like many of the other trees nearby, this one was naked of leaves.

"That's really high up," she said. "Doesn't it look cold to you?"

"Yep."

"I can't believe he sleeps up there sometimes."

"Maybe it beats the alternative."

She felt an old bitterness welling up. "Have you called CPS about this family?"

"They've been out. And I'm keeping my eye on things." Jack's tone was serious, and he said it like a promise.

Fiona looked at him, wondering if he really knew what to watch for. Did Brady's mother pass out on the sofa with a lit cigarette dangling from her fingers? Did she ever raise a hand to her son? Did her boyfriends?

Or were some of them a little *too* friendly?

Fiona tromped over to the tree and gripped the first rung of the makeshift ladder. The wood looked old, but solid. It appeared as though Brady had appropriated his building materials from someone's picket fence.

She started climbing.

"What the hell are you doing?"

She tested her weight on the next rung. "I want to see what Brady saw."

Jack stood beneath her, hands planted on his hips, as she made her way up. "It's going to really piss me off if you break your neck up there."

Fiona finally reached the top and hoisted herself onto the platform. From this vantage point, she had an unobstructed view of the whole pasture as well as a strip of highway and most of the nearby houses. From his fort, Brady would be able to see his mother's visitors coming and going. He most certainly would have had a good view of the killer dumping the body. The killer's transportation, though, was another matter.

"It's hard to see the highway from here," she reported. "If the guy parked beside those bushes near the road, the car would have been hidden."

Fiona made her way back down. She had nearly reached the bottom when her foot missed a rung. She lost her balance, and Jack caught her arm and pulled her upright just before she landed on her still-sore tailbone.

"Thanks," she said, steadying herself.

He stared down at her, and she saw the flare of anger she'd seen at the press conference.

"What?"

He dropped her arm and strode back to the truck.

"Jack?"

He jerked open the passenger's-side door. "Let's go."

She walked to the pickup, determined not to lose her cool like she had down by the lake yesterday. She stopped in front of him. "What is your problem?"

He looked down at her, stone-faced.

"I'm here to help, in case you haven't noticed. It's not my fault your sheriff went and alienated the witness."

"Get in. You're going to freeze out here."

She ignored him. "Brady could still come around, you know. In the meantime, you'll just have to work other leads. What did you find out over at Viper's place?"

"Get in," he repeated, "or I'm going to put you in."

She climbed into the truck and jerked the door closed.

He was so obnoxious sometimes. And controlling, as if he didn't have to share information with anybody, as if he could do everything on his own. No wonder his biggest case was getting wrestled away from him.

He yanked his door open and swung into the driver's seat. Then he fired up the truck and pulled onto the highway.

He glanced at her. "You know, I thought I asked you to stay out of all this. Now you're down here, more involved than ever."

"This isn't about you. The FBI asked me to get involved."

He shook his head and stared through the windshield. She noticed his hands tightening on the steering wheel, and she looked away. Pastures and barbed-wire fences sailed by as they sped down the road.

"My car's at county headquarters," she said. "You can drop me off."

He sent her a smoldering look. His gaze dropped to her chest, and she didn't know whether he was checking out her breasts or remembering the shirt he'd loaned her.

"If you need your shirt back, I can run into the bathroom and change."

He faced forward then and muttered something.

"What?"

He swerved onto the shoulder, slammed on the brakes, and shoved the truck into park. Then he lifted her right up out of her seat and hauled her over the console, into his lap. The steering wheel pressed into her back as she stared down at him in shock.

"I'm not dropping you off," he said. "And I want my shirt back. Now."

CHAPTER

14

N ow?"
   He kissed her, hard, and the roughness of it sent a sharp thrill through her entire body. His mouth moved down her neck, and he pulled the flannel aside so he could suck on the skin just above her collarbone. A tightening, tingling sensation flooded through her, and while she was distracted by it, he lifted her hips again, expertly shifting them until she was straddling him.

"Jack."

He fitted her against him, and she heard herself moan at the feel of it. His hands moved up to tangle in her hair, and then he kissed her mouth again, practically inhaling her. She inhaled him right back, wondering how they'd ever gotten their wires so crossed, and then not caring at all because everything felt so good. His hand moved down the front of her shirt—*his* shirt—popping open the buttons.

"Oh my God, *Jack.*"

"Hmm?" He loosened the shirt, and the air chilled her skin. She felt the hot wetness of his mouth through her bra, and she forgot everything except pressing herself as close to him as possible. He pulled the lace away with his thumbs, and her blood started to burn as he nipped at her skin. She combed her fingers through his short hair, wanting to make him stop and make him keep going at the same time. A car roared past on the highway, and he looked up from her naked breasts.

Their gazes locked, and some diabolical instinct made her rock herself against him. He tipped his head back against the seat and looked pained. "We need a motel room."

The lust evaporated, and she pulled the sides of his shirt together. The flannel was soft against her bare skin, and she couldn't believe she was *straddling* this man in his truck.

"What?"

"Nothing." She tried to look impassive.

"Honey, we can't do this here. I'm the friggin' chief of police. I'd never hear the end of it."

"What about your house?"

He hesitated—just a second too long—and she felt a stab of disappointment.

"The motel's closer." He slid his hands up her shoulders, resting them on either side of her neck. "Half a mile, tops."

She bit her lip and looked down at him. She couldn't do this. She didn't want to check into some cheap motel with him and have to nurse a bruised ego when he got dressed and left an hour later.

He cupped the side of her face with his hand. "Does it really matter to you?"

She nodded.

He closed his eyes briefly, sighing. Then he took the two shirttails and tied them together at her belly button. "Stay way the hell over there, then. It's a ten-minute drive."

Seven minutes later, he whipped into a gravel driveway in the middle of nowhere. They'd been surrounded by farmland, and then—inexplicably—there was this little white house.

"You live here?"

He shoved the gearshift into park. "Yep." He hopped out and came around to her side as she sat there gazing at his home. It was a thirties-era one-story cottage flanked by two enormous oak trees.

He pulled her door open and practically dragged her out of the truck.

"When was this built?" she asked, as he tugged her up the sidewalk. The deck on the front looked new, but the pier-and-beam construction and the age of the trees told her he wasn't the original owner. He led her by the hand up the stairs and pulled open the screen door, then thrust his key in the lock.

"Is it postwar?"

He shoved the door open and then scooped her off her feet. "Save the history lesson. I want you naked."

The screen door slammed behind them, and he kicked the wooden one shut. She draped her arms around his neck and rested her cheek against his shirt. He smelled good, like he always smelled. Like Jack. Her eyes adjusted to the dim lighting, and she realized he was carrying her through a kitchen, then a short corridor, and into a bedroom. With no ceremony whatsoever, he dumped her on the bed and started pulling off his boots. They thudded heavily to the floor, and then she heard the rip of Velcro. He'd been wearing an ankle holster, she saw, as he switched on a lamp and placed his gun on the dresser. His shirt came off next, and she tried not to embarrass herself by saying *oh my God,* but that's exactly what she was thinking. She propped up on her elbows to admire his perfectly sculpted chest, and smiled because he was completely at ease in his house and in his body. She toed off her shoes.

Then he knelt beside her on the bed and tugged loose the knot of her shirt. Soon her smile faded as he really got down to business, making her body quiver under the heat of his mouth. No one had ever wanted her like this, and she felt swept away on a tide of need and emotions. This man was strong and insistent and hot for *her*, for some crazy reason, and she couldn't do anything but feel the craving deep inside her body and the certainty that she was in way over her head.

He pulled the shirt from her arms and stared into her eyes as he slid a big, warm hand around her rib cage to unhook her bra. He slipped it off and dropped it on the floor. Then he unbuttoned her jeans, and she stiffened.

"What?" he asked.

"Nothing."

He nuzzled her temple and touched her body through the denim. "Don't tense up on me, now."

"I'm not."

But he called her bluff by easing down her zipper and then standing at the end of the bed to pull off her jeans. Next came her panties, and a warm blush spread over her skin as his gaze moved slowly over her body. She gripped the bedspread, trying to calm her nerves as he looked at her with that glint in his eyes.

Suddenly, she couldn't stand it anymore, and she knelt at the end of the bed and reached for *his* jeans, but he caught her hand. "Not yet," he said, and kissed her.

She flattened herself against his chest, loving the contrast of his hair against her smooth skin. She felt the hammer of his heart and realized he wasn't nearly as calm as he wanted her to think. The knowledge spurred her on, and she pulled him back onto the bed, right on top of her.

"Fiona."

She wrapped her legs around him, bringing him hard against her. She sank her fingers into his skin and kissed him until her body ached.

"Just hold on." His voice was strained.

She squeezed. A groan came from deep in his chest, and she felt gloriously empowered. His knuckles brushed against her as he hurried to free himself from his jeans. He reached over her, and she heard a drawer scrape open and the tearing of foil. She waited, on the verge of meltdown, struggling not to bite a hole in her lip. And then he thrust into her, and she cried out at the shock of it.

"Sorry." He winced. "Just . . . give me a second."

She looked up at him, at the desperate need on his face, and she didn't have a second to give. With every fiber of her body, she pulled him closer. His muscles tensed under her hands, and she felt the wonderful power of him pounding and pounding into her.

"Fiona . . ."

"*Yes.*"

And in a searing, white-hot moment, it was over.

Jack stared down at her, mortified beyond words. Even the blissed-out expression on her face couldn't fool him into believing she'd actually enjoyed that. He pushed up from the bed, surprised when she locked her legs around him to keep him from moving. He did the obligatory kiss on the forehead, and she finally let go.

A few moments later, he flopped onto his back beside her and dropped an arm over his eyes with a groan. The mattress shifted next to him as she turned onto her side.

"Fiona." Shit, what could he say? He opened his eyes and looked at her. A damp curl clung to her neck, and her cheeks were tinged pink. She looked so goddamn pretty, and he'd just turned in his worst sexual performance in at least a decade, probably more.

She stroked a finger down his chest, and he caught her hand. "I'll make it up to you," he said.

Her eyebrows tipped up. "Make what up?"

"*That*." Christ, it would be easier if she just elbowed him in the ribs and told him, tough shit, he was all out of chances.

Instead, she brought his hand to her lips and kissed his knuckle, which was still blue from pummeling Hoyt's face. Then she nestled into the crook of his arm and sighed. They lay there for a few minutes, her breath warm against his chest as his heart rate returned to normal.

"Jack?" she murmured.

"Yeah?"

"Your house is really cold."

It wasn't just cold, it was arctic. He'd hardly been home in days, and the heater had been turned off. But the damn thing barely worked anyway, so instead of hassling with it, he scooped up her knees and swept the bedspread and sheet down. Then he pulled the covers back up over them both and hooked an arm around her waist.

"Thanks." Her voice sounded sleepy, and he prayed she wouldn't drift off before he managed to salvage at least a shred of pride. He pulled her body back against him, and she made a soft, mewing sound.

Something pinched inside his chest. For a while, he just lay there with his mind swirling. He couldn't believe this had happened. And with her, of all people.

Her hair tickled his chin as she snuggled closer. He wished he could turn back the clock. Ten minutes would do it. Five, even.

She mumbled something incoherent.

"Huh?"

"You *do* have rabbits." She gave him a drowsy look over her shoulder. "I saw the cage on your porch."

"They're my nieces'." God, were they really talking about this? "My nephew's allergic, so they live here."

"That's sweet."

Sweet. Not the word he wanted to hear right about now.

Her shoulders hunched as she stifled a yawn. She was tired. So was he. The last two weeks had been a marathon. What he needed was just a few minutes' rest, and he'd be back in the game.

He kissed her ear and whispered a promise to her, but she didn't hear it. She was already out cold.

John D. Alvin was a shit.

Courtney watched him through the windshield, taking in the tailored dark suit, the red power tie, the French cuffs that showed a flash of gold at his wrist.

Courtney was no detective. She wasn't *psychic*, like Fiona. But it didn't take a crystal ball to figure out John D. Alvin was a lying prick. And he'd assumed she was too stupid to figure it out. He'd thought he could lie to her, take what he wanted, and then be done with her.

But if there was one thing Courtney couldn't stand, it was asshole men who thought she was stupid.

She shoved open the door of her '98 clunker and stepped out onto the sidewalk. She stood and watched from just yards away as John *David* Alvin handed his Porsche keys to the valet and escorted *Mrs.* John David Alvin into the restaurant.

"Pig," Courtney muttered. He walked in ahead of his wife, like the dickhead that he was, and didn't even bother to hold the door.

Not that she felt sorry for the woman. She drove a white Jag convertible and lived in a mansion in Lakeway, a freaking *golf* resort just west of Austin. The woman probably knew precisely what kind of jerk she'd married. What wife didn't?

The valet jumped into the Porsche and headed south down Congress Avenue. Courtney got back into her Buick and followed him. She took a swig from her bottle of Grey Goose—a little liquid courage for the rest of the night's activities.

After Googling David on the Internet and finding no Dallas attorneys by that name, she'd followed up on a hunch. The hunch had led her to the swank Austin offices of John D. Alvin, Attorney-at-Law. And what had she seen in the parking lot? A shiny red Carrera with which she was intimately familiar.

She'd waited outside his office, a ball of hatred forming in her stomach. Then she'd followed him home in rush-hour traffic and watched him pull up to the mansion he shared with his wife.

She'd felt sick. Then stupid. Then sick all over again

when she'd spotted the pink Big Wheel abandoned in the driveway.

She took another swig of vodka and felt better, somehow, as it burned a path down her throat. *Hey, baby, I've got something for ya.*

Taillights glowed in front of her, and the Carrera turned into a half-empty lot. The valet parked between two Beamers as Courtney drove past and turned into an alley. She parked. Then she sat there for a few minutes, staring at her lap and remembering the Barbie Big Wheel she'd had when she was a kid. It had been a hand-me-down from Fiona, and Courtney loved to pedal it around the run-down apartment complex where they'd lived in Los Angeles.

Her stomach churned.

She took a last, long swill of vodka. Then she scrounged up her supplies and got out of the car.

Her breath turned to frost in front of her mouth. She'd forgotten a coat. The alley smelled like vomit, and she made her way to the street on legs not quite steady.

"Shit!" she yelped, stumbling over a beer bottle. She glanced around, but saw no one. This side street was vacant except for a few cars at meters. She crossed the parking lot to the gleaming Porsche.

She dropped her supplies into a pile and stared down, trying to remember what to do first. She'd had a plan earlier, but it was fuzzy now, a little vague around the edges. She needed to think. The hammer seemed to be calling out to her, so she picked it up, tested the weight of it in her hand, and took the first swing.

The sound was musical. Glass fell at her feet like snow, and she smiled. She made her way around the car, ignoring the alarm wailing in her ears. She felt euphoric. Gleeful. She took another swing, and then another. Each brought a shower of ice, and another little thrill. *I've got something for ya.* She rounded to the passenger's side, stopped to stare inside at the leather upholstery. It had felt good against her skin, warm and rich. The hammer slipped from her hand, and she teetered on her heels.

She shrugged off the dizziness and crouched down for the can. She shook it beside her ear, making the bead inside clatter over the wail of the alarm. She stood up. The car blurred in front of her. She held her hand out and saw that it was trembling, but then the hissing came, and she felt steadier, more powerful. She could do this. She moved around the car and thought of the picture she made— Courtney the *artist*! Courtney the *painter*! A giggle escaped, and then another. She bent over, laughing hysterically, and her cheeks felt freezing and she realized they were wet. Her legs folded under her and the can rolled away, and she lay there, sobbing on the asphalt, as the wailing closed in.

Fiona jolted awake at the noise. Another call . . .

Something moved beside her, and she jumped, startled to realize she wasn't alone.

She was in Jack's bed. She was in Graingerville. And the shrilling telephone would not be for her.

Jack snatched the receiver off the nightstand. "Bowman."

He listened a moment and then got out of bed to scoop his jeans off the floor. He fumbled in the dark with the denim.

"Shit. Yeah, it's here." He sighed. "Ringer's off. I was in a press conference. Why? What's up?" And after a brief pause, "When?"

Fiona watched his naked silhouette in the near darkness. At some point, Jack had turned out the lamp. At some point, he'd shucked his jeans and climbed under the covers with her. They'd fallen asleep, and now it was—she glanced at his alarm clock—11:14. And judging from Jack's rigid posture and terse words, he wouldn't be coming back to bed any time soon.

He ended the call and pulled on his jeans, and Fiona knew what he would say even before he said it.

"I've got to go in."

She'd spoken the same words on more than one occasion over the years, usually to a boyfriend who didn't understand the round-the-clock demands of her job. She guessed Jack hated pouters as much as she did, so she didn't say anything, but she did give in to the self-conscious urge to tuck the sheet up under her arms.

He jammed his feet into boots, not even bothering with socks.

Worry gripped her. "Is it Marissa?"

"No." He pulled his shirt on, buttoned up quickly. "That was Carlos. He needs my help with something."

This was just the scene she'd wanted to avoid in a motel room. Silly her, for thinking it wouldn't have played out the same way at his house. Cops could never stay, not for very long anyway. And they never told you where they were going.

She knew, because it was the same for her. Why burden the normal people in your life with an unpleasantness they could neither fathom nor understand?

He paused in the doorway. "Will you be here when I get back?"

No kiss good-bye.

"That's a good assumption. I don't have a car." She heard the bite in her voice and wished she hadn't let it come through.

"Oh. Right."

"Just bring my purse and my art case in, would you? They're on the floor of your truck, and my cell phone's in one of them."

He stood still for a second, and she wished she could read his face in the dimness. Was he replaying the frantic moments that had made her forget her stuff in his pickup? Or maybe he was feeling guilty for leaving her alone like this.

"I'll be back as soon as I can." And with a quick rap on the door frame, he was gone.

Lucy was waiting outside for him when he arrived. She wore a barn jacket over blue satin pajamas. Her gaze raked over him, and her lips pressed into a thin line.

"Sorry to drag you out of *bed*."

"What are you doing out here?" he demanded, mounting the porch steps. "Where're your brothers?"

"Everyone's got the night shift except Dolores." She held the door open. "And he's not there anymore. I've been watching."

"You couldn't watch from behind a locked door? What the hell—" Jack halted when he saw Sebastian curled up on the living room sofa with his teddy bear.

"Hi, Jack."

"Hi, sport."

"Sebastian couldn't sleep," Lucy said pointedly. She locked the door, and then crossed the living room. "Come back here and I'll show you that thing I was talking about."

She led him to her workroom at the back of the house, where she typically slept on the pull-out couch. She didn't turn on any lights, but simply crossed to the wall of windows stretching across the back of the room.

"He was over there." She gazed out the window, nodded. "Under the oak tree."

Jack looked out the window. "Are you sure it was a person? Maybe it was a cow got loose from the Nelson place. Or a deer."

She turned to face him. "Do cows smoke cigarettes?"

Jack shifted his gaze back outside.

"I got up to get a drink of water. Sebastian found me in the kitchen. He said he couldn't sleep. He said the shadow man was there again."

"The shadow man."

"He said he watches the house sometimes. Always at night, from under that tree. And yes, tonight's the first I've heard of it."

Jack tried not to show a reaction, but an old, long-buried fury was pushing its way to the surface.

"Stay here," he said.

He unlocked the back door and shoved it open. He didn't see anyone outside, but he slipped the gun from his waistband just in case. The familiar weight and shape of it in his hand helped him think like a cop instead of a protective boyfriend.

The night was dark and cold, the moon a thin slice of

silver up high in the sky. It was a good night for stalking someone, a good night to move around undetected.

Jack tromped across the grass and ducked between two lengths of barbed wire, taking care not to snag his jacket. This was Nelson land, and the farmer kept a couple dozen head of cattle in an adjacent pasture. Jack stopped beneath the oak and pulled a small Mag-Lite from his pocket. He scanned the ground around the tree, pausing the beam on something small and white. A cigarette butt. Flattened with something—probably a shoe—against the root of the tree. Jack crouched down.

The cigarette butt bothered him beyond the fact that it corroborated Lucy's story. Why leave it? Why go to the trouble to watch someone, or stalk someone, under cover of darkness, and then risk the glow and smell of a cigarette? And why leave the butt behind?

Why kill a young girl, then dump her body near a well-traveled highway? Why kidnap the daughter of a prominent politician? If the mission was to rape and kill, or simply to kill to cover up a rape, why leave a trail for the cops?

Unless part of the mission was to screw with the cops. Or with the public at large. Or maybe a certain segment of the public that would feel intimidated by the selection of these particular victims.

The Arrellandos fell into that segment. And maybe tonight's visit was just one more way to terrorize.

Jack took a pair of latex gloves from his jacket pocket and snapped them on. The HPD had taught him always to come prepared, and the habit hadn't faded in Graingerville. Jack carefully picked up the cigarette and dropped it into one of the small brown bags he kept folded in his pocket. It was a cold night, meaning a higher likelihood the subject would have been wearing gloves, and also a lower likelihood he would have had sweat and oil on his hands that would leave behind a good print. But he would have left saliva, and now that the FBI was involved, Jack might actually find a way to get the shit analyzed in a lab in the next year or so.

Jack tucked the bag into his pocket, and then resumed his flashlight sweep for any further clues. He spent ten more minutes walking a grid pattern and was about to call it quits when the back door squeaked open. Lucy came down the steps and walked toward him, arms wrapped around herself to ward off the frigid wind that whipped across the pasture.

"Find anything?"

"Maybe. You should go back inside."

She shrugged. "We both know he's not here anymore."

"We don't know that."

"Yes, we do."

"When does your family get home?"

"Morning." She cocked her head to the side. "Go home, Jack. You don't really want to be here."

He switched off his flashlight and shoved it in his pocket.

"You just fucked her, didn't you?"

He sighed. "Lucy—"

"I can tell. I remember that look." She turned and trudged back toward the house. When she reached the door, she glanced back over her shoulder. "It's okay, Jack. Next time I'll call the sheriff."

CHAPTER

15

It always amazed Nathan how stupid the bad guys could be. He stared down at the report on his desk, shaking his head at the utter idiocy of it. Tonight's perpetrator, a seventeen-year-old gangbanger, had decided to knock off a sandwich shop on the east side of town. Kid thinks he has a clever plan: he plunks a twenty down on the counter, asks for change, and when the cashier—a young Vietnamese woman—opens the drawer, he sticks a gun in her face and tells her to hand over all the cash. She complies. He leaves the store feeling like hot shit, probably ready to go celebrate with his buddies, but a black-and-white pulls up just as he's rushing through the door with a semiautomatic pistol in his hand. The kid panics, squeezes off a round that totally misses the cops, but hits the middle-aged computer programmer who's sitting at a stoplight less than a block away.

And the irony of it all? The kid left his original twenty on the counter and made off with a grand total of eighteen dollars and eighty-seven cents. It would have been funny if it weren't so fucking tragic.

The computer guy expired an hour later from a gunshot wound to the chest.

Nathan rubbed his eyes. Some days he hated this job.

"You *are* here."

Nathan glanced up to see a guy from the burglary squad standing beside his desk.

"Everyone's looking for you."

"Yeah, why's that?" He could already feel the acid pooling in his stomach.

"Got a chick down in reception. She's raising all kinds of hell, says she wants to talk to someone in charge. Says her sister works homicide for us."

Nathan frowned. "There aren't any women in homicide."

"I know." He smiled. "But you may want to go talk to this girl. She's got a trash mouth and a body like you wouldn't believe."

"What's she in for?"

"No idea."

"So why do I want to talk to her?"

The guy shrugged. "She says she knows you. Oh, and her name's Corey. Or Courtney. Yeah, that's it. Courtney Glass."

Jack's house was old and drafty, full of creaks and moans that made it impossible to sleep. Fiona pulled the blankets up around her neck and berated herself for the string of poor decisions that had gotten her to this point.

She'd slept with Jack. Finally. And while part of her reveled in it, another part of her was already making the case for Never Doing It Again. He hadn't kissed her good-bye, and she hated that it mattered to her. She hated that she actually *liked* this man and had thought his feelings for her went beyond the I-need-to-get-laid variety.

A car motored down the highway, and Fiona tensed, hoping it was him. But it passed by without slowing.

She sighed. She despised this. The little woman waiting at home for her man. The tip of her nose felt cold, and she wanted Jack's warm, muscled body to spoon with her again. She wanted the weight of his arm slung over her waist as she slept.

This was a disaster. She should never have given in to lust.

Except it had been the best sex of her—amazingly sheltered, she now realized—life. So she didn't totally regret it. But she regretted where she was right now, alone in his house, shivering beneath sheets and blankets that smelled deliciously like Jack Bowman, and Jack Bowman was off fighting bad guys with Carlos.

Her purse vibrated on the nightstand, and Fiona squeezed her eyes shut. Not again. Jack had left her stuff on his kitchen table, and when Fiona had gone to retrieve her phone, she'd seen that it was set to vibrate from the press conference, and that APD had called twice since ten o'clock. She just wasn't up for it tonight. She had no transportation and no desire to hear about a case she couldn't get to all the way in Austin.

But what if it was Jack?

She took the purse from the nightstand and checked her phone. APD, just as she'd suspected. She waited to see whether they'd leave a message.

The screen door gave a high rasp, then thudded quietly against the doorjamb. He was back, *finally*.

But what about his truck?

An icy bolt of fear shot through her as she realized she hadn't heard it. Every cell in her body froze, and she strained for sound.

Nothing.

Had she imagined the screen door? No way. She wanted to call Jack's name . . . but what if it wasn't him? What if it was a burglar who thought no one was here? Or an intruder who knew someone *was* here, alone and naked in this house?

She sprang out of the bed. She grabbed her purse and shoved her phone into it, beside the Ruger. Where were her clothes? She spotted something dark draped over a chair and snatched it up. Clutching everything to her chest, she tiptoed to the closet. The door stood ajar, and she squeezed inside.

The closet was crowded. She backed against some clothes and heard hangers scrape against the rack. She tried to stay still.

Who was here?

The house was silent, except for the pounding of her heart.

Had she *imagined* the sound? Was she *that* off kilter? She remembered her unfounded panic over that man in the convenience store. She took a deep breath and tried to think rationally. Everything was still. The closet smelled of fabric softener, and leather, and fresh dirt. She felt the toes of Jack's sneakers under her feet.

Creak.

Her pulse leaped. This was not her imagination. Someone was in the house with her, and she hadn't heard Jack's truck. She wrestled into the sweatshirt she'd grabbed off the chair and slid the Ruger from her purse.

Don't panic. Don't freak out. It could be Jack. Maybe someone had dropped him off down the road, and he was being quiet because he didn't want to wake her. Maybe it was Jack's neighbor or a friend. Or a niece or nephew sneaking around his house in the middle of the night. None of those explanations made sense, but—

Creak.

Oh, God. She tried to swallow, but her mouth was like parchment. Her lungs burned, and her heart pounded. She held the Ruger, pointed down, hoping like hell she wouldn't make a terrible mistake.

And then *squeak, slap*—the door slammed shut.

Her breath whooshed out. She stepped out of the closet, scurried to the window, and parted the blinds. The high-wattage security lights illuminated nothing but an empty field. She dashed across the room and tried another window. Emptiness.

In the far distance, she heard an engine growl to life. She ran from the bedroom to the opposite side of the house where the windows faced the highway, but she couldn't *see* anything. There were no headlights on the road. Her heart thudded wildly as the noise faded into nothing.

It was well after midnight before Nathan finally called it a day. It has been a hellacious tour, capped off with an hour-long stint downstairs as he called in a truckload of favors to have Fiona's sister cut loose from a vandalism rap. The task had been made easier by the fact that John D. Whosit, whose car she trashed, didn't want to press charges and wanted the incident kept quiet. What *hadn't* helped matters was Fiona's sister being drunk as a skunk and shouting obscenities at the guards while Nathan sweet-talked the jail supervisor.

Shit, what a night.

Nathan swung out of the parking lot and thought about home. He needed a pizza, and a Scotch, and some mindless television. He pulled up to a light and tried to remember the contents of his freezer.

The woman standing on the corner caught his attention. Courtney Glass. She was tall and slender, and wearing way too few clothes for the weather and the neighborhood. She sidled up to Sugar, the 250-pound hooker who frequented this corner, and struck up a conversation. Sugar reached between her humongous breasts and pulled out a lighter.

"Fuck," he muttered, and leaned over to roll down the passenger's-side window.

Courtney gave Sugar a cigarette, and the two lit up together like old pals.

"Hey," Nathan yelled, and Courtney turned around. "What do you think you're doing?"

She sashayed over on her mile-high heels. She looked steadier on her feet than she had an hour ago, but that wasn't saying much. She leaned a forearm on the window of his car, and Nathan tried not to stare down her shirt. She was Fiona's kid sister, for Christ's sake.

"What are you doing, Courtney?"

She sucked on her cigarette, blew out the smoke. "Waiting for the bus."

"You can't stand out here. It isn't safe."

"I'm four blocks from a police station."

"Get in the car."

She laughed then, a low throaty sound.

"I mean it."

She stood up and crossed her arms. "Thanks, but I'm fine."

"Like hell. It's thirty degrees out. You don't even have a coat."

She tossed a look over her shoulder at the bus stop where Sugar stood, advertising her wares. "Neither does she. She's doing all right."

"Courtney." His patience was slipping. "I'm trying to be nice here. For Fiona's sake. But I'm not going to tell you again." He leaned over and pushed open the door.

Courtney tossed her cigarette away, finally, and slid her tight little butt into the passenger's seat. She yanked the door shut, then leaned out the window. "Hey, Sug! You need a ride somewhere?"

Sugar flashed a smile and waved them off.

"This isn't a taxi service," he said, pulling away from the corner.

Courtney rolled her eyes. "Don't be a dickhead. She's nice."

"What, you two are friends now?"

She shrugged. "I met her in the holding cell. She's got three kids at home with her sick mother. Give her a break."

Nathan shook his head. He'd jumped through hoops of fire to get this girl released tonight, and by way of thanks she calls him a penis.

"Where to?" he asked.

"Lamar and Ninth."

"You live with Fiona?" This was news. Nathan hadn't even known Fiona had a sister before tonight, much less one who lived with her.

"It's only temporary."

Nathan hung a right and headed toward Fiona's loft in the trendy part of downtown.

Courtney ran a hand over the dashboard of his restored '66 Mustang and whistled her appreciation.

"You sure you're a cop?"

"Fifteen years."

She slid her hand over the upholstery, gave a little bounce. "This is *sweet*. My dad drove a piece-of-shit Pontiac."

"Your dad was a cop?"

Courtney fiddled with the radio. "San Antonio PD. Fiona never told you?"

Nathan knew Fiona had spent the early part of her childhood in Texas, but he'd had no idea her father had been on the job. It was an odd thing for her to have left out. Cops were a fraternity of sorts.

"She never mentioned it."

Courtney rolled her eyes. "Typical. She doesn't talk much about it. He was killed in the line of duty."

"I'm sorry."

"Thanks, but I barely knew him. My mom pulled up stakes and moved to California after it happened."

Nathan eyed Courtney as she scrolled through radio stations. She was a beautiful woman. Barely. She was twenty-six years old. Too young, he thought, to be dousing herself with all that makeup and hairspray. She'd look better with some decent clothes and less of that crap on her face. And tonight's detour into Inebriation Land hadn't helped. Both her knees were skinned, and her silky turquoise shirt was torn at the elbow.

He turned down the radio. "So what happened with the Carrera? You got something against imports?"

Nathan had figured out the situation on his own, but he

wanted to hear what she would say. To his surprise, she suddenly looked contrite.

"I don't know what I was thinking." She folded her hands in her lap. "I just—" She gazed out the window, and he hoped she wasn't going to turn on the waterworks. "I don't know. I was just mad. I hate being lied to."

Nathan shot her a sidelong glance. "You really didn't know he was married?"

She snorted. "I didn't even know his real name until today. He fed me this big story, and I bought the whole thing." She turned to look at him, and he noticed the mascara smears under her eyes. "Thanks for bailing me out."

"I didn't really bail you out. I got the charges to go away before you got too deep in the system. There's a difference."

Fiona's building came into view, and Nathan double-parked near the entrance. He went around to open Courtney's door. The Mustang was pretty low to the ground, and women had trouble getting out of it, especially in heels. He took her hand, getting an eyeful of her killer legs as she emerged. He looked away.

Fiona's neighborhood was quiet tonight. The street was empty except for a yuppie-looking guy out walking his Labrador.

Nathan accompanied Courtney to the door. "So Fiona's gone, I take it? She didn't answer her phone."

Courtney stopped. She folded her arms under her breasts and eyed him hotly. "I'm not going to screw you."

"Come again?"

"I appreciate the help tonight, but I'm not going to sleep with you."

Nathan stood there, stunned. "I never thought you would."

She tipped her head to the side, as if trying to gauge his honesty. Jesus Christ, she was serious.

"Well . . . good night." He took a step back from her and shoved his hands in his pockets. "Stay out of trouble. Leave the painting to your sister."

He turned and walked back to the Mustang, where he could wait for her to get in safely without making her uncomfortable.

"Nathan?"

He turned around. "Yeah?"

"Sorry I called you a dickhead."

"I've been called worse."

She smiled timidly. It didn't fit with the clothes or the attitude, but there it was. "Thanks for helping me," she said.

"Sure thing, kid. Hey, you know the difference between a porcupine and a Porsche?"

She gave him a wary look. "What?"

"A porcupine has pricks on the outside."

It took a second to register, and then she grinned and pulled open the door.

Jack left Lucy's in a sour mood. It felt pretty low to be sleeping with someone he'd hired to help work his ex-girlfriend's rape case. He knew it was bad. Hurtful. He never would have brought it up with Lucy, but she was good at reading him, always had been.

His phone buzzed from the console, and he saw his home number on caller ID. Damn it, he'd been gone over an hour.

"I'm on my way," he told Fiona.

"Where have you been? I called the station!"

Her voice sounded funny. "I was finishing up with Carlos. What's up?" He waited a beat. Then another. "Fiona? You there?"

"You've had a break-in."

"A *what*?"

"A break-in. It's where an intruder enters the premises and—"

"What happened? Are you hurt?"

"I'm fine."

"I'm five minutes away." Three if he floored it. He never should have left her alone. "Tell me what happened. Tell me everything. Are you sure you're all right?"

Jack pictured Hoyt Dixon kicking the door in, and his blood started to boil.

"I was in bed. After you left."

God, she'd been naked. He'd left her there naked and alone, and someone had broken in.

"I heard the door opening—"

"Which one?"

"The back."

"It was locked. How'd they get it open?" Jack hit a curve, and the truck skidded. He regained control.

"I don't know."

"Then what?"

"I hid in your closet. Then I heard a footstep. And then I heard the door squeak, and they were gone."

"That's it? That's all that happened?"

"That's it."

"Did they take anything?"

"I don't think so."

"Did they break anything?"

"I don't think so."

Okay. This was odd. "Any chance it wasn't the door you heard? Maybe you heard a gate slamming? Something outside?"

The silence stretched out. "It wasn't outside. It was the *back door*."

All right, so she was pissed. Couldn't be helped. He needed to understand what happened. He specifically remembered locking the back door.

"And then what?"

"Then I called the station," she said coolly. "And Carlos came over."

Carlos. *Shit*.

"Put him on."

Shit, shit, shit.

"J.B.? Where are you?"

"Is she really okay? Tell me straight."

"Seems fine to me."

"Any sign of forced entry?"

"Nope. Nothing."

"I don't get it."

He heaved a sigh. "Neither do I, Chief. Hold on."

Jack waited while Carlos exchanged some muffled words with Fiona.

"I gotta go, J.B. She needs a ride to her vehicle."

"Stall her."

"No can do. She really wants to go home."

"*Stall* her, will you? I'm almost there. Fill out a report or something." She was pissed, and in typical Fiona fashion, she was taking off.

"We done that already. I can't keep the lady against her will, and I can tell you right now, her will is to leave. I don't know what you done, but she's out the door already, waiting by the unit."

"Just . . . drive slow. I'll try and catch her at her car."

Ten minutes and about a hundred moving violations later, Jack squealed into the parking lot of the Grainger County Administrative Building. Fiona was tossing her art case into the backseat of her Honda, and Carlos looked to be doing his damnedest to slow her down. He stood beside the hybrid, probably making inane small talk as she climbed into the car. She shot Jack an icy look as he pulled up beside her and hopped out.

"Thanks, Carlos," he said. "I can handle it from here."

Carlos raised an eyebrow in a clear vote of no confidence and got back in his car.

Jack caught Fiona's door just as she was pulling it closed. "Hold on. I want to hear what happened."

"Read the report." She started the engine. "Carlos was very thorough. No sign of forced entry. No footprints. No tire marks. Nothing stolen. Nothing broken. I must have imagined it."

She tugged the door, and Jack blocked it. He crouched down next to her, and she looked straight out the windshield.

"I'm sorry I wasn't there."

"That's okay. You were working, obviously. With Carlos."

"Talk to me. I want to understand what happened."

She put the car in gear. "I repeat: read the report. Now do you mind? I've had a long day, and I could really use some sleep tonight."

She wouldn't look at him. He crouched there, right beside her, and she wouldn't even make eye contact. He saw the slight quiver in her chin as she fought with her emotions. Shit, she'd been alone and frightened of something— he didn't really know for sure what. And then he'd lied to her and questioned her credibility.

"I'm sorry you were scared."

She still wouldn't look at him. A single tear slid down her cheek. He reached up to wipe it away, and she cringed.

"Come home. We'll talk about it."

"It's not my home, Jack." Finally she looked at him. "And I don't want to talk to you."

CHAPTER
16

The white hybrid Jack spotted on the way into work could belong to only one person. He swerved into the parking lot of Lorraine's Diner and elbowed his way through her breakfast crowd until he sighted Fiona seated way at the back. She wore the beige suit from yesterday, and her hair pulled back in a tight ponytail. She glanced up as Jack neared her table. Her face remained neutral, but she shifted her art case to the space beside her.

He slid into the vinyl bench across from her. "Thought you went back to Austin."

"Evidently I didn't."

"Where'd you sleep last night?"

"The motel." She gazed down at her menu. "I'm leaving shortly, though. I'd hoped to meet with Brady this morning, but it's not going to work out. His mom says he's got a stomach virus."

"Can I get y'all some coffee?"

Jack looked up at the waitress. "That'd be great, thanks. And two eggs, sunny-side up. Side of sausage." Jack gave Fiona a look that said, *Tough luck, babe. You're gonna have to talk to me.*

She sighed. "Coffee, please," she told the waitress. "And toast."

Jack watched the armor come up. She filed her menu away behind the napkin dispenser, squared her shoulders, and tipped her chin up. She knew he'd stopped by here to corner her.

"I shouldn't have lied to you."

"It's immaterial."

He leaned back against the booth. "You always talk like a lawyer when you're upset?"

"I'm not upset."

The coffee arrived, and Jack watched as she added creamer, delicately peeling back the foil lids of the containers and meticulously stacking them off to the side when she was through. He downed a sip of his strong black coffee and decided to change tactics.

"I was at Lucy's," he said. "She had a disturbance at her house and wanted me to come see about it."

"Interesting. Why didn't you just tell me that?"

"I didn't think you'd understand."

"I understand completely. Who else would she call to check out her disturbances in the middle of the night? There's no reason to lie about it, as if there's something to cover up."

Jack was pretty sure there were several layers of meaning to what she'd just said, but he was running on very little sleep and didn't feel up to analyzing it.

"What was Lucy's disturbance?" she asked.

Jack paused a moment, then decided to go with honesty. "She says she saw someone sneaking around her place last night."

Her eyebrows tipped up. "Did he try to break in?"

"Nope."

"Did *you* see him?"

"Nope."

She pursed her lips. "Two delusional women in one night. Must be something in the water."

"I didn't say she was delusional. I don't think *you're* delusional. I just don't understand what happened. I know I locked the door, so I don't see how someone could have just walked in."

"When did you lock it?"

"Huh?"

"The door. *When* did you lock it? You left twice, remember? Once to get my stuff out of your truck and once to go to Lucy's."

Jack's shoulders tensed as he realized what she was saying. She thought he'd been careless. She thought he'd left her alone in an unlocked house while he'd rushed off to see about Lucy. That's not how he remembered it, but he had to admit it was possible. He'd been half asleep and in a hurry.

"You think the incidents are related," he stated.

"I don't know. Do you?"

"I don't know." Sebastian's "shadow man" could be anybody, but Jack didn't like the timing. He felt grateful now that Fiona was going back to Austin.

Their food arrived, and Fiona tore her triangle of toast in half. She buttered it with polite little swipes of her knife. She looked so cool and prim, and suddenly he remembered the way she'd looked, bare-breasted and flushed, in his lap yesterday. And then underneath him in his bed.

"I'm coming to Austin," he said. "I want to see you again."

She nibbled her toast. Swallowed. Took a sip of coffee. "When are you coming?"

"When are you available?"

That got her. She didn't like the label, and her eyes sparked. "I'm not. I told you before, I've got a gallery showing—"

"I want a do-over." He gave her a hot, lingering look that conveyed the kind of do-over he had in mind. He needed time—much more time—to show her he wasn't the man she'd seen last night. Last night he'd lied, and been insensitive, and been much too quick on the trigger. That wasn't the real him, and it was important that she know it.

He *needed* her to know it.

Her hands fluttered over her toast, and he could tell he'd made her uncomfortable.

"I don't think that's a good idea," she said.

"Why not?"

"Because. This isn't going anywhere, and I'm not good at casual sex."

"You were great last night."

Her cheeks reddened, and the freckles on her nose stood out.

"I hope I'm not interrupting."

They glanced up to see Agent Santos standing a few feet from their table. He had a gray trench coat draped over his arm and was holding one of Lorraine's to-go cups. "Mind if I . . . ?"

"Certainly." Fiona moved her art case out of the way and scooted over to make room for him beside her. Jack gritted his teeth as the agent slid right in.

"When is your interview?" Santos asked her.

"It's canceled. He has a stomach virus. Or so his mother says."

Santos's brow furrowed. He took a sip of his coffee, but didn't say anything. Then he looked at Jack, reached over the table, and offered a hand. "Ray Santos, FBI."

Jack shook his hand. "Jack Bowman, Graingerville PD."

"I know."

"Any word on those lab results?" Jack asked him.

"So far, no match."

"Match for what?" Fiona asked.

"The DNA evidence recovered from Natalie Fuentes," Jack provided. "We were hoping he might already be in the database."

"He's not," Santos said. "But that isn't necessarily conclusive because we've got backlogs you wouldn't believe. There're tens of thousands of samples out there, just haven't been entered yet."

Jack shook his head.

"Blame the politicians," Santos said. "Our labs can't keep up with all the new laws on the books."

"What about prints?" Jack asked. "You run them through IAFIS?"

Fiona's eyebrows snapped together. "You have fingerprints? From where?"

"Marissa's car," Jack told her. He exchanged a look with Santos that said Fiona was in the loop. Yes, she was an outside consultant, but she could be trusted.

"Marissa's blood was found in her car," Santos said in a low voice. The booth behind them was empty, but Lorraine was busy this morning. "We also found prints from a thumb and index finger on the rearview mirror, also in Marissa's blood."

"So he got in her car, adjusted her mirror, and *drove* her somewhere?" Fiona asked.

"Most likely," Jack said. "Why else adjust the mirror? But he wouldn't have gotten far on a bad tire. He probably just pulled the car farther off the road than it was originally. We found it at a bend in the highway, near some trees."

"The prints aren't consistent with the victim's," Santos said. "So we believe they belong to her abductor, that he got blood on his hands when he subdued her with force, possibly a blow to the head. We were expecting the prints to tell us something, but so far that hasn't been the case."

Jack shook his head. "And you got a thumbprint? That's what the sheriff said."

"That's correct."

Fiona's gaze moved from one investigator to the other, and Jack could see her following the logic. "That print should be in the DPS database," she said. "If this man has a Texas license, you should have a record of him."

"You'd think," Jack said. "So maybe he's from out of state—which I don't believe, personally—or he doesn't mind operating a vehicle without a license. My money's on the second one."

Santos leaned forward, resting his elbows on the table. "You sound like you're working a theory. What is it?"

Jack watched him a moment. He'd expected to hate this guy, but so far, he was okay. He was soliciting help from the locals, which Jack approved of, and he wasn't walking around with a monster ego. Jack was still waiting for some psychobabble.

"I think he's local," Jack said. "For a lot of reasons, many which have to do with an unsolved rape case we've got from more than a decade ago."

"Maria Luz Arrellando." Santos nodded. "I read the report. And you think they're connected because of the MO? The cordage?"

"That and some other things. The victimology."

Santos cocked his head to the side. He was listening, at least seemingly, with an open mind. Jack found this remarkable because he knew Randy and his father-in-law had been working hard lately to make the Graingerville police chief into something of a pariah. They didn't want Jack horning in on their publicity.

"I think we've got a loner," Jack continued. "A white supremacist type who probably doesn't have much use for the government. This guy's not going to stand in line and pay a fee to be fingerprinted and granted a license so he can move around freely—something he believes is his God-given right. I think he's local, because of his familiarity with the land and the roads around here. I think he knows just where to pick up his victims, just where to take them to stay out of sight. But he's got to be a hermit, or else somebody would have recognized him from Fiona's picture by now. It's a good drawing. She's the best in the business."

Fiona glanced at him, obviously startled by the compliment.

"Agreed," Santos said, looking at Fiona. "Your drawings are always right on the mark."

She looked down, clearly uncomfortable with the praise. Jack didn't understand how a woman with her gift could be so modest.

"I think he chooses his victims carefully, and that he stalks them first." Jack watched Fiona's reaction. If his words spooked her, she didn't let on. "Once he knows who he wants, for whatever reason, I think he lies in wait, like he probably did with Maria Luz. Or he uses some scam, like the flat tire, to get the victim in a vulnerable position. I suspect if we ever find Natalie's car, we'll find evidence she ran into some sort of trouble that led to her abduction."

Santos nodded. "So you believe he's smart and organized."

"Don't you?"

"The evidence seems to point that way. And he's not using the victim's car, that we know. It was a Hyundai Elantra, right? That's not consistent with the tread marks from the crime scenes."

"That's right," Jack said. "I think he has his own vehicle. Maybe more than one. I think he has his own base of operations. Maybe more than one. And I think he's escalating. I think it's no accident he picked a politician's daughter, a Latina. I think it's part of his message. I haven't figured out the weather thing yet."

"The weather?" Santos asked.

"All the victims went missing during a cold snap. Temperatures in the twenties or lower."

The agent nodded, and Jack felt faintly smug that he'd picked up something the FBI hadn't, even if he had no idea what it meant.

Jack didn't share the rest of what he was thinking. He didn't tell Fiona he suspected the man skulking around the Arrellandos' last night and the person who had somehow entered his house was their guy. And that if he was on the prowl again, that did not bode well for Marissa Pico.

Santos leaned back against the booth and looked pensive. Jack locked gazes with Fiona. His analysis seemed to come as a surprise to her, and Jack bit back a sarcastic comment. Hell, he'd been on this case for two weeks—eleven years and two weeks if you counted Lucy's attack. Did she think he hadn't developed a profile of the subject by now? Jack didn't need a fancy degree or a stint at Quantico to be a good detective. It was what he did. It was what he excelled at. And just because his current job came with a big title didn't mean he'd forgotten how to roll up his sleeves and work a case.

"We've been channeling a lot of resources into domestic terrorism, both foreign and home-grown," Santos said.

" 'We' meaning the FBI?" Jack asked.

"And Homeland Security. There's been increased activity from a number of hate groups in the Southwest lately. I'll see if we've got our eye on anyone in particular who lives close to here."

"You've infiltrated the groups," Jack stated, not bothering to conceal his skepticism.

"Some. The agencies vary, but there are people working undercover. I'll see what I can find out."

Jack shook his head, wishing the FBI had been involved weeks ago. Amazing the resources that could be brought to bear when someone rich and powerful got involved.

"I agree with the hate-crime angle, but I'm not sure it's completely about race," Santos continued. "I think there's more to his motive."

"Such as?" Jack asked.

"These crimes are up close and personal. They demonstrate a high degree of emotion. Maybe he picks his victims because of race, but I think there has to be more behind his rage. I think there's some personal element to it that we're missing. His MO says he's conflicted about these women."

"Yeah, well, maybe someone can write a thesis about him someday," Jack said. "Me, I'd mainly like to catch him."

Santos didn't acknowledge the jab. He reached into his suit jacket and pulled out his cell phone, which had started to ring. "Excuse me," he said, sliding out of the booth. "I need to take this."

When he was gone, Jack stared at Fiona. He felt both relieved and frustrated that she was going back to Austin soon.

"Well." She took out her wallet and placed some bills on the table. "I think I'll try Brady one more time before I go. See if he's feeling better."

She rummaged through her purse and then her art case, purposely avoiding Jack's gaze.

"I meant what I said about coming to Austin. As soon as I can get away."

"Where is my phone?" she muttered, jerking a sketch pad out of her case and slapping it on the table. "I swear I just had it."

"Fiona."

She pulled out a pencil case, frowning when her hand got tangled up in some black string. "What in the world . . . ?"

Jack watched her untangling the string and noticed the dried black substance and the green peeking through in places. His stomach fell out.

"Stop," he ordered.

She pulled at the twine, and he clamped a hand over her wrist. "*Stop*, goddamn it!"

Santos was back at the table again, jabbering about something, as Jack stared at the blood-stiffened twine tangled around Fiona's hand. The sick fuck had put it in her art case.

Jack looked up at Santos and finally tuned in to what he was saying. Something about Marissa Pico. Something about a body—

"We've got a crime scene unit heading over there right now. You want to ride with me?" The agent frowned down at Fiona's hand. "What's all that?"

"Souvenir," Jack said. "It's from him."

When they arrived at Rancho Pico, the crime scene technicians were already there.

"Body was reported by a deliveryman," Santos told Jack, parking his car on the shoulder of the highway. "He'd just dropped off a shipment of tractor parts when he saw it from his truck. Called the sheriff's office on his mobile phone."

The scene was being guarded by a uniform from Randy's office, while another sheriff's deputy set up orange and white blockades just inside the entrance to the ranch. Jack glanced at everyone else milling around, but didn't see a single familiar face.

Santos picked his way over the cattle guard in his shiny black shoes. He flashed his credentials at the guard and proceeded down the gravel road. Jack tossed Randy's guy a scowl as he followed the agent, paying close attention to the tracks marring the muddy road. It was a damp morning, and the possibility existed of recovering tire imprints.

A woman in a white jumpsuit approached Santos. She wore latex gloves, and two of her fingertips were smeared with blood.

"We've got a brunette female of undetermined age. Multiple stab wounds to the chest. Mutilation to the hands and feet."

Santos glanced at Jack, and he suspected the agent was thinking the same thing he was—that their man had altered his routine.

Santos followed the woman to a clump of trees just inside the ranch's entrance. The body was lying in a ditch between the road and the barbed-wire fence. Even from a distance, Jack could see this was a clear case of overkill. The victim had been beaten severely about the face, making her unrecognizable. The stab wounds didn't appear to have bled very much, and Jack guessed they had been inflicted postmortem, but the ME could determine that for sure. Jack assumed this was a strangling, but the severity of the injuries made it impossible for him to tell at a glance.

"He's escalating," Santos said, and pulled a phone out of his pocket.

Suddenly the *whip, whip* of a chopper drew near, and the ground around them began to swirl with leaves and debris. Jack looked up to see a helicopter descending to hover just above the crime scene, kicking up just about every scrap of evidence they might have hoped to find on or around the body.

Jack turned to Santos. "Did you leak this?"

The agent scowled up at the network logo on the side of the chopper. "No." Then he glanced over Jack's shoulder. "You might want to ask your sheriff."

Jack spun around and saw Randy Rudd standing in front of the barricade, gesturing dramatically and talking to a reporter and cameraman. A white news van was parked haphazardly on the side of the highway, and another bar-reled down the road toward them. In a matter of moments, this place would be a total zoo.

"Anyone talked to the Picos yet?" Jack demanded.

"No."

Jack strode past the barricade and shouldered Randy out of the way. "Is that your chopper?"

The bright-eyed reporter looked startled, and then gazed up at the helicopter in question. "It's Channel Six," she said. "We're Thirteen."

Jack made a note of which station to call and raise holy hell. "We have no comment at this time," he snapped. "Now get your ass off this property, or I'll have you arrested."

The reporter's jaw dropped. Then she seemed to recover, and gave her cameraman a quick glance to see if he'd caught it on film.

"Now, just wait a minute—"

Jack whirled around. "We've got a crime scene to pre-serve. You mind if we do some police work here, 'stead of strutting for the cameras?"

Randy's face turned beet red, and Jack glanced past him just in time to see Bob Spivey climbing out of his silver Cadillac and strolling up to the barricade. Jack took in the scene: the mayor, the sheriff, a cluster of police vehicles with the wrought-iron Rancho Pico arch stretched over it all, like a perfect set for an episode of *CSI: Texas*. Jack wanted to throttle someone.

He picked Spivey. "Your brain-dead son-in-law's hold-ing a press conference, and we haven't even removed the body yet! You've got the Pico ranch on camera, and they haven't even been notified!"

"Calm down." The mayor glanced nervously over Jack's shoulder, and Jack knew someone was filming.

"Who called the media, Bob? Was it you? Was it him?" Jack thrust a finger at Randy, who had resumed his performance in front of a steadily increasing number of TV reporters. "Do you realize the complications this creates for investigators? For the prosecution team down the road? We've got evidence flying all over creation while your son-in-law's up there giving sound bites. He's one helluva lawman." As Jack said this, a black Range Rover skidded to a halt just inside the gates, and a man in a blue tracksuit jumped out and ran toward the forensic techs huddled around the body. Senator Pico. Good God Almighty, and the cameras were rolling. Agent Santos intercepted the man and held him by the shoulders as he squealed like a stuck pig.

"This is a disgrace." Jack glared at the mayor. "You make me sick."

"You're fired, Jack."

"*What?*"

"You're off the case and off the job."

It hit him like a sucker punch. "You can't fire me. I was hired by the city council!"

Spivey's eyes blazed with triumph. "Take a look at the Graingerville Municipal Code, Article Twelve, Section Three. I *can* fire you, and I *am* firing you." He straightened his hat and dusted his lapel. "Have your badge and your gun on my desk by the end of today."

CHAPTER
17

The break sounded like rifle fire.

Two solids dropped, and Jack watched with satisfaction as a third ricocheted off the cushion and rolled into the pocket closest to Nathan. It felt good to smack the hell out of something, even if it wasn't Randy Rudd. Jack studied the table, then leaned over and took a combination shot that sank the one and the seven.

"I need another drink." Nathan rested his empty bottle on a nearby table and signaled the waitress.

Jack botched his next shot and swore as Nathan took aim at the twelve, which had been an outright gift. He sank it just as the drinks arrived.

"Here's to shit jobs, and being rid of them," Nathan said, raising his bottle. "That Mayberry gig never suited you anyway."

Jack scowled. He'd never considered being chief of police a shit job, but Nathan was just trying to spin it. He'd been doing his best to snap Jack out of his black mood for the past hour.

Nathan was playing second fiddle tonight, and he knew it, but he was too good a friend to give him crap about it on this particular occasion. Jack had driven to Austin to see Fiona and had been more than a little pissed when her door—like her phone—went unanswered after repeated attempts. So he'd called Nathan, deciding if he couldn't console himself with a warm, soft woman, he could do it whipping his friend's ass at pool.

Or maybe not. Nathan pulled off a jump shot, and Jack cursed.

Nathan leaned down again and sent him a look. "Thought I'd throw the game just to cheer you up?"

"That was dumb luck."

By way of retort, he sank another stripe. He eyed Jack smugly as he chalked his cue. "Where is she tonight?"

Jack didn't pretend to misunderstand. He never talked about his sex life, but some things Nathan just knew.

"Out." Jack swilled his beer.

"She's a nice woman. Watch your step, though, or she'll send you packing."

Jack fumed from the corner. It felt like she'd already sent him. And he should be grateful, really. Hot sex, he wanted. Relationship headaches, he did not need.

What he needed right now was a job.

Nathan rounded the table, studying the layout. "You met her sister yet?"

"Yeah. She's a babe."

Nathan lined up his shot. "She's a train wreck."

"That, too."

The fourteen glided into the corner pocket nearest Jack.

"I spent some time with her the other night," Nathan said. "She told me their old man was on the job in San Antonio. Got killed responding to a liquor store holdup. I looked up the incident."

Jack frowned. "Fiona never mentioned it."

"Not much of a talker."

Jack stared at the table, subconsciously strategizing about the game as he processed this new information. Fiona's father had been a cop. In Texas. Several pieces of the Fiona puzzle fell into place, and Jack felt relieved for some reason.

Fiona rarely talked about her parents. From a few offhand comments, he'd gathered that her mom had a drinking problem and that they weren't close. The only male relative she ever mentioned was her grandfather.

Jack watched his friend, who had been a colleague and mentor to Fiona for two years. They'd worked on some grueling cases together, Jack knew, and Nathan had probably seen her with her guard down.

Jack cleared his throat. "You ever wonder why she's so good at what she does? Rape vics and kids?"

He glanced up from the table, catching Jack's meaning. Jack let it hang there in case Nathan was struggling with some sort of ethical dilemma.

"It's crossed my mind. She's never told me anything, though." Nathan took a cross-bank shot at the eleven, but it petered out shy of the pocket. "You're the detective. Go find out."

Jack scoffed. He wasn't a detective anymore. He wasn't even a cop anymore, and they both knew it.

Jack took aim at the three, but put too much power behind it and scratched.

"Fuck." He looked up to see Nathan watching with annoyance. "What?"

"You're not really quitting, are you?"

"I don't have a choice."

"Bullshit." Nathan took control of the table, systematically clearing the remaining stripes as Jack's blood pressure elevated. He shouldn't have come here. He'd known exactly what sort of advice he'd get by hanging out with Nathan tonight.

"You think I should ask for my job back."

Nathan squinted at the eight. Shook his head.

"Then what?"

"You know what. Left corner." He tapped the cue ball, and the eight tumbled into the corner pocket. Nathan straightened away from the table. He gave Jack the cut-the-crap look that had always reminded him of his father. "You're a homicide dick, Jack. Always have been. Don't give up now, not when you're this close."

Jack stared down at the table, knowing Nathan was right. The bitch of it was, though, he didn't know what to do about it. He was a detective without a case. He didn't even have a *badge*, for fuck's sake. How was he supposed to apprehend a serial killer? It was the single most important case of his career, and he'd failed. Completely.

Jack drained his beer.

"Go find Fiona," Nathan said. "She'll tell you the same thing."

Another thrashing at the pool table didn't improve Jack's mood. Fiona wasn't home. She wouldn't answer her phone. He'd lost forty bucks to Nathan and another twenty at the bar. Jack made one last attempt to track her down at her apartment, but no one was there. He'd just decided to head back to Graingerville when he passed an Exxon station on Lamar Street and did a double take. Pulled up to one of the pumps was a white Honda and, beside it, a familiar redhead.

Jack made a quick U-turn and swerved into the lot just as she was lighting a cigarette. He walked up to her from behind. "Not a smart place to light up."

Courtney jumped and whirled around.

"Shit!" She clasped her hand to her chest. "Why do you keep *doing* that?"

"What?"

"Sneaking up on me!" She stuffed a lighter into her pocket. She wore a knee-length black trench coat and a pair of shoes that looked painful.

"You seen Fiona?"

"No." She spun around and jerked the nozzle free, then slammed it back into place when she realized she'd forgotten to pop the gas cap. With a huff, she leaned back into the car.

Jack pulled out his wallet and swiped a credit card. Then he inserted the nozzle and leaned against the door to watch the numbers scroll.

Courtney took a drag of her cigarette. Her nails were painted bright white at the tips. "I have a credit card for that."

"Oh yeah? Is it yours or Fiona's?"

She crossed her arms, clearly annoyed that he had her number. Jack had younger sisters, too. He watched the gallons add up.

Courtney dropped her cigarette onto the concrete and snuffed it out with the toe of her shoe. "She wouldn't want you doing that. She's very *liberated* that way."

He shrugged. "I figure I owe her a few tanks of gas. She's

been driving back and forth to Graingerville to help me with my case."

Courtney licked her lips. After a few moments looking him up and down, she swayed closer. Jack couldn't tell what, if anything, she had on under that trench coat, and he suspected that was the point.

"Fiona's busy tonight," she purred, hooking her fingers in the pocket of his jacket. "You could hang out with me, though."

He gazed down at her. She'd done something with her makeup, and her eyes reminded him of a cat's. She shifted her body, brushing his thigh with hers.

"Knock it off, Courtney. Where is she?"

She dropped the coy look and stepped back. "She's busy."

"So you said." Jack reached for the squeegee and dragged it over Fiona's dirty windshield. Her car looked like it had been on a cross-country road trip. "You know *where* she's busy? Or when she's getting home?" It wasn't lost on him that if Courtney was driving her car, she had to have another mode of transportation. Maybe she was on a date.

Jack yanked the squeegee across the glass a few more times, trying not to let the thought of Fiona out with another man bother him. It was totally fine. They didn't have a relationship, really. He didn't know what they had.

"You really want to know where to find her?"

"Yes." He jammed the squeegee back in the holder. Something mischievous flickered in Courtney's eyes, and he knew she was up to something.

Or Fiona was up to something.

"Spill it. We're freezing our tails off here."

She smiled. "Well, I don't know for *sure*, but it's a good bet you'll find her at the Continental Club."

Fiona loathed the Continental Club. It was loud and crowded and filled with people in faux grunge. She'd come here on a mission, and as soon as she accomplished it, she intended to leave.

A guitar whined. Fiona sat at the bar, nursing a whiskey sour and wishing the alt-country singer at the microphone would wrap up his set. Aaron had a fairly decent voice and looks that could have sold magazines. But the tattered cowboy hat and three-day stubble were just a bit over the top for Fiona's tastes.

She stirred her drink. Going out tonight had been a mistake. She wasn't up for the music scene right now, not when every one of her thoughts was consumed with work. Or Jack. Or working with Jack. All week she'd tried to focus on other things, but her mind kept returning to Graingerville. She wondered how the investigation was going. She wondered how the Picos were doing. She wondered if she'd ever see Jack again, or if he'd buried himself in his case, intending to forget about her.

She'd tried to forget about *him* by retreating to her studio. She'd spent hours with her paints and brushes until she was ready to collapse. But her normal escape route hadn't worked this time, and her thoughts kept covering the same ground.

The bartender stopped by to check her drink. Fiona smiled and tried to muster some conversation. It was no use. She didn't feel like chitchat. She checked her watch and then cast an impatient glance toward the stage.

"Tell me you didn't ruin that bourbon with fruit juice."

Fiona jerked her head around. Jack leaned against the bar, watching her.

"What are you doing here?"

"Just catching the show."

He wore Levi's, and his scarred leather jacket and boots that had probably stepped in many more cow patties than the ones worn by the man crooning into the mic.

This was going to be ugly.

"How'd you find me?"

The muscle in his jaw twitched. "I'm an ace detective."

She looked at him closely. Something was wrong. She hoped to God it wasn't another missing girl.

"What're you drinking?" He eyed her glass, and then his gaze slid to the half-empty beer bottle just a few inches away from it.

"Whiskey sour."

He winced.

"What?"

"Somebody needs to teach you how to drink." He flagged the bartender. "Jack Daniel's. Straight up."

Fiona stole a glance at the stage where Aaron was alternating among the three guitar chords in his repertoire. He caught her eye over the heads of the other patrons and then fixed his attention on Jack.

She needed to get out of here.

The bartender delivered the bourbon. Jack tossed back a sip, then offered it to Fiona. "See? No need to mix it with lemonade."

"Really, Jack, how'd you know I was here?"

"Bumped into Courtney." He turned to face the club.

His stance was relaxed, but he seemed tense. He was scanning the crowd, possibly for the owner of the half-finished Heineken. He glanced down at her legs. "Those are nice boots. You look good tonight."

Fiona gulped her drink. She was on her second whiskey sour, which had helped make the past hour bearable. Seeing her ex tonight had pushed her to the limit.

And now she had Jack to deal with. Quickly. Before this song ended. She reached for his drink and took a sip. It scalded its way down her throat and set fire to her stomach. She could *not* tolerate this stuff straight.

He watched her, and she caught it again—that hard glint in his eyes.

"What's wrong?" she asked.

"Nothing."

"You drove all the way up here just to see me? In the midst of your homicide investigation?"

He looked away. His gaze paused on Aaron, who was watching their exchange as he muddled through the last few bars of his song. Jack looked back at Fiona.

"It's not my investigation anymore. I got canned yesterday."

"You got . . . *what?*"

"Fired."

Fiona studied his face and realized he was telling the truth. This wasn't a joke. "But . . . but who's going to take over the case?"

He shrugged. "The sheriff, I guess. It's his anyway."

"But . . ." Fiona's throat tightened. "That guy's an idiot! He'll never figure it out. And if he does, he's sure to botch it up."

Jack turned to face the man approaching them from across the room. "Your friend's back," he said.

Oh, God.

Aaron stopped in front of Fiona and crossed his arms. He looked like a petulant child—which he was, really—and Fiona couldn't believe she'd dated him for more than a year. So much for her attempt to break her cop habit with someone "artsy." She watched Jack and Aaron taking each other's measure and wondered what Jack would say if she told him she'd slept with someone who habitually borrowed her eyelash curler.

"Jack Bowman, meet Aaron Rhodes." She grabbed her purse and fished out a twenty. "Aaron, we were just leaving."

Jack extended a hand, and Aaron, being Aaron, responded with a half-assed squeeze.

Fiona's pulse skittered. It was amazing, seeing them together like this. It made everything so *clear*. She picked up her glass and poured the last sip of whiskey sour down her throat. God. Oh, hell. *When* had she gone and fallen in love with Jack Bowman?

Aaron looked at her. "I thought we were having a drink later."

"No, you had your ears turned off again." Fiona put her money on the bar and held out her hand, palm up. "I'm leaving."

Aaron's eyes narrowed. If Jack hadn't been standing there, he probably would have called her a bitch. And she probably would have let it go because she was *that* determined not to let him get a rise out of her ever again.

Aaron reached into the pocket of his artfully torn jeans and yanked out a key chain. He shook his head as he pulled off her apartment key and slapped it onto her palm.

Fiona dropped it into her purse. Then she pushed her way through the crowd and escaped out the door. The cold air lashed her cheeks, and she suddenly remembered her coat, draped over the bar stool. She turned on her heel and saw Jack walking behind her, the coat bunched under his arm. He stopped beside her. Without saying anything, he held the coat up and helped her into it.

"Thank you."

They started down the sidewalk. Fiona focused on the cracks in the pavement. She was in her stiletto boots tonight, and it wouldn't do to catch a heel.

Jack shoved his hands into his pockets. "Are you sleeping with him?"

"That's not your business."

"If you're sleeping with me, it is."

She stopped beside him. "Is this it? Are we having the relationship talk now? I'm not sure you want to do this tonight, because I'm tipsy, and you look mad enough to hit something."

He glanced away from her. Then he looked down at his boots and took a deep breath.

"Fuck." He raked his hands through his hair, then glanced up, apologetic. "Sorry. It's been a shit week."

The anger inside her softened. "Did you really get fired?"

"I really did."

"What are you going to do?"

"I have no fucking idea."

She could see him fighting to rein in his emotions. It had to be humiliating, getting fired from a job in your own hometown. Especially a town as small as Graingerville, where gossip was served up like iced tea at every meal. And what would he do now? He'd been a cop all his adult life. It went beyond a livelihood for him. It was his identity.

Her father had been the same way. Fiona had been young, but she remembered. Vividly. The job had meant everything to him, even more than his family.

"Aaron and I are over," she told him. "I just came by to get my key."

Jack nodded. "Good."

They started walking again. She wanted to ask him about Lucy. She wanted to know if he still loved her, if they still had a sexual relationship. But she couldn't bring herself to do it. It would hurt too much if he lied to her again.

"You got your Ruger with you?" Jack nodded at her purse.

"Yes. Why?"

"I think our guy sticks to his comfort zone, but I don't like his interest in you." He stopped and turned to face her. "Keep your gun with you. Always. And don't go out alone."

Apparently, Jack didn't realize the twine incident had terrified her.

"If you're trying to scare me, don't bother," she said. "The FBI still has my art case. Santos says the blood on the twine in it belonged to Marissa. He thinks the killer planted it there to intimidate investigators. It worked. I'm intimidated."

"You need to be vigilant," Jack said sternly.

"I am."

They resumed their pace, and she saw him glancing at her shoes again. "What's your sister doing tonight?" he asked.

"You tell me."

"Last I saw her, she was stocking up on beer and snacks with your gas card."

Fiona closed her eyes and sighed. She never should have let Courtney move in, but she'd been powerless to say no. It was always like that. The more trouble Courtney got in, the more Fiona felt responsible.

"Why do you let her walk all over you?" Jack asked. "Just kick her out if she's driving you nuts."

"It's complicated."

"She said something about going to Jordan's." He stopped and tugged her around to face him. He brushed a lock of hair from her shoulder. "Does that mean she's gone for the night? Because I really, *really* want to get you alone."

Her stomach fluttered as she looked up at him. What was she doing, letting herself feel like this? Maybe it was the whiskey. Or maybe it was the man.

"That's probably not a good idea."

He pulled her against him, and she nestled into the warmth of his chest. Definitely the man.

"It's a great idea." He kissed the top of her head. "Come on, I'll show you."

Sullivan crouched down beside the burgundy Mercury Cougar and peeled back the tarp. Keith Janovic stared up at him with empty eyes.

"Two to the chest?" Sullivan asked the officer in charge.

"That's right."

The lights on the nearby patrol car gave Janovic's skin a freakish hue—red, blue, red, blue. The colors coupled with the wide-eyed stare made him look like some morbid cartoon, almost animated.

But the man sprawled out on the frontage road was very dead. And whatever knowledge he'd had stored in his twisted brain would go with him to the grave.

Sullivan stood up. It was a miserable ending to a miserable case. Annie Sherwood had spent nearly three weeks agonizing over her daughter's whereabouts, and now the one person who could have brought her closure was gone.

"How's the patrolman?" Sullivan asked, referring to the cop who had pulled Janovic over on a bad taillight.

"Made it to the ER," the officer reported. "He's in surgery now. We're waiting to hear."

A seemingly routine traffic stop had gone awry when the officer had asked for a driver's license and then turned to take it back to his vehicle. Janovic had climbed out of the Mercury and pulled a gun, resulting in the exchange that left Janovic dead and the cop severely wounded.

No such thing as a routine traffic stop.

Sullivan peered inside the car, which had already been searched for clues. Several had been found, including a girl's hair band beneath the front seat and a disturbingly large bloodstain on the carpet lining the trunk.

Like the other silent, stone-faced cops working the scene tonight, Sullivan knew that the blood likely belonged to Shelby.

The door of the vehicle stood open. It had a gray cloth interior, with trash and newspapers littering the floorboards. Sullivan reached a gloved hand inside and carefully picked up the McDonald's bag sitting on the passenger's seat. Thirty minutes ago, he'd been coming off a twelve-hour shift with no break. He'd been ravenous. Now just glancing at the half-eaten burger inside the bag made his stomach lurch.

"Interesting order," he said.

"What's that?" The cop walked over and shone a flashlight into the bag.

"Big Mac. Large Coca-Cola. Two medium fries."

"Yeah, so?"

Sullivan looked up. "What's the largest size available at Mickey D's?"

The officer shrugged. "Hell if I know. My wife never lets me eat there. Hypertension." He patted his gut.

"You see *Supersize Me*?"

The officer stared at him blankly.

Sullivan replaced the bag on the passenger's seat and stepped away from the car.

Eighteen days.

It had been eighteen days since anyone had seen Shelby Sherwood alive. A week ago Janovic had paid cash for a motel room in Meridian, Mississippi. The next day his face had been all over the news, and he'd skipped town. Every witness account had him driving a burgundy sedan and traveling alone. Janovic's last known cell phone call had been to a personal psychic three days ago. It was picked up by a cell tower in Shreveport.

Sullivan crunched across the gravel and stepped into the grass. He smelled pinesap from the towering trees lining the highway, a two-lane road that snaked south from Shreveport through eastern Louisiana. Had Janovic been heading for Mexico? The coast? Sullivan didn't like the combination of a child predator and several million acres of swampland.

He wondered whether the perp had picked Louisiana, or if he was just passing through.

So many questions remained, but the one concerning his location had finally been answered.

Sullivan pulled his cell phone from his coat pocket. Acid roiled in his stomach as he stared down at the display.

He couldn't do it.

It was cowardly to postpone the inevitable, but he wasn't ready to call Annie Sherwood. He needed a friendly voice first, someone who could ease him into the task that was the very worst part of his job. There was only one person he knew who fit the bill, and he scrolled through his directory until he found her number.

Jack started undressing her in the elevator. Underneath her coat, which was interesting.

He jerked her shirt up, unclasped her bra and shoved it aside, and by the time the doors dinged open, Fiona was so dizzy she could barely stand.

"She'd better be gone." Jack pulled her coat together and tugged her into the hallway.

"You don't seem to like my sister much."

He towed her down the corridor and cast a glace over his shoulder. "I like her fine."

"But . . . ?"

He stopped in front of the door and backed her against it so he could kiss her neck some more. "You smell good."

Fiona pushed against his chest. "Out with it. What have you got against Courtney?"

He tipped his head back and groaned. "Can we talk about this later?"

"Did she come on to you?"

His brows arched. "She *told* you?"

"No." Fiona poked through her purse for her key. "She does that with everyone. She's not serious. It's just her way of screening my boyfriends."

"*Screening* your boyfriends? She practically threw herself at me. *Twice.* Does she have any idea how dangerous—"

She jerked his head down for a kiss. After a few scorching moments, she pulled away. "Later. The lights are out and the music's off, so I think we're good."

Jack's hand stayed under her shirt, fondling her breast, as she turned the key in the lock and shoved open the door.

Score! Empty apartment. His thoughts must have been the same, because before she knew it, he had her on her back on the sofa. He wrestled her coat off, then his, and tossed them on the floor.

"Did you lock it?"

"Yeah." He kissed her. Half the work was already done, so it didn't take him long to get rid of her clothes. Her shirt landed on top of her coat. And then her bra.

He pushed up on his palms and looked down at her. The only light came from a fixture in the kitchen, but she could see his expression. Lust again. With something else she hadn't figured out yet.

"I'm pacing myself this time."

She smiled.

"I mean it," he said. "Don't bother with your tricks. I know what you're up to." He knelt beside her and slid down her stretchy black skirt until she was left in just underwear and boots.

"Excuse me?" She covered her breasts with her hands. "My *tricks?*"

He ignored her breasts and dove for her navel. "I love these boots. These can stay." He kissed a path down her abdomen, and she squirmed.

"Wait."

He wasn't listening, so she sat up.

"No fair. I'm the only one naked here."

He smiled slowly as his gaze moved over her. Then he sat back on his heels so she could pull his shirttail from his jeans. She took her time undoing the buttons, following her hands with little kisses and nips. She loved his chest. She loved his body. She loved the way he smelled, the way he moved—everything.

And she wouldn't think right now about how stupid that made her.

His shirt joined hers on the floor, and she stifled the whimper in her throat that would have told him how absolutely beautiful she thought he was. A man with a body like his didn't need compliments.

"That's it for now," he said, easing her back against the cushions.

"Why?" His chest hair rasped against her skin, and she pulled him closer. He felt warm and good.

"You rushed me last time. I've been walking around with a wounded ego for days." He settled in for a long, deep kiss, and when he finally stopped, she smiled up at him.

"Not too wounded." She arched her hips, and the flare of desire in his eyes made her feel giddy.

He tucked one of her knees up by his hip and took her

mouth again. She lost herself in the heat of it, in the way his body fit against her and made her throb everywhere. She felt what she'd felt the first time, this aching pull that she couldn't get enough of.

"Fiona?"

"Hmm."

"That's you."

She opened her eyes. "What?"

He gazed down at her in the dimness. "The phone. It's yours."

She glanced over at the pile of coats and heard her ringtone.

"I'll turn it off." She reached over and burrowed into her pocket. But when she pulled out the phone to silence it, she saw a familiar number on the screen.

"Hello?"

Sighing, Jack sat up.

"Fiona, it's Garrett."

"What happened?"

The silence stretched out, and she knew. She reached for the throw on the sofa arm and wrapped it around her shoulders while she listened to him talk. She heard him out and managed to give him a brief pep talk before he got off the phone with her to call Annie.

Fiona glanced at Jack. She'd expected him to be annoyed, but he simply sat there, watching her.

"That was the agent I worked with in Atlanta."

"I caught that."

She turned off her phone and tossed it on the coffee table. "Not good news."

A shiver moved through her, and she gathered the blanket closer. Jack tried to slide an arm around her shoulders, and she popped up from the sofa.

"Excuse me."

She walked over to her bed. The problem with a loft apartment was the lack of privacy. It was the main reason she hadn't wanted Courtney here. She sank onto the bed with her back to Jack and went to work on her boots, which were a pain to get out of. Finally, she yanked them off and tossed them into the corner. She dropped her blanket on the bed and stood up to pull on her green satin robe. She hoped Jack would get the message.

She heard his boots scraping softly across the floor behind her, and her shoulders tensed. Before she could think of something to say, his arms slid around her waist, and he pulled her back against him.

"I'm feeling really tired. Why don't we—"

"Shh ..." His breath was warm against her neck, and she knew he meant to kiss her.

"Please don't."

They stood there, motionless, as she tried to smother her impulse. She wanted to tell him to back off, to get the hell away, that she needed to be alone. But this wasn't about him, and he'd think she was a lunatic.

"Relax," he said. "I just want to hold you."

She didn't want to be held. But she didn't want to be mean, either, so she pretended not to care. A bitter lump rose up in her throat, and she tried to swallow it down.

"I know how you feel."

She snorted.

"Fiona." His voice was gentle, but firm. "You're not the only one who's ever had a case go down the toilet."

A case. Shelby Sherwood was a case. Like so many others she'd worked on over the years. The little girl had a goddamn case number attached to her name.

She pushed Jack's arms away and whirled around.

"You know something? This case *sucks*. All my cases *suck*. You know why? Because they're all the same." She was shaking with rage, and she didn't care. Jack just tucked his hands in his pockets and watched her.

"Every time I get called in to draw a perp, it's a man. Some demented, fucked-up, sick-in-the-head man. And you know what? Every time I get called in to draw a victim, it's a child or a woman. Someone's mother or daughter or sister who's been killed and thrown away like garbage. *These* are the cases I get. She was ten, Jack. *Ten!* What kind of person *does* that? I can't understand it."

"They're the cases we all get," he said quietly. "It's the nature of the job."

"I hate this job! I don't want this job! And every time I try to stop, someone pulls me back into it."

"No they don't."

"*Yes,* they do. You did it. Nathan does it. GPD. APD. FBI. Everyone."

He sat on the bed and looked at her. "No one forces you to do this. You do it because you're good at it and you feel obligated—same reasons I do."

She stared at him, her frustration expanding because she knew he was right.

He was *right*. No one forced her to do what she did. She

made her own choices, and it had been her choice to put her painting on the back burner so she could continue with police work. It was her choice every time she answered the phone and went out on a call.

"Come here." He caught her hand and pulled her toward the bed.

"Jack, I'm tired."

"Just sit down."

She sank down beside him and rubbed her eyes. She really was tired. It wasn't just an excuse; she felt exhausted all of a sudden.

He lifted his hand and combed it through her hair. Then he trailed it down her back and started tracing patterns up and down her spine through the robe. His touch was feather soft, and it should have tickled, but, actually, it felt good. The tension gradually drained out, and she rested her head on his shoulder.

"Lie back," he whispered.

She sat up, tense again. He slid his hand up her neck and tucked a lock of hair behind her ear. "Let me do this for you." He kissed her temple. "I've been wanting to do this for you."

She looked at him in the dimness, and her heart jumped into her throat. His low, husky voice made everything inside her go warm. She wished she could be with him and let him touch her and make her forget about everything, especially the guilt she was feeling just for being alive. She ran her fingers through his hair and kissed him, and then they were easing back on the bed together, and she closed her eyes and pretended she was floating on a cloud. He parted her robe and slid it off her shoulders. She felt his hands, his lips, his breath brushing over her skin. He plumped her breast in his palm and lingered over it with his mouth, playing with her, teasing her, letting his stubble scrape the skin there. He moved to the other side and she felt the heat of his hand sliding under the silk between her legs. She clenched her thighs together and murmured something, but it was incoherent, even to her. The throbbing started again, that deep, hot pulsing that went everywhere, and she wrapped her arms around him to pull him closer. Their legs tangled, denim and skin, and they were wrestling with each other for control.

"Wait."

"Shh . . ." He touched her and kissed her with a rhythm she loved, and time spun out as she gave herself over to the sensation. The first wave came suddenly, pitching her whole body into a shudder. She found his mouth with hers and kissed him as the perfection of the moment poured through her veins.

When she opened her eyes, he was watching her intently. She smiled up at him and slid her hand down for his jeans. He helped her this time, not taking his eyes off her as he pulled off his boots, stripped down, and knelt between her legs.

It would show on her face, she knew. All those feelings he'd let loose, she knew he could see them there, so she closed her eyes and turned her head.

"Look at me."

She did, and those piercing blue eyes stared down at her. He saw everything, like he always did. She pulled him into her, catching her breath at the thick, sweet pain. His skin was damp with sweat, and she felt the tension in his muscles as he tried to hold back.

"Easy," he said, and adjusted her legs.

But she didn't want him to hold back anything, and she pulled him even closer. "I love you," she whispered.

He went still, and her stomach plummeted when she looked up at the shock on his face.

Oh, God, what had she done? She closed her eyes and tried to block it out.

She moved beneath him, hoping to distract him with her body, which seemed to work. He kissed her forehead, then her cheek, then her mouth, as they started rocking together, building a sensual rhythm that fit both of them perfectly. Time stretched out and out, and she knew he was trying to prove something, and suddenly she couldn't wait anymore.

She rolled to the side.

He looked startled, then intrigued, when she eased herself on top of him and pinned his wrists to the mattress, just like he'd pinned hers in the back room at Becker's.

A smile spread across his face, and he let her take over with the pace she wanted, the one he'd shown her the first time when he was so consumed with her, he hadn't been able to stop. It was like that now, as he gripped her hips and moved with her, and all his control started to give way. Finally, it snapped, and for the span of that too-short, shimmering moment, she knew he was hers.

CHAPTER
18

He trailed his finger up her back, then down again, up and down. She tucked her head under his chin, pressing her ear against his chest so she could hear his heartbeat slow. The moments crept by. The room was silent except for their breathing and the faint hum of traffic four floors below. The quiet started to bear down on her, and she began to get self-conscious about her weight on him, so she sat up.

He lifted an eyebrow as she reached for her robe.

"Just a sec," she said, and slipped into the bathroom. She let the water run as she took a few minutes to sort out what had just happened.

She'd told him. She hadn't planned to, but it had popped out, and now she felt queasy because he hadn't said anything back. She stared at her reflection in the bathroom mirror and braced herself for the very real possibility that she might have just ruined everything. He wasn't callous enough to hurt her with words—at least she didn't think so—but she could definitely imagine his hurting her by simply walking away.

She should have kept her mouth shut.

After stalling for another few minutes and primping—as if that would help—she stepped out of the bathroom.

He was leaning back against the headboard, his fingers laced together behind his head. He'd turned on a light. The sheet was tucked around his waist, and as he watched her walk toward him, she tried to read his expression.

"I like this one."

She followed his gaze to the bookcase dividing her bedroom area from the studio. He'd taken her most recent painting and propped it there, where he could see it from the bed. She glanced up at the track lighting. He'd adjusted one of the fixtures to spotlight the picture as if it were hanging in a gallery.

She cleared her throat. "It's for the show. I'm taking it in tomorrow."

He stared at the painting until she started to get antsy. Did he recognize the subject matter? Probably not—it was too abstract.

"It's good," he said.

"It's late."

He looked at her quizzically as she slipped into the bed beside him. He wasn't getting dressed and making excuses to leave. That was a good sign. He wanted to talk about art. Or maybe he just wanted a change of subject, but she could go with that.

"I was supposed to have it to the gallery last week for framing. It's the focal point of my show. The opening's in two days, and the paint's barely dry."

"Two days?" He slid an arm around her shoulders and pulled her against him. "I didn't realize it was so soon."

"You didn't ask."

It was a cheap shot, but she couldn't resist. Since their

first meeting, he had blown off the importance of her show.

"It's actually a pre-opening," she explained. "Some local collectors. A few media. The gallery owner is a friend, and he's trying to introduce me to some of his contacts. He's set up this private wine and cheese thing, and after that, it'll be open to the public."

Gazing at her painting with a critical eye, she decided she liked it. The vibrant reds and golds contrasted with the serene blues of the water. Everything swirled together like yin and yang, so that viewers might not realize they were looking at a school of fish.

Fiona decided to take off the robe. It seemed pointless, and it was in the way. She tossed it on the floor and settled against his chest. He stroked his fingers up and down her arm, and a knot formed in her stomach.

"You're kind of like Georgia O'Keeffe," he said, "but with water instead of flowers."

Fiona jerked her head back to look at him. Never in a thousand years would she have guessed he knew anything about art.

He must have caught her surprised look, because he rolled his eyes. "Hey, I went to college. I took art history."

Everything she was thinking probably would have sounded insulting, so she kept quiet.

"I like how you do close-ups," he continued. "Sometimes I don't even know what I'm looking at until I've stared at it a while. Like those ones here before. River scenes, right?"

She bit her lip. She'd had no idea he'd paid any attention. "The Blanco River. It's near my grandfather's house."

She didn't know what else to say, so she just closed her

eyes and rested her cheek on him. They weren't going to talk about what she'd said. That was okay. The moment had passed, and it seemed out of place now.

Her chest felt sore, but she didn't want to think about it. Her feelings were too raw at the moment to prod and analyze. She could do that later, when she was alone.

For now, she just wanted to fall asleep beside him and dream about the remote possibility he'd still be there in the morning.

Jack woke early and felt the weight of Fiona's arm draped across his chest. He removed it carefully, eased out of bed, and walked silently to the bathroom. Everything she had in there smelled girly, but he took a quick shower anyway and threw on his jeans. Then he padded barefoot into her kitchen and started opening cabinets.

Well, holy shit. The granola girl from California was a junk-food addict.

Shaking his head, Jack grabbed a box and started putting together breakfast. Juice, cereal, milk. He hunted up some coffee filters and got a pot going. She didn't have any eggs, so he settled for toast. Sex always made him hungry, and this morning he was famished.

"Hi."

He glanced up from the toast he was buttering to see Fiona standing on the other side of the counter.

"Morning." He put a plate of toast in front of her. She looked at it warily, but didn't comment. She had on that green thing again. Her hair looked good, all loose and curly around her shoulders, and he couldn't resist leaning over to peck her lips. "Looks like you need coffee."

She sank onto a bar stool. "You're cooking."

"Not really." He opened a few cabinets.

"Above the TV."

He found a couple of mugs and poured the coffee. She didn't have cream, so he added milk to hers and put it in front of her. Then he filled two bowls with cereal and poured milk over each, tossing the empty carton into the trash can under her sink when he was through.

"You got a grocery list somewhere?" he asked.

She just stared at him.

"Better have some caffeine. You look like a zombie."

"By the phone," she muttered, and took a sip.

He looked beside the phone and found the list. He knew she'd have one; she was a highly organized woman. He scribbled down "milk" and "eggs" before taking the bowls of cereal to the bar. He sat on the stool beside her and scooped up a bite.

She watched him, wide-eyed.

"What?" He paused, spoon in the air.

"You threw away the milk carton."

"It was empty."

"You put 'milk' on my grocery list."

He rested his spoon on the bowl. "Are you okay?"

"I don't know."

"You're looking at me like I just killed your cat."

"I don't have a cat."

"Thank God for that. I hate the damn things." He kissed her nose. "Eat your Cocoa Puffs."

She took a tentative bite and then stirred her cereal until the milk turned brown. He wondered if she was going to bring up last night, what she'd said while they were in bed together. He hoped not. He didn't want to talk about it, and it would be much easier for her to corner him into a big discussion now, in the light of day, than it had been right after sex.

Jack heard the lock tumble and turned around. Courtney stood in the doorway, and for once he was glad to see her.

"Well, well." She dumped an oversize black purse on the floor and tossed her trench coat on the bench by the door. "Good morning, *Jack*. I see you found my sister."

"Morning," he said.

The mystery from last night was solved: she was wearing a short black dress. Her hair and makeup looked tired, but she seemed energetic as she flounced across the kitchen to help herself to some coffee.

She leaned back against the counter and eyed Jack over the rim of her mug. Her gaze dropped to his pecs, and he tried not to shift in his seat.

"So," she said. "You're friends with Nathan. I guess that means my secret's out."

"What secret?" Fiona asked.

"You want to fill her in, Jack?"

"I have no idea what you're talking about."

Courtney's expression turned suspicious. "Nathan didn't tell you?"

"Tell him what?"

Jack glanced at Fiona, who shot him a glare.

He held his hands up. "Hey, I don't know anything."

"You're serious?" Courtney put down her coffee. "Nathan really didn't tell you?"

"He really didn't."

"Tell him *what*?" Fiona was getting upset now.

"Nothing." Courtney strode out of the kitchen. "I just need to grab a few things, and I'll be out of your way.

"Hey, good news, Fi. We're supposed to get a warm front tomorrow. You're almost rid of me." She took some clothes from her sister's closet and shut herself in the bathroom.

"Do you know what she's talking about?" Fiona demanded. "Don't lie."

"No idea. I wouldn't lie to you."

Her eyebrows arched.

"Going forward," he clarified. "I won't lie to you."

Shit, now what had he done? He'd just made a promise that would be hell to keep.

Not that it mattered. She could tell when he was lying anyway.

Jack downed a few more bites of soggy cereal, then got up and took his bowl to the sink. "I've got to go."

She followed him into the bedroom area, where he shrugged into his wrinkled shirt and buttoned it.

"Are you busy today?" she asked.

"Yeah." He smiled. "Thought I'd put my résumé together." She pursed her lips.

Shit, this was already tougher than he'd thought.

"Also, I might work on the case some." He pulled on socks. "Look into a few things."

Soon as he got his boots on, she followed him to the door and opened it. She was trying not to cling, he could tell. Suddenly, what she'd said to him last night was like a presence in the room.

He stepped into the hallway and dragged her with him. Those hazel eyes were glistening, and he knew he needed to hightail it out of there.

He pulled on his jacket. "You never invited me to your show."

She bit her lip.

"I don't know much about art, but I'd like to be there."

"It's kind of a drive for you," she said reasonably. "Four hours round-trip."

"I know."

"Don't feel like you have to or anything."

From the look on her face, he knew he'd been right. This was a big deal to her. If he came, he'd be committing to something more than just a few hours of mingling with art snobs.

"Tell me where and when. I'll do my best to make it."

"The Fuller Gallery on Fifth Street," she said. "Tomorrow at five."

"Fuller on Fifth. Got it." He pulled her into a kiss, but she wasn't into it. She'd gone into protective mode again, so he let go of her.

"Take care, now," he said. "I'll probably see you tomorrow."

Courtney had perched herself on the kitchen counter and was chomping on an apple. She'd changed into Fiona's Austin City Limits T-shirt, and Fiona made a mental note to make sure it didn't wind up in her sister's duffel when she left.

"What happened with Nathan?" she asked, picking up her coffee. Jack had made it too strong, but she needed the jolt.

"Don't worry about it."

"Courtney."

She rolled her eyes. "Can't you let anything *go*?"

Fiona waited.

"Fine." Courtney hopped down from the counter. "I had a little brush with the cops last week. Nathan helped me out."

Nathan helped her out. Not a good sign. "What does that mean, exactly? A 'little brush'?"

Courtney bit into her apple, stalling.

"Tell me the truth."

She swallowed. "I kind of trashed David's car."

"What? *Why?*"

She tossed the core in the sink. "His name's not David. And he's married."

"Courtney!" Fiona gaped at her. "*How* could you do that?"

"I didn't know, okay? And I already feel like shit, so don't pile on. You can save the lecture."

Fiona's stomach filled with dread. "How did Nathan get involved?"

"After I got arrested—"

"Arrested?"

"Hey!" Courtney plunked a hand on her hip. "I said no lectures. I don't need any more grief about this. Nathan pulled some strings, and it basically went away, all right?"

Fiona looked at her sister. Did she have any idea how much trouble she could be in? An arrest—even a minor one—was a serious hassle, not to mention an expense.

"Are you sure it's cleared up? Do we need to get you a lawyer or something?"

Courtney scoffed. "No more lawyers. Ever." She sank onto a bar stool. "Enough about me. I want to hear what's going on with you."

Fiona sat down on the stool beside her. If Nathan had dealt with it, then it was dealt with. He had a lot of pull within the department, and he would have said something to her if Courtney had a serious problem. Fiona was surprised he hadn't mentioned anything before now, but maybe he'd been sworn to secrecy.

"So?" Courtney asked, raising her eyebrows. "What's up with Jack?"

Fiona folded her arms on the counter and rested her head on them. "I told him I'm in love with him."

"What?"

She closed her eyes. "During sex."

"Omigod, are you *crazy*? You're kidding, right? No way you really told him that."

"I'm not kidding."

"And what did he say?"

"Nothing." Fiona looked up at her. "I ruined it, didn't I?"

Courtney bit her lip.

"Be honest."

"Well." She tipped her head to the side, weighing the odds. "He seems polite."

"Yeah."

"And sort of old-fashioned."

"Yeah. So what?"

"So you'll probably get the courtesy call in about a week." She shrugged. "He'll maybe make a date or something. Then cancel because something comes up."

Fiona plunked her head down. "I can't believe I'm such an idiot."

Courtney patted her back. "Neither can I."

Take care, now.

She'd told him she loved him, and what were his parting words yesterday? *Take care, now.*

Fiona pushed through the door to her building. The bright afternoon sun greeted her, and it actually felt nice outside for the first time in weeks. She unbuttoned her coat and looked toward the street in front of her parking garage. People were out biking and jogging and walking dogs, soaking up the Saturday afternoon. The whole city, it seemed, was coming out of hibernation. She strode out to Lamar Street and stopped to turn her face upward. It was one of those crisp, clear days, the sky so blue it looked as if it had been painted with pigment straight from the tube. The gallery wasn't far, so she decided to go on foot.

Her crushed-velvet dress swished around her legs as she walked. She'd bought it especially for this occasion. It had a scoop neckline and long sleeves, and the fabric clung to her body while the deep violet color set off the gold in her hair. She felt pretty. Beautiful, even. And her pulse picked up as she wondered whether Jack would make it to her show.

It was silly to be thinking about him at a time like this, but she couldn't help it. She was in love with the man. She didn't know whether he loved her back, but she thought he might. Even if he wouldn't talk about it, she'd seen something in his face while they'd made love. And then he'd offered to come here, to see her opening, knowing full well how immensely important it was to her.

Of course, he might just have been being nice.

It was even possible he'd made the offer merely to distract her from an awkward conversation about the L-word. Maybe he had no intention of coming at all.

Fiona stopped at the corner and waited for the light to change. She took a deep breath and tried to steel herself. Today was *her* day. *Hers.* And if Jack didn't make it, she'd just deal. There would be plenty of other people to talk to. And Courtney would be there for moral support. Her sister was a flake sometimes, but she came through when it really mattered.

Fiona's phone sang out, and she pulled it from her pocket just as the stoplight turned green. She didn't recognize the number.

"Hello?"

"Is this Fiona?"

She could hardly hear over the traffic. "Yes."

"It's—" Static. "I have to—" More static.

"I can barely hear you," she said loudly. "Can you speak up?"

"It's *Brady*."

"Brady Cox?"

"You said I could call. You gave me your number."

Her hand tightened on the phone. "It's fine, Brady. What's wrong?"

"Nothing." But his voice sounded nervous. "I just thought of something, and I thought, you know, I should call you."

Horns blared. Fiona realized the light had changed and she was planted in the middle of the intersection. She hurried to the corner. "What is it? What did you think of?" She ducked into a doorway to get away from the people and the traffic noise.

"I remembered the truck," he said. "I was at the grocery store with my mom, and I heard this engine, and it sounded familiar, and I looked over, and there it was. Diesel engine and everything."

"A truck." Fiona's heart pounded. "The one driven by the man we drew together? You saw it?"

The phone was silent for a moment.

"Brady?"

"I dunno. Maybe not the *same* truck. But just like it. I remember now. I remember everything. I was thinking you could come over, and we could, like, draw it all."

Her heart raced. The perp's vehicle would be a major break. She had to tell Jack. Or Agent Santos, since Jack had been kicked off the case.

"Brady, listen to me. It's good that you called me. I'm going to give you a phone number, okay? Of a man who's working on this case. I want you to tell him everything you told me, and then *describe* the truck to him. Tell him everything you can."

Silence.

"Brady?"

"I want to tell *you*. I want *you* to draw it."

Fiona glanced at her watch, exasperated. It was nearly three. Her opening started in two hours, and this couldn't happen right now.

"Brady. Listen. I'm tied up right now. The soonest I can get there is tomorrow. But it's very, *very* important that you tell someone about the truck as soon as possible, all right? I need you to call this investigator. He's a very nice man—"

Click.

"Brady?"

He'd hung up.

"*Damn* it." She stomped her foot and stared at her phone. She scrolled through to find the number, but paused before pressing the Callback button. It wouldn't matter. Brady was one of the most headstrong kids she'd ever worked with. If he didn't want to talk to someone besides her, he wasn't going to.

"Damn it, damn it, damn it!"

Fiona whirled around and looked down the street. In the distance, she saw the Fuller Gallery's black awning. She'd been there yesterday, and she knew that two of her best paintings hung in the window. Her photograph sat on an easel in the foyer, and her Blanco River series was mounted all over the walls. The painting closest to her heart, the fish composition that she'd first visualized during her dinner with Jack, was spotlighted on the main wall, a four-by-six-foot testament to the turmoil permeating her life.

And the gallery owner who had bent over backward to help her get her start was waiting there, amid all of it, to go over last-minute details before her big debut.

Fiona's hands shook as she stuffed her phone inside her purse and turned around.

CHAPTER

19

Nathan knocked on Fiona's door and waited patiently. The stereo was on, so he knew someone was home. He knocked again, louder.

Finally, the door pulled open, and there stood Courtney.

"Fiona's not here."

Nathan looked her up and down. "You always answer the door that way?"

She glanced down at her silky black robe and shrugged. Then she turned around and disappeared into the apartment.

Nathan followed. "You know where she is?"

"Out." She bent over beside the bed and pulled a duffel bag out from under it. For the second time this week, Nathan was rendered speechless by her legs. He watched from a comfortable distance away as she tossed the bag on the bed and unzipped it.

She glanced up at him. "Hey, bring me that laundry basket, would you?"

A basket heaped with clothes was sitting on the coffee table. He picked it up and ferried it to the bed.

"Thanks." Courtney eyed the gun at his hip. He wore the

holster with his usual dress slacks and a tie. "You on your way to work?"

"Home, actually."

She dumped the basket upside down and started sorting everything into piles. "You try her cell phone?"

"No answer. You know where I can find her? It's important."

"She's at her art show. I'm heading over there, too, soon as I get dressed." She finished sorting, and Nathan watched, riveted, as she scooped up a pile of lacy lingerie and stuffed it into the duffel. Her gaze met his over the bag, and he suddenly had a burning desire to know what she planned to wear tonight. "You want to give me a message? I can pass it along when I see her."

"No, I need to talk to her." He pulled a plastic bag from his pocket and sighed. It was the letter Fiona had given him, the one that had taken weeks to get back from the lab. He placed it on the dresser.

"What's that?"

"A note she got in the mail. I had it analyzed."

Courtney walked over to the dresser and picked up the bag. Through the plastic, she read the words, and her face paled.

"Couldn't get anything useful from the prints, but I did some research, and the postmark makes me think it has to do with one of her high-profile cases—a serial rapist who's doing time in L.A. County. The guy's got family in the town outside Dallas where this was mailed."

"A serial rapist. Charming. Last time it was gang members." She dropped the bag on the dresser and crossed her arms. "Are you aware that she uprooted her life and moved fifteen hundred miles to get away from this kind of crap?"

"Yes."

"It's no wonder she's so stressed out all the time. She needs a break. Why don't you guys leave her alone?"

"I wish I could," he said honestly. "But the cases don't stop coming, and she's the best we got."

Jack flipped his wallet out on the counter and took out a few twenties to pay for his gas and some Gatorade. The pimply-faced kid at the register stared at him, as if he'd never seen a guy in a suit before.

Jack reached into his coat pocket and pulled out a sketch, the one he'd taken to carrying around everywhere he went.

"This man look familiar to you?"

The kid cast a brief glance at Fiona's drawing and shrugged.

"That a yes or a no?"

He smacked his gum a few times, then shook his head. "Nope."

Jack collected his change. He noticed the bulletin board behind the counter where flyers were posted advertising flea markets and river-rafting tours. Jack slid the sketch across the counter. He had a whole stack of them in his truck.

"Tack this up there, will you?"

The kid looked down at the ugly mug. "I probably should talk to my manager? He's in back."

Jack checked his watch. If he didn't get on the road soon, he was going to be late to Austin. But this gas station was at a high-volume intersection, and he wanted a drawing posted.

His phone buzzed, and he dug it from his pocket. Fiona.

He whipped out an old business card, which wasn't nearly as impressive as whipping out a badge. "Get your manager. Hurry."

The kid disappeared, and Jack answered his phone. "Hey, I need to call you back."

"Wait. Where are you?"

"On the interstate. About halfway to Austin."

"Turn around."

"What?"

"Turn around. I'm coming to you."

"Why?"

"I need to talk to Brady Cox," she said. "He remembers the truck he saw from his tree fort."

"What about your show?"

"They'll have it without me."

He paused a moment to make sure she was serious. "But this is your big chance. It could be a onetime opportunity."

She was quiet on the other end, and he figured she knew this already.

"I need to talk to Brady," she repeated. "He knows something important."

Jack felt someone hovering near him, and he glanced over to see an old guy standing too close, gnawing on a stick of beef jerky.

"Okay, so talk to him," Jack said. "But how about over the phone? Or I'll bring him to you. You shouldn't come down here."

"Jack, this is my job. I'll interview him at the station house, if it makes you feel better, but I'm coming."

"Fiona—"

"I have to go now."

"Wait." Goddamn it. She was the most mule-headed woman he'd ever known. "Call me soon as you get to town. And keep your gun handy."

Jack disconnected, and the white-haired guy shuffled up to the counter. He continued to chew his jerky as he gazed down at the picture until Jack half expected his dentures to fall out.

"I knew it," the man said. "That's the spitting image of Melvin."

Jack's pulse skipped. "Who's Melvin?"

"Ah, what's the last name?" He removed the cap from his head and rubbed the age spots at his temple. "Husky fella. Works at the hunting bureau."

"Melvin *Schenck*? With Texas Parks and Wildlife?"

The watery gray eyes lit up. "Yeah, that's the one. Course he's a lot heavier now."

Jack had met Melvin and knew he wasn't their guy. He was a few decades too old and too tall to match the witnesses' descriptions. But Jack's mind started to race with possibilities. The Parks and Wildlife Bureau had really dragged its feet on that list of deer licensees. And their regional office was in Borough County, where Lucy had been picked up by hunters all those years ago.

"Does Melvin have a son?" Jack asked. "Or maybe a nephew?"

The man frowned at the drawing, scratching his head some more. "I don't rightly know. Seems like he had a family once. Seem to recall his wife died. Then he lost his farm. Or maybe that was someone else, fell on hard times. I couldn't say for sure one way or the other."

Jack took a moment to jot down the man's contact information on his gas receipt and then stuffed it in his pocket.

"Thanks," he told him. "You've been a big help."

Jack plowed through the doors and got back in his truck. He needed a computer, ASAP, not to mention a team of detectives to help him run down this lead.

He probably wouldn't get either, but he could damn well try.

Within fifteen minutes of arriving in Graingerville, Fiona learned two things: Jack really *had* been booted off the case completely, and Randy Rudd was an even bigger moron than she'd originally thought. The sheriff seemed to believe sitting behind closed doors in his office was going to miraculously bring a killer to justice.

The one glimmer of good news was that someone—most likely Agent Santos—had realized Brady Cox and Lucy Arrellando were the prosecution's key—and possibly *only*—witnesses, should the case go to trial. Both of them had been placed under protective surveillance for the time being.

The bad news was, Randy's office was in charge of the job, and the territorial sheriff made it known to Fiona through his assistant, Myrna, that it would be impossible for her to interview Brady at the Graingerville Police Station. More pissing wars with Jack, Fiona guessed.

So she set off to visit the house. She'd promised Jack she'd be careful, and she figured working in the presence of a sheriff's deputy qualified as taking precautions.

The deputy was sitting in his unit in front of Brady's home when Fiona pulled up. He was engrossed in a magazine and barely bothered to wave as Fiona got out of her car and walked to the door.

"Nice security," she muttered as she rang the bell.

No one answered, and she tried again. And again. Finally, she strode over to the deputy's car and tapped on the glass.

He glanced up, startled, from his *Sports Illustrated* swimsuit issue, and rolled down the window.

"Sorry to interrupt," she said sweetly, "but you wouldn't happen to know where the witness is, would you?"

He frowned. "The mom left. Said she was running late for work."

"And Brady? You know it's the boy, not his mother, who will be called to testify if this case goes to trial. You might want to think about guarding *him*."

The deputy scowled. "Who are you?"

"I'm a forensic artist here to interview Brady about the case."

He shoved open the door, hauled himself out of the car, and ambled up the sidewalk. Without so much as a knock, he entered the house. He took a quick tour of the tiny home and then returned to the front door, where he fisted his hands on his hips. "He was just here a while ago."

Fuming, Fiona pulled out her phone and called Santos.

"It's Fiona," she said, crossing the kitchen and pushing open the back door. She glanced up at Brady's fort and saw that it was empty. "They lost the witness."

"What do you mean *lost*?"

"I came over to interview Brady. He called me this afternoon to tell me he remembers the vehicle, and he wanted us to sit down and draw it together. I'm at his house now, and he's gone, right out from under the sheriff's nose."

Santos said something in Spanish that didn't sound kind, and then, "You try his mother?"

"She's at work, according to this surveillance guy. She waits tables at IHOP. Listen, I don't like this. Someone needs to check on Lucy." Fiona noticed the narrow, muddy tire track on the house's back porch. Maybe Brady was on his bike, which at least meant he'd probably left of his own volition.

"He's disappeared before," Fiona said. "But still, I'm nervous. We need to find him."

"I'm on it," Santos said, and disconnected.

Fiona did a quick search of the house, on the off chance that the deputy had missed something. No sign of Brady, but several rolls of quarters lay on his bed, along with half a dozen empty coin wrappers and a lonely gym sock. She didn't see its match.

By the time she made her way to the front of the house, the deputy was leaning against his patrol car talking on the phone as a black SUV pulled up to the curb. Randy Rudd, in all his ten-gallon glory, got out and approached his deputy for what looked like a reaming out. Fiona stood off to the side, pretending not to eavesdrop, and waited for the sheriff to finish.

Finally, Randy looked her way. His gaze paused on her cleavage before he managed to notice her face. "And you are . . . ?"

"Fiona Glass. The forensic artist. I spoke with your assistant."

His gaze dropped again, and Fiona crossed her arms. *This* was why she wore suits all the time.

"His bike is missing," she said curtly. "I think we should contact his mother, see if she can tell us his favorite hangouts. And if she doesn't know, maybe she could at least supply the name of a friend of Brady's who could tell us."

The sheriff nodded. "Thank you, ma'am, but we've got it under control." He turned to his deputy. "You check all the playgrounds. I'll get another man driving through town, see if we don't spot him."

Fiona's mouth fell open. "*Playgrounds?* Sheriff, have you met this kid?" She knew he had, the day Brady had called him a bonehead asswipe. "I think it's highly unlikely he's playing on the slides. It looks like he took some quarters from his room—"

Randy hooked his thumbs on his gun belt and stepped in front of her, shading her with the brim of his hat. "Ma'am, you can go now. This is a law enforcement matter. Hadn't got nothing to do with art."

Fiona felt her cheeks flush. She jerked her keys from her purse. "Fine. Hey, if you see Brady, tell him I agree with his assessment of you."

Jack grabbed the sheets off the printer and booked it for the door. As he left the station house, he winked at Sharon, whose worried expression told him she knew he was up to something. Using Carlos's computer while he was out on a dinner break wasn't exactly aboveboard. But, shit, what were they going to do, fire him?

Jack returned to his truck, which he'd parked discreetly at the side of the building. He cranked the engine to life, all the while scanning the papers in his lap. This was good stuff.

Nothing definitive, but good. He had an address to check out. And he had the pull factor.

The pull factor was something from his homicide days, when he and Nathan had worked for the HPD.

It was pretty straightforward: when you were staring at a pile of paperwork, or a crime scene, or whatever, and a certain piece of evidence just kept dragging your attention away from all the rest, even if you didn't know why, *that* was the pull factor.

The last known address for Melvin Karl Schenck was like that. It didn't feel right, for some reason, and Jack wanted to check it out.

The passenger's-side door jerked open, and Carlos got in.

"Hey there, Chief."

Jack scowled. "I'm not chief anymore. You are."

He popped a toothpick in his mouth. "Whatcha got there?"

"Do yourself a favor," Jack said. "Go right back to work and pretend you didn't see me."

Carlos didn't budge.

"Damn it, I'm serious. You could lose your job over this. You got kids to think about."

"You're looking for our perp, right? I figure that's my job."

"Carlos—"

"Save it, J.B. I'm coming. Tell me what you got."

Jack handed over the papers and thrust the truck in gear. "Rap sheet for Melvin Schenck. Operating a vehicle without a license. A couple DUIs. A domestic."

Carlos looked over the papers as Jack pulled onto the highway.

"All this shit's from ten, twenty years ago. Looks like he cleaned up his act."

"Yeah, after his wife died."

Carlos raised his eyebrows.

"Hunting accident. I found a newspaper article about it, but I didn't bother getting a copy."

"This guy's in his sixties," Carlos pointed out. "Too old to fit the profile."

"A witness says he's the spitting image of our suspect sketch, so I'm looking for a younger male relative."

"Hey, you ever think to hand this over to Randy? Or the feds?"

"I intend to," Jack said. "Soon as I see whether there's anything to hand over. Right now we're just taking a little road trip."

Fiona scoured the video arcade at Dot's Truck Stop but didn't see any nine-year-old kids toting a sock full of quarters. She cut through their kitschy gift shop, taking a quick peek down all the snack aisles, and decided to try Dairy Queen. Also, she should probably call Jack. She'd agreed to call when she arrived in town, but she hadn't gotten around to it, mainly because she knew he'd tell her to get her butt to the station house and stay there until the cops located Brady.

Which was unlikely to happen with Randy in charge.

Fiona walked briskly toward her car. It was nearing dusk, and getting chilly again. Her exhibition would be well under way by now, and just thinking about it tied her stomach in knots. She'd definitely burned a bridge this afternoon when she'd told the gallery manager she wasn't coming.

Fiona neared her Honda and noticed a kid with a purple bicycle on the other side of the giant parking lot. He was crouched beside the air station, attaching a hose to the front tire of the bike.

"Brady!" she yelled, walking closer. It was definitely him. "Hey, *Brady!*" But he couldn't hear over the hiss of brakes and the grumble of truck engines.

A white pickup pulled in, obscuring her view. Her footsteps quickened.

"Brady!" She broke into a trot. What was that truck doing?

The driver heaved the bike into the truck bed, then jumped behind the wheel and roared off.

"Brady!"

Fiona's heart skipped. He was gone. Must have been shoved in through the driver's-side door.

The truck squealed away, and she sprinted for her car.

CHAPTER

20

"This address seem hinky to you?" Jack asked Carlos as they sped down the highway.

Graingerville's newly appointed acting chief of police took the sticky note and frowned.

"I MapQuested it," Jack added. "Got a post office in Meyersberg. That was it."

"Live Oak Trace? Isn't this out toward that big oil field? Del Toro Minerals or something?"

"That's what I thought, too," Jack said, nearing the turnoff.

Sure enough, several miles down the caliche road, they detected hydrogen sulfide, what Fiona had called the rotten egg smell. In the waning daylight, Jack looked beyond the barbed-wire fence and saw half a dozen bobbing pump jacks. Less than a mile later, a rusted gate came into view and then a weathered wooden sign: DEL TORO MINERALS. TRESPASSERS WILL BE PROSECUTED.

Jack wasn't discouraged by the message so much as a complete lack of lights, mailboxes, or any other sign of residents within miles. He followed the road another few miles until it dead-ended at a metal gate. About fifty yards back from the fence sat a small, dilapidated farmhouse. Kudzu had overtaken the western side of it, and the windows were boarded up with weathered plywood.

Carlos took out his cell phone. "Don't look like Melvin lives here. At least not anymore."

Without asking for Jack's approval—which he didn't need, Jack reminded himself—he called Santos. After giving the agent a quick update, he clicked off.

"Says he'll check it out," Carlos reported. "Let me have a look at that paperwork."

Jack handed it over and pointed his truck back toward the main highway. He was getting that tingly feeling in his spine, the one he hadn't had since his last homicide case in Houston had come together. Jack had learned early on that the *why* plus the *how* usually equaled the *who* in any investigation. And a motive beyond simple racism was starting to take shape in his mind. The Schencks had been farmers some time in the past, but they'd "fallen on hard times," as the gas station guy put it, and sold out to an oil company, one that had apparently profited from land the Schencks had once considered theirs. And what could cause a farmer to fall on hard times? A crapload of things, including a sudden cold snap, the kind that could transform months of a backbreaking work into acres of rotting mush in a matter of days. Maybe someone in the Schenck family had a violent temper—one that was set off by weather that reminded him of all the shit he'd been through in his life that was somebody else's fault.

But, hell, what did Jack know? Maybe his theory was just a bunch of psychological mumbo-jumbo, and their killer simply got off on torturing women.

"Here's something," Carlos said, flipping through the

printouts. "Melvin's got a tattoo. Double lightning bolts, same as Lowell."

Jack frowned. "Lowell has a tattoo? Where?"

"On his chest. Big-ass thing, probably eight inches tall. But you wouldn't see it unless he's got his shirt off."

I hate body art. You couldn't pay me enough to let some nut job near me with a needle.

Jack looked at Carlos, still not sure he believed him. "You've seen Lowell with his shirt off?"

Carlos pulled out his toothpick. "Yeah, Fourth of July picnic couple years back. Flag football. It was my kid who noticed it. Asked me if it had something to do with Harry Potter."

"It's not a literary reference," Jack said grimly.

"What's it mean?"

"Double lightning bolt stands for *SS*. As in Nazi henchmen." Jack pounded the steering wheel. "Holy shit, I can't believe I didn't catch it."

"What's that?"

"Lowell. He's fucking involved."

When she called, Jack answered on the first ring. "Where are you?" he demanded.

"Brady's been kidnapped."

"What?"

"By the killer, I think." Fiona struggled to keep the panic out of her voice, but she was nearly hyperventilating as she raced down the highway. "They're in a white Ford pickup, license plate C-C-Z-6-something-or-other. The plate's muddy. I can't see the rest."

"You're *following* them? Are you freaking crazy?"

She didn't bother arguing. "We're on Dry Creek Road heading west."

"Dry Creek Road. Viper lives around there."

"I know." She clutched the steering wheel. "I'm hanging back now so he won't notice me. But it's getting harder because there's not a lot of traffic way out here."

"Pull over. Call 911. Then call—"

"I already did. I called Santos, too, but the call dropped. He's trying to get together a hostage-rescue team. I haven't been able to get through again, so I thought I'd try you. Okay, I just passed a sign. I'm entering Borough County."

"Borough County," Jack repeated, and she heard a muffled voice. He was talking to someone. "Yeah, she's tailing them. There's a map in that glove box. Fiona?"

"I'm here." It was getting dark now, too dark for landmarks. She hadn't turned on her headlights, because she didn't want to attract attention, but she was about to have no choice.

"Wherever you are, just pull over. I'm on my way. We'll be there soon."

"Okay, he's turning." Fiona slowed nearly to a stop. The pickup was merely a distant pair of taillights on the horizon, but she didn't dare get closer. She just hoped she'd be able to spot the turnoff in the darkness.

More mumbling and crinkling of paper. It sounded like Jack and someone were looking at a map.

Straining her eyes, she spotted what might be a road up ahead. Relief flooded through her, then apprehension. "I think I see the turnoff."

"Fiona, you need to stop."

"Okay, I've got the turn, but no sign. I'm making a right. North. It's a gravel road—*ouch!*"

"What's wrong?"

"I just hit a bump. Shoot, this is really tough—hey wait, there's a low-water bridge. Jack? Are you getting this?"

Muffled arguing on the other end. It sounded like Carlos, or maybe Lowell.

"Jack? Did you get that? I don't have a road sign, but there's a low-water crossing."

"I got it."

"Okay, the taillights are gone now. I think there's a bend up ahead. Maybe a driveway or a gate—"

"Fiona. Honey, please listen to me." She heard the strain in his voice, and she tried to block it out. Like her churning stomach. Like the fact that she was tailing a serial killer to his home. "I need you to turn your car around right now. Go back to the main highway. Put your hazards on—"

"Jack, did you hear what I said? He has *Brady*! I need to see where they go."

"Stop it, goddamn it!" His voice leaped an octave. "Are you out of your *mind*? This guy's dangerous! Shit. Carlos, read me that crossroad, will you? Fiona, we'll be there soon. Just *stop*, okay? If you want to help, call Santos. Give him all the information you just gave me."

She tried to discern the road, but this was the country, black as tar, and the moon wasn't visible yet. If she careened into a river or a tree, she couldn't help anyone.

"Okay, I'll call Santos." She eased her foot off the gas,

and her throat tightened as she thought of Brady. "But you have to hurry."

Jack was sweating bullets by the time he disconnected. "Fucking hell!" He flung his phone onto the dashboard. "She followed him down that road. She's probably almost at his fucking driveway."

"I don't know about this, Chief."

"What? What don't you know?" Jack tore his eyes off the highway to see Carlos bent over the map.

"We got two choices. Viper's digs, and then there's Lowell."

"What about him?"

Carlos shook his head, and Jack felt, suddenly, like his chest was too small for his hammering heart. He was going to have a heart attack, right here, doing ninety-five-fucking-miles-per-hour down the highway.

She'd *followed* him.

"Dry Creek Road. Lowell lives out that way, too. Don't know the address, exactly, but it's something out there. Don't you remember how he's always bitching about the drive?"

Jack clenched his teeth together until his gums hurt. "Check the map again," he said finally. "She said a low-water bridge. There's one on there? A river? A creek? Something?"

"This don't have bridges on it."

"Fuck!"

"There's Mesquite Creek to the north, but it parallels the whole damn highway. Any road off of there's likely to cross it." Carlos looked up at Jack. "So we got two choices. Viper or Lowell."

Jack gripped the steering wheel. He didn't have a clue

what Viper looked like because he'd sent Lowell to check him out instead of handling it personally. But Fiona had flashed the suspect sketch at Viper's workplace, and no one had recognized him.

And then there was Lowell, who didn't look anything like the sketch, but who had been lying to Jack since the investigation began. Maybe it was a joint operation or a cover-up of some sort. Lowell had been volunteering his help, right and left, since the beginning. He'd been the one to finally get Melvin to hand over that list. He'd answered phones on the night the suspect sketch was released. He'd checked out the tattoo artist. He'd checked out the tire tread.

Jack's gut burned as he pictured Lowell's signature at the bottom of Lucy's police report. He'd been a rookie then. Barely a year on the job, and he'd interviewed Jack's girl-friend about her attack at the hands of some racist scumbag. Maybe Lowell had gotten turned on just hearing about it. Maybe he'd purposely screwed up the composite, slapped the thing together—as Fiona had said—like Mr. Potato Head. Maybe he hadn't given a damn whether they ever caught the guy. Or, shit, maybe they were buddies.

"Call Lowell," Jack said, watching the speedometer creep up. Ninety-eight. One hundred. He was going too fast to talk and drive. "We need to find out what the hell's going on."

"Agreed. But what do you plan to ask him? We know he's not the murderer. Looks nothing like the sketch. All we know is he's got some tattoo—"

"We know he's not the one who dumped the body and who attacked Lucy, but that doesn't mean he's not involved some other way. And he lied. That means he's hiding something. He's had his hands all over this case from the get-go."

Carlos shook his head. "I don't like looking at a cop for this."

Neither did Jack. And maybe Carlos was right. Maybe Jack was jumping to conclusions. But the reality was, they had to make a decision. Soon. And as much as it pained him, Jack had to let Carlos take the lead.

"You're chief now," Jack said. "This decision's yours."

Carlos chewed his toothpick vigorously as they raced down the highway. They passed an ENTERING BOROUGH COUNTY sign, and Carlos looked at the map again. He put in a call to the station house, and after a brief exchange with Sharon, he hung up.

"Lowell's AWOL," Carlos announced. "And I've got an address."

Fiona sat in her Honda with sweat streaming down her back. Her skin was hot under all that velvet, and her heart was pounding. No Santos. Still. And she couldn't call Jack again. She fidgeted with the bracelet at her wrist and tried to decide what to do.

A dog barked in the distance. Through the windshield, she saw a glow of lights just above the tree line. It was a house, probably. A house where someone had Brady.

Was it Viper's house? She didn't know. She didn't know anything, really, except that sitting here doing nothing was making her insane. She couldn't do this. She couldn't just *sit* here, not when a child was in danger so close by.

Her chest tightened, and she closed her eyes. She felt like a kid again, in a tiny apartment in Los Angeles, a place with shag carpeting and paper-thin walls. She remembered the darkness, the sounds, the frantic pounding of her heart then, too, as she lay there, terrified to get out of bed and go do something about what she sensed was happening in the next room. Courtney had forgiven her years ago, but Fiona would never forgive herself.

She couldn't just sit here like this. But what could she do?

Inspiration struck suddenly, and her eyes flew open. She started her car again. She did a careful, three-point turn, and made an agonizingly slow journey back to the main highway. She kept the headlights off and prayed for divine guidance as the car dipped down and rolled across the low-water bridge. She couldn't see a thing past her dashboard, and even the faint glow of the instrument panel made her nervous. At least her Honda was quiet, relatively speaking. She bumped along slowly, and when she felt the surface beneath her change from dirt to asphalt, she turned right and pulled onto the shoulder. Then she grabbed her phone from the console and got out of the car.

Using the phone like a flashlight, she held it low to the ground and made her way to the juncture where the two roads met. After a few moments of stumbling around, she found a post and, atop it, the very thing she was searching for.

A mailbox. Painted like a flag.

Lowell wasn't home, and no one else seemed to be either. The man lived in a small clapboard one-story that reminded Jack of his own place, except Lowell's was a dump. Trash bags littered the porch, and the screen on the front door was nearly torn out. Evidently the man hadn't done a lick of maintenance work since his divorce two Christmases ago—a divorce that, according to Lowell, had been amicable.

But what did Jack know, really? An hour ago, he would have sworn he knew each and every one of his direct reports. Now, all bets were off.

Jack looked around. He listened. But the place was silent, save the rustle of too-tall grass in the nighttime breeze. There were no vehicles in sight, and the house was locked up tight as a drum.

Carlos came around from the back porch, clutching his service weapon. "Nothing. Don't think anyone's here."

Jack itched to leave. He felt certain they were in the wrong location, but Lowell's rickety wooden storage shed kept drawing his attention. A lone yellow lightbulb shone above the door. The structure was eight-by-ten, or thereabouts, and the hardware on the door looked a hell of a lot newer than the rest of the shed.

"Fancy lock," Jack commented, and trekked across the yard.

Carlos pulled out a flashlight and followed him. He shone it on the window to the shed and confirmed Jack's suspicion that the pane of glass had been painted black.

"What do you think he keeps in there?"

"No warrant," Carlos reminded him.

Jack planted his hands on his hips and stared at the shed for a few seconds. He picked up a rock and—

"Jack."

—hummed it straight through the windowpane. Then he took out his mini Mag-Lite and shone it inside.

"Holy shit," he muttered.

Carlos walked up behind him, and they both gazed inside at a blue Hyundai Elantra.

But even more startling than the car was the rank odor wafting through the broken pane of glass.

Carlos coughed. "I know that smell."

"Go back to the truck, Chief."

"Why?"

Jack rounded the shed. "Because you don't want to be a witness when I bust down this door." He gave the door a sharp kick and sent splinters flying.

"Fucking A," Jack said, reading the vehicle tag. "It's her car. Right here. We've had a BOLO on this for ten days."

Jack glanced in all the car's windows, then walked to the trunk. "Hand me that tire iron."

But Carlos had a better idea. He jerked his shirttail out and used it to keep from leaving prints as he opened the door. Then he leaned down and popped the trunk button.

Jack shone his light in. "Holy Christ."

"What you got?"

The stench about knocked him over, and the *sight* . . . Both bullet wounds to the forehead were neat, clean, but the torso was another matter. It looked like a giant snake had been gutted. Jack stepped back and tried not to retch.

"J.B.? What is it?"

"I think I found Viper."

Jack whipped back onto the highway, leaving Lowell's house in the dust.

"What are we, twenty? Twenty-five miles out?"

Carlos checked the map as his phone buzzed.

"Santos," he told Jack, and answered it. Carlos gave the agent a brief rundown of what they'd discovered in Lowell's shed. He was vague about how, exactly, Lowell's window had come to be broken, and after a few minutes of listening, he glanced at Jack. "Sure, he's right here." He passed over the phone.

Jack took it. "Yeah?"

"It's Santos. I need you to call Fiona. She'll listen to you. Convince her to stay away from that house. I've run a check on the Schenck family, and I think I've got our suspect."

"Talk fast."

"We're looking at Scott Schenck, thirty-eight, occupation unknown. Born in Meyersberg, Texas, graduated high school there. Last known address was an RV park in Maricopa County, Arizona. Turns out, we've got a thin file on this guy already. He tried to volunteer for a civilian militia group there, but was asked to leave by the leader of that organization because he didn't, quote, 'work well with others.' "

"There's a surprise."

"Attracted the attention of a couple of undercover agents several years ago when he started showing up to Aryan Nations meetings in Utah and Arizona. He's since dropped off the radar. No tax return, nothing."

"Sounds like a model citizen," Jack said.

"Here's something else. I've got a fax in my hand from San Antonio PD, where Schenck used to live with a—get this—*Gabriela Vega*. She filed a restraining order against him twelve years ago. Told police they'd broken up, and he wouldn't leave her alone. Six months later, Gabriela Vega turned up dead from a gunshot wound to the forehead, but the autopsy concluded it was self-inflicted."

"GSW to the forehead. Same as Viper."

"Yeah, I know," Santos said. "The police initially questioned Schenck, but he had an alibi, apparently. We're talking about a dangerous person with a highly volatile temper. If there's anything you can say to Fiona to get her away from there, you need to say it now. Last I talked to her, she seemed to be on a quest to get her witness out of harm's way."

"Got it." He disconnected and returned the phone to Carlos. Then Jack took out his cellular and dialed Fiona. It took him two tries because his hands were shaking all over the place.

His stomach somersaulted until, finally, she answered.

"Where are you? Are you all right?"

"I was just about to call you," she said. "I found the mailbox with the Confederate flag. This is Viper's house. I think he's the one who took Brady. I didn't get a good look, but—"

"Viper's dead." He let the words hang there a moment, hoping they would scare some sense into her. "Two bullets to the forehead. And then he was gutted with a knife and stuffed in Natalie's trunk."

"Natalie Fuentes?"

"You got it. Now listen up, Fiona. No more arguments. Carlos and I have an ETA of fifteen minutes, and Santos is on his way with a hostage-rescue team. You're in the way, and you need to get gone."

He heard a whimper on the other end of the phone.

"Fiona?"

"I just . . . Brady's in there. Right now. What if we're too late?"

"You can't save everyone." Goddamn it, she wasn't listening. "You're not responsible for every kid in trouble."

"Sometimes you are." Her voice wobbled, and he knew she was crying.

"Is this about Courtney? Is this about some bullshit from your past? Because if you really love your sister, you won't do this." *If you really love me, you won't do this.*

"I'm sorry, Jack." And she clicked off.

Fiona pulled the Ruger from her purse and checked it. It was loaded. She tossed the handbag on her front seat and quietly closed the car door. She wanted both hands free to hold her gun, so she stuffed the cell phone into her bra, safe and sound. Knowing Jack would call again, she'd switched the power off so she wouldn't lose her life over an inopportune snippet of Vivaldi.

She took a deep breath and looked around. It was dark. Very. The persistent barking in the distance sent a thread of fear down her spine. Fiona rubbed the scar at her neck, and tried to put the dog out of her mind as she crept over to the scrub bushes lining the road. For the *n*th time today, she regretted her attire. The soles of her Ferragamo pumps crunched on the gravel, but she didn't want to kick them off in case the ground was covered with sticker burrs. Her dress snagged on some bushes, and she stooped to tug it free.

Despite what Jack thought, she didn't have a death wish. She had no intention of getting anywhere near Brady's kidnapper if there was any way to avoid it. Santos was bringing in a trained hostage-rescue team. Her goal was to keep tabs on the situation and hopefully learn Brady's location so she could tell Santos as soon as possible. That was all.

Unless, of course, someone tried to hurt Brady. If that

happened . . . well, she didn't know exactly. She gripped the Ruger tightly and tiptoed up the road.

"Drop it."

She gasped and whirled around.

"You got three seconds."

She stood petrified, too scared even to breathe. The voice came out of nowhere, and her gaze couldn't penetrate the darkness.

"Two."

She glanced down at the bright red pinprick flickering across her chest. Wherever he was, he had a bead on her.

"One."

She dropped the gun.

CHAPTER

21

"Slow down, Chief."

Jack shot Carlos a look as they rocketed down the highway. The speedometer was pushing one hundred, but the road wouldn't come fast enough.

"Where's that turnoff?"

"Eight, ten more miles," Carlos said. The phone in his hand buzzed, and he answered it. From what Jack overheard, it sounded like Santos again, wanting an update.

"HRT's on its way," Carlos announced after hanging up. "They're coming by chopper. Team's out of San Antonio, though, so it could take a while. Santos is en route to Viper's, probably be there in twenty minutes."

Jack tried to visualize the logistics. A helo full of SWAT jocks would drop down on the house where Fiona was skulking around, probably peeking in windows. She stood an excellent chance of getting caught in the cross fire, and that was if she *hadn't* already managed to get noticed by the bad guys. This was a guaranteed goatfuck.

"It's not like they're just gonna burst in, guns blazing," Carlos said, reading his mind. "Not with civilians involved."

Civilians. Jack scoffed. This opinionated, resourceful,

hardheaded woman who'd turned his world upside down was a *civilian*. She had no business being involved in this mess, but she was right in the middle of it. And why? Because he'd put her there.

If anything happened to her, he'd never forgive himself.

"Pop that glove box," he said. "Make sure my SIG's loaded."

Jack focused on the road, blinking the sweat from his eyes, as he heard the click and slide of Carlos checking his backup piece. Jack's department-issued Glock was in a weapons locker at the station house. He was a civilian now, too, and the knowledge grated on him.

"When we get there," Carlos said, "you need to stay on the sidelines."

Jack grunted.

"I mean it, J.B. You got no authority here—"

"You can have the arrest. I just need Fiona."

"I'm not talking about an arrest. I'm talking about you getting your ass shot off on my watch. It's not gonna happen."

"I know it's not." Jack held his hand out for the weapon. Carlos passed it over, and Jack tucked it into the back of his pants, where his black leather belt held it snugly against his spine. He wished he had a holster, but when he'd put on his only suit this afternoon, he'd been expecting to spend the evening at a freaking art gallery.

"*Locote,*" Carlos muttered.

"What's that?"

"You," he snapped. "Still thinking with your dick."

Fiona's breath rasped in and out as he moved closer. The red spot on her chest expanded until it was as big as a quarter, a fiery preview of the hole he would blow in her if she decided to move.

But she couldn't move. She couldn't think. She couldn't do anything besides stand, immobile, as his shape materialized out of the shadows. He was silhouetted faintly in the middle of the road, and he held a mean-looking gun level with his shoulder. An assault rifle, she guessed, judging from the size of it.

He scooped her Ruger off the ground, and then let the rifle dangle at his side. She saw now that he wore it on a strap slung across his body.

The man was short. Stocky. And broad-shouldered, just as Lucy had described him. She remembered all the other things Lucy had described, and her knees wanted to buckle.

He tucked the Ruger into the back of his pants and then pulled something from his pocket. "You're trespassing."

"I was just—"

Pain shot through her as he wrenched her arm behind her back. He lashed her wrists together with some kind of cord and pulled it taut, until her skin burned. She sucked in a breath, and he jerked her hands higher, bringing tears to her eyes.

"That hurt?" He dropped her hands, and her breath whooshed out. He jabbed her in the shoulder blade with his gun. "Better toughen up. We got a long way to go."

He prodded her again, and she stumbled over the gravel. They moved toward the house, getting closer to the barking with every step. She could have wept at the irony. Some psychopath was shoving her around with an assault rifle, and all she could think of was a pair of sharp canines sinking into her flesh. The scar at her neck seemed to burn, and her breath came shallower. She had to concentrate on her footsteps to keep from losing it.

They rounded a grove of trees, and the building came into view. It was a brick ranch house with an attached garage. The weedy yard was illuminated by a pair of floodlights, one on each corner of the home. Some sort of aluminum camper sat off to the side, under a tree.

And standing at the screen door was a monstrous-looking dog, barking wildly and pawing at the mesh. Fiona halted.

The gun barrel jabbed her back. "Up the stairs."

"Call off your dog."

He sneered behind her. "Don't like dogs, huh?"

She didn't say anything, and the dog kept up the racket. Finally, the man gave a sharp whistle, and it stopped.

She glanced over her shoulder and sucked in a breath. In the glare of the floodlights, she got her first good look at him—wide nose, deep-set eyes, square jaw. Identical to her sketch down to the pockmarked skin. It was as if her drawing had sprung to life—the Pygmalion story, except this artist definitely wouldn't fall in love with her creation.

"Move," he ordered.

She gulped and mounted the front step. "What kind of dog is that?"

"Rottweiler." He reached around her and pulled open the screen door. The dog scurried forward and nosed her crotch.

"Heel!"

She wasn't sure if he meant her or the dog, but the dog obeyed. Another prod, and Fiona stepped over the threshold. The dog's chops hung open, displaying a mouthful of menacing teeth and a copious supply of drool. The man stepped in behind her.

The door squeaked shut, and Fiona watched, shocked, as he pulled a Milk Bone from his pocket and dropped it into the dog's snapping jaws. He glanced at Fiona.

"Back bedroom."

Her blood ran cold.

"Now."

She darted her gaze around, desperate for any kind of help. Another person. A weapon. A distraction. All she saw was an unkempt living room and a kitchen blanketed with dirty dishes and beer cans. The place smelled like sour milk and marijuana.

He watched her, drumming his fingers on the gun barrel at his side. "Don't make me say things twice."

Fiona glanced at the darkened corridor on the far side of the room. Brady might be back there.

She moved toward the hall, sidestepping a stack of *Skin & Ink* magazines and an abandoned water bong on the living room floor. She wondered if her and Brady's chances were better if their captor was stoned. His eyes were bloodshot, but that could just be the intensity of the past few days. If Jack and Santos were right, this man was escalating. He'd killed at least two people in the past five days and kidnapped an innocent little boy and now a police consultant. Not prudent behavior. He was becoming manic and bloodthirsty and sloppy about covering his tracks. He was unraveling.

Fiona felt his presence behind her as she walked down the carpeted hallway. There were three doors. The first was closed, and the second stood partly ajar, revealing a room crammed with stools and a padded table. Viper's home office?

"Last one."

She stopped at the last door and waited as he reached

around her to open it. It was pitch-black inside, and her body tensed.

She turned to face him, and stared into his eyes. *Make him see you as human. Establish a connection.* She didn't know where the thoughts came from, she just knew she should heed them.

"Could you loosen my bindings, please? My arms hurt."

He looked her over, his gaze lingering on her neck, and she wondered if he was visualizing his thick fingers wrapped around it. She took a step back.

Suddenly the butt of the gun came up. She toppled backward, into the darkness, and the door banged shut.

Jack's phone hummed, and the number on the screen caught him by surprise. It hadn't even occurred to him to check on Lucy after hearing about Brady.

"Are you all right?"

"So nice of you to call," she said. "And yes, I'm fine."

"Sorry, Luce, but it's been crazy. I'm on my way—"

"I know where you are. I've got a sheriff's deputy parked in my kitchen, and he's been on the phone for the past ten minutes. Sounds like this is coming to a head."

Jack skidded around a bend, and Carlos braced a hand on the dashboard. Their turnoff was supposed to be just up ahead.

"I've got some friendly advice, Jack."

He eased his foot off the gas so he wouldn't fly past the turn. Any second now—

"We're still friends, right?"

Shit. "This isn't a good time, Lucy. I'll call you later."

"There might not *be* a later, if you're doing what I think you're doing."

"Huh?"

"You're on a mission, right? Rescue the girl? Settle an old score? Get your head blown off?"

"Lucy—"

"Shut up, Jack. I know you. Probably better than anybody. So listen when I tell you he's not worth it. You already lost your job. Don't lose your life, too. Let the FBI bring him in. You can stand next to me someday and watch him get the needle, but don't do anything stupid. You don't need to be a hero."

"On your left," Carlos said.

Jack slammed on the brakes and bumped his chin on the steering wheel as the truck squealed to a halt. "Shit!"

Lucy sighed. "Too bad you never listen to good advice."

"I listened." He did a quick U-turn and brought the truck to a stop just yards away from Viper's mailbox. Jack cursed himself. If he'd followed up on this lead himself, he might have prevented this whole fiasco.

"You probably don't get this, Jack, but I really do love you. I want you to be happy. I want *me* to be happy. I can handle losing you to someone else, but I can't handle going to your funeral."

Jack thrust the truck into park. Lucy had the crappiest timing of anyone he knew. "I gotta go. And stop planning my funeral. Jesus. This'll all work out."

He hoped.

"Maybe," she said bitterly. "But I'm a pessimist."

Fiona lay sprawled on the carpet, trying to get her wind back. She'd fallen awkwardly on her arm, and it hurt. Badly. She didn't think it was broken, but she was certain she'd have bruises tomorrow.

If she was alive tomorrow.

She sat up and looked around, frustrated once again by the darkness and her bindings. The hallway outside was dim, but she could just make out a strip of gray beneath the door. On the far side of the room were faint, thin stripes of light peeking through miniblinds. There had to be a light switch somewhere, probably beside the door. She scooted over to it, and used the wall to help lever herself up. She rubbed her good shoulder against the Sheetrock and finally bumped into a switch. Using her chin, she flipped it up.

Still dark.

She heard a faint *thud* nearby.

"Brady?" she hissed.

Another thud.

"Brady, where are you?" She followed the dull sounds until her shoulder brushed up against another door frame. Maybe a closet. Or a bathroom. She turned her back to it and groped around with her bound hands until she found the doorknob. She twisted it.

The door was unlocked, thank goodness, and she pulled it open. "Brady, it's Fiona. Is that you?"

There was a grunt, and something bumped against her leg.

She crouched down. "Is there something over your mouth?"

Another sound that she took for a yes.

"Lie down, okay?" She kept her voice low. "I'll see what I can do, but my hands are tied up, so bear with me, all right?"

She felt soft fabric over bony arms. Probably a T-shirt. Then a shoulder, a chin. There was something smooth stretched over his face, and she imagined it was duct tape.

"Did he tape your mouth?" She managed to peel back a

corner. It was definitely some sort of tape. "This is going to hurt, okay? But I'll do it fast. Stay still. And stay quiet, even when it stings."

She tried to get a good grip on the edge of the tape, then steadied herself and yanked straight up as quickly as she could. She heard a moan and felt a hot rush of breath on her hands.

"I'm sorry," she whispered. "Are you okay? We have to talk quietly."

He didn't say anything for a moment, but she could hear his breath wheezing in and out. Was he asthmatic? She didn't know anything about his health history.

"Brady, are you hurt? Can you talk?"

"Yeah," he rasped. "I'm just . . . I dunno. I feel weird. He made me drink something."

"What did it taste like?"

"Maybe . . . grape? It was sweet. Some kinda medicine, I think."

Fiona's mind raced. Lucy had been drugged with what she thought was cough syrup. The fact that Brady's tasted fruity was probably good. Maybe it was a children's formula.

"I know you're groggy, but try to think. Do you know if there's a light switch or a lamp somewhere?"

"There's a light in here. He turned it on when he first put me in. This closet's full of clothes and sports equipment and stuff."

Fiona pushed to her feet.

"One of those pull switches. With the chain."

She stumbled farther into the closet and moved her head around until she felt something metal brush against her cheek. She managed to capture it in her teeth and pull.

Light.

Brady was curled on the floor. He squinted up at her, and she saw purple stains on his T-shirt, probably the medicine. She didn't see any blood, but his hands were secured behind his back with silver duct tape.

Duct tape was good. She could tear it, unlike twine, which they were going to need something sharp to get through.

Barking erupted from the front of the house, and they exchanged fearful looks. They probably didn't have much time.

"We have to hurry," she said, crouching down. "I'm going to try and tear your bindings. Then we can look for something sharp to cut mine. Or maybe you can undo the knots."

As she worked frantically on the tape, she heard a screen door slap shut. Then voices.

"Someone's here," Brady said.

The voices got louder, and Fiona strained to make out the words. It sounded like an argument. The dog had quieted, though.

This wasn't the cavalry coming to rescue them. This was someone who knew the killer.

Finally, she tore through the top layer of tape. Then the next. At last, she pulled the sticky scraps loose and dropped them to the floor.

"Ah ..." He winced as he moved his arms around.

"I know it hurts, but can you stand up?"

The arguing in the other room intensified. Fiona really wanted to listen to get a handle on what was going on.

"Look for something sharp to cut my hands free, okay? I'll be right back." She stumbled across the room, bumping into what felt like a bed, before reaching the door. She pressed her ear to it.

"They're fucking *Anglos*, for Christ's sake! What the fuck?"

Fiona didn't recognize the voice.

"You've lost sight of the big picture." Her captor sounded eerily calm compared to the other man.

"What picture? That you're a total dumb ass?"

Fiona turned to Brady. "Have you found anything?" she whispered.

"No."

More arguing in the living room. "—and I never signed on for a kid. *Never.*"

"The enemy takes many forms."

Fiona shrank back from the door. They needed to get out of here. Her gaze darted to the window covered with miniblinds. But what about the dog? Surely it would begin barking its head off if they started creeping around outside.

"You're crazy, you know that?" a voice boomed. "I'm done! I don't owe your dad any more favors, and I'll be damned if I . . . what are you doing?"

The Honda was empty. Jack made a quick search of the vicinity around it, and didn't find any clues.

"She must be at the house," he told Carlos. "Let's split up. You go—"

Pop!

"What was that?" But Jack knew it was a gunshot. Coming from the direction of the house. He turned to Carlos. "Let's move!"

Brady looked terror-stricken. Fiona glanced at him, then back at the door as she struggled to think straight. They had to get out.

She rushed to the window. "Over here. Help me."

Brady looked as though he might puke, but he staggered to the window and pulled up the blinds. It was a simple lock, and he undid it quickly. He tried pulling the pane up, but it wouldn't budge.

"What's wrong?"

"I don't know," he said.

"Maybe it's painted shut." Fiona glanced around anxiously. The front of the house was silent.

"There's a baseball bat in the closet," Brady said.

"Get it."

It couldn't have been more than two minutes later when the bedroom door burst open. Light from the hallway poured into the pitch-dark room.

"You. On your feet." The man stepped toward her, and Fiona recognized the Ruger aimed straight at her face. "Where's the boy?"

"What boy?" Fiona pushed her shoulders back against the bed and struggled to stand.

He seized her arm and jerked her up. "The kid. What'd you do with him?"

"I don't know—" Her eyebrow exploded with pain as the butt of the gun smashed into her face.

"Don't lie to me, bitch!" He lunged for the closet, yanked open the door, and pulled the light switch. The storage space was crowded with clothes and boxes and sporting gear, but no Brady. He scowled at Fiona and then his gaze landed on the window behind her. A chilly gust drifted in, stirring the blinds.

He stepped forward and touched the gun to her forehead. The barrel was still warm.

"I should kill you right now."

CHAPTER

22

Jack plunged through the underbrush with Carlos at his heels. Carlos was talking into his phone, demanding backup, but Jack could tell it wasn't coming fast enough.

Finally the house came into view. Jack halted behind the cover of a cedar tree and motioned for Carlos to keep quiet as he surveyed the situation.

Two vehicles—a white pickup and a beige Suburban. Jack recognized the Suburban.

"Lowell's here," Carlos said.

"This complicates things. He'll be armed. He'll—"

An engine roared to life behind the house. "Someone's taking off!" Jack said, panicking.

"You think they're still inside? Fiona and Brady?"

"I don't know. I heard *one* shot. Either one of them could be in there, injured or worse."

Carlos craned his neck to look at the house. "Or they could be getting away."

Jack envisioned Fiona bleeding out on the floor, right this second. "I'm going in," he said. "Go see if you can get a visual on the vehicle. I'm guessing it's Viper's."

Carlos took off around the side of the house. Jack bolted across the front lawn and ducked for cover behind the Suburban. After a second of silence, he made a run for the door. He plastered himself against the wall beside it, and listened intently.

Nothing. Not even a growl from that dog they'd heard barking like crazy just minutes before. The wooden door stood open, and Jack predicted the screen door would be unlatched. He readied his weapon.

In one swift motion, he yanked the door open and entered low, ready to fire. He did a 180-degree sweep of the room.

Silence greeted him. And Lowell, lying on a carpet soaked with blood.

Fiona cowered against the side of the SUV, struggling to put as much space as possible between herself and the dog. The Rottweiler rested his nose against her seat and rumbled deep in his throat.

"Max senses your fear," the man told her. "It gives him the advantage."

Was he serious? Max already had a mouth full of advantages and a master who was holding her at gunpoint. She thought of leaping out of the speeding Tahoe, but she couldn't get her bound hands around to the door handle without attracting attention.

Establish a connection. She gulped down the bile clogging her throat and tried to breathe.

"What's your name?" she asked.

He ignored her as they continued to bump and bounce over the terrain. As far as she could tell, they weren't on any road, and yet he seemed to know where they were going. He also didn't seem to care about mowing down cacti and scrub bushes to get there.

"Where are we going?" she asked.

He cocked his head to the side, as if considering it. "People underestimate dogs' intelligence. Take Max, for instance. His IQ's probably higher than yours."

Okay, non sequitur. Fiona darted a glance at Max, whose rump was settled on the backseat. His ears had perked up, and he seemed to know he was being talked about. What a genius.

"How long have you had Max?"

He sighed. "You know, you need a license to catch a fish, but any asshole can just walk into a pound and get a dog?" He shook his head. "That's what's wrong with this country; no one has any perspective."

All right, this guy had a screw loose. But she'd already known that.

"What's your name?" she asked again.

He shot her a cool look. "What do you care?"

She cared a lot, considering the sacrifices she'd made to help crack this case open. But beyond that, she needed to establish a rapport with him.

"I'm Fiona."

The SUV rattled as they crossed a cattle guard. Suddenly he braked and put it in park. "Hey, Fiona. Shut the fuck up, okay? We're not buddies."

Max growled from the backseat, as if to agree.

"Why don't you let me go?"

"I don't think so." His eyes narrowed, making him look truly predatory. She'd seen his handiwork up close and knew he was capable of unspeakable cruelty. And now he was so near, she could smell his sweat.

"Why am I here?" Her heart pounded against her ribs as she waited for an answer.

"Thanks to you, *Fiona*, my picture's posted at every gas station and police department in this godforsaken state." He dug into his pocket and produced what looked like a polished animal bone. He popped out a blade, and she inhaled sharply.

"I'm going underground. And if I run into trouble, you're my bargaining chip. Gimme your hands."

She eyed the blade and decided the black stuff on it was dried blood.

He jerked her around and started sawing away at the bindings. The twine loosened, and pain flooded the nerve endings in her arms and wrists.

He scooted onto the console. "Climb over me. You're driving."

"Me? Why?"

He used one hand to fold and put away the knife, and the other to point the Ruger. "Because I said so."

This was her chance. She had to do something. But trying to wrestle the gun away would be suicide. Maybe she could make a run—

"Now."

Fiona climbed over him, trying to conceal her left hand as she plunged it into her bra. Her fingers closed around her cell phone, and she tugged it out.

"This better be an automatic," she babbled, grasping for a distraction. "I never learned how to drive a standard transmission." She plopped into the driver's seat and tucked the phone into the folds of her skirt. Her black bra was showing now, and she hoped he wouldn't notice and get curious.

"Take a left," he said. "And hurry it up. We don't have all night."

She shifted into drive and took a cautious left onto a

paved roadway. She didn't see any signs, but it no longer looked like they were on private property.

"Faster."

She pressed the gas pedal, trying to look comfortable behind the wheel, so he wouldn't notice when she dropped her hand into her lap. She needed to activate her phone and press redial, but she had to think of something to cover the noise. Brady was back at the house, hiding under the bed, and she needed to get a message to someone before a SWAT team showed up and started shooting the place to bits. She had no idea what their procedures were, but she knew it wasn't safe for a dazed little boy to be on the scene when they arrived.

"I'm feeling nauseous," she said. "Can we pull over?"

"No."

They kept driving, and she tried to look ill. "Please . . . Would you open the window at least? I think I'm going to throw up if I don't get some air."

He looked at her with disgust and then lowered the window a few inches on his side. Max helped with the distraction by scrambling out of the backseat and jumping into the man's lap so he could poke his nose out.

"Thank you, that's much better," she gushed. "Sometimes I get carsick."

She stared straight ahead, stiffly, and hoped he hadn't just heard the telltale beep of her phone coming to life.

Jack and Santos sprinted back to the truck.

"Suspect is fleeing," Carlos yelled into the phone. "And we got an officer down. I repeat, officer down. We need immediate assistance."

Jack jumped behind the wheel and started the truck. Before Carlos had even closed the door, he was hurtling down the highway. "I need the cross street that picks up Route 964. If they went north across this property, that's bound to be where they end up."

"Chopper's almost here," Carlos told Jack. And then into the phone, "That's right, *no* hostages. I repeat, both hostages still missing." He snatched the map off the floor and bent over it. "You need Buck Ridge Trail. Should be the next one up. Hang a right."

The sign came into view. Jack made a sharp right and then gunned it. His phone started buzzing, and he jerked it out of his pocket.

"Sweet Christ, it's her." He punched the Talk button. "Where are you?"

She didn't answer, and he realized she might not be able to talk.

"Shh!" He motioned for Carlos to shut up and then pressed the phone to his ear.

". . . I think this is wrong." Fiona's voice was barely audible. "I mean, are you sure this is *west*? It feels like north to me. Or maybe east."

She was with him. Right now. *She's with him,* Jack mouthed.

Carlos gestured for him to put the phone on mute. Good plan. He did, and tried like hell to pay attention to the road, and the phone, and whatever the guy was saying. But the only voice he could hear was Fiona's, and even that was barely a murmur.

But she was alive.

His shoulders sagged from relief over that one shred of information.

Jack spotted the sign for Route 964 and hooked a right. If he guessed correctly, this road paralleled the back of Viper's property.

"Okay, okay . . . But I don't want to get pulled over."

"I think they're heading west," Jack whispered, even though the phone was muted.

"Shit, we'll pass 'em."

The words were just out of his mouth when a pair of headlights came into view up the highway.

"That might be them," Jack said. "Call Santos and let him know. Maybe they can set up a roadblock."

The headlights were coming fast. Much too fast. Jack slowed down and strained to listen.

She was saying something about Brady. About a window. She was probably talking about the bedroom window. It had been broken, but the opening wasn't sizable enough for a person to fit through.

"Can you blame him?" she was asking. "Kids get scared easily. If it had been me, I would have been hiding under the bed."

"She's trying to tell us something," Jack said. "I think Brady's under a bed somewhere. Tell Santos. Make sure whoever goes in there knows to look for a kid. Probably hiding."

Just then the car flashed its headlights and flew past.

Jack jerked his head around. "It's them. Shit, I think she's driving. She must have recognized my truck."

He eased off the accelerator and watched the taillights in his rearview mirror. He was tempted to pull an immediate U-turn, but he didn't want to tip the guy off. The SUV faded over a rise, and Jack slammed on the brakes. His truck fishtailed to a stop, and he turned it around.

"What's the plan, J.B.?"

Jack killed the headlights and stomped on the pedal. "We're going after them."

She felt his gaze burning into her like a laser.

He'd caught the lights thing. It had been a risk to do it, and now she'd provoked him.

"You think you're smarter than me, don't you? You think I don't know what you're doing, you little bitch?"

She stared straight ahead and gripped the steering wheel. Her gamble had failed. She'd thought the truck might have been Jack, but its taillights had disappeared in the rearview mirror.

"You fuck with me, there's consequences. That's something you need to learn." He jabbed a finger at the control panel, and Fiona looked down, puzzled.

The cigarette lighter. She shot him a glance and saw his lip curl into a smile. Lucy had told her about that smile, about how every time she saw it, she knew something horrible was coming.

Fiona shifted her gaze to the road and tried to breathe. She had to get away. . . .

Click. The lighter popped out, and he reached for it. He held it up, admiring the glowing coil at the end.

Fiona swerved off the highway and jammed on the brakes. The SUV pitched down, and up, and metal scraped against metal as they careened into the barbed-wire fence. Yelps and curses exploded beside her, and her body snapped forward, then back again.

For an instant, everything was still.

Adrenaline flooded her veins, and she shoved open the

door. She tumbled out, landing on all fours, and then tripped to her feet. Barks rang in her ears. She ran, heart thundering, as fast as her legs could go.

Jack screeched to a halt just behind the wreckage and jumped out of the truck, SIG in hand. Where was Fiona? The driver's-side door stood open, but—

Pop! Pop!

"Take cover!" Carlos yelled, ducking behind the door on his side. "Where's the shooter?"

"I don't know!" And where was Fiona?

"Police! Drop the gun!" Carlos bellowed.

The windshield shattered.

"Get behind the engine block!" Jack shouted, and Carlos dove back into the cab and elbow-crawled over the seat. With three tons of metal between them and the gunman, they crouched on the street. Furious barks sounded nearby.

"Couldn't see him," Carlos said, panting. "Think he's still in there?"

"I don't know. Did you see Fiona?"

He shook his head. Then he jerked out his phone and placed an urgent call for backup.

Jack eased toward the front bumper and peered over the hood. Where was she? He couldn't see worth shit.

"Duck inside the cab and flip my brights," he told Carlos. "I'll try and get a shot from behind the glare. Wait for my signal."

Jack steadied his arms on the hood and waited. He had to be 100 percent sure. If he mistook the target . . . Sweat streamed down his temples, and he took a deep breath and nodded.

The lights flashed on, and a shadow moved inside the wreck. Jack's trigger finger flinched, but he wasn't certain.

Pop!

He leaped back, like he'd been singed. "Son of a *bitch!*" He slid down and leaned against the tire well, clutching his shoulder.

"You're *hit?*"

"Bastard nicked me." Jack squeezed his eyes shut.

"You sure it's just a nick?"

No. "Yeah, I'm sure."

"Shit, it's bleeding everywhere."

"Forget it." Damn, how had this happened? He'd thought he had the advantage. He looked at Carlos. "We need a new plan. How about—"

"Down!"

Carlos jerked him to the pavement, and rifle fire reverberated all around them. Jack swung his weapon toward the noise, but the shooter was down already, sprawled in front of the pickup.

"You got him!"

"Did you see that?" Carlos sputtered. "A fucking AK-47! He tried to Swiss cheese us!"

"I think he's alive." Jack trained his weapon on the gunman and approached warily. Sure enough, one of the arms moved, like he was reaching for something.

With lightning speed, Carlos had him rolled on his stomach with his hands cuffed. Blood was pouring from the man's right leg.

Jack hurdled the guy and rushed to the SUV.

It was empty except for a pissed-off Rottweiler. Someone had leashed it to the door handle, probably to keep it from ruining the stealth attack.

"Fiona!" Jack ran in front of the wreck and glanced around frantically. The vehicle's high beams made a surreal white landscape of weeds and rocks and fence posts, but Fiona was nowhere. Where could she be? She must have fled right after impact.

Just before bullets had started flying.

"Fiona!" Desperate, he turned around in circles. Maybe she was hiding. Maybe she'd run the other way.

And then he spotted her. A dark heap at the bottom of the ditch.

He sprinted over and dropped to his knees. She lay on her side in the leaves and muck. "Fiona? Oh, Jesus." Her eyelids fluttered, then closed. He turned back toward Carlos. *"We need an ambulance!"*

Gently, he rolled her onto her back. Her hair was sticky and warm. "Fiona? Can you hear me?" He ran his hands over her face, her head, her neck, searching for the source of all the blood. It seemed to be gushing from a spot near her ear. "Honey, stay with me."

Jack ripped off his bloodied shirt and wadded it into a ball. He pressed it against her head as a stream of incoherent words spilled out of him. He didn't know what he was saying, only that he was pleading with her and willing her to hear him.

"Fiona, hold on."

Her eyes opened then, and Jack's heart lurched. She murmured something.

"What?" He leaned closer.

"I'm ... scared."

"It's okay. Help's coming." Sirens wailed faintly in the distance, but they never seemed to get close.

God, her full, beautiful lips were gray. Her eyes were wide with shock.

"Stay with me, now." He picked up her hand and pressed it flat against his chest. "Help's coming, okay? Just hold on."

CHAPTER

23

Shelby Sherwood was hungry.

And not the small, quiet hungry, like when you went to bed without dinner. This hungry was fierce, like an animal with teeth and claws wrestling her insides.

She took another two steps and sank down beside a broken log. She felt dizzy. She tipped her head back and stared up at the pine trees, high as skyscrapers, and wished for something to eat.

An extra-cheese pizza from Dino's. She'd eat it straight out of the box and wouldn't share a single piece with Colter.

Well, maybe one.

A new pain twisted her stomach, and the thing she'd been trying to forget about for days and nights and weeks popped back into her head.

I want to go home.

But she didn't know where home was. She only knew it wasn't here.

She looked up at the sunbeams coming down through the branches. The beams were white and thick, and made her think about God. She'd been thinking about God a lot lately and wondering if her dad was with Him up in heaven right now, looking down at her.

She'd heard her grandma talking once, saying her dad was a sinner because he drank too much and never went to church. Her mom had argued, but Shelby knew her grandma was right—at least about the drinking and the church part.

But Shelby thought maybe God was different from that. Maybe He understood about the bad things, like her dad's drinking, and the way she sometimes lied to her mom, and the way she'd sneaked onto the computer when she wasn't allowed. Shelby knew she'd brought all this on herself, but she hoped maybe God didn't see it like that.

Shelby closed her eyes and let the sun warm her face. Her cheeks felt cold from the tears she couldn't quit making, and her stomach started to twist again.

She rubbed the hair away from her face and got up. She had to find food. It had been four days since she'd eaten much of anything, and three days since the man had left, saying he'd be back with hamburgers. He'd stayed gone a long time—longer than ever before—and Shelby had thought she should try to get away from the cabin. He'd nailed the windows shut and locked the door with a key and told her don't make trouble, or she'd be sorry.

And he'd made her sorry before, so she'd believed him. But when morning came, and he still wasn't back, she'd decided to try anyhow.

Shelby walked on through the forest now, looking for blackberries or dewberries, like she and Colter used to pick near their grandma's house. She didn't want to remember the man anymore. She hated thinking of his ugly hands and his stinky breath in her face. She hated everything about him.

I want to go home.

She pushed the thought away again and kept walking. The ground was soft under her Skechers, and her feet were so numb, she almost didn't feel the blisters anymore.

The bushes rustled, and she looked along the edges of the path. She'd seen squirrels and chipmunks and even a rabbit, but not a single other person since she'd left the cabin. She didn't mind. Sleeping alone on the moss and leaves was better than being back there.

Shelby's legs wobbled, but she kept going. She didn't want to stop yet, not until she'd found something to eat. Maybe if she listened hard, she'd at least find a stream to drink out of. So she walked and listened. The trees started to thin out, and the ground wasn't as soft. Something white and lacy up ahead made her stop.

A mayhaw tree. Her grandma had mayhaws. She gathered the berries every year for jelly and cooked them up in her big soup pot. Shelby liked to watch as she poured the red juice into jars that said *Ball* on the sides.

She got close to the tree. It was small, like a midget compared to the big pines. She didn't see any berries—just flowers—but she grasped the trunk with both hands and started shaking. She shook and shook and the flowers came down like snowflakes.

"What you doing to my tree, child?"

Shelby spun around. At first she didn't see the woman. Her skinny brown body and her baggy brown clothes blended right in with the tree trunks.

"Fruit don't come for a while yet. You just shakin' the flowers loose."

Shelby stepped back as the woman came close. She squinted down at Shelby from underneath a straw hat.

"You a mess, girl."

"I was just . . ." Shelby glanced at the tree. "I was looking for berries."

The woman worked something around in her mouth. She turned and spit on the ground. She squinted some more and leaned her head to the side. "You hungry?"

Shelby nodded.

"Come on, now."

She waited a second and then followed the woman down the windy path to a brighter place where all the trees were short. There was a cabin up on blocks with white-flowering mayhaws all around it.

"You set there on the porch."

Shelby dropped onto the lowest wooden step and rubbed her palms on her jeans. Her hands were dirty. Her face was probably dirty. Her hair hung around her head like string, and she needed a toothbrush.

But then she heard oil spitting, and the smell of bacon made her forget all that. Her mouth started to water. She ran her tongue over the empty place where her tooth had used to be, the one he'd knocked out that first day. She didn't like thinking about that day, but sometimes she couldn't help it because her tongue kept touching the empty spot. Her shoulders got tight, and she glanced into the cabin. Maybe this wasn't a good idea. Maybe she should run back into the woods.

But her stomach growled again, so she stayed, and the woman came onto the porch with a blue tin plate and cup.

"Careful, now. Coffee's hot." She put the cup and plate next to Shelby, and sat down on the highest step.

Shelby looked at the food and wanted to cry. Two pieces of bread, smeared with butter and jelly. Three strips of bacon. She snatched one up and stuffed the whole thing in her mouth. After a few chews, she picked up the bread.

The woman watched her from under the hat. "That's the best mayhaw jelly in Sabine Parish. I sell more jars than Miss Mayhaw and Southern Best combined."

Shelby chewed the bread, feeling bad for hardly even tasting it.

The woman looked out at her yard. "People be saying these is miracle trees. Not supposed to bloom another three weeks yet. And after all that cold, we thought they might not bloom at all. Now here it is February, we got flowers everyplace."

The woman looked at her a long time, and Shelby tried to slow down, but her mouth seemed to be moving on its own.

"Where your people, girl? You out here alone?"

Shelby looked down. She swallowed. She didn't know what to say, so she picked up another piece of bacon.

The woman turned to her yard again.

"Miracle trees. Humph!" She made an arc of spit into the dirt. "We make our own miracles round here. Been through droughts and mealybugs, Katrina and Rita. Only thing kept my business going was a generator and a deep freezer and a strong back to haul it all up outta the flood."

Shelby didn't like coffee, but her mouth felt dry, so she drank some. It was warm, and the bitterness made her shudder.

"You that Georgia girl."

Shelby froze.

"People be looking for you. Just yesterday, some FBI man was asking 'bout you down at the gas station. Someone seen the car you was in over at the campground. Whole town's talking 'bout it."

She couldn't breathe. The food made a big, greasy ball in her stomach, and she thought she'd throw up. She glanced at the woods.

The woman reached out and placed a brown hand over hers. "Don't be scared now." Her voice was soft. "Ain't no one gonna hurt you here."

With her other hand, she pulled a cell phone out of her pocket. It was big and gray like a remote control.

"You got someone to call, baby? I can do it for you if you want."

She turned Shelby's palm up and pressed the phone into it. Shelby stared down, and her thumb seemed to remember the numbers. She lifted it to her ear.

The loud beeps made her jump.

"Dial one first, child. You in the piney woods of Louisiana."

Shelby tried again and waited through the rings. Then came her mother's voice, and she felt dizzy again.

"Mom, it's me." And the tears burst out. "I want to come home."

Fiona felt heavy, everywhere. She tried to move her arm, and then her leg, but every limb seemed cemented to the ground.

She wasn't on the ground. She was on something firm, but soft, and her head was slightly higher than the rest. She smelled Band-Aids. She opened her eyes and winced at the glaring light. Suddenly her skull seemed to squeeze, and she moaned.

Her arm lifted, and something warm enveloped her hand. It felt familiar. She remembered that warmth around her hand sometime before. When? It had been just after the bright lights and the pinpricks and the man with the blue mask.

"You awake?"

She opened her eyes again. This time Jack's big, dark form blocked the glare from the lamp beside her bed.

But it wasn't her bed. She darted her gaze around and panicked. She tried to sit up. The bolt of pain was so intense it sucked the breath out of her.

"Lay back."

"Where . . . ?" She didn't have enough air to finish the thought. Her throat felt dry.

"You're in the hospital." His voice was close. "They got you all taken care of now. You're going to be fine."

He squeezed her hand, and the heat of his fingers made her realize how cold the rest of her was.

"I'm cold."

He dropped her hand for a moment, and she panicked again. But then a thick blanket came up around her shoulders.

"Better?"

She tried to nod, which was a huge mistake. Someone seemed to be whacking her forehead with a mallet. She groaned and closed her eyes.

The commotion increased inside the room. She heard Jack's voice, and a woman, and then there was another man talking, and she slid back into darkness.

She opened her eyes again, and the room was brighter. Strangely, though, it wasn't nearly as painful as before. She let her gaze trail around slowly, taking in the pale blue walls, the brown curtains pulled closed, the table littered with coffee cups. On a beige recliner sat a giant red purse.

"Well, well! Look who's up!" Courtney appeared in her field of vision. She had a smile plastered on her face and black smudges under her eyes.

"Hi." Fiona's throat had never felt so dry. "Is there . . . water?"

"One venti water, coming right up." She rushed over to the sink and filled a pink plastic cup. "So, you decided to rejoin the world. Guess the drugs wore off, huh? I've been lobbying for you, but they're stingy around here."

She came back and nudged the straw between Fiona's lips. The water tasted wonderful. She wanted a hose.

"Don't overdo it." Courtney pulled the cup away much too soon. She was smiling, but Fiona saw the signs of strain. Her hair looked greasy, and she wasn't even wearing lipstick this morning.

It was morning, wasn't it? She remembered the room being darker before, and she remembered Jack's hand.

"Where's Jack?"

"Hmm, you mean my new favorite person? The man who rescued my sister from a homicidal maniac and plays a mean game of Texas Hold 'Em?" Courtney returned the plastic cup to the table. "I sent him out for sandwiches. He looks like death warmed over. He's hardly left the hospital in three days."

Three days. But . . .

"Apparently having your girlfriend get shot in the *head* and Life Flighted away takes a toll on a guy. Imagine that? I told him it was no biggie, but he's been kind of edgy about it."

Fiona let the words sink in. She'd been shot in the head? Was that why her skull felt two sizes too small?

Courtney sat on the bed, taking care not to pull the tube

hooked up to Fiona's arm. It trailed up to a clear plastic bag filled with some sort of liquid. The drugs that were making her thoughts fuzzy, probably.

She picked up Fiona's hand with her pale, slender fingers. Her hand was cool and small—not at all like Jack's—but amazingly comforting.

"God, Fiona." Her voice quavered. "You scared the *shit* out of me. Don't do that again, okay? To me *or* Jack. I've never seen a man so stricken as when I walked in this place and he was standing there with your blood all over him. And he had his own injury to worry about, but he wouldn't let anyone near him until he found out about you."

Fiona's stomach tightened. "What injury?"

"That psycho shot him in the shoulder. Straight through the muscle, so he was lucky. He says it's fine, but I'm sure it hurts like a bitch."

Jack had been shot. And it was *her* fault. She felt a stab of guilt, worse even than her headache, which was excruciating.

"How do you feel?"

Fiona closed her eyes. "Remember your twenty-first birthday? The tequila shooters? It's that hangover, times ten." She reached up and hesitantly touched the bandage at her forehead. "What happened, exactly?"

"You want the English version?" Courtney's voice was steadier now. "Because I can get Dr. McDreamy back here to give it to you in medispeak, but it would just piss you off like it did me."

A nurse popped her head in and smiled.

"Temperature check," she said, bustling in to poke and prod Fiona with various instruments.

"Bottom line, you were insanely lucky," Courtney said. "Bullet grazed your scalp just above your left ear. Eight stitches. You're having an extremely bad hair day, but it's not fatal. The real damage came when you tripped and conked yourself out on a rock. You suffered a concussion, but the doctor thinks you'll be fine by the end of today." Courtney stood up and stepped aside so the nurse could check the IV. "In other bullshit, you've got an ugly purple bruise on your chest, two cut wrists, and a nasty black eye. Jack and I are not amused."

Courtney crossed her arms and stared down at her. "But if you ask me nicely, I *might* consider helping you out with that haircut. And some makeup, too. You look like crap."

"Thanks."

"Anytime."

The nurse left, and Courtney shoved her purse on the floor and flopped onto the recliner. "FYI, I've taken charge of your social life. You've had two phone calls from a Garrett Sullivan, a visit from Nathan, a bouquet of carnations from someone by the name of 'Brady's Mom,' and two drop-ins by a Special Agent Santos, who says he needs to *debrief* you as soon as possible, and who also happens to be a total hottie. He can debrief me, if you're not up to it."

Fiona blinked at her. "Wow."

"Tell me about it. I had no idea you had so many men in your orbit. I'm thinking of becoming a cop." She glanced over her shoulder as a male voice drifted in from the hallway. "Okay, here's McDreamy. Look alive, okay? We want to get you home."

CHAPTER
24

In what Fiona felt pretty sure was a conspiracy, Courtney disappeared when it was time for Fiona to be discharged, meaning she faced an uncomfortable car ride with Jack all alone.

She didn't know what to say to him. Every time she looked over and saw the bulge of the bandage underneath his T-shirt, she wanted to cry. He'd been shot. Because of her. And in a horrible twist of fate, the weapon had been *her* Ruger, which she'd personally loaded.

"You comfortable?" Jack adjusted the air vents toward her. "If you're too warm, I'll turn it down."

"I'm fine."

The hovering was another thing. For the past twenty-four hours, he hadn't let her do anything for herself, not even go to the bathroom. She'd had to kick him out of there, cheeks flaming, so she could pee without an audience. He seemed to have appointed himself her personal bodyguard. And nursemaid. And chauffeur.

They pulled into her garage, and Jack slid the Honda into a parking space close to the door. Fiona looked around.

"Where's your truck?"

"In the shop," he said. "Should be ready soon. Just needed some bodywork."

Bodywork? This was one of the many things she'd had yet to hear about. Jack had been sparing with the details from Saturday night, and she knew they needed to have a talk soon and just get it all out there.

At least Santos had given her the overview during her debriefing. The man who'd killed Natalie and Marissa and attacked Lucy was behind bars. His name was Scott Schenck, and his DNA matched samples recovered from the victims' bodies. Schenck hadn't started cooperating with authorities yet, but they were biding their time, hoping to wheedle a confession out of him eventually, along with the whereabouts of Veronica Morales.

Jack helped Fiona out of the car. They made it up to her apartment without incident, and he held her elbow while she stepped over the threshold, as if she were some frail old lady. After easing her coat off and hanging it, he went to put her overnight bag on the bed. He placed the bouquet of carnations on her dresser beside a vase of long-stemmed yellow roses that could only be from him. Fiona bit her lip and looked away.

It felt strange to be home. The faint smell of linseed oil and turpentine was wonderfully familiar, but somehow everything seemed different. Her gaze landed on the leather jacket hanging on the hook near the door. Stowed neatly on the floor below it was a pair of cowboy boots.

Fiona walked straight to the couch and sat down. She felt queasy and wondered if it was the Vicodin. She rested her head on the sofa arm.

"You okay?" Jack gazed down at her, his brow furrowed.

"Just tired."

"You need a pill?"

"No," she sighed. "I just need to close my eyes a sec."

She did, and when she opened them next, she was staring at her alarm clock. Seven fifty-one. Somehow, she'd ended up in bed beneath the covers. She glanced at the window. It was light out.

Seven fifty-one A.M. She bolted upright, and her head seemed to implode. She sat motionless for a moment, until the pain faded.

She'd slept for fifteen *hours*. She looked down and realized she'd awakened at some point to put on a nightshirt and move to the bed. The memory was muddy. She resolved to pitch the rest of her Vicodin prescription in the trash this morning.

She heard the bathroom sink running and swung her legs out of bed. She smelled shaving cream as she crossed her apartment to discover a beautiful, half-naked man in her bathroom. He leaned close to the mirror and dragged a razor expertly over his jaw.

"Morning, sunshine." He winked at her in the mirror.

"I can't believe I slept so long." She gazed into the mirror and was struck dumb by how *bad* she looked. The left side of her forehead was purple, with tinges of green around the edges. And Courtney's assessment of her hair had been generous. With all the stitches showing, she looked like Frankenstein. Courtney thought she could fix it with a good haircut, but Fiona thought nothing short of a wig would help.

She tugged her hair over the wound self-consciously and caught Jack's gaze in the mirror. Her attention was drawn to the fresh white bandage taped to his shoulder. It was smaller than yesterday's, but she still couldn't stand to look at it. *Flesh wound.* What a load of bull. Why did he have to be so stoic about everything?

Jack rinsed the razor and tapped it against the sink, then pulled a towel off the rack.

"I've got appointments today." He toweled off his face. "Courtney said she'd stop by on her lunch break and check in on you."

"That's not necessary," Fiona said, and followed him into the bedroom. He opened the closet, and she was startled to see a row of men's shirts hanging neatly on the rack. Jack pulled some black slacks off a hanger and stepped into them. Then he reached for a starched white shirt and shrugged it on. Fiona lifted her eyebrows and then had to remind herself to minimize facial expressions today.

"What appointments?" she asked.

He reached up to the top shelf of her closet—the one she couldn't access without a stool—and she noticed a pair of men's sneakers that hadn't been there a week ago. Beside it was a pair of black dress shoes. He took the dress shoes down, along with a black leather belt.

"Job interviews," he said. "I've got two meetings with people from the D.A.'s office this morning. Then I need to swing down to Graingerville and pick up some stuff. Files. My computer. Things like that."

Her sluggish brain waded through the part about the computer until she got back to the first thing. "Job interviews? You're trying to get a *job* here?"

He opened the dresser drawer that previously had been hijacked by Courtney and pulled out some black socks.

Fiona noticed a heap of boxer briefs as he closed the drawer.

He'd moved in. She spun around to the closet and inventoried its contents again. A shelf once occupied by her sweaters now held a stack of men's undershirts.

"You're moving here? Like, to Austin?"

He sat on the bed and pulled on his socks, watching her intently. "That's right."

"But . . . what about your house?"

"I'm selling it." He rested his ankle on his knee and tied his shoe.

"But . . . what about your family? What about your rabbits?"

The side of his mouth ticked up. "They'll be fine. I can visit."

Fiona's head was spinning. This was happening too fast. He couldn't just sell his house and get a job here! Those were the kind of life events that took months and years to plan for.

"But don't you think we should talk about this? I mean, moving to Austin is a big deal. What if we're not compatible? What if"—she waved a hand back and forth between them—"what if we get sick of each other?" *What if you don't love me?*

He stood up and rested his palms on her shoulders. Gently, he bent down and kissed her lips. "You sick of me already?"

"No."

"Good. Because I intend to be around awhile."

She stepped back and folded her arms over her chest. God, she *hated* this nightshirt. Where had it come from? She couldn't believe she was having this conversation looking this terrible. "I just mean . . . This is a big deal. I was under the impression you wanted to be a homicide detective again."

"I never said that."

"Yeah, but you're a *cop*."

His jaw tightened. "There's an opening for an investigator at the D.A.'s. office. I think I'd be good at it."

"But . . . it always seemed like—" A realization came to her and she covered her mouth with her hand. "It's me, isn't it? You can't get a police job anymore because of me."

He frowned. "How do you figure that?"

"Your injury." Guilt swirled around in her stomach. "If you hadn't gotten shot with *my* gun, you could apply for any job you wanted."

He put his hands on his hips. They were narrow hips, compared to his broad shoulders, and she wasn't used to seeing them without a gun tucked nearby. He'd always been a cop, and she'd ruined it for him.

"Don't," he said. "I see where you're going with this, and just don't, okay? You need to rest today. Next week you have to get back in the classroom, and you need to be all healed up. Why don't you hang out on the sofa today and watch TV?"

"Hang out on the sofa." She followed him into the kitchen. He pulled open her fridge, and she was shocked to see it stocked full. Orange juice, Gatorade, milk, eggs. Fat-free yogurt and Diet Cokes, which were for her, obviously. There was even a salad kit and a cellophane-covered casserole dish.

He grabbed a Gatorade.

"Who made casserole?"

He smiled. "It's from my mom. She wanted you to have a speedy recovery, so she sent King Ranch chicken."

"Your mother made me casserole."

"Us." He took a swig of Gatorade.

"You told your mother you were moving to Austin to be with me. Away from your family, and your house, and the town you've lived in your whole life."

He put the Gatorade on the counter. "I haven't lived there my whole life. And a house is just a house. It's no big deal. I can get one in Austin once I get my equity out."

"Houses in Austin are expensive."

"I've got savings."

She didn't know what to say. She couldn't speak. It was all too much. What if he uprooted and moved to Austin and then hated her after a week? What if he was fickle, like Aaron?

"I think," she said, clasping her hands in front of her, "that it would be wise to discuss all this some more before you pursue such a drastic course of action."

He shook his head. "There you go again, with the lawyer talk."

"I'm just being logical."

He circled his arms around her, very gently, and pulled her against him. "Please don't worry about all this today, okay? You need to get healthy. I need to land a job. Once we get those two things taken care of, we can have the relationship talk you've been hankering for. But right now, I'm running late."

He kissed her mouth briefly, and then headed for the door.

"But ..."

"Oh, and don't be surprised if there's a delivery today. I'm expecting a package."

Relationship talk. He hadn't even told her he loved her.

And now he was acting like they had a future together. And she was *stupidly* allowing herself to feel happy about the idea. "But . . ."

The door closed behind him.

Fiona went into the living room and dropped down on the couch.

Jack had moved in with her. Just like that. He wanted a job in Austin and a house and a relationship with her. It was all of her deepest-buried yearnings come true, and she felt absolutely terrified.

She reached for the remote and flipped on the TV sitting atop her bookcase.

The *TV.*

Along with clothes, boots, and King Ranch chicken, he'd brought his TV. It was tuned to ESPN, of course. She shook her head and began mindlessly surfing channels.

Jack loved her. He hadn't said it this morning, but she knew it in her heart. She couldn't remember precisely, but she had this unshakable feeling that he'd said the words, over and over, while she lay in the ditch bleeding. She was almost sure he'd said the words again at the hospital, in the dark, as he'd kissed her hand and she'd felt stubble against her fingertips. It was coming back now—Jack Bowman hunched bedside her, telling her he loved her and she was going to be okay.

Suddenly her gaze focused on the screen, on a straight-haired young woman standing at a podium. She'd lost so much weight, she looked anorexic, but an enormous smile lit up her face.

Annie Sherwood.

Fiona sat forward and turned up the volume. The CNN newscaster was talking about miracles, and the camera panned over to a solemn little girl with brown hair and eyes just like Annie's. She was sitting beside Colter.

"God in heaven," Fiona murmured, reaching for her phone. *This* was why Sullivan had called four times since Saturday.

Shelby Sherwood had beaten the odds.

Fiona stirred awake as Jack slipped into bed. He eased up behind her and pulled her against the warm hardness of his chest.

"Sorry I'm late," he said, his voice low.

"You're not." She nestled her head back against him. "It's early. I just couldn't keep my eyes open. How was Graingerville?"

"Good." His hands strayed under the slinky black thing that was an improvement over last night's sleep shirt.

"Did you see the news today?"

He kissed her neck. "Shelby Sherwood. I caught it on the radio."

"I talked to my friend at the FBI. I'm going to start taking cases again."

She felt his body tense, and she waited for an argument.

"You can take some time off," he said. "Give your painting a year or two."

"You know I can't do that. I don't *want* to do that."

He sighed. "I know. I even understand, I think."

She rolled toward him, and for a moment they just stared at each other in the dimness.

"I have a surprise." He propped up on an elbow. "And why do you look guilty all of a sudden?"

She bit her lip. "I'm sorry. I couldn't resist opening it."

"You mean my package came? From the Fuller Gallery?"

She arched up and kissed him. "It's my favorite painting. How did you know?"

"I pay attention."

"It was expensive. You didn't need to do that," she said, although she was secretly glad he had. The idea of parting with her fish painting had been bothering her.

"I've wanted it since I first saw it." He flattened his palm over her stomach. "But that's not the surprise."

"What is it?" And as she looked up into his face, she knew. "You got the job."

He smiled.

Half of her felt euphoric, but the other half was filled with anxiety. He'd be moving to Austin now for certain. "Are you sure we're not rushing this? Maybe we need more time. We've just been through a trauma—"

"Stop." His face was serious now. "I let someone I cared about push me away once before, and it's not going to happen again. I love you too much."

Fiona smiled, and the happiness started to crowd out the worry. "I love you, too. And you're sure this is what you want?"

"Yes." He leaned down and kissed her. "This is exactly what I want."

Pocket Star Books
proudly presents

Whisper of Warning

Coming soon
from Pocket Star Books

Turn the page for a preview of
Whisper of Warning . . .

Courtney Glass whipped into the gravel lot and cursed the man-toad who'd invited her here. This was August. Texas. It was ninety-nine degrees outside, and any halfway-sane person was holed up in an air-conditioned building right now, not parked at a deserted hike-and-bike trail, hoping to score after lunch.

Did he think this was romantic? Spontaneous, maybe? Despite the Ivy League diploma, John David Alvin could be a real idiot.

Courtney huffed out a breath and flipped down the vanity mirror. Idiot or not, she wanted to look good. Looking good was the best revenge, especially when it came to ex-boyfriends.

But the Beauty Gods weren't smiling on her today. The humidity had turned her hair limp, and her makeup was practically melting off. She dug through her purse, seeking inspiration, but finding little. She blotted her forehead with a tissue and fluffed her hair. She started to put on lipstick, then decided to hell with it. Who cared if she impressed David? He was the last person she wanted to see right now. She shouldn't even be here, really, but his insistent messages were driving her crazy. They needed to hash this thing out, once and for all.

A flash of movement in the rearview mirror caught her eye. He was here. She watched the black Porsche Cayenne glide up alongside her. He'd traded in the red Carrera, apparently, which shouldn't have come as a surprise. Suddenly nervous, she cast a glance around her car, a Buick Skylark that was a hulking testament to the emptiness of her bank account. Courtney could work wonders with drugstore cosmetics and she was a bloodhound for treasures in a thrift shop, but this car was beyond help. Until she climbed out of credit card debt, she was stuck in a '98 clunker with a temperamental AC. She turned up the power now and adjusted the vents.

David sat in his SUV but didn't get out. Courtney could feel his gaze on her while she cleared clutter off the front seat. She refused to make eye contact. This was *his* meeting, and he was going to have to come to her. She didn't relish the thought of talking to him in her heap, but she wasn't stupid enough to give up her home-field advantage by getting into his Porsche.

His door opened and closed with that luxury-car *click*. From the corner of her eye, she saw him fist his hands on his hips. She set her chin. She could match wills with him any day of the week. Sweat beaded between her breasts as she waited, silently, gazing through the windshield at the dragonflies playing in the sunshine.

Finally the door squeaked open, and he slid into the passenger seat. He wore a crisp white shirt with monogrammed cuffs, a red power tie, and his usual dark pants. In an instant, the Skylark smelled like Drakkar Noir.

Courtney looked at him with disgust as she rolled down her window.

"Well?"

"Well, what?" she shot back. "You called me."

"I most certainly did not."

"Text message. Whatever." God, he was such a prick. Just smelling him again made her want to retch.

He gave her an annoyed look. "I don't have time for this shit. This is bordering on harassment."

"Harassment?"

Suddenly the back door jerked open. Courtney turned around and found herself face-to-face with a black ski mask.

The man pulled a gun out of his pants and pointed it at David's nose. "Gimme your phone."

All the breath whooshed out of Courtney's lungs. She gaped at the gray eyes glaring out from holes in the mask.

He jabbed the gun at David's neck. "Now, asshole!"

She glanced at her ex-boyfriend. His arrogance had morphed into fear, and he wasn't moving. *Do it!* she tried to tell him mentally, but he was frozen. At last, he braced one hand on the dashboard and jammed the other into his front pocket.

She cast a panicked look outside. No one. This was unreal. It was the middle of the day. Granted, it was hotter than hell outside, but there had to be someone—

The barrel swung toward her, and her stomach dropped out.

"Yours, too."

She stared at the twisting pink mouth and tried to process the words. Hers, too. Her phone. He wanted her phone. Did he want her money, also? Her phone was in her purse, along with her Mace.

"Let's go!"

David tossed his phone at him, and it landed with a clatter on the back floorboard. The man scooped it up and shoved it in the pocket of his tracksuit.

Then the masked head turned toward her. "*Now,* or I'll blow his fucking brains out."

David went pale. He sent her a desperate look. "*Hurry,* Courtney!"

Her purse was near her feet. On the floor. And her Mace was in there. She dragged the bag into her lap and thrust her hand inside. She groped for the tube of pepper spray, but couldn't find it amid all the junk she lugged around. *I can't die yet. There's so much I haven't done.*

"Now!" The eyes watching her through the cutouts squinted.

Her clammy fingers closed around the phone, and she pulled it free. She held it out to him.

Time stretched out as the phone hovered there in her trembling hand. He reached for it. He wore tight black gloves, and she knew—with sudden certainty—this was going to end badly.

ABOUT THE AUTHOR

Laura Griffin started her career in journalism before venturing into the world of romantic suspense with her debut novel for Pocket Books, *One Last Breath*, and its sequel, *One Wrong Step*. Her articles have appeared in numerous newspapers and magazines, and her fiction has garnered awards from writing competitions throughout the country. Laura currently lives in Austin, where she is working on her fourth book for Pocket. Visit her website at www.lauragriffin.com.